MW00985255

Advance praise for The Green Phoenix

"So much of imperial Chinese history is an enigma; a world we, as outsiders, are shut out off. Alice Poon's novelised life of the Empress Dowager Xiaozhuang fictionally pulls back the curtain on Manchu court life and lets us step into a forbidden world."

— *Paul French, author of Midnight in Peking*

"Alice Poon has written a masterpiece of Chinese history little known in the West. It's a story of love, betrayal and loyalty, and shows how one woman inspired the reunification of China. For so long the West has fixated on the end of the Qing dynasty, but as Poon beautifully recreates in her book, the real heroine of the Qing is the Empress Dowager Xiaozhuang. Never before has this story been told in English, and it's arguably the most important historical novel of early Qing Dynasty China."

— *Susan Blumberg-Kason, author of Good Chinese Wife: A Love Affair with China Gone Wrong*

"The Green Phoenix illuminates the complex, sweeping history of the Qing rise to power with captivating scenes of intimacy, conflict, loss, and triumph. Through the story of Mongolian-born Empress Dowager Xiaozhuang, Alice Poon delivers a lush and deeply informed look at the multicultural origins of China's last dynasty"

—*Elsa Hart, author of Jade Dragon Mountain and The White Mirror*

THE GREEN PHOENIX

Alice Poon

The Green Phoenix

By Alice Poon

ISBN-13: 978-988-8422-56-2

Cover design: Jason Wong

FICTION / Historical

EB091

Published by Earnshaw Books Ltd. (Hong Kong)

PART 1

Destiny

One

ELATION CREEPS UP on her as the steppe looms out of the darkness. In an instant, she is treading on the velvety softness of the vibrant green grass. Its unique fragrance, carried by the wind, makes her heart croon as it used to. Verdant pastures ripple out around her in all directions to join hands with the dazzling blue sky. To her, the color and scent of grass are most redolent of Mother Nature and are the perfect balm for her heart and soul. In the next instant, she is the untamed child atop her white-maned Jirgal in a wild dash toward the horizon, her plaits flying happily after her. One moment they are scaling golden sand dune after sand dune; the next sailing across a sea of jade greens. They finally come to a stop in a valley filled with lavender lilies, and horse and child share a moment of warming ecstasy.

"Am I really back home?" she moaned in a faint voice, stirring feebly in her sickbed. Then, in a nebulous haze, the scene shifted, and time glided forward to the year of her wedding…

The bridal procession is led by a troupe of horseback guardsmen with Wukeshan at its head. Trailing behind are the flower-decorated bridal carriage drawn by two sturdy stallions draped in ceremonial red cloth and a string of ten camels carrying huge wooden chests containing the bridal dowry and provisions. Her beloved Jirgal carries the maid and trots gaily alongside the carriage, oblivious to the sadness that fills the vessel on wheels. Even in her desolation, she is grateful Sumalagu is with her, and does not mind the maid peeping in through the carriage window once in a while to check on her.

The procession treks across a mosaic landscape of vastly divergent terrains. An expanse of barren sand hills meets with a wide stretch of river marshes rich in flora and fauna. Nor is it strange that a large patch of jade green grassland lies right next to a windswept stony desert with sporadic springs, which then gives way further along to yet another swathe of lush pastures. The humbling vastness of this changing landscape fills her with renewed respect and affection. She wants nothing but to sear the images onto her memory, so that this land will forever be a part of her.

From time to time, the travelers make stops to take light snacks of dried apricots, roasted chestnuts and biscuits, with water to quench the thirst. In the evening, the riders try their best to find pastures near brooks or in sheltered dells to set up camp. Their animals are let free to graze while they cook over an open fire and replenish their water, if water is to be found.

After many days of tiresome journeying, early one morning, Wukeshan pokes his head inside the carriage to announce, with clear excitement in his voice: "Mukden is in sight, dear sister! We'll reach the capital by sundown!"

In recent months, Bumbutai had floated through life like a phantom, numb to feelings and desires. Why hadn't Dorgon replied to her letter? Why had he left her Borjigit home the previous winter without saying farewell? Her maid's repeated pleas had buzzed in her ears unheard: "You're harming your beautiful eyes with this non-stop crying, my precious! Won't you at least take some milk? You've not eaten for two whole days already. If you go on starving yourself like this, you'll end up with a flat chest!"

Then slowly, she had allowed Sumalagu to persuade her to

prepare for her new life. She had written frequently to Aunt Jere to seek her guidance and advice on Jurchen lifestyle and etiquette. She had buried herself in Jurchen and Han Chinese folk literature, practiced Chinese calligraphy every day and learned to do needlework from Sumalagu.

The maid took a good look at the bride. "You simply look ravishing!" she exclaimed.

Bumbutai had chosen to wear her favorite dark blue brocaded fur-lined *deel* over a purple silk robe girdled with a sapphire sash. She knew well enough how the color of the *deel* set off the lustrous shine of her eyes beautifully. But she also believed Sumalagu was right in saying that people who happened to see those frosty eyes now would probably think they belonged to a seasoned young woman rather than an unworldly adolescent.

Letting out a long sigh as she caught a glimpse of the outside view, she noticed Sumalagu was clasping her hands together in a silent prayer. She mutely thanked her maid for not nagging her when she had earlier insisted on donning Mongolian garb and wearing plaits for the journey. This was the last time she could do that.

Aunt Jere's letters prepared her well on what to expect at her wedding. Upon arrival at the Mukden Palaces, the bridal group would rest for a day and then would have to help with the decoration of the wedding hall and the sorting of wedding gifts. The ceremony would be held on the third day.

"Your bridal garment is a wide-sleeved, high-neck and knee-length red silk robe embroidered in silver and gold peonies, to be worn over a full-length red satin skirt," her letter said.

"It is a Jurchen custom to wear undergarments. This is an open cross-collar pink silk shift paired with loose silk underpants. Your hair will be coiled into two knots at the nape of your neck, fastened by pearl hairpins, and topped by a bridal headdress made of pearls, pink gems and blue feather inlays framed in silver, all wired into the shape of a flowery coronet, with a veil of hanging bead strands. On each ear you will be wearing three earrings. Again, this is the custom for Jurchen brides. The amount of decorative jewelry in the headdress is a symbol of the social status of the wearer. A concubine's jewelry is naturally less valuable than that for the wife, and the quantity and type of gems also depend on how much she is favored by her new groom. In your case, I can tell you that your groom is quite smitten with you… Once in your new home, you will have to quickly learn how to walk in Jurchen high-heeled shoes…" Aunt Jere spared no details in her rambling letters.

These trivial thoughts flicked through her mind and then slipped away like spilled water. The questions that had left her hanging in the air were stealing their way back now to taunt her. She had been so sure that Dorgon, the young and charming Jurchen Beile and half-brother of Aunt Jere's husband, had special feelings for her, as she had for him. Was she mistaken after all? Or could it be that he already had a special someone?

The late spring sun was in languish descent as the procession meandered through the outer town's cobblestoned streets. Bumbutai looked out from her carriage to savor a view of the place.

"This was once populated by Han Chinese," Wukeshan explained to her. "After Nurhaci seized the town, the Han people were forcibly evicted." The Jurchen nobility had taken up residence in the tidy rows of courtyard houses with gleaming ceramic-tiled roofs and terra cotta walls. Brightly lit lanterns painted in red and gold adorned the front porches. Some larger houses had a pair of sculpted stone lions guarding the main gate.

"The homes look so imposing and different from our Mongolian *gers*," Bumbutai said with awe.

"Little sister, this is civilized culture. Once we get passed the gate to the inner town, we'll find the Palaces of the Aisin Gioro clan. Those buildings should be even grander." Wukeshan beamed good-naturedly.

Her heart went out to the Hans who had been uprooted from their homes. How odd that her fate and theirs should be aligned! Wasn't she being forcibly uprooted, just like them? But at least she didn't have to suffer their woe of being enslaved to work the farms for the Jurchens, the invaders and new masters of the town.

She had learned from books that the Jurchens were now a sedentary tribe that had adapted to crop farming a long time ago, although some still preferred livestock breeding like the Khorchin Mongols. Only a small number adhered to nomadic hunting and ice-fishing.

"By Nurhaci's orders, the Jurchens have just developed their new script based on the Mongolian writing system," Wukeshan added. "For centuries, though, they have been practicing Han Confucian customs. Shamanism is traditionally their primary religion, but they are also well exposed to Buddhism and Taoism." He pointed to a Buddhist temple at the far end of the street they were traveling on.

"I am already familiar with the new Jurchen script, thanks to Suma," she said pensively. "I hope someone will teach me Han history and the Four Books and Five Classics."

Jere was fond of Bumbutai and had especially assigned two Han maids-in-waiting to serve her. They were named Siu Mui and Siu Fa, twin sisters who had been sold as slaves to Hong Taiji's household. Her temporary residence was set up inside the Library Hall, consisting of an antechamber and a large bed chamber, just off the main study hall.

As her entourage arrived at the Hall entrance, the two maids bustled over to welcome her and ushered her to the bath area, which was adjoined to the bed chamber and partitioned off by an opaque, double-paneled, silk-mounted screen. Behind the screen a wooden tub of steaming hot water perfumed with rose petals was waiting for her.

After taking a soothing bath, she met Aunt Jere in the antechamber. All smiles, the aunt handed her personal gifts from Hong Taiji, contained in a shimmering box made from seashells and lined in velvet. They included a pair of green jade tasseled hairpins, three pairs of emerald earrings and two bracelets made with emeralds and pearls. Jere told her, not without a trace of jealousy, that Hong Taiji had given her, the wife, the same amount of jewelry at her wedding, except that hers were made of rubies instead of emeralds. She also showed her the bejeweled bridal coronet, the lavish bridal dress and undergarments.

"You can try the garments on tomorrow. They should fit perfectly. I made doubly sure the seamstress followed the measurements that your mother gave me during my home visit last winter," Jere said sweetly. Fighting her fatigue, Bumbutai graciously repeated words of thanks to her aunt for overseeing the wedding preparations. As soon as Jere stepped out of the chambers, she retired straight to her bed without casting a second look at the bridal gear.

After a good night's rest, she spent the next day exploring the phalanxes of packed bookshelves that lined the walls of the study hall. "This is indeed a treasure trove of knowledge," she sighed as she skimmed some of the Chinese classics. Her private viewing of the library refreshed her spirits like a shower of spring rain.

At the break of dawn on the big day, Siu Mui and Siu Fa came in to help their mistress with the hair dressing. Sumalagu looked on in quiet bewilderment. She had never in her entire life seen anything as sophisticated as these bridal garments. She also saw that her mistress was not particularly pleased with such a complicated style of dress.

The first thing that Bumbutai asked her friend and maid about was her pet mare.

"Did they put Jirgal in a nice clean stable? Did they feed her fresh grass?"

"Yes, Jirgal is comfortable and well-fed. Don't worry about her, my precious. It's your big day and you needn't worry about lifting one little finger. Just look beautiful and leave the rest to us."

"Oh, Suma, I'm so glad you're here with me. Otherwise, I think I would have died from homesickness already. Everything is so strange here."

"Venerable Mistress, if there is anything we could do to help you feel more comfortable, pray tell us," Siu Mui said shyly, and Siu Fa nodded innocently in agreement. Bumbutai's heart melted at these words, and she spoke to the maids in fluent Chinese:

"How old are you two, Siu Mui, Siu Fa?"

"We're both twelve years old. Siu Fa came one hour after me," Siu Mui replied courteously, slightly bemused that her mistress could speak Chinese so well.

"Oh, then we're all of the same age! What a coincidence!"

"Venerable Mistress, we're only maids and are not supposed to speak unless spoken to. But we want to say that we've never seen anyone as beautiful as you. Please do not be angry at us for daring to say this."

"Siu Mui, Siu Fa, how can I be angry at you for saying such a sweet thing? You two girls are very pretty too. And how I admire your deft hands!" The twin maids giggled softly at hearing this and became much more relaxed. Siu Mui ventured further, while twisting a braid of hair into a coil:

"What does the name Jirgal mean, Venerable Mistress? It sounds foreign to me."

"Oh, it means 'happiness'. It's quite a common Mongolian name. What do 'Siu Mui' and 'Siu Fa' mean?"

"My name means 'Little Plum Blossom' in Chinese, and my sister's name means 'Little Flower'," Siu Mui replied, as she was fastening one knot of hair with a pearl hairpin that Siu Fa had just handed her.

"That's what I thought. What pretty names!" she said with an absentminded smile, frowning at the bejeweled bridal coronet.

Within a short while, the twin maids finished making the double hair buns and were adjusting the coronet. Then Sumalagu warned them of the approaching hour of the bridal sedan's arrival, and bade them to hurry with the dressing of the bride.

Bumbutai looked forlornly into the bronze mirror which the maids had just placed in front of her. She was on the verge of crying when she saw the gaudy and unnatural hairdo reflected in the mirror.

At this instant, out of nowhere, a tall young man in metal armor suddenly bolted into the reflection. She flinched. Joy, anger and vexation all at once flushed over her. Their gazes locked steadfastly on each other in the mirror for a long time. Her heart pranced like an untamed horse on the loose. Seeing this, Sumalagu bade the twin maids leave and, with knitted brows, also stepped outside, closing the door behind her.

That winter night on the Mongolian steppe, Dorgon had handed Sumalagu his written reply to Bumbutai's letter, suggesting that they make a betrothal vow to each other the next morning, at dawn. He said in the letter that he would be waiting for her under the tallest poplar tree by the river, along which they had strolled that morning. He waited there from dawn until noon. She never appeared. Completely crestfallen, he left the

Borjigit compound without saying farewell to his hosts.

"Congratulations, my dear sister," he taunted in a barbed tone.

"I have no idea why you chose this moment to appear, My Lord," she retorted with an equally sour note.

"Haven't I the right to have a good look at my brother's bride?"

"My Lord, you are quite drunk."

"Yes, I do nothing but drink these days because I am heartbroken. But this is your big day. So it is an occasion to drink to, is it not?" He wobbled as he slurred out the words, his face a bilious green.

"Suma, Siu Mui, Siu Fa, please come in and help the Beile to a chair. Suma, please bring him some ginseng tea."

"I've come to wish you happiness on your wedding day. What wrong have I done now?"

He would not quiet down and struggled to stay upright. The three maids with a concerted effort bundled him out to the antechamber, where they sat him down in a chair. Sumalagu served him hot ginseng tea while the other two helped Bumbutai to dress. The bridal sedan was waiting at the Library Hall entrance.

For the rest of the day, Bumbutai was so wrapped up in the wedding rituals that she hardly had a spare moment to reflect on Dorgon's sudden appearance. When her curtained bridal sedan arrived at Hong Taiji's Palace, the head palace maid approached the sedan, crouched down and gruffly bade her climb onto her back. A bride's slippers must not touch the ground because dirt would taint her purity.

With the bride on her back, the head maid stepped nimbly over a tin plate containing burning incense before entering the Palace via a side entrance. Rites forbade concubines from entering the household through the main entrance on the wedding day, a privilege reserved for the first wife. The incense was supposed to rid the bride of all evil spirits that might be accompanying her. It was no help that Jere had briefed her in advance about these strange rituals. Bumbutai felt humiliated and ill at ease. The head maid, with a surly face and bristling eyebrows, acted so roughly that it made her wince with each step.

Once inside the main hall, which was overflowing with wedding guests, she was ushered over to perform tea offerings, first to Nurhaci and Lady Abahai, then to Hong Taiji and Jere, and then to all the Beiles and Princesses in the royal family. With each tea offering, she had to kneel and bow three times to the recipient. By the time it was all done, her head was spinning and her knees ached terribly. She felt relieved, though, that Dorgon had not bothered to show up.

After the tea ritual, wedding guests were seated and served a sumptuous feast of roasted mutton, roasted piglets, stuffed geese and ducks, and all kinds of dumplings, sweet pastries and sweet soups. When the third course was served, at the head maid's prompting, Bumbutai rose with her new groom to do the rounds of wine toasting to the guests. Then followed a variety of ceremonial entertainments, which began with ribbon dancing and ended with a martial arts performance.

When the feast was near its end, the head maid scurried across the hall to fetch Bumbutai and grabbed her already-bruised arm so hard that it almost made her cry. Once outside, she pushed and shoved her into the bridal sedan that was waiting to take her back to the Library Hall. She was to wait in her bed chamber for her groom. Hong Taiji, who preferred to keep his emotional distance, never allowed his wife or any of his concubines to share his own bed, even on wedding nights. Sumalagu had earlier brought from the royal kitchen a few dishes of Manchu Sanzi cakes, linden leaf cakes and candied fritters and left them on the side table for her, but she had no appetite for them.

Alone at last, she began to ponder Dorgon's words. What did he mean by heartbroken? Why would he feel heartbroken if he had not even bothered to reply to her letter? Yet, for all her heartache, she never stopped pining for him. His appearance that morning rekindled a spark of life in her heart.

Now another appalling dark thought emerged. Her mother's words haunted her: "Whatever your groom does to you on the wedding night, you have to submit, even if he hurts you. A woman always endures the act in silence." She also remembered her sister's warning. "You will feel sharp pains if the man is aggressive in his ways. Your girlhood will be savagely ripped away. But it will be over in no time. From that instant on, your body belongs solely to the groom. You will be just one of his many woman slaves. He will expect to see blood as proof of your virginity, which was a part of the arrangement when the marriage negotiations took place." On that thought, she cringed uncontrollably.

Heavy footsteps could be heard drawing near. The erratic thump of her heart almost deafened her. She did not know where to lay her eyes and unknowingly rested them on her coronet, which she had earlier placed on the chair beside the freshly-made bridal bed. Debating whether or not to put it back on her head, she recalled what Siu Mui had told her that morning. The blue inlays were made of feathers plucked from captured kingfishers. The poor beautiful birds! That mere idea was revolting to her. "I'm never going to wear it again," she thought. "I don't care if I'm breaking the custom." She bit her lip rebelliously. Seated on the edge of the bed in her flimsy shift and underpants, she simply could not stop her knees from knocking together.

Before she knew it, the bed chamber doors swung open with

a bang and in barged the massive hulk of her new husband. He was visibly steady in his gait and did not show any sign of drunkenness. As he approached the bed, he threw his fur-lined surcoat on the floor, leaving on only his yellow hemp robe. Then he plumped himself down beside his new bride and looked steadily into her eyes. He stretched out his large warm hands to cup her tiny cold ones as if he wanted to pass on his body heat to her. Her eyes had nowhere to wander and she had no choice but to gaze into his. She was baffled to find they had a strange coercing charm. He held her hands until her body stopped shaking and said in as gentle a voice as he could manage:

"My sweet Bumbutai, you must be feeling homesick these past days. I know that feeling. How would you like some distraction? How about taking lessons in Chinese literature and history together with me?" His tone was wheedling, like a parent to a child.

"I'm going to ask Scholar Fan to give us lessons each morning in the study hall. You will have your afternoons free to go riding with Jirgal in the nearby woods, read to your heart's content, practice calligraphy or learn Chinese ribbon dancing. What do you say to that?"

She could not believe her ears. From gossip she had heard, this man was in the habit of ordering the execution of a soldier for breaking the slightest military rule. Could it be true that he was actually trying to please her, a new concubine? He had had concubines before whom he treated with his notorious ill temper. It was true, though, that he still showed some respect for Jere, his Number One Wife after his first wife died. But that was probably an exception. For a moment, she was at a loss as to how to respond to this unexpected kindness. After an awkward pause, she stammered:

"My Lord, you are very kind… and thoughtful. I would love

to... take lessons with you." Then, venturing further like a child who gets its way with its first cajoling attempt, she asked, "Will I really be free to do all the things you said?"

"I give you my word. You were born a free spirit. I must see to it that nothing wears that spirit down. If you are happy, I am happy."

"I am most grateful to you, My Lord. There is actually another favor that I would like to ask of you. The everyday headdress and high heels... these are not suitable for horse-riding. Could I please be exempted from wearing them while outdoors?"

"Of course, my sweet girl. You don't have to wear anything that you don't like. Just keep your plaits and wear whatever clothes that you wish, even Han dresses. I'll have the most beautiful silk and satin sent to you and you can pick your favorite colors. Then Sumalagu can make new dresses for you. Only promise me that you'll show me how you look in the new dresses once they're made." His eyes scanned her thinly-clad body and he seemed affected by her bony form.

After a moment's silence, he stretched himself, yawned and rose to leave. He bent his thick-set body to pick up his surcoat and put it back on, saying, as if to himself:

"Tonight is our wedding night. I will sleep in the antechamber instead of going back to my Palace, just to avoid gossip. You can keep your bed chamber doors latched if you like. And I won't be coming to you at night again. I trust I will see you in class tomorrow. And... you need to eat more."

Bumbutai was left entirely lost for words. She could not believe that she had actually escaped her ghastly fate. To be sure, she was not just dreaming, she pinched her unbruised arm several times. Satisfied at last, she murmured repeated thanks to Eternal Blue Sky.

While in the antechamber where Sumalagu was setting up a

bed for him, Hong Taiji said to the maid with feigned menace: "If you ever let Dorgon anywhere near Bumbutai again, I'll have you flogged." Then he softened his tone and added: "But you did well with that letter. I'm grateful to you."

Sumalagu did not feel the least bit intimidated by this man, knowing he had a soft spot for her.

"My Lord, it was my oversight this morning. It will not happen again. I hope you will keep your word and treat my mistress well."

TWO

ABOVE THE BOUNDLESS steppes that straddled the unforgiving Gobi, the sky habitually sported an unremitting blue. Every now and then coltish white clouds and playful black hawks would break in to tease the resolute blue. This was the ancestral home of the nomadic Mongols. As Mongolian folklore went, once upon a time by the shores of a placid lake on the crest of Burkhan Khaldun (the mountain that Genghis Khan ordained as sacred), Blue Grey Wolf had mated with Beautiful Red Doe. The first child in Mongolian history was then born. Their divine protectors, Eternal Blue Sky and Mother Earth, have ever since been singing their sweet lullaby to soothe and revitalize the roaming Mongol descendants. All Mongols have since been worshipping the spirit of freedom in their souls. These were the lands that cradled a Borjigit daughter who was destined to steer three peoples to safe shores.

On the rolling steppe south of the Gobi, burly grey winter had just stepped over the threshold, all set to stay well past his welcome as always. Coming from a distance, a burst of laughter like jingling silver bells rang through the snow-carpeted lakeside marshland. The lake within sight was a dormant sheet of cobalt ice, reflecting a pale blue sky decorated with wisps of cottony clouds. Echoes of the laughter, as soft as snowflakes, fell weightless on the sleepy marshland and melted away. Dreamy silence lingered as though not a wisp of air had disturbed it.

A little while later, silence gave way as the rhythmic clacking of two horses' hooves on the frosted earth drew near, accompanied by a sweet melodic song. The intruding sounds of humanity startled the resident marmots out of their cozy burrows, and stirred into vigilance their few visiting friends: two bushy-tailed sables, a furry beaver and two slender gazelles, gathered around the lake to rest from the morning's labor of pre-hibernation food hunting. The song's lyrics were in Mongolian and could be clearly heard as the horses came closer at a canter:

We make our fair-faced daughters
Sit in the two-wheeled cart,
Harnessed to a black camel,
For you who will become Khans,
And send them off at a trot,
On the throne of queens;
We make them sit together with you.

Astride on a white Mongolian mare sat a spirited young girl, riding alongside a strong young man atop a dark brown stallion. The man's leathery attire was that of a Mongolian warrior. The young girl was clad in a purple felt tunic with same color leggings, topped by a luxuriously brocaded black-and-purple fur-trimmed *deel*, and shod in a pair of knee-high soft leather boots. Her silken black hair was dressed into two braids. Round the crown of her head she wore a multi-colored woven band from which red bead strands hung down the two sides of her face and the back of her head. From the richness of the material of her *deel*, one could tell that she must either be a *beki* from an aristocratic Mongol clan or a princess of royal Jurchen descent. Wisps of her shiny black hair whipped about her white face as the blustery winter gusts threw their weight around. Her defiant cheeks, lit up by a pair of sparkling elongated eyes (which the Hans would call "phoenix eyes"), were of a luminous rosy pink. Though reddened by the harsh cold, her delicate straight nose looked pretty, and her sensual pink lips and slim oval face would have made one mistake her for a Han maiden from Suzhou or Hangzhou.

Then her face suddenly froze into alertness as the canter slowed down to a trot. Her dark eyes radiated a sharp gleam of excitement. Spotting a lonesome grey wolf cub on the edge of the frozen lake, she winked at her brother and silently drew an arrow from the leather quiver strapped across her shoulder. She took aim with her gilded bow while her brother looked on, slightly amused. Svelt as she was, she had a steady and firm grasp on the bow. Her upright poise on the saddle looked elegant with a hint of boyishness. It appeared as if she had had much training in archery and horseback riding skills.

At this moment she was so absorbed with the cub that she hardly noticed the two horseback hunters who had arrived on the scene. They were quietly watching her from beside a denuded thorn bush about twenty yards away to her left. The two men were in plush Jurchen garb and wore fur-trimmed woolen hats. The young warrior, his eyes fixed on his sister, did not seem the least perturbed by their presence.

Motioning her white horse with a light pat to move a few steps towards the lake, she carefully took aim again from the new position. Her confident face said that she could hit the target in one single shot. The solitary wolf cub was apparently ignorant of the impending danger. Then it turned its head around at the critical moment to stare the girl in the eyes, and the cub's wide-eyed watery gaze caught her unguarded and stopped her action in its tracks. Its beautiful, mesmerizing eyes made her exclaim in silence. Probably its mother was desperately looking for it now.

On that surmise, her taut arms relaxed and she lowered the bow, letting it rest on her lap. With a slightly wistful look she turned towards her brother, Wukeshan, and said:

"Eternal Blue Sky is merciful and does not wish me to end his life. I hope he'll find a beautiful mate one day. I do believe humans should respect animals' right to live."

"My dear sister, it seems to me you are just not cut out for hunting. But as your coach, I'll say you're one exceptionally good archer."

"How else can we prove we're the worthy descendants of Khasar's?" she said with a proud tilt of her head, sending her bead strands into a lively bounce.

"Haha, I can't argue with that. But your natural flair clearly lies in languages."

"It's sweet of you to say that, my good brother. You're right though, hunting is not for me." She nodded in agreement. "The reason I took up the sport was because I wanted to show everybody that girls can excel in archery like boys, not because I had any taste for hunting. I would much prefer reading and writing any time. But…." turning to her mare, she whispered into its ear: "we still love gallivanting around looking for lavender lilies, don't we now, my precious Jirgal?" She rubbed her hand on the mare's neck and gave it a loving pat. The meek beast responded with an affectionate grunt.

As soon as she had put the arrow back in the quiver, she heard a loud booing followed by raucous laughter from the direction of the thorn bush. This irritated her so much that she would have shouted back a riposte had Wukeshan not put his hand up in time to stop her.

"My dear Bumbutai, they are the Jurchen *Beiles* from the royal family of Nurhaci," he confided to her. "The older one is Hong Taiji, the husband of our Aunt Jere. The younger one is his half-brother Dorgon. When Aunt Jere married ten years ago, you were only one year old, so you didn't have a chance to meet our in-laws at the wedding. They have come with Aunt Jere on a family visit. I would advise you to behave properly towards them, little sister."

"It is they who did not behave well. They were rude to jeer at me," retorted Bumbutai, her face blushing into a deep pink.

"I'm sure they didn't mean anything ill, Sister. Be a good girl now, let's go and greet them," coaxed Wukeshan, who doted on his young sister.

At the introduction, it was young Dorgon who spoke first.

"You must be Wukeshan," he said with breathless excitement. "I'm delighted to meet you. Jere has often talked about you and it seems as if I've known you for a long time." He turned to Bumbutai and smiled, fixing his melting glance on her. "And this beautiful young girl here must be Bumbutai. Very pleased to meet you. This is my older brother, Hong Taiji. Jere has gone on ahead in a carriage as she couldn't wait to meet with her father and brother."

When Bumbutai's eyes met those of Dorgon's, a rattling thrill grabbed her from head to toe. Never in her life had she met any boy as good-looking and as well-built as this new-found distant relative. He had a high forehead, thick bushy brows over impenetrably dark eyes that exuded sincere warmth, an uncompromising angular jaw line and a cool aquiline nose. With an erect and muscular body, he had the physique of a superbly-trained warrior. Noticing a fresh red scar just above his left brow, she imagined admiringly how he must have fought valiantly in some recent battle. His smooth skin indicated that he was in his early teens, probably a year or two older than she.

Flustered by his animated gaze, she was not her usual talkative self and could only cast down her eyes in a blush. After an awkward silence which lasted as if for a lifetime, she finally collected herself and addressed the two Beiles politely in Jurchen language, which she had learned from her maid-in-waiting and intimate friend, Sumalagu.

"It is with great pleasure that we welcome you to our land. My brother Wukeshan was just telling me about your visit. We are honored to have you. Please let us guide you to our humble abode, where we can serve you warm mare's milk and hot meat stew."

Bumbutai dutifully performed what Mongolian etiquette required of females, but her lingering blush didn't escape Wukeshan's eyes. He sighed and went up to converse with Hong Taiji. Bumbutai stole a furtive glance his way and noticed his big moustache and swarthy face, which made her feel strangely uneasy. In no time, though, her playful nature took over and she challenged the lad to a horseback race around the frozen lake.

Dorgon accepted the challenge with an amiable chortle. His chestnut-colored stallion had never lost a race. For this competition, though, he pulled back his reins on purpose to let the girl lead. Jirgal did the best she could but her rival never lagged behind by more than half a length. At the finishing line, where Dorgon's stallion was just a horse's head behind, he clapped his hands ecstatically along with the spectators. She appreciated his gesture and responded with a smile and a sweet toss of her head, tinged with feigned reproach.

The two hosts and their two guests then rode along at a slow trot towards the Borjigit family compound, which nestled in a nearby sheltered valley through which a half-frozen river coursed, feeding into the lake. On the way, they passed by villages made up of clusters of *gers* and of tracts along the flat banks of the river teeming with horses, oxen, sheep, deer and camels.

On one of the larger expanses, two young boys, seven or eight years old, were practicing shooting at moving targets with arrows from atop racing horses. Nearby, a bunch of smaller kids were jumping on and off their young horses and cavorting with each other in a chatter of sunny ebullience. Bumbutai was heartily affected by the romp and beamed her young companion a knowing smile that said: *no doubt you're itching to join the fun.* He seemed to get her silent message and acknowledged it with a nod and a big grin. They both knew that now was not the occasion to behave with childish indiscretion.

The two youngsters, riding in front, were just happy to drown their senses in the vista of lyrical scenes that rolled by. Heartened and eager for conversation, she asked him in a timid voice:

"Do you believe in animal spirits?"

"Sure I do. I'm a Shamanist. They are here to protect us from harm."

"I'm a Shamanist too!" She exclaimed, unable to hide her excitement and curiosity. "Which animal spirit is your guardian?"

"My guardian spirit is the golden eagle. Do you know which one yours is?"

"My grandpa told me that it's the sand fox...."

"Oh, sand fox.... you're one of my favorite preys then," he chuckled teasingly.

After a moment of reflection, she replied boldly:

"Um, I'm not so sure. Don't you know that in the world of animal spirits, there are no predators or preys? As far as I know, all spirits rank equal in that world."

She shot him a smug glance, satisfied to see he was stumped. Then she adroitly changed the subject and asked him how he got the wound above his brow.

For the rest of the journey, oblivious of the two adults behind, they carried on their incessant light-hearted banter. Even in a stranger's eyes, the two were clearly lost in their own halcyon maze of magic.

The lyrics of the song that she had earlier sung reflected a long-held Mongolian core value. She had known from a tender age that she would be married to a great khan one day, not just from what she had read, but also from what her grandfather had told her when she was growing up. She must be well prepared to be the right hand of either a ruling khan or a future one. "You need not understand why I arrange marriages for the Borjigit daughters, young girl. You only need to know that whatever I do is for the welfare of the Khorchin Mongols. It is your duty to obey my wishes," her grandfather had once told her. She had often heard Manggusi tell stories of vicious territorial wars among different Mongolian tribes. Those stories had always distressed her to the point of tears. Now a little older, she began to see why he valued peace so much.

Bumbutai was the younger of two Princesses born to Prince Jaisang of the noble Borjigit clan. Her older sister Harjol had, against Manggusi's wishes, secretly married a Mongol warrior named Zhuolin, and had left the homestead a few years earlier. Though she had been too young to understand the matter, she had nonetheless admired Harjol for her audacity.

At the age of four, she had started learning archery and horseback riding from Wukeshan, apart from taking language lessons. Her mother, a half Han, had also been teaching her Chinese calligraphy and folk literature. Her grandfather was her teacher in Mongolian script and history, while Sumalagu, an adopted war orphan of mixed Jurchen and Mongolian parentage, was her tutor in Jurchen language and culture. This wide scope of learning grounded her well in all three cultures, though she was fond of telling herself: "I was born a Mongolian. I will always be a Mongolian."

She had always idolized both Genghis Khan and his brother Khasar, from whom her line descended. What impressed her most was Genghis' loyal love for his wife Borte and his keen sense of fairness towards the weaker sex and the poor. "Equal sharing of power and responsibilities between the two sexes is crucial to maintaining familial and social harmony," Genghis had once said. Those words were branded in her mind. But life would later teach her that in some cultures the notion was just wishful thinking.

Manggusi had been keen on befriending the newly-risen Jurchen Empire in the neighboring territory under Nurhaci's rule, for the sake of peace and safeguarding his tribe's land and other interests. Peace had a price. Happily, he had the means to pay for it – the Borjigit clan was famous for its beautiful and desirable women. Hence, his life-time mission was to marry off his daughters and granddaughters to royal Jurchen Princes in exchange for the new Empire's perpetual protection.

Nurhaci, as Khan of the Jurchen Empire, was on the other hand equally able to benefit from the matrimonial bonds. These ties gave him easy access to a ready supply of Mongolian warhorses and horseback warriors. Such military reserves would come in handy someday. He saw China under the wobbling Ming Dynasty as fair game. It was just a matter of time before he made a kill. Manggusi understood the Jurchens' needs perfectly. Hong Taiji was a dauntless warrior representing Nurhaci in these cross-border negotiations. He was now Fourth Beile sitting on the Jurchen Empire's ruling council. Manggusi was betting on his becoming the next Khan one day.

On an open and spacious clearing which backed onto a thick copse by the river, a row of south-facing *gers* were neatly ranged. These portable dome-shaped tents were made of durable felt mounted over a birch wood framework of poles. In the middle stood the largest one, the inside of which was lit by a bright oil lamp hanging from the domed ceiling. Wukesan lifted the heavy door flap of this tent to let Hong Taiji and Dorgon through. Seeing the guests enter, Manggusi and his son Jaisang rose to their feet to bid them welcome.

"My dear son, it's been a long time." The Khorchin Clan Chief hugged his son-in-law warmly, then turned to Dorgon and gave him an affectionate pat on the shoulder: "Young lad, make yourself at home."

Jaisang's wife already had a pan of mare's milk on the stove and was pouring it into five porcelain serving bowls. In a crouching position, she offered the bowls to each of the guests first, then to the three male hosts. At the head of the low table sat Manggusi, whose rugged but kind face wore an amiable grin. Flanking him were Hong Taiji on one side and Dorgon on the other. Jaisang and Wukesan were seated at the opposite end near the entrance. The older men began talking about the recent battles fought between the Jurchens and the Chakhar Mongols.

When the third round of mare's milk was served, on a hint from Manggusi, Wukeshan invited Dorgon to go outside for a tour of the compound. A short while later, the wife also rose and made for the door, leaving the three men to their confidential talk.

She went back to her own tent where Bumbutai was helping with the cooking of the meat stew. Aunt Jere had just come in looking for her sister-in-law and could scarcely hide her excitement when she saw Jaisang's wife enter.

"My dear sister, I'm so happy for you. There's great news for your daughter," she gushed in heartfelt joy. "Bumbutai is going to have a husband and I can count on her company in Mukden soon, all thanks to Pa's arrangement. There's going to be a grand wedding. Unfortunately, the new Palace will not yet be ready by then. That's the only imperfection. But I can assure you that everything else will be just splendid!" Then, turning to her niece, she added earnestly, "Oh, sweet Bumbutai, you're going to be a bride soon! I can't wait for you to come and join me."

Bumbutai, whose mind had been somewhere else all evening, at first didn't get what her aunt was saying. Then the words hit home, and her heart raced, guessing that a betrothal match was being made for her and Dorgon. This thought made her blush into a deep purple in the glowing firelight. Her heart was almost leaping to her mouth. She wanted to shout out her bliss to Eternal Blue Sky.

"Oh Ma, can I go and look for my dancing garment, because I want to rehearse for a dance that I'm going to perform for our guests tomorrow night," she begged. Her mother teased her for being coquettish and shooed her away.

Once inside her own tent, she searched frantically for her favorite dancing costume ensemble, which consisted of a green silk pleated long skirt and an embroidered black velvet vest. She found the skirt but not the vest and was on the verge of bursting into tears. Then she saw Sumalagu come in holding the vest and remembered that her maid had taken it away to sew two loosened buttons back on. She jumped up to kiss her on the cheeks. Sumalagu responded with a puzzled frown. The two girls had grown up together and there was no secret they wouldn't share with each other.

"I believe Grandpa is going to betroth me to a Jurchen Prince," she exclaimed, revealing her thoughts in a blushing glow to her best friend, "He's the brother-in-law of Aunt Jere's. I met him and my uncle this afternoon on the marshland near the lake. I, er,... I think he'll be nice to me.... I'm going to perform the Mongolian waltz tomorrow night for our guests. Oh, Suma, I'm so happy that I know I won't be able to sleep tonight!"

"So that's what it is! Look at you, you can't wait to become somebody's bride. Shame, shame!" The maid couldn't resist teasing her mistress, but almost immediately added sadly: "You'll be so far away from home. Oh, I can't bear the thought of you leaving me. … But first let me scout around for more tidings for you."

Sumalagu was always the one with witty ideas and was always looking out for her mistress.

Throughout the night, Bumbutai's mind kept turning over and over the marshland scene and Aunt Jere's words. Dorgon's florid face was circling in her head all night. She was sure that Hong Taiji was the one who had made the boorish gesture that afternoon. Pursing her lips at the thought, she muttered: "What a brute of a husband that Aunt Jere is married to!" She almost felt guilty about her imminent good fortune.

THREE

THE NEXT MORNING Dorgon came to Bumbutai's *ger* to take her for a walk, as he had promised the night before. She told him of her favorite haunt by the river, and led him by the hand through the copse, a cluster of lush pine trees which breathed out an exhilarating perfume, and a small patch of gaunt rosemary.

"My favorite flower is the lavender mountain lily," she said gaily, picking up a sprig of the fragrant herb. "But it only grows in the summer. And my favorite bird is the swallow." When she received no answer, she looked up into his ebony eyes and saw that they reflected pools of warm light. Then she added softly: "Did you know the mountain lily is a sign of dedication when given to a good friend?"

"No, I didn't know that," he answered, "And why do you love swallows?"

"Because I've often read about them in Chinese poems. They are a symbol of home and happiness."

It was a calm and beautiful night. The gusts that had blown fiercely the previous day had died down and the bluish-black celestial canopy was alive with a riot of twinkling stars crowding around a shapely new moon. The night air was invigoratingly crisp and fresh. As if drawn to an imminent revelry, the stars hung so low that they appeared ready to tumble down any time to join the fun. The camp ground in front of Manggusi's *ger* was abuzz with excitement as maids went about setting up makeshift tables and benches in preparation for the Princess's horseback dance and poetry recital performance. Flaming torches were placed in between spectator benches that circled the dancing area. Mare's milk, roasted pumpkin seeds and sweet biscuits were laid out on wooden tables behind the benches.

Wukeshan was Bumbutai's dancing partner. This had a somewhat calming effect on her, although her heart was still thumping wildly. They had done this Mongolian waltz many times before in front of guests and had always won big applause from the audiences. Mounted on their separate horses now, they started circling each other in a three-step cadence, timed to a traditional song played by a band of musicians strumming on their *morin khuur*, the horsehead fiddles. The steps would pick up speed with the progress of music.

With her silky hair woven into two loose plaits and each tied at the end with a purple ribbon, and dressed in her flowing green skirt and black velvet vest over a purple felt tunic, she looked deliciously attractive. Her elegant poise on horseback had an air that dripped dewy freshness. Her every movement, be it the choreographed swinging of her slender arms, or rhythmic clapping of her hands, was exquisitely graceful and in sync with Jirgal's steps, which matched those of Wukeshan's stallion. It gripped the audience's attention as the horses' steps gathered pace. The sweet blossoming smile never left her face during the entire dance. Aware of where Dorgon was seated, she uncontrollably threw him glances whenever her posture allowed it. As the dance progressed, she saw Dorgon craning his neck to follow her, but something kept distracting her. Hong Taiji's craving eyes seemed bent on having her pinioned.

When the dance came to an end, the bewitched audience broke out in thunderous applause. Having agilely dismounted, Bumbutai held her brother's hand and went before the two guests to take a gracious bow. She looked up and met Dorgon's eyes. They were singing a silent tune of adoration. She blushed and her shiny dark eyes responded with a flowering smile. Dorgon rose and stepped up to her, handing her an ink drawing of a pair of swallows hovering over a bunch of mountain lilies. Looking intently at the drawing, she was amazed at how very nicely it was done. The birds and flowers almost jumped off the paper. Too overwhelmed for words, she could only manage an awestruck look with slightly parted lips.

All this time, Hong Taiji looked on and remained silent with a deadpan face. On Jaisang's signal, Wukeshan went up to him and sat down to distract him with conversation. Meanwhile, Bumbutai retreated to a corner to prepare for her Chinese poetry recital.

She had chosen a popular lyric poem by the Song Dynasty poet Su Shi, entitled *Reminiscing Red Cliffs.* The poem was about the life and romance of Zhou Yu, a heroic and chivalrous general from the Three Kingdoms era. In a clear voice she performed the recital in impeccable Chinese, all the while holding the drawing that Dorgon had just given her:

The Great Yangtze scurries forever east,
Many an ancient hero buried in its sweep.
West of the old forts, they say,
Was fought Zhou Yu's Battle of Red Cliffs.
Rampant cliffs that pierced clouds,
Angry waves that ripped shores, churning up snowy foam.
Such a picturesque country,
So full of gallant men in times of old.
Thinking of Zhou in that distant past,
He must have looked valiant, with Xiaoqiao his new bride;
Feather fan in hand, hair tied in silk,

His enemies crushed to dust as he joked.
Such was my dreamy tour; mock me as maudlin,
But I'm just a young white-haired bloke.
Life is but a dream; let me offer wine to the river moon.

When she finished reciting the poem, Hong Taiji stood up and clapped his hands passionately, and this started a round of applause from the amazed audience. Bumbutai was taken aback by his enthused reaction as she had never imagined that a Jurchen Beile would understand Chinese poetry. Secretly she sneered, thinking he was probably imagining himself as the charming Zhou Yu. She then looked at Dorgon and was amused by his puzzled look. The next thing she saw was Hong Taiji whispering something into her grandfather's ear which made him break into a hearty guffaw. Determined not to let the audience's response bother her, she took her bow with cool poise.

As she walked back to her tent, she wondered how many in the audience understood that the poem was about a pivotal Chinese historical event in the Three Kingdoms era. In the decisive naval battle, Cao Cao, the arrogant warlord of the State of Wei, lost his entire fleet of warships and was forced to acknowledge the States of Wu (under Sun Quan with Zhou Yu as his chief adviser) and Shu (under Liu Bei) as the equals of Wei. Zhou Yu had always been her literary hero.

Sumalagu, who had been standing in an obscure corner watching the whole scene, hastily followed her Princess. Once inside Bumbutai's tent, she sat down glumly on a stool. She was thinking hard how to break the news to her elated mistress.

Still reeling from the earlier titillating eye contact with Dorgon, Bumbutai was blind to her maid's presence. She started humming a folk song while poring intently over his drawing. Then with eyes closed, she flopped dreamily onto her soft bed covered in beaver fur. Her mind was hankering after the image of his half-manly, half-boyish face. When she next opened her eyes, she saw Sumalagu staring down at her with a pitiful expression. She sensed something was very wrong and instantly sat up straight.

The maid took her mistress's hands into her own and said in a low voice:

"My precious girl, I have bad news."

"What is it? What kind of bad news, Suma? Tell me right away, please."

"Please promise to be calm.... Your grandfather.... has betrothed you to Hong Taiji as his concubine. The date of your wedding has been fixed for next spring."

Those startling words hammered her so hard that it choked her breathing. For the next short while, she remained gagged. Her face changed from a vivid pink into a livid white. Sumalagu put her arms around her and rocked her from side to side like an infant. Abruptly Bumbutai broke loose from her maid's embrace and bounced off her bed, crying in a strained voice:

"No, I can't accept this. I don't even like Hong Taiji. He is twenty years older than I and he already has Aunt Jere. It's not fair. I will fight like Harjol and be the master of my fate. She got her way in the end, didn't she?"

She began pacing the tent agitatedly.

"Please calm yourself, Bumbutai. Don't you remember that Harjol's elopement almost killed your grandfather? You know very well that even to this day he still refuses to see her when she visits with her husband. He has put all his hope and expectations on you. Do you really have the heart to thrust a knife into him? He barely survived the last wound. He is already seventy years old. This time, he may not be so lucky."

"But what about my life and my happiness?" Bumbutai said

defiantly. "I only want to marry someone I like. Is it too much to ask? At least Harjol is happy." She was not about to back down. A rivulet of tears ran down her face.

"And what about the safety and well-being of the whole tribe and the Borjigit clan? Have you forgotten everything that your grandfather has taught you? Do you want your tribesmen go to war year after year? Do you want them to go to premature deaths and their wives and children to become war slaves?"

"Please stop, Sumalagu! I order you to stop speaking. That's enough!" she screamed. She sobbed even more loudly, her tears falling in a torrent.

"I love you like a sister, Bumbutai, and I always will, because I am forever indebted to your kind family for adopting me. I do want you to be happy. But happiness can mean you do your part to save the lives of hundreds of thousands of people, like the Goddess of Mercy. Happiness can mean you make good use of your knowledge to help your future husband in his quest to become a great Khan. Do you understand what I am trying to say? You were born to be a great Khatun!"

"But there's something magical between Dorgon and me…. I can't explain it. I've never felt anything like this… It seems like he came to wake me up from a long dull slumber…." she paused. Moroseness shrouded her tear-streaked face as the reality sank in. After a long pause, she finally said: "But I do understand what you mean."

"Maybe in time you'll get to like Hong Taiji more. At least he appreciates Chinese poetry. I hear that he is well versed in Chinese history and classical literature. But let's not worry too much for now. Your wedding won't take place until next spring, after you've turned twelve." Sumalagu tried her best to sooth her heartbroken Princess, stroking her hair tenderly as she spoke.

"I'll ask Grandpa to let you accompany me. I can't, and I

won't go without you," she murmured helplessly.

The two girls were embracing each other when Wukeshan entered quietly. He signaled for Sumulagu to leave. Sitting down on the edge of the bed, he patted Bumbutai's hand and said gently:

"My precious sister, you've heard."

"I want to die, my good brother."

"What for? Don't be silly. I knew from the way you blushed yesterday that you have fallen for Dorgon. But I can assure you that that kind of feeling will pass quickly. You're going to start a whole new life in an exciting new place. The Jurchen Princes are in possession of immense wealth and abundant luxuries that you've never even dreamed of," he paused a little and, seeing calmness return to his sister's face, he continued.

"The man who's going to be your husband is a great and kind man and I'm sure he'll lavish on you the most extravagant gifts and jewelry. Much more than that, he's going to be a great Khan who will one day rule over the Jurchens, the Hans and the Mongols. Do you even begin to realize what that means to you? Why has he picked you to be his concubine? Because he sees so much potential in you being his Khatun and his right hand. You are a prodigy who is well exposed to all three cultures. Once you become his consort, not only will your future well-being be secure, but so will the future prosperity of all Khorchin Mongols."

"I know, I know. It's my duty as a Mongol Princess. It is my destiny." She was almost loathing her birth now, but she knew her brother was speaking the truth.

"I will personally be your guard on your journey to Mukden and will see to it that you are nicely settled before I come back. It would be most ideal if Hong Taiji is good enough to offer me a military post within the Mukden Court, in which case I could be close to you. If not, I promise I will visit you at least twice a year."

In Bumbutai's intimate world, Wukeshan was one in whom she had complete trust and whose wisdom she would never doubt. Still, she resented his allusion to the prospect of her personal enrichment. He should know she never cared for jewelry or riches. But she believed his other arguments were valid. Turning her mind to her senile grandfather, who she knew had spent all his life brokering peace for his tribe, she found herself relenting. Somehow she would have to erase all thoughts of Dorgon from her mind. But there was something she must find out first.

After Wukeshan stepped out of the tent, Bumbutai took out a fine brush pen, a plate of black ink and a sheet of parchment, and began writing a letter to Dorgon in the Jurchen script:

"Venerable Beile,

I suppose by now you must have heard the news. My grandpa has decided to betroth me to Hong Taiji as his concubine. The wedding ceremony will be held next spring.

My eyes are full of tears even as I am writing. I had to write to you because I am desperate for you to hear my heart's voice. The moment I first laid eyes on you, I sensed something strange and beautiful was happening. My life suddenly burst into a million twinkling stars. You may think I'm naïve to say this, but this was how I truly felt. Sadly, the heavens are cruel and are determined to take away my stars.

I will not be able to show you a smile from my heart when I see you again, or to look into your eyes the way I did. I will even have to pretend that I don't feel anything. Because I will soon be your sister-in-law and I will never be happy again.

I'm not sure how you feel about me, Dorgon, and I'm dying to know the answer. Even if you don't write me back, please just give me a token and I will be content. I will keep the letter or token close to me until the day I die. But if you send nothing to me, I will also understand. These past two days have been the happiest of my life. I will be forever grateful to you. My heart is yours to keep forever, and I only have one heart to give.

With eternal affections,
Bumbutai"

When she had finished writing, she cut out a lock of her hair and put it inside the folded letter, wrapping all in a piece of pink silk kerchief that had a blue swallow embroidered on it. Then she fastened the bundle with a purple ribbon. She called out to Sumalagu and gave her the bundle to deliver to Dorgon immediately, bidding her to wait for an answer, which would either be a letter or a token, unless she was told that there would be no answer at all. In either case, she was to report back without delay.

Four

Once back in Mukden, Hong Taiji gave instructions to Jere to start making preparations for the wedding and to set up Bumbutai's temporary living quarters. As the new Palatial Complex was still under construction, he intended to have the new bride live inside his personal Library Hall, which was situated to the right side of his temporary Palace. It was appropriate, as Jere's Palace was to the left. He felt sure that his large archive of books in Jurchen, Chinese and Mongolian would make Bumbutai happy. He also told Jere to make a list of wedding gifts that were to be delivered to the Borjigit family after the Chinese New Year. As for gifts for the bride, he would personally make a selection.

Since becoming Fourth Beile at the age of twenty-two, a title he had earned by winning numerous battles against weaker Jurchen tribes, he had been gaining ever more trust and respect from his father Nurhaci. He, together with First Beile Daisan, Second Beile Jirgalang and Third Beile Manggultai, had helped Nurhaci unite all Jurchen tribes under the Khan's leadership. With their help, Nurhaci had established the Later Jin Dynasty (in deference to the Great Jin Dynasty of the twelfth and thirteenth centuries). By the sixth year of his reign, Nurhaci had captured the Chinese outpost town of Shenyang, beyond the Shanhai Pass north of Beijing and had named it Mukden, *the Rising Capital.*

The Four Great Beiles were effectively the ruling council of this Later Jin Empire and held supreme military power through the Eight Banner system. Daisan, the eldest son, was the Banner Chief of the Plain Red Banner and Border Red Banner. Ajige and Dodo (blood brothers of Dorgon's) held the Plain Yellow and Border Yellow respectively. The three brothers, though not Great Beiles, were all born of Lady Abahai, Nurhaci's favorite consort. Manggultai, an older son by another consort, headed the Plain Blue Banner, while Jirgalang, a nephew, was Chief of the Border Blue Banner. Hong Taiji was entrusted with both the Plain White and Border White.

The numbers of troops and their efficacy under the Eight Banner system ranged in this descending order: Plain Red, Border Red, Plain Yellow, Border Yellow, Plain Blue, Border Blue, Plain White, Border White. So in terms of military strength, Hong Taiji was the weakest of all the Princes, and he knew he was not Nurhaci's favorite son, even though he had his trust. He also knew that his position could become precarious overnight because he didn't have a mother to protect him.

He would never forget what his mother had said to him in her dying breath: "Son, the safest way to survive in this treacherous court is to become Khan yourself. I'm sorry I won't be around to protect you any longer. You have to mind for yourself…." He wept in his heart whenever he recalled her last words. He had no doubt Lady Abahai had been the cause of his mother's death. He had only been eleven then, and had hated the Consort ever since. As Ajige, Dorgon and Dodo grew up, they became Nurhaci's favorite sons because of their bravery in battle. Pangs of jealousy occasionally stabbed at him.

Lady Monggo, Hong Taiji's mother, had been a kind-hearted and refined lady of great literary talent. Nurhaci had admired her greatly before the arrival of Lady Abahai. But from a brutish man's perspective, cultural charm was no match for physical beauty in a woman. Lady Abahai's sparkling youthfulness had in no time conquered Nurhaci's heart and bearing him three strong sons had added even more merit to her credit. The sense of being deserted had plagued Lady Monggo to the point of debilitation.

After her death, Hong Taiji secretly made a vow to become Nurhaci's successor. Whether it was for self-preservation, or to fulfill his ambition, or both, he alone could answer. He had read enough Chinese history to be convinced that power was the only effective armor in an Imperial Court. The incident of Xuanwu Gate in the Tang Dynasty, in which a prince had murdered his throne-vying siblings, had firmly lodged in his mind.

Guided by his youthful perceptions, he had long identified Daisan as his first enemy, if only because he was the most likely to be made a Crown Prince, being the oldest of his half-brothers. Jirgalang was only a nephew and therefore posed no threat. Manggultai was a drunk and lacked fighting skills. The other key adversaries would naturally be Lady Abahai and her three sons.

In his efforts to discredit Daisan in Nurhaci's eyes, Hong Taiji had gone to great lengths. He had spun a rumor of an ongoing love affair between Daisan and Lady Abahai, conspiring with a young concubine of Nurhaci's who was jealous of the favorite Consort. Bearing false witness to an amorous meeting of the two framed victims, she had convinced Nurhaci of the story, and he had banished Lady Abahai from his Palace for a while. But afterwards he all but forgave her. Was it due to his doubts about the truthfulness of the case, or to a desperate need for conjugal love? It would never be known. In the end, Lady Abahai was reinstated in the Palace.

While on the surface, his chicanery seemed to have failed, it did have the desired threatening effect on Daisan. After the incident, he became much less motivated in the competition for Nurhaci's favor. That aside, Daisan had also been quite unnerved when his father ruthlessly ordered the execution of his elder brother for flouting a military order.

"Daisan is just a weak-willed wimp. I'll have him under my thumb if and when I choose to," Hong Taiji thought with impudence.

Sensing that his military power was inadequate, Hong Taiji had been mulling the establishment of a standby cavalry of Mongolian warriors who would be loyal to him alone. To this end, he had been building up ties with Manggusi of the Borjigit clan. The Clan Chief had given Jere to him as his primary wife in exchange for his promise of full protection for the borders of the Khorchin Mongols' tribal state. To secure Manggusi's promise to supply warriors and horses when needed, Hong Taiji had pledged to him a portion of any loot and seized land whenever he captured an unfriendly Mongolian tribal state.

On a recent visit to the Borjigit home, he had assured Manggusi that he was aiming for no less than the Jurchen throne. Manggusi had said to him: "Bumbutai is my favorite granddaughter and she's a jewel of a talent. I wouldn't offer her to you if I didn't think you would become the next Khan."

When he thought of Bumbutai, his tough facial features softened. The girl's natural youthful beauty and scintillating intelligence had captured his heart. She would be such a prize to him. But something was nagging at the back of his mind. Whatever it was, he was firm in the belief that the end justified the means. Yet, he seemed unable to shake one scene from his head.

One night, Sumalagu was leaving the guest tent where Dorgon was staying, carrying inside her *deel* the reply letter that Dorgon had given her. Without her knowledge, Hong Taiji had followed her there from Bumbutai's tent. As it had happened, he had been standing outside Bumbutai's tent and had overheard her instructions to Sumalagu about her letter. He jumped from the darkness to intercept the maid.

"The letter please, Sumalagu. You know very well that Dorgon's letter would only do harm to your Princess." He knew how close the two girls were. "She is going to be my concubine soon. Dorgon is young and brash and doesn't know what he's doing. What good will it do her if she can't be loyal to me and serve me with her whole heart? You are a clever girl and I'm sure you know how to protect your mistress's welfare."

Sumalagu had looked into his eyes as she retrieved the letter from her bosom and handed it over to him.

Since the wedding, Hong Taiji had been busy supervising the completion of the new Imperial Palatial Complex in the capital. He was mindful that the new premises would serve as an important symbol of the Jurchens' new found power and prestige. Also on his mind were plans to launch a major attack on the strategic Chinese town of Ningyuan in Liaodong Province. If captured, the town would facilitate an incursion into China proper through the nearby Shanhai Pass. In his mind, China was the greatest prize in sight, with Mongolia coming second. To get his hand on that coveted prize, he badly needed military aid.

Hong Taiji was in no hurry to possess his new bride's body. He was a patient man. When he felt the moment was right, he would take her whole, body and soul. He would wait for her to come round to loving him of her own free will. But that didn't mean he could let down his guard where Dorgon was concerned. He knew it would be unwise to have his lovelorn half-brother around in Court and decided to send him far away on a military errand. As there were unending skirmishes with the Chakhar Mongols, Hong Taiji ordered Dorgon to join the Plain Yellow Banner cavalry headed by Ajige, his elder brother, whose assigned mission was to end those skirmishes once and for all.

He had long had his eyes on the Plain Yellow and Border

Yellow Banner cavalry headed by Ajige and Dodo, whose warriors were much better trained and equipped than his own Plain White and Border White ones, let alone the outnumbering in men. If he were to gain an edge over the tenacious Ming Imperial Army at Ningyuan, he would need those better trained cavalrymen plus the help of his secret Mongolian ally. Hong Taiji had always taken extra caution not to let Dorgon or any of his other half-brothers know about his secret weapon, because as far as he was concerned, they were as much his enemies as the Ming soldiers.

The Ming Court at this juncture was plagued by a subversive eunuch faction who had powerful sway over the Emperor. These corrupt eunuchs were vehemently opposed to fighting with the Jurchens, because wars had to be financed by the Court's treasury, which they looked upon as their private coffer. The silver and gold bars were fast disappearing from the treasury as the greedy eunuchs kept stuffing their own pockets. For this reason, the commander in charge of the Ming forces at Ningyuan, the formidable General Yuan Chonghuan, an avowed advocate of taking the offensive against the Jurchens, was their principal nemesis.

In General Yuan's view, Ningyuan was a well-fortified stronghold only a short way beyond the protective Great Wall. From there, a counter-attack could easily be launched with his new artillery weaponry: iron cannons produced using the latest technology from Portuguese Macau. Neither Nurhaci nor any of the Four Great Beiles was aware of such deadly weapons being in the Ming arsenal.

Little by little, Bumbutai was beginning to shed her homesick feelings. During the morning classes, she discovered that Hong Taiji had a sharp mind and a prodigious memory, which she greatly admired. He showed an apparent liking for Sun Tzu's

The Art of War, especially the part about using spies. He had the whole book imprinted on his memory.

Bumbutai, who had also read the book, one day remarked in a chat with him: "It's interesting that many of Sun Tzu's war strategems resemble those used by Genghis Khan."

Her comment immediately spiked his interest, and he wondered aloud how he could get hold of a copy of Genghis' secret journal. It so happened the journal was the Borjigit clan's ancestral document and she knew it by heart. To show her gratitude for the favors he had granted her, she quietly worked on a translation into Jurchen. During one morning lesson, when Scholar Fan turned his face aside to cough, she quickly slipped him the translated copy with a secretive smile.

Hong Taiji flipped through the work, his stolid face melting into a childish grin.

"You are making me very happy, my precious," he whispered in mirth.

Later that day, Scholar Fan revealed to Bumbutai: "I've never seen the Fourth Beile in such a good mood."

By the time summer arrived, Sumalagu had finished making three ensemble sets of Han-style half-sleeved waistcoats and pleated long skirts from the bales of floral patterned silk in sky blue, jade green and violet that Bumbutai had selected. She loved these colors because they reminded her fondly of the Mongolian sky, the grasslands and the lavender lilies, and jade green was her favorite.

One evening, after dining with Hong Taiji in the antechamber, Bumbutai asked him to close his eyes and retreated into her bed chamber. When she re-appeared before him, she was dressed in a sky blue silk ensemble, twirling in a pre-rehearsed Chinese feather-fan dance. The body-fitting waistcoat clung snugly to her supple form. It made her look deliciously womanly. She didn't put any make-up on or wear any jewelry. Her hair was braided in two girlish plaits tied with color-matching ribbons.

Hong Taiji loved her new look so much that he said to Sumalagu: "You are a masterful seamstress, Suma. Your sewing skills have set off the womanish trait in your mistress!" Delving into his sleeve pocket in a guffaw, he took out two silver bars and gave them to the maid. He seemed reluctant to leave after the dance, but at length rose to retire to his own Palace.

The next day he granted Wukeshan the honorary title of Prince of the First Rank of the Jurchen Court, which meant that he could set up residence in Mukden and be near his sister. This sent her into a jubilant mood.

Before Bumbutai realized it, her first year in Mukden was coming to an end. But it was not until three years later that their marriage would be consummated. Before that would happen though, Hong Taiji would first be swept up in a blood-spilling power play.

In the spring of the eleventh year of Nurhaci's reign, the seventh of the Tianqi Emperor's reign, the Ming eunuchs recommended a new military commander to the Emperor. Upon arrival at the Ningyuan stronghold, this new commander showed General Yuan an imperial edict and ordered that the main defending forces retreat inside the Great Wall and abandon all the territories beyond the Great Wall. This order contradicted General Yuan's intention of strengthening the defense of Ningyuan. Being an ultra-loyal subject to the Emperor, he could not bring himself to disobey the imperial edict. Thus, he was left with only 10,000 soldiers to hold the fort at Ningyuan.

The Jurchen sentinel immediately reported the situation to Nurhaci. The Jurchen Khan saw this as his golden opportunity to launch the long-awaited attack. He picked Daisan, Hong Taiji and Manggultai as his commanding generals and led a troop of

100,000 in an all-out offensive. The cavalrymen traveled for days to reach Ningyuan and upon arrival, took up an attack position.

But General Yuan was not one to give up easily. He wrote a defiant letter in his own blood to Nurhaci vowing to fight the enemy to the death of his last soldier. At the same time he sent orders to the Great Wall guards to execute any soldier who was coward enough to become a deserter. Being the patriot he was, he immediately gained the staunch support of Ningyuan's residents. Most of the males volunteered as civilian fighters. Their feisty spirit gave an immediate boost to army morale.

In the battlefield, the two sides fought ferociously for two days. With the help of the iron cannons, which could fire shots of forty pounds, the Ming artillery inflicted heavy casualties on the Jurchen cavalry. These cannons had been newly made in a foundry in Beijing under the supervision of a German Jesuit priest, Johann Adam Schall von Bell. They proved to be the vital weapon in the Ming army's arsenal.

On the third day on the battle front, Nurhaci galloped in the leading position of the central column, flanked on the right and left by Daisan's and Hong Taiji's troops. He was waving the section with scaling ladders forward with a Jurchen flag, determined to breach the defences of the Ningyuan fortress.

A swishing sound fell on his ears and before he knew it, a cannon shot blasted right in front of him and split his chest open. He slumped to the ground, bleeding profusely. As Daisan saw him fall, he jumped from his horse and rushed up to his wounded father. Nurhaci had already fainted and was lying motionless, sprawled over the crumpled, blood-drenched flag. Daisan picked him up swiftly and carried him on his own horse away from the frontline.

Hong Taiji took over as Chief Commander. He and his stunned soldiers braved the cannon fire for another short while before fear overcame them all. Scores of his cavalrymen lost the will to fight and turned their horses round to flee. Seeing that there was no point in losing more lives, Hong Taiji ordered a full retreat back to Mukden.

FIVE

ONCE BACK IN MUKDEN, the brothers summoned the finest herbalists in the capital to Nurhaci's Palace. By the time the herbalists had managed to stop the bleeding, he had already lost far too much blood. The huge blood loss didn't kill him immediately but was serious enough to make him bedridden. Lady Abahai spent all her time by his sick bed, nursing him day and night.

Several months passed, and the Khan's condition showed no improvement. Seeing their father in such a precarious state, Daisan called a meeting of the Four Great Beiles to discuss the succession issue. He addressed the meeting by saying that the previous night he had had a talk with Lady Abahai.

"She told me that the Khan was slipping fast and that we should be prepared for the worst. She said that his last conscious words were that he wishes for Dorgon to succeed him if he doesn't recover."

"But we all know that the Khan has always embraced the merit system," Hong Taiji snorted in disdain. "Dorgon has little war credit to show. I am sure the Bannermen will revolt if he's made the next Khan." He looked around at the others. "You are not taking that woman's words seriously, I hope." His piercing gaze made Daisan shift uneasily in his chair.

"You definitely have a point there, brother!" he declared. "Dorgon is far too young. I thought Lady Abahai was most likely too distressed. She may have made things up." He was quick to say what Hong Taiji wanted to hear. "But she is still our stepmother. If she insists…." He threw his hands up to show he was in a bind. He had been hoping to sit on the fence until he could feel which way the wind was blowing, but he was not one who could withstand pressure.

Manggultai, as usual, had no strong opinions of his own and was happy to look to Daisan for guidance.

"I agree with Daisan," he said. "Women's words are not to be trusted, but we have to respect her as our stepmother." He shook his head in a pensive manner, as if in deep thought.

Hong Taiji ignored him. "So you are suggesting that it's better to risk the Bannermen's wrath than to thwart a boldfaced woman's ambitions?" he demanded of Daisan.

"Of course not… I was just saying….," His face whitened as he stammered. "We have always listened to your sound advice. Whatever you deem fit, we're willing and happy to follow."

Jirgalang remained reticent throughout. He knew better than to cross Hong Taiji. Besides, being only a nephew, he was clear where he stood in this matter.

Hong Taiji had always perceived Lady Abahai and her three young sons as the major stumbling block to his ambitions. Knowing full well that an open confrontation might bring about circumstances beyond his control, he decided to opt for a safer and more devious way out of the impasse. First, he would feign humility and disinterest in claiming the throne for himself. He would try to convince the other three Great Beiles that the best way to solve the succession problem would be for the Four Great Beiles to share the throne equally. They had been the *de facto* Ruling Council all along, and such an arrangement would meet with little resistance from the Eight Banners. Once this proposal was accepted, he would unsheathe his hidden dagger.

The end always justifies the means, even means of the most wicked sort, he would say.

In both Han and Jurchen culture and history, favorite consorts who had sons had always carried political sway on Court matters, especially when one of their sons was made the crown prince or put on the throne. It was customary for such consorts to practice nepotism, even long before the throne came within their control. In extreme cases, such practices brought about the eventual subversion of the royal Court. Hong Taiji saw the problem with this custom, how it prevented true talent from making contributions to the state, and he was determined to put an end to it. Removing Lady Abahai, who was beginning to build up her own network of allies, would mean killing two birds with one stone. As for her three sons, he planned to win them over.

In the seventh lunar month, Nurhaci's condition took a turn for the worse. Hong Taiji deliberately sent Ajige, Dorgon and Dodo on a military mission to fight the Chakhar Mongols. By this time, he had already made a secret pact with the other three Great Beiles to share power equally as Co-Rulers upon Nurhaci's death.

One night in the following month, a shrill scream shot out from Nurhaci's Palace, tearing through the crisp autumn air. Sumalagu bolted into Bumbutai's bed chamber to deliver the sad but unsurprising news. A moment later, Bumbutai was summoned to Lady Abahai's Palace. All women of the royal household were congregating there in white mourning robes.

In her mid-thirties, Lady Abahai still looked very fresh and attractive. Her white cloth mourning garment made her look vulnerable. Seeing the hapless pallor of her tear-stained face, Bumbutai felt pity for her. This woman had just lost her main prop in life. A Consort's fate is just the flimsy shadow of her husband's. With her once-powerful husband now walking among the dead, Lady Abahai's future was becoming perilous, if she had a future at all.

In a glum mood, the grieving widow led the procession of royal women towards the Throne Hall. There, in the center, a bier had been set up on which lay the casket that contained the corpse of the Jurchen hero. White lanterns were hung on both sides of the entrance. Inside the Hall, white candles were lit all around the bier. A ghostly white light fluttered over the faces of the male mourning crowd.

As soon as the women took up their kneeling position on both sides of the bier, Daisan rose up and addressed the crowd, holding a piece of paper in his hand:

"This is a painful day for our family and for the whole Jurchen tribe. We have lost a great ruler. A man who re-wrote our history. A man of unequaled valor and wisdom. A man who fought all his life to unite our tribe and who ruled with foresight. Fortunate for us, though, he made his wish known while he was alive, and his wish is for the Four Great Beiles to continue to rule jointly after his death. The four new Rulers will be headed by Hong Taiji. By consensus, the Four Great Beiles have voted to respect Nurhaci's wish and to take over the throne with immediate effect. If there is any objection to this succession arrangement, please let it be made known now."

Dead silence echoed in the Hall. Then a weak husky voice floated up from the female throng on the right:

"My three sons are on their way back from the battlefield right this moment. My late husband indicated clearly to me that he wants Dorgon to succeed him. I would plead with the Four Great Beiles to delay making any move until my sons have arrived."

The crowd stirred in a buzzing murmur on hearing this daring affront.

"Lady Abahai, the late Khan had his wishes written down. This cannot be disputed. I have the paper in my hand. In fact, I was about to announce the other important wish of his."

Daisan paused deliberately to look around him and, detecting no dissent, he continued to speak with a solemn expression: "Our great Khan foresaw the immense pain that his death would inevitably inflict on his beloved Concubine. His last wish is for Lady Abahai to escort him into the realm of ancestors." Then, turning to the widow, he said: "As for what you just said, the late Khan did state on paper that your three sons would all be appointed to a Private Council to assist the Four New Rulers."

A loud gasp erupted amongst the mourners. Lady Abahai could no longer keep her calm. She burst into a cataract of tears while muttering her vain protests. On the order of Hong Taiji, who had all this while remained silent, two strong maids went up and hustled the wailing widow out of the Throne Hall.

A chill went down Bumbutai's spine on witnessing this grim tragedy. She had never imagined that a helpless widow could be subjected to such calculated cruelty for political convenience. The whole event made her shudder with revulsion. What would Dorgon and his brothers do when they heard the news? She bit her lips in anguish. But it was there in writing. So probably no one could argue with that.

That very night, the Four Beiles appeared in Lady Abahai's bed chambers to carry out their late father's last wish. It would be prudent to do it before the return of her three sons to Mukden, which was expected the next morning. They knelt before Lady Abahai and pleaded with her to submit to the late Khan's wish. The thirty-six-year-old widow looked collected and calm, having accepted her fate. She said in a steady voice:

"I was married to the Venerable Khan at the age of twelve. I spent many joyous years in his company and was blessed with his affections and his many favors. It will be my honor to follow him into the land of our ancestors as he wished. Before I do that,

I have only one request: I am entrusting into your care my three young children and I beseech you to treat them with kindness. Can I have your word that you will never do them any harm?"

"You have our word. There is nothing more for you to worry about. We beseech you to begin your journey to rejoin our Khan," answered Daisan.

"I will get dressed properly. Please allow me just one moment."

A moment later she reappeared from the inner chamber in her glamorous red bridal robe. She sat down at her dressing table to powder her face. Manggultai and Jirgalang crept up from behind and strangled her with a bowstring. Her flailing hands scratched the air madly for a full minute before she went limp.

In a dark corner outside, two strong men were manhandling Nurhaci's lower-ranked concubine who had helped Hong Taiji to spread the tale of an adulterous affair between Daisan and Lady Abahai. They were putting the noose of a white rope around her neck after telling her that she had been selected to accompany the favorite Concubine.

When dawn broke, three stallions raced at lightening speed towards the Throne Hall. Having dismounted, the three brothers disarmed themselves and brusquely threw on the white mourning garments that were laid out for them at the entrance. They went up to the casket and fell to their knees, breaking into loud wails.

Not seeing their mother among the mourners, Dorgon was the first to raise the unwelcome question: "Where is our mother?" His frantic gaze swept the entire Hall. Daisan stepped forward and told him in a stutter what had happened the previous night. The young Beile almost went berserk. He lunged at Hong Taiji like a raging bull and would have strangled him with his bare hands were he not restrained by Jirgalang and Manggultai. When

Dorgon had calmed down a bit, Daisan showed him and his two full brothers Nurhaci's handwritten will. The three brothers then fell into silence, but could hardly hide their bitter resentment.

Two days later, inside the antechamber, Bumbutai was serving Hong Taiji a dinner of Chinese dishes, which were his favorite. She was pensive the whole evening and didn't say much. Hong Taiji couldn't help asking what it was that was bothering her.

"Was it really necessary to waste two human lives, even if it was written in the late Khan's will?" she blurted out. "The new Rulers could well have granted them a reprieve, if only to show magnanimity. Being a widow, Lady Abahai could hardly be a threat to the Four Rulers."

To her, it just didn't make any sense that Nurhaci would want to deliberately deprive his favorite sons of their mother. On the succession issue, though, she was ready to believe the arrangement was indeed his wish.

Not at all used to the slightest reproach, Hong Taiji felt badly stung by this sharp observation. His face instantly creased into a scowl.

"Woman, don't you ever dare talk to me about Court matters again, unless on my request," he shouted. "You have to know your place. Consorts who commit such a misdemeanor should be punished by flogging and banished from the Palace."

Hong Taiji's anger was so humiliating to Bumbutai that it made her eyes brim with tears. For the first time she saw savagery in his eyes. She knew she had touched a raw nerve but she didn't regret speaking her mind. It was just plain cowardice to murder a defenseless woman. Seeing the tears, the new Khan's face relaxed somewhat and, lifting her chin, he changed to a coaxing tone:

"Come now, my sweet Bumbutai. I didn't mean to frighten you. Please stop crying. You're making my heart ache!"

"I beg you to forgive me, Venerable Khan. I will observe court rules more carefully. This will never happen again. Please don't be angry with me," she pleaded in a meek voice. She lowered her eyes and sobbed. She knew that tears were her shield. She also learned a lesson in man-woman relationships: that a man can become unreasonably hostile if challenged intellectually.

"Rulers have to be obeyed absolutely. All lurking threats of betrayal or disloyalty have to be nipped in the bud," Hong Taiji continued. "You may be too young to understand these things. Your most important duty is to give unquestioning support to whatever I do and to indulge me with your affections. I could banish you to a retreat house for flouting a court rule. Do you understand me?"

"You are kind to explain all this to me, Venerable Khan. I will obey you and serve you well with all my heart."

But she still silently questioned the morality of expending two human lives out of the mere suspicion of disloyalty. She had heard about Hong Taiji's old grudges against Lady Abahai and could understand his need for self-preservation, but she feared that this killing of the mother would sow seeds of hatred in the three sons' heart, which would only spawn more bitter strife in the Court. Hatred is a destroyer of the human spirit, a poisonous burden to carry on one's shoulder. She wished so much that Hong Taiji could see he had made a terrible mistake. At this point, though, she was still in the total dark about the story of Nurhaci's will.

In the ninth lunar month, the enthronement ceremony was held in the Throne Hall. Four dragon seats were placed on a line all facing south on the raised dais. It symbolized an equal ranking of royal prestige for all Four Rulers. Hong Taiji also used this opportunity to mend his relationship with his three half-brothers by putting them on his Private Council and granting them new residences in Mukden. Extending an olive branch to Dorgon, he promoted him to the prestigious position of Deputy Commander of the Imperial Guards as a reward for his military success against the Chakhar and Khalkha Mongols. Out of self-interest though, he appointed his eldest son Hooge, who had much less military merits than Dorgon, to the position of Chief Commander.

In the months that followed, Hong Taiji set his heart on taking Ningyuan and avenging his father's death. He knew that in order to capture Ningyuan, the first thing he would need to do was to eliminate General Yuan. Aware of the long-term animosity between the Ming eunuchs and General Yuan, he thought it best to leverage that division to his own advantage. Recalling the Sun Tzu stratagem of using spies, he planted his own eyes and ears inside General Yuan's military camp to gather information. Meanwhile, he drew up a detailed plan to set up a decoy that would rid him of his Han arch-enemy once and for all.

Six

Hong Taiji spent two years laying a solid foundation for his rule by establishing more lenient policies in the treatment of his Chinese subjects and in recruiting more Chinese talent to fill official posts. Being a lover of Confucian philosophy himself, he had readily accepted Bumbutai's advice to hire Han Confucian scholars to important Court and military posts. Hong Taiji understood that for a minority race to successfully rule over the Han population, the key was to win over the hearts of the people. With this in mind, he made a special statute that forbade the Jurchen noblemen from grabbing Chinese farmers' land. Another edict was issued to abolish the oppressive vassal system.

One late morning, after a lesson had ended, Bumbutai came up with an idea, which she shared with her husband.

"Scholar Fan is well versed in Chinese military theories and no one knows the geography of China better than he. Don't you think he would make a good adviser on your military council?"

Hong Taiji inwardly exclaimed: "What a clever idea! Why haven't I thought of it before?"

He had been planning an assault on various Chinese towns on the border but had delayed the action because he and his men were unfamiliar with the landscape.

"I will appoint him to the council right this moment," he said with unconcealed excitement.

Not forgetting that his Plain and Border White Banner cavalry were inferior to those of the Plain and Border Yellow Banners, Hong Taiji asked Daisan to make a formal request on his behalf to Ajige and Dodo for an exchange of Banner cavalry. None of the three brothers raised any objection to the request, and the exchange went ahead smoothly. Seizing a long-awaited chance to depose Manggultai, Hong Taiji used misconduct as an excuse and managed to grab control of his Plain Blue Banner cavalry as well.

In the first month of the third year of his reign, Hong Taiji wrote a long emotional letter to General Yuan asking for a truce. Yuan presented the letter to Ming Emperor Chongzhen, an eighteen-year-old who had ascended the throne two years previously. The young emperor was very pleased, assuming that the Jurchens' miserable defeat at the Battle of Ningyuen was the cause for the truce request. He immediately promoted General Yuan to the post of Governor for the town of Ningyuan. Two months later, however, Hong Taiji's troops made a surprise second attack on the town. The Ming army won, but in the process General Yuan was discredited in the eyes of the Ming Emperor out of no fault of his own. This was exactly what Hong Taiji had intended.

That winter, Hong Taiji led troops consisting of the Jurchen and Mongolian Eight Banner cavalry totaling 100,000 men and descended upon the Ming capital of Beijing. Emperor Chongzhen ordered General Yuan to come to the rescue and the two sides fought bloody battles in the suburbs of Beijing for days. Yuan managed to prevent the Jurchen troops from reaching the capital's citadel walls.

Two Ming eunuchs were captured during the fighting and, on Scholar Fan's advice, they were put inside one of the military camps under loose guard. One night, two Chinese soldiers on the Jurchen side wandered over to just outside that camp, chatting loudly. One told the other that he had learned that orders had been received to retreat the next day, as Hong Taiji had made a secret truce pact with General Yuan. Later that night, the two eunuchs were given an opportunity to flee the Jurchen camp. And the following day, Hong Taiji's troops quietly retreated. Yuan feared that the retreat might be a trap and decided not to chase after the enemy.

The two eunuchs went straight back to the Ming Palace and reported what they had heard to the chief eunuch, who promptly presented an exaggerated version to the Emperor. The report focused on Yuan's supposedly traitorous agreement with the enemy and his obvious reluctance to defend Beijing. Earlier, General Yuan had ordered the execution of one of the Emperor's favorite generals for a grave military offense without first consulting the Emperor. That had already greatly ruffled his feathers. The chief eunuch naturally didn't lose the chance to latch onto that to further fan the young Emperor's suspicions of Yuan.

Hong Taiji's ruse worked as he had expected. One sweltering late summer day in the fourth year of his reign, also the fourth year of the reign of the Ming Emperor Chongzhen, a big crowd gathered in the main execution ground of the city of Beijing. A prisoner was being taken there in a wooden cage on a wheeled cart, with his neck and two hands locked in three holes of a wooden pillory. Two guards led the way in front of the cart with another two pushing it at the rear. His hair was in a tangle, his clothes in rags, and his bloodied face and body showed apparent signs of torture. But he stood upright in his cage and his face shone with pride. The final punishment he was going to be subjected to was one of the cruelest, as the mere name suggested: "Death by a thousand cuts."

A feral, blood-curdling cacophony rose from the crowd. "Let each of us have a piece of this traitor!" some shouted shrilly.

Little if any sympathy was visible on the faces in the crowd. Still less did the deadpan-faced executioner show on his, as he toyed with the newly-sharpened knife. The cart stopped between the wood-framed scaffold and a makeshift counter, behind which sat the Court Official of Public Execution.

In the middle of the scaffold was a pole, and the masked executioner was leaning idly against it. Two of the guards unlocked the cage and pulled out the prisoner. As they led him up the few steps to the scaffold, his knees buckled from weakness and they had to carry him to the top. The Court Official stood up and asked loudly whether the prisoner had any last words to say. The prisoner looked around him and then stared intensely at the crowd below. In a steadfast voice, he recited this poem that he had written in his prison cell:

My life and career have come to ruin,
Half my dreamed honors will never be.
My death will yet spur valiant men to show,
My patriotic soul will still guard Liaodong.

When Hong Taiji later received a report of that day's happening from his spies in the Ming camp, he secretly rejoiced that this fatal blunder by the Ming Emperor would for sure sound the death knell for the Ming Court. Patriotism rewarded with cruel death— what would the other army generals think? He could not but feel the deepest respect for General Yuan, who reportedly took half a day to pass over to the netherworld. He even felt disgusted when he was told how the foolish fanatic crowd had grabbed at the slices of flesh until all that was left was Yuan's head. One of the two guards who had carried Yuan up the platform still possessed a shred of decency and took the head and later gave it a proper burial in a remote spot beyond the city walls.

Bumbutai flinched on hearing what had happened to General Yuan, and had an intuitive premonition of the coming collapse of the Ming Court. In human history, beastly cruelty always heralds and precedes the collapse of a ruler. This and other overt signs were too obvious to overlook.

In the following year, Hong Taiji beseiged the fortress town of Dalinghe in Liaodong Province. He brought with him Daisan, Ajige and Dodo as his commanding generals. Instead of launching a head-on attack on the fortress, he ordered Daisan and his troops to surround it tightly. At the same time, he sent Ajige and Dodo with their men to attack the nearby smaller villages, forcing the residents to seek refuge and spread fear among the Dalinghe population inside the town. As the number of refugees increased, food became scarce and chaos ensued. At last the town fortress had no option but to raise a white flag.

Upon entering the fortress, Hong Taiji accepted with alacrity the surrender of ten famous Ming generals. He later made a point in holding a grand feast on the spot to welcome the surrendering generals and their families. He also put all these Ming generals under the command of Scholar Fan, who was easily able to strike up a rapport with them.

The new Imperial Palaces in Mukden finally neared completion during his sixth year as Khan. The complex was modeled after the Forbidden City in Beijing and had one hundred and fourteen buildings and twenty gardens in total. The grand Dazheng Hall (the new Throne Hall) in the Eastern Section looked out on a long pathway, which was flanked by a range of Banner Chief Pavilions. In the Central Section snuggled the Emperor's residence and Inner Palaces for his harem, interspersed with landscaped gardens and terraces. The Western Section housed large theaters, libraries and banquet halls.

Hong Taiji intended for the occupation of the new premises to take place after he secured absolute power and the title of Emperor. Prior to that, he would focus his energies on warfare and Court administration matters, thereby accruing credits for his later claim to absolute power. As of now, his large dragon seat was the only one facing south in the Throne Hall, with the remaining three placed at an angle, no longer on the same line.

Since seizing the title of Khan the year after his father's death, Hong Taiji had been hoping Bumbutai would offer herself to him voluntarily. To his dismay, that had not happened. It was in the late summer of the following year that he would find out the reason for her lack of intimacy towards him. One afternoon, he was in a good mood and wanted to take Bumbutai for a horseback ride in the woods. He was not in the habit of visiting her during the afternoon and was going to give her a surprise. As he was crossing the garden area that fronted the Library Hall, he saw from a short distance Dorgon and Bumbutai sitting close to each other on a stone bench under a sprawling oak tree. Dorgon had one arm around her waist and was using his other hand to caress her face. He backed noiselessly like a prowling leopard into a shady spot behind a hedge and continued to watch. They were holding hands and her head was leaning on his shoulder.

Hong Taiji's face instantly changed from a ruddy red to a copper green. Blinding fury uncoiled in his guts. With clenched fists and furrowed brow, he retraced his steps without making a sound.

That night, after extracting everything from Sumalagu without punishing her, he barked at his chief eunuch: "Fetch Bumbutai. I want her to serve me tonight."

Now that he was Khan, he no longer deigned to visit the chambers of his consorts at night. Instead, they would be carried to him, stripped for security reasons. The chief eunuch did as he was told, went over to the Library Hall and delivered the summons. Knowing this was Bumbutai's first time, he personally gave instructions to Siu Mui and Siu Fa to bathe Bumbutai and prepare her for the Khan.

Bumbutai knew that this day would come sooner or later. She had prayed to Eternal Blue Sky to delay it for as long as possible, but now she had to face it. While being bathed in the tub of perfumed warm water, she wept at the thought of what was going to happen to her. But there was no escape now. In despair, she let her mind wander off to the day when she had met Dorgon for the second time since her arrival in Mukden. It was in the previous spring, when he had returned from a battle in Mongolia.

On that slightly breezy spring day, Dorgon had appeared out of the blue at her antechamber. In Sumalagu's presence, he had bluntly questioned Bumbutai as to why she hadn't shown up for their assignation in the copse. She cast a puzzled look at Sumalagu, who reluctantly related the whole truth about the fate of Dorgon's letter, seized by Hong Taiji. Finally, the great conundrum was unraveled and the lovers had wept together in a passionate embrace, each having long pined for the other's touch.

"My sweet Bumbutai, now that the truth is out, I am content," said Dorgon. "All these years I could hardly take my mind off you. I realize there's nothing we can do to change your fate now. But as long as our hearts are one, there is nothing anybody can do to change that either. We are young, and we can afford to wait."

"Venerable Beile, I am yours in heart and soul and will always be. Eternal Blue Sky willing, I vow to offer you my whole self on a future date, if you don't mind waiting," she had answered, shaken by sobs and torn by desolation.

"There is no one I hate more than Hong Taiji! He murdered my mother and snatched you from me. Life is so unfair. But I will grit my teeth for now. The day will come when I will avenge my mother and make you all mine."

"My love, you mustn't torture yourself so! Hatred only serves to destroy the spirit. I assure you, the right time will come for us. Be patient and don't give up hope."

"I can be patient. But my love, please don't ask me to shed my hatred. He thinks he can fool us into believing that Nurhaci's will was authentic. Daisan told me the truth in confidence some time ago. Hong Taiji knows in his heart that he is an illegitimate ruler. But he has the upper hand now, as he has Daisan's support and a tight grip on the military. My brothers and I will play along for now."

Bumbutai had been flustered to learn about the forging of Nurhaci's will.

"Is there anything he wouldn't do to get his way?" she muttered.

From that moment on, her esteem for the Khan had plummeted. Whatever affection she had previously felt for him had dissipated. All her love would henceforth be reserved for Dorgon alone.

After bathing their lady in the perfumed bath, Siu Mui and Siu Fa undid her plaits and combed her cascading hair to a smooth sheen. Mutely they coated her face with a powder made from crushed pearls, gently rubbed her body with fragrant oil, put on her emerald earrings and dressed her in a loose-fitting white robe of pashmina wool. They then presented her in the antechamber, where the chief eunuch and another younger eunuch were waiting. The two eunuchs had spread a large quilted blanket on the floor and bade Bumbutai to take off her robe and lie on the blanket. Mechanically they rolled up the blanket and carried the bundle out to the palanquin that was waiting outside the Hall. Once inside Hong Taiji's bed chamber, the eunuchs put the bundle on the edge of the bed and unrolled the blanket. They then helped the Khan undress and bowed themselves out.

He couldn't keep his eyes off the nude body that glowed with dewy exuberance. She had a fuller form now than what he remembered from the wedding night. Her waist still looked tiny, her limbs perfectly proportioned. He had had other virgins before, but had never before felt so consumed with passion as he did now. Time had acted as a whetstone. Staring down on her nakedness, he said gruffly: "You are mine, and you always will be."

In the summer of the third year of Hong Taiji's reign, Bumbutai bore him their first daughter. The only one who felt happy on that occasion was Wukeshan, as he was really looking forward to betrothing his infant son to Bumbutai's first born daughter. Insensitive to his sister's dejection, Wukeshan announced that Manggusi, at Hong Taiji's behest, had just given their half-sister Little Jade to Dorgon in marriage. This news pushed Bumbutai into a bout of melancholy.

Two years later, while the Khan was away fighting the Battle of Dalinghe, one late autumn night, Dorgon stumbled into Bumbutai's bed chamber, stinking of alcohol. He hadn't seen her after their meeting in the Library Hall garden and was missing her badly. The Khan had chosen to station him in Inner Mongolia to keep an eye on the Chakhar Mongols. He had sneaked back to Mukden on a relief break and had begged her to allow him stay the night in her scented chamber, promising not to touch her. The next morning he found himself on his own bed, feeling groggy and not having a trace of memory of what had taken place the night before.

When the Khan returned victorious a month later, he

summoned Bumbutai to his bed. In the late summer of the following year, Bumbutai gave birth to another daughter. She felt strangely content over her birth and personally picked the Han name "Shuhui" for the newborn, which meant kindness and wisdom.

Soon after, Hong Taiji, still in a buoyant mood over his victory at the Battle of Dalinghe, demanded her conjugal services frequently. She conceived again and just ten months later gave birth to her third daughter without much ado. Now even Wukeshan was beginning to be worried about Bumbutai for her failure to produce a male heir for the Khan.

During the years of pregnancy and childbirth, Bumbutai became gradually attuned to reality. While accepting her fate as Hong Taiji's child-bearing woman, she strived to build herself an emotional and spiritual sanctum through the books that she found in the Library. She pored through the Chinese Four Books and Five Classics. She would make herself useful to the Khan, she told herself. In the process of acquiring new knowledge, she became a more self-possessed person and an intelligent adviser to him. She gave him the loyalty, deference and feminine support that he sought, but her heart was off-limits. She never shared her intimate feelings with him and always kept an emotional distance. Her inner world was a locked boudoir, the key to which was meant for no men but one.

Hong Taiji inwardly seethed. He could do as he pleased with her body, but it was an empty shell without an accessible soul. Outwardly, though, he appeared to be content with her giving advice on Court matters. In the Battle of Dalinghe, it was she who reminded him that Genghis Khan had often used siege tactics. Another piece of advice of hers that he had put into practice was the encouragement of interracial marriages between Jurchen, Mongolian and Han commoners. She also convinced him that promoting peace and social harmony was a paramount priority for the Empire.

There were times, though, that he wanted to strangle her fragile white neck. Her stiffened face and body gave him no pleasure in bed. He sought warmth and tenderness, but she always closed up her heart tightly like a clam. He began hating her. There was another thing that was really bothering him, and that was that she still failed to give him a son, and Jere continued to be childless.

SEVEN

SHORTLY AFTER GIVING birth to her third daughter, Bumbutai received a letter from her mother in Mongolia saying that Harjol had been widowed as her husband Zhuolin had been killed in a battle. Harjol wanted to come and visit her in Mukden and Bumbutai immediately sent a reply welcoming her sister's visit.

Harjol was four years older than Bumbutai and was the more beautiful of the two. She was also the favorite of their father, who gave her the name of Harjol, which meant "white jade". When she had insisted against Manggusi's wishes on marrying Zhuolin, a Mongolian warrior who had been her childhood playmate, Jaisang had quietly given her a mare and a coffer of silver bars so she could elope. Manggusi, who had been planning for Harjol to be given to Hong Taiji as a concubine, had been infuriated by her brazen act and had been on the verge of disowning her.

In their childhood days, Bumbutai had been close to Harjol. She had always envied Harjol's dreamy crescent-moon eyes which always looked like they were smiling. The features of her heart-shaped face were well proportioned, as was her willowy figure. Bumbutai, being herself a nimble dancer, had always adored Harjol's effortless dancing grace, which no girl in the whole Borjigit clan could match. Whenever Harjol performed a dance, the entire audience, especially the men, would be intoxicated.

When Bumbutai informed Hong Taiji about Harjol's imminent

visit, he appeared delighted. A thought immediately dawned on Bumbutai, that Harjol could become a welcome distraction for Hong Taiji and could even share her burden of child-bearing. If Harjol could produce a son, it would secure Hong Taiji's royal lineage, in which the Mongolian Borjigit clan would share an equal part. She felt sure that her grandfather was thinking the same thought too.

On the day of her arrival, both Hong Taiji and Bumbutai went to the Mukden inner town gate to welcome her. She brought with her two horse-drawn carts filled with sable, beaver and mink furs, together with five stallions from the Borjigit clan's ranches. At twenty-five, she had flawless milky skin and bewitching facial features, apart from a lithe figure. She was wearing a dark green fur-lined pashmina wool cape with a violet brocaded robe underneath. Alighting with an air of regal charm from her carriage, she walked towards the host and hostess in a naturally seductive gait.

As soon as Hong Taiji set eyes on Harjol, he was struck by her stunning beauty to the point where words failed him. Bumbutai came to his rescue by exchanging warm greetings with her elder sister. The royal couple invited Harjol to ride in their own carriage and led the guest's entourage back to the Palaces. On the way, Bumbutai and Harjol twittered like little girls, ignoring Hong Taiji's presence. When he had a chance to interrupt, he only managed to ask the meaning of the name Harjol in Mongolian. When he was told that it meant "white jade", he appeared happy with the answer and fell into silence again. The two sisters were glad to continue their chat undisturbed. Bumbutai couldn't help noticing that Hong Taiji was stealing furtive glances at Harjol.

A temporary bed chamber had been made for Harjol in the study lounge of the Library Hall, off from Bumbutai's antechamber. Harjol was surprised not to find Bumbutai's daughters around. Bumbutai explained to her that it was the rules of the Inner Palaces that royal newborn infants would be taken from the birth mothers as soon as delivered and nursed in a Residence reserved for royal infants. When the infants became toddlers, they were cared for by other concubines who would act as foster mothers. Bumbutai's two older daughters, one four-year-old and the other one-year-old, were living with an older concubine, while her newborn baby daughter was still in the care of a wet nurse in the infant nursery.

"What strange rules! Can you visit your daughters any time you want?"

"Only for a short time each day. I'll take you to visit them tomorrow, after you've paid a visit to Aunt Jere. But you must be dead tired now. I'll ask Siu Fa to prepare your bath. After you've taken your bath, we could have a light dinner and then you can go straight to bed."

"Bumbutai, are you happy here?"

"As happy as I could expect to be. Hong Taiji is kind to me and I get to study and learn like a scholar. What about you? How was your life with Zhuolin when he was alive?"

Bumbutai did not want to reveal her innermost secret about Dorgon, not even to Harjol.

"I had a blissful life with Zhuolin," her sister replied. "After his death, I dreaded going to bed alone for nearly three months. I thought I would wallow in grief forever, but the healing started soon after I took up Buddhism a couple of months ago. My mind is finally at peace now."

"I'm so glad to hear that, Harjol. Hong Taiji is a fervent believer in Buddhism. You two may have something in common to talk about. You know, I've always envied you for the love you and Zhuolin shared. And the way you stood up to Grandpa! I wish I had that kind of courage."

"If I were to do it all over again, I would still follow my heart and do the same thing."

"But sometimes life forces your hand… What about duty to your family and state?"

"I only know that if I didn't follow my heart, I'd end up being utterly miserable. For me, being loved by a man is everything… Buddhism teaches love too, but of course that's a more noble kind of love. I'm still striving to understand it."

Siu Fa came in at this moment to tell her mistress that the guest's bath was ready.

"We'll have all the time to talk during your stay here. I'm so happy to see you."

"I'm happy to see you too, little sister. Funny to see how little we've changed. You are still your old serious-minded self, all this talk about duty. No wonder people think that you're the older sister!"

The next evening, on Hong Taiji's invitation, Harjol showed up with Bumbutai at a grand feast held in her honor. The sisters surprised the Khan by offering to dance a Chinese ribbon duo dance, which they had rehearsed in the afternoon. At the end of the performance, Hong Taiji applauded heartily.

In order to let Harjol have time alone with Hong Taiji, Bumbutai made an excuse to retire early towards the end of the feast.

There was a little awkwardness at first, but once they started talking about Buddhism, a natural kinship sparked between them. Harjol happened to be just as interested and well versed in Jurchen history as Bumbutai, and knowingly led Hong Taiji into a field of knowledge that was close to his heart.

"We Mongolians have always admired the Jurchens for being the valiant warriors they are, dating way back in history." She knew that to please a man, boosting his ego was the surest way. "Your brave ancestors ruled over northern China under the Great Jin Dynasty long before our Kublai Khan established the Yuan Dynasty. But even the founders of the Great Jin pale in comparison with your Aisin Gioro clan in the ability to unite, lead and rule. The Great Jin Dynasty Founders were cruel and shortsighted and just did not understand the importance of benevolent rule. Their fledgling dynasty was thus soon crushed along with Southern Song of China when our ancestors rose to power. But the Mongolian Yuan Dynasty in the end fared no better, for much the same reason."

"You have good insight there," Hong Taiji replied. "The Yuan Dynasty had a short span of life because the Mongolian rulers failed to win the hearts of the Hans."

He was amazed that a woman as delicate as Harjol could talk with such virtuosity on such a complex historical subject.

"Grandpa told me long ago that he is confident of your becoming the eventual great ruler of all of Mongolia, China and Manchuria, because you have all the qualities of a visionary leader."

"Your grandpa was kind to say that, Harjol. As a matter of fact, there is much in common between Mongolians and Jurchens in terms of warfare ability. Both races are unparalleled horse riders and archers. But neither race in the past had the necessary cultural understanding of the conquered race that was needed to sustain its rule. My one and only idol has always been Genghis Khan. No one from either race has yet surpassed him in vision, bravery and intelligence. Even my father, brilliant as he was, tended to treat the conquered in a tyrannical way. I don't deny that my cherished dream is to be that perfect ruler, but I'm not so arrogant as to claim I'm entirely worthy of your grandfather's praise."

Hong Taiji had never previously uttered the secret thought

about his father to anyone, not even to Bumbutai.

"You are far too modest, Venerable Khan. If you are not worthy, then I don't know who is. Uniting the three races under one single state will be for the greater good. Mongolia has long been in need of a capable leader, as has China. Besides, any person who believes in Buddha is one with a kind heart. I will ask Buddha to help you reach your goals."

Though tired of people around him behaving in an obsequious manner, he had come to regard that as normal. Even Bumbutai would not always be forthright with him. But the humane side of him never stopped pining for true companionship. In speaking from the heart with unbridled candor, Harjol was like a splash of sweet rain on parched land. He knew he had just found a roost for his solitary soul.

"Harjol, your words are the sweetest I've heard. Ahh, 'Harjol', what a beautiful name! White jade! It is a most fitting name for you."

"You are the first man who has said that to me. It's very kind of you, Venerable Khan," she blushed into a deep pink as she lowered her crescent eyes in shyness. The Khan saw it as a sign of the seduction to come.

He rose from his eat and stepped over to Harjol. "I've never seen a woman more beautiful than you, or sweeter," he whispered in her ear. "Buddha is merciful and has sent you to mend my poor wounded heart."

"Venerable Khan, I am sure I don't deserve such high praise… It's getting late and I should retire." She thought the best strategy was to exit now.

The next afternoon, when Hong Taiji had finished attending to Court matters, he took Harjol on a private tour of the new Inner Palaces at the Palatial Complex.

Harjol was so impressed by the meticulously landscaped

gardens and the ornate Palace interiors, that she exclaimed aloud her awe at every discovery. Her childish rapture and natural laughter caught Hong Taiji like a fever and made him feel twenty years younger. He asked her to pick the Palace that she liked best. She pointed to the one that had sky-blue glazed-tile rooftops and pale gold exterior walls, with an ornamental dark blue ceramic marquee. This Palace happened to be closest to the Emperor's Residence. He was pleased that she made that choice.

For the remaining days of her sojourn, Hong Taiji could not keep himself away and found time to be with her every afternoon. She seemed equally excited to see him each time.

Bumbutai was quietly watching the pair and could foresee the outcome. Two days before Harjol's intended departure, Bumbutai wrote to her grandfather and mother and told them all that was happening between the Khan and her sister, bidding them to get Harjol's dowry ready well ahead of time.

On the day Harjol was to leave, Hong Taiji came to her bed chamber and gave her as a token of admiration a precious bracelet of eighteen white jade beads with a pendant of two large pink pearls. It was a Buddhist prayer bracelet that had been kept in the Court's national treasure chest. Then he took her in his royal carriage which rolled at a slow trot to the town gate. There he bade her farewell as she mounted her own carriage. He stood there till her carriage entirely disappeared into the winding folds of the carriage track.

The following spring, Harjol's bridal procession followed the same route as Bumbutai's nine years before, and was also led by Wukeshan. Manggusi had been so pleased with this event that he had given special orders for an extra generous dowry to accompany Harjol. The wedding at Mukden was the grandest that Hong Taiji had ever held for any of his brides. The jewelry that Harjol received from her new husband included a pair of white jade tasseled hair pins, three pairs of white jade and pink pearl earrings and two bracelets of white jade beads.

The new royal couple thereafter led a life of bliss. Following the wedding, no other Consort was ever summoned to the Khan's bed chambers. Hong Taiji reserved all his love for this Mongolian gem of a bride. Harjol's showering of tender love on her husband rejuvenated him, turning him into a young lion at heart. Bumbutai secretly rejoiced that Hong Taiji now had a woman to satisfy his emotional and physical needs. She prayed that Harjol would soon conceive and bear a son.

Hong Taiji did not let his new found love occupy all his time and energy. Shortly after the wedding ceremony, he led his troops in an assault on China's Shanxi Province. In the following year, he concentrated his military power on the unfriendly tribes of Inner Mongolia and attained victory after victory. By the end of the ninth year of his reign, the whole of the Mongolian steppe south of the Gobi had come under Jurchen control. He took as his trophy Consorts the two widows of the Chakhar Mongol leader, Ligden Khan. Ligden Khan's successor offered Hong Taiji the Yuan Dynasty's Heavenly Jade Seal as a gesture of submission and loyalty. Hong Taiji thought it an opportune time to officially change the tribal name from "Jurchen" to "Manchu", so as to distinguish his reign from his father's.

EIGHT

THE FOLLOWING YEAR was an important milestone in Hong Taiji's reign. In the spring, he ordered a grand ceremony to be held in the new Dazheng Hall to mark the Empire's official dynastic name change from "Later Jin" to "Qing". The reason for the name change was that the word "Jin" in "Later Jin" would remind the Hans of the previous much-resented Jurchen rule in the 12th century of northern China. Another reason was that the character "Jin" (meaning gold) had a metal element which was blamed by the soothsayers for persistent strife among the royal brothers, whereas the character "Qing" (meaning clear) carried a water element and was expected to usher in more harmony for the royal family. Hong Taiji also designated "Aisin Gioro" as the official Imperial clan of the Manchus.

The ceremony was attended by all Aisin Gioro male clan members as well as Court officials and Bannermen of the Manchu Eight Banners and the Mongolian Eight Banners. Before entering the Hall, Hong Taiji, crowned with a gold-rimmed crimson velvet hat and dressed in a golden yellow silk Imperial robe embroidered with a pair of dragons in front and one at the back and girthed with a gold-trimmed sash, offered incense to the Heavens and ancestors at an altar which had been set up on the wide marble stair landing. The landing was atop an expansive flight of marble steps overlooking the grand pathway, where cavalrymen and foot soldiers carrying banners lined up on both sides. He then went inside the Hall and stepped up onto the throne dais. Turning around to face the gathered audience, he seated himself on the golden Throne Seat placed in the middle.

In making obeisance to the new Emperor, all the attendees in the Hall kneeled three times and bowed their heads nine times in front of the marble steps leading up the dais, while chanting "Long live our Emperor". With a sweeping stroke of his hand, he signaled for them to rise. The Director of Protocol had planned this ceremony based on the Ming Imperial Court's ceremonial rites to the minutest detail. He now proceeded to read out a statute which bestowed the temple name of "Taizong" on the new Emperor. Under Han customs, this name was normally used for the first emperor of an Imperial lineage.

Daisan put on a congenial smile throughout the rites while Jirgalang wore a nonchalant expression. Manggultai had not been invited because of his recent demotion to the post of an ordinary cavalryman. Dorgon, Ajige and Dodo had come with great reluctance, their impassive faces masking visceral hatred. Bumbutai had begged Dorgon to persuade his brothers to attend without fail. No one understood Hong Taiji better than she. He would take an overt snub as a sign of challenge and perfidy.

Underneath the apparent calmness, the struggle for absolute power had never ceased. Daisan and Manggultai had long been unhappy about Hong Taiji's efforts to cut their entitlements and privileges. They had previously had the discretionary power to horde war loot as they pleased, but Hong Taiji had recently issued an edict banning all their discretionary powers, and commanding that all war loot must first be brought back to the Court. His Private Council was authorized to propose on the method of distribution, on which he alone had the final say.

Manggultai had a quick temper and did not bother to hide his contempt, unaware that by doing so he was playing right into Hong Taiji's hands. The Emperor banned him first from his Private Council and then further demoted him to the rank of an ordinary cavalryman. Jirgalang's brother Amin disobeyed the new order and was imprisoned. Daisan and Jirgalang appeared docile on the surface and submitted to Hong Taiji's autocratic rule. Still, that didn't stop the Emperor from eventually stripping all the Eight Manchu Banner Chiefs of decision-making power. His Private Council now included Scholar Fan and a handful of newly-recruited Han officials, who gave enthusiastic support to his centralization of power.

With the inaugural use of Dazheng Hall, the other parts of the Imperial Complex were also opened. He hadn't forgetten Harjol's wish and promptly assigned to her the Palace of her choice, which was the largest and most lavishly decorated of all the Inner Palaces. This Palace was on the east side of the Emperor's Residence, while the Empress's Palace was located on the west.

That summer, Hong Taiji issued an edict for the establishment of a Code of Etiquette for the Inner Court based loosely on the Ming Chinese Code. In honor of the Khorchin Mongols, he granted Jere the most prestigious title of Empress, giving her the Qingning Palace (Palace of Celestial Peace) and putting her in charge of the affairs of the Inner Palaces. The title of Consort was bestowed on four of his Concubines. Harjol got the title of Consort Chen of the Guansui Palace (Palace of the Swans) and the two Mongolian widows of Ligden Khan from the Chakhar tribe were titled Consorts of Lingzhi Palace and Yanqing Palace respectively. Bumbutai became Consort Zhuang of Yongfu Palace (Palace of Eternal Comfort).The order of the title grants conspicuously showed Harjol's name right after Empress Jere's and heading all the other Consorts. Bumbutai ranked last.

Hong Taiji had specifically chosen the name Guansui for

Harjol's Palace. The name came from the first poem in the Chinese Book of Poetry, in which swans were used as a symbol to eulogize the life bond of a love couple.

As if empowered by the magic of love, the Emperor won three major battles in a row against the Chakhar Mongols and brought the whole of Inner Mongolia under his control. Bumbutai had never seen him happier.

Neither did he show any qualms about flaunting his happy life with his beloved Consort. Harjol was always seated right beside him in all Court banquets, large or small. He never took any Consort but her with him on his hunting trips. His chief eunuch delivered the Emperor's bed partner summoning tag to no one but Harjol. All the eunuchs and maids-in-waiting had special orders to take extra care to serve the favorite Consort well. There was to be no limit to her household expenses. Her clothes were made of the most luxurious fabrics, the food she was served the finest possible, and the flowers for her Palace the most beautiful and freshest.

Bumbutai couldn't help but wonder if the Emperor's showy doting on her sister didn't partly stem from a vindictive desire to sting her. Much as she welcomed the idea of being left alone to live peacefully, she nevertheless had to face the dismal prospect of unending solitude. She had no idea, then, of the depth of his wrath.

As for Harjol, she initially still showed some courtesy towards her younger sister. But as she started to master the art of wrapping the Emperor round her little finger, she became more distant and even insolent towards Bumbutai.

Yongfu Palace was the smallest of all Inner Palaces and the farthest from the Emperor's Residence. The exterior garden walls were of modest purple-painted terra cotta and the roof tiles were a demure dark blue. The front porch was of plain oak wood, coated with lacquer. The interior had three modestly furnished but airy main chambers: one lounge with latticed windows on opposite sides, one antechamber and one bed chamber at the back. There were annexed rooms in the backyard that served as the maids' quarters. Bumbutai loved the understated elegance of her Palace. What pleased her most was the large garden fronting the lounge. It had a small pond in one corner near the front porch, filled with white lotuses. Two weeping willows stood guard on either side of the pond. The lounge looked out on a large flower bed, where she could tend to her favorite lavender lilies.

To her, a large open space where she could keep in close touch with the sky was much more important than an embellished interior. She thought the name of the Palace, "Eternal Comfort," was very pleasing too, because it did bring her a little peace of mind. Still, the Emperor's stark coldness towards her was like an angry undercurrent that wouldn't leave her at ease. She was twenty-three years old and had to taste what living widowhood was like.

One hot summer day, when she was watering her favorite lilies, a maid from Empress Jere's Palace came and announced that her presence was required at once at the Imperial Clan court. She hastily tidied herself up and hurried over with Siu Fa tagging along.

Once inside, she was astounded to find that a trial was in progress. She saw two chained prisoners kneeling on the floor: a low-ranked young Concubine and a young cavalryman. Empress Jere was presiding at the interrogation and all Consorts and Concubines were present as observers, except for Consort Chen, her sister. The pair were accused of adultery. They both looked distraught and deeply frightened.

In a rigid and hard voice Empress Jere said: "Your shameful deed has besmirched the Emperor's honor and the honor of the clan. I cannot allow this kind of despicable conduct to ever happen again in the Inner Palaces. For this reason, all other sister Consorts and Concubines have been invited here to observe the punishment. I now sentence you both to a beating of sixty strokes each with a large stick. Then you, sister, will be banished to life confinement in the retreat house, and you, young man, will be exiled for life outside the borders."

Bumbutai couldn't remember having ever before heard Jere speaking in such a harsh tone. On hearing the sentence, the accused Concubine fainted and slumped to the floor. The cavalryman leaned over to prop her up. He then pleaded in a plaintive voice with the Empress to let him take all the hundred and twenty strokes, sparing the Concubine. After mulling for a while, the Empress granted his plea. Then she ordered two eunuchs to execute the beating at once.

All the Consorts and Concubines cringed in trepidation when they saw the man being pinned down on a bench and hard blows landing on his buttocks and legs. He gave out hair-raising screams as blood seeped through his pants. The guilty Concubine promptly passed out again.

As Bumbutai watched the cruel beating, a chill passed down her spine. A gruesome picture rose in her head. She saw a crippled Dorgon staggering towards her, his leggings drenched in blood. The blood kept squirting from his mangled legs. Her whole body shivered violently like willow branches caught in a wild gust. Later she would learn that the Empress was already showing leniency. The usual punishment involved one hundred strokes each, which could mean a maimed lower body or even death. In the present case, the poor cavalryman could well be crippled for life even if he could survive the hundred and twenty strokes.

That night, Bumbutai tossed and turned in her bed and

couldn't sleep a wink. Anxiety roiled inside her. The grisly image of a maimed Dorgon kept churning in her brain. At last she could no longer bear being alone. She got out of bed and fumbled her way to Sumalagu's bed chamber in the backyard to wake her.

"Suma, Suma, please wake up. I need to talk to you," she pleaded between sobs.

"What is it, my mistress? What has happened?" Sumalagu bounced up from her sleeping position, much alarmed.

"I couldn't sleep. I kept having these monstrous thoughts about Dorgon and me."

"You must try to calm yourself. I will fetch you a cup of ginseng tea. But you must return to your own bed chamber, because it's much warmer than here. I'll sleep on the floor right beside your bed if you like."

The maid quickly threw on her day garment and accompanied the stricken mistress back to her own chamber. Once back there, Bumbutai broke down in a deluge of tears in her maid's embrace.

"I fear for myself and for Dorgon..... But today's event was just so grotesque. It doesn't bode well. The Concubine was so young. She must have been very lonely and in need of a man's love. That poor girl, I pity her so much. It's not her fault really." Big drops of tears continued to roll down her chin.

"I know, I know, my precious," the maid whispered soothingly. "It's the fault of the stupid rules of the Inner Palaces. The Emperor can have countless women, but they all have to share that one man, and infidelity on their part is punishable by death or near death. But you have done nothing, nothing at all, that has broken those rules. You mustn't let your silly thoughts run wild."

"But sometimes I do feel unbearably lonely. In times like those, I would fantasize being in Dorgon's company ..." She blushed and could not go on.

"I know how you feel about Beile Dorgon, my good mistress. It's too bad that the Emperor knows it too." She released a deep sigh, wanting to say something and then stopped. After a pause, she continued:

"I heard from the Empress's maid that the Empress was under special orders from the Emperor to conduct today's interrogation in full presence of his harem.... He had made particular mention of your name."

This shocking revelation twisted Bumbutai's guts. So it was a deliberate warning from him. She had thus far known him to be a possessive person, but going so far as to terrorize her over a letter written before her marriage was beyond comprehension. She was not aware that he had spied on her intimate rendezvous with Dorgon in the Library Hall garden.

"You must be very careful not to give him any more reason to suspect your conduct," Sumalagu gave her a comforting brush on the back.

"If he wants to trick me, there are a million ways he can do that, no matter how much care I take," Bumbutai shot back. "I am nothing more than a bird trapped in a gilded cage." Her eyes reflected a glint of bitterness and rebellion.

"He is only a lion with a wounded heart seeking some kind of outlet for his hurt pride," Sumalagu replied, trying to deflect her mistress's concerns. "Sooner or later he'll come to terms with the fact that love cannot be forced."

"I hope so. I've been trying so hard to give him whatever I can give. How can he be so cruel? I'm sure Harjol is giving him the happiness he was seeking. Isn't that enough?"

"This phase will soon blow over, especially now that he is the Emperor with supreme authority."

"I do hope you're right, Suma."

Back in the first year of his reign, Hong Taiji had tried and failed to conquer the Joseon Dynasty of Korea. After he was anointed the first Manchu Emperor, he purposely sent an expedition of delegates to Seoul to seek their recognition of his new Imperial reign. But with the back-up of the Ming Imperial Army, King Injo of the Joseon Kingdom showed disdain for the Manchu Emperor and impudently tried to ambush the delegates. This incensed Hong Taiji.

Now in the early winter of the tenth year of his reign, he appointed Dorgon as the commanding general, and together they led an army of 120,000 into Korea. King Injo and his royal family tried to escape to Ganghwa Island as Korean kings traditionally did when attacked by an enemy. The King's attempted escape was foiled by the Manchu army although other members of the royal family managed to flee to the island while King Injo took refuge at the Namhan Mountain Fortress. Hong Taiji used his familiar siege tactics and soon those inside the Fortress ran out of food and ammunition. Meanwhile, Dorgon descended upon Ganghwa Island to capture King Injo's family and consorts. Ming China made a token effort, sending a miniscule rescue force, which, by a streak of bad luck, was wiped out by a storm at sea. In the end, King Injo had no option but to surrender.

On a platform that was specifically built for the surrender ritual, Hong Taiji forced King Injo to repeat the humiliating act of kneeling and bowing to him many times.

Back at Mukden, Hong Taiji rewarded Dorgon handsomely for the military success over Korea. He gave him one-tenth of the loot, reserving the other nine-tenths for distribution among the Eight Manchu Banner Chiefs and the Eight Mongolian Banner Chiefs.

On the night of his return, the Emperor signaled to his chief eunuch that he desired Consort Chen, that is, Harjol. The favorite Consort had been expecting the call and had been soaking in a bath filled with fragrant rose petals, knowing that the Emperor loved this fragrance on her body.

When the chief eunuch came for her, she gave him a bar of gold, together with a small packet containing some horny goat weed in powder form. He took them with a smile and said he would return as soon as possible. Meanwhile, Harjol's maids dressed her in a white robe made of sheer material imported from Europe and applied the finest make-up to her face. They adorned her hair with her white jade-tasseled hairpins and put on her white jade earrings.

That night, the lanterns inside the Emperor's bed chamber remained lit until very late. Two months later, Harjol's Palace was abuzz with excitement. The Emperor was informed that his favorite Consort was with child.

NINE

HONG TAIJI HAD BY this time already had seven sons born to him. But none of them had won his heart. The intensity of his love for Harjol could be easily read from his reaction to the news of her first pregnancy. It was both a Chinese and Jurchen custom never to celebrate an early pregnancy. The belief was that it was a boasting of good luck which would arouse jealousy in the gods and hence jinx the birth or the infancy. But the Emperor decided to ignore that custom, partly because he was too enamored with Harjol not to do something to reward her, and partly because he felt that he, as the supreme ruler of three races, should not deign to submit to such superstition.

He thus ordered a grand celebration to be held at the Guansui Palace. On top of that, he showered Harjol with luxurious gifts ranging from mink fur capes and jewelry set in precious gems, to expensive silks, perfumes, flowers and delicacy dishes. He also assigned two maids to give the Consort daily massages and to attend to her slightest whim. No other Consort or Concubine from his harem had ever been pampered this way.

For Bumbutai, this news was good news too, as it seemed that Sumalagu's prediction was coming true. The bad phase was finally over and Hong Taiji's frostiness towards her was starting to melt somewhat. She wrote to her parents with the joyous news and prayed hard to Eternal Blue Sky to let Harjol carry a son in her womb. At the same time, in the deep recesses of her heart, she was yearning for the day that Dorgon and she could be joined in union too, although something told her she had nothing to look forward to except a fanciful dream.

Leaving the celebration feast at Guansui Palace, Bumbutai made her way back to her own Palace. While passing through an orchid garden, she saw Dorgon moving towards her. She wanted to dodge away to avoid him but it was too late. He stopped by her side, quickly shoved a piece of paper into her hand, then disappeared from her sight. She kept walking until she was inside the garden walls of her own Palace. Her heart still beating fast from the encounter, she sat down on a porcelain stool underneath the drooping willow branches and opened the handwritten note:

"Meet me tomorrow night in your garden at the first Palace gong beat."

She paced too and fro in her scented garden for a long time, thinking about the note. She was yearning to see him, but she knew she should not. It would be too dangerous. What should she do? Should she send Sumalagu to take a note of refusal to him?

Under the rules of the Inner Palaces, no male except for the eunuchs was allowed to remain inside the Imperial Palace Complex after nightfall, when the brass-studded Main Gates would be slammed shut and an Imperial sentry would stand guard until the next morning. The first gong beat signified the first security call announcing the impending closure of the Main Gates. There would be a lapse of an hour between the first and second, and between the second and last gong beat. At the last gong beat the Inner Court would be off limits.

Dorgon lived in a large mansion just a short walk from the Palace Complex. If she agreed to the meeting, it would mean that he could spend a little less than two hours with her at the most and then he would have to make for the Main Gates, allowing time to walk from her Palace, which was located not far from the Gates.

Hong Taiji would definitely not be visiting her at night time, and it was also out of the question that she would be summoned to his bed chamber, now that Consort Chen enjoyed sole custody of him in her Palace. It was three days before Chinese New Year, and many workmen and tradesmen would be busy with their work inside the Complex until the time of the Main Gates' closing. The eunuchs and maids from other Palaces would be occupied with festive preparations inside their households and would not come near the Yongfu Palace. That would mean the chance of Dorgon being seen on his entry and exit was quite remote, if he were sensible enough to disguise himself as an ordinary workman. After thinking it through carefully, Bumbutai decided that their meeting should be quite safe.

The next evening, Bumbutai asked Siu Mui to serve her an early meal, saying she would like to retire to bed early as she had a headache. After the meal, she relieved the two young maids of their duties and sent them to their own quarters. When she was alone with Sumalagu, she told her that Dorgon was coming to see her and asked her to keep watch at the garden gate when the two of them had gone indoors.

At the appointed time, Dorgon slipped unnoticed into the garden, dressed in workmen's clothing, with dirt smeared on the face. Bumbutai took his hand and led him inside her lounge. Having seated him on the lacquered red wood couch by the window, she served him hot jasmine tea. A shaft of moonlight peered through the window to spread a silvery sheen on the lounge floor, imbuing the room with moody calmness.

"You've lost weight, my love," he said, touching her face gently as she sat down beside him. On hearing such intimate words, all her pent-up emotions were unleashed like a violent tempest, and she burst into tears.

"He was so mean to threaten me with that most wicked drama, all because of jealousy over the letter I had written to you." Her tears, once unleashed, could not be stemmed.

"I know, I understand. Hush, hush, my sweet love. I heard about the Clan court case. He is such a sick man." He instinctively put his arms around her and wiped away her tears with his fingers. "It's not just the letter," he added. "He actually saw us cuddling in the Library Hall garden that day. Later he got everything out of Sumalagu. Somehow the information got out, and I heard it from Wukeshan when we were out on a campaign a couple of years ago."

She nodded. "Oh, so now I can see why he acts so spitefully towards me." She dried her tears on her sleeve, recalling the fury in his eyes on the night she had been deflowered. In the dark recess of her mind loomed a secret that she would guard with her own life. Not even Dorgon could be let in on it. Having regained her composure, she continued:

"I did all I could to keep him satisfied before Harjol came, but there was just no way to please him. It's only since he found out that Harjol was pregnant that he began to thaw a bit towards me."

"Bumbutai, do you remember what you said to me before? Our time will come. I believed you then and I still do. So please don't give up hope."

"Yes, I will hang on for your sake, my love. He was mad at me because he couldn't have my heart. Now that he has found his own true love, he will spare me, I hope."

"How I wish I could protect you from him! It breaks my heart to see you suffer like this."

"I've always known that a great part of my destiny would

involve duty. But I didn'r realize it would be so hard to give up love for duty. It's impossible for me to get you out of my mind."

"The more I know you, the more I love and respect you, sweet Bumbutai. You've been such a great spiritual prop to me. I can't go on without you," he lifted her moistened face and kissed her hard on the lips.

"How has he been treating you?"

"After the war in Korea, he tried to win me over by lavishing gifts on me. But just as he did before to please me and my brothers, it's all a show. He is good to us for only one reason: we are all good at fighting and he needs us to wage his wars. And he knows in his heart what he owes me in particular."

Sumalagu had laid out several dishes of sweetmeats on the table, and Bumbutai got up to serve them to her lover. Just then, they heard the sound of the second gong beat. Watching her gliding towards him, he seized her by the tiny waist and pulled her close to him. He lifted her up effortlessly and carried her into her bed chamber. As he started to unbutton her waistcoat, she struggled to sit up on her bed.

"No, no, please don't do this, Dorgon. It could bring ruin on both of us. We must try to keep our heads. He has not touched me once over the last two years, and if I get pregnant, it will be the end of us!"

Those words froze him in his act. He buried his head in Bumbutai's bosom and cried in anguish. She stroke his face tenderly and kissed away his tears.

A pattering of hurried steps outside the chamber could be heard. Then a knock on the chamber door. They heard Sumalagu whisper through the door chink:

"Venerable Beile, you must leave right now through the backyard door. Please hurry. A man is coming to the garden gate. It's too dark and I couldn't identify him."

Dorgon jumped up from the bed, kissed Bumbutai on the forehead and dashed out. Sumalagu led him out into the backyard and opened the yard gate for him. Then she rushed back to the front gate.

Her mistress was talking to Wukeshan in the garden. He had come to deliver the news of the passing of their grandfather. He asked his sister's advice on whether or not they should disclose this mournful news to the Emperor and Harjol. After contemplating for a long time, Bumbutai decided that it would be best to keep it quiet for the moment. She feared that if such bad news led to any mishap in Harjol's pregnancy, it might give the Emperor an excuse to find a scapegoat.

Then Wukeshan took out a small package from his sleeve and handed it to Bumbutai.

"On his sickbed, our Grandpa told me to give this to you," he said. "This jade seal is the Borjigit clan's heirloom. You are to safe-keep it and pass it on to the first male issue from Hong Taiji and one of the Borjigit Princesses."

The news of Manggusi's death left Bumbutai devastated, and she thought about how, on top of not being able to mourn her beloved grandfather in her homeland, she would have to put on a false merry face when around the Emperor and Harjol.

Wukeshan said a few words to comfort her and then turned just before leaving.

"Sister, do watch your step," he warned. "I wouldn't do anything stupid."

After he left, she remained in the garden, not wanting to go indoors. She looked up at the dark vaulted sky. Heavy clouds were devouring the full moon as if to portend her bleary future. An unbearable sense of isolation engulfed her. A sudden yearning to hide in her mother's embrace rushed up to fill her entire being. The word "duty" had never weighed heavier on her heart than at that very moment. She crouched down and curled up her body, wishing there was a cocoon into which she could vanish.

In the early summer of the following year, the Emperor ordered a Buddhist ritual to pray for the safe delivery of the royal infant, whose birth was expected in about three months. Led by Empress Jere, all Consorts and Concubines wearing violet silk robes filed into the Guansui Palace garden. They chanted psalms as they circled the altar, which was placed in the middle of the garden. At the altar three Buddhist monks offered joss sticks to the effigy of the Goddess of Mercy and burned strips of yellow paper with wishes written on them.

Half-way through the ritual, the Emperor's entrance was announced. His eunuchs helped him to be seated in a canopied wing chair to observe the ritual. His eyes loitered for a moment and fell on Bumbutai, whose face he had not seen for a long while. What he saw now pleased him a great deal. She still had a strikingly handsome face and a supple figure. The violet color of her robe set off her luminous complexion to a pearly shade. Her gracefulness and understated charm brushed over him like a fresh breeze. If Harjol could be likened to a pink peony in full bloom, then Bumbutai would be a budding white lily. How could he have neglected such beauty?

In the evening, the Emperor gave special orders to his chief eunuch that he wanted Bumbutai in his bed chamber for the night. If Harjol should ask for his whereabouts, he was in the study hall reading Court papers. He had endured his dry spell for long enough.

On the Imperial bed, Bumbutai closed her eyes and tried hard to conjure up images that could distract her. When it was over, the Emperor said despairingly:

"You are my woman. Why can't you give me your heart?"

"Your Imperial Highness, every part of me is yours. My

only wish is to give you pleasure. If I have failed, I beg your forgiveness."

"Your heart is somewhere else. Don't take me for a fool. I am the Emperor and your husband. I have a right to you as a whole. If your heart betrays me, I can punish you."

"If it pleases Your Imperial Highness, I willingly submit to your punishment," she replied in a soft voice, unfazed by his threat. It was in moments like this that she wished she had bristles on her body.

"Don't you know that I could never harm you? My heart was set on you from the first time I saw you, Bumbutai. Do you know how hurt I felt the night you bedded me for the first time? You couldn't even look me in the eyes." A shadow of deep dolor darted across his face as he spoke. After a long pause, he continued: "But it doesn't matter now. Your important duty is to bear me a son, because I want this son to inherit your wisdom and my bravery."

"I know very well that is my duty, Your Imperial Highness."

"How I hope Harjol will bear me a son. I need capable sons to inherit the fruit of my lifetime conquests. How perfect it would be if you could be as devoted to me as your sister. You two are the most intelligent of all my women, you in particular." That dark shadow again swam across his deeply furrowed forehead. The candle flickers cast uneven shades on his face and made him look haggard.

"My mother told me when she was dying that I wouldn't be safe until I became a Khan. I had to do whatever was necessary to get to that position. In the process I might have hurt some people. Now that I am in that position, I have tried to make amends. But I also need to pass the fruit of my labor to posterity. My Empire and my subjects need a great successor. He must be able to realize my dream – of uniting the three races under the

Qing – in case the heavens summon me earlier than expected….."

Bumbutai's heart softened as she heard such heartfelt words from him. The man had deeper feelings than he let on. Only he had too much pride and was in the habit of hiding his emotions. No amount of love could assuage his innate fears and burden of guilt. Instinct urged her to respond to the fickle warmth that this cold-faced man had just shown. She snuggled up to console him, and he took her again, this time with much tenderness. She felt she understood him better now, and she could even be kind to him. But she only had one heart to give, and it had long been taken.

Three months later, the Emperor had a strange dream one night. In the dream his father Nurhaci came to tell him to look up to the sky. As he looked up, he saw tiers of beautiful rose-colored clouds floating around and above them a small chink of blue sky, which shifted in and out of sight, until it disappeared altogether. A wild wind blew and the ethereal clouds dispersed. Then out of nowhere a ball of fire rose up, burning brightly. It startled and woke him. He felt an ominous unease.

He told Daisan about his dream and asked what he made of it. Daisan said that fire was always a good sign because it symbolized heat and life, deliberately ignoring the first part of the dream. The Emperor's mind was somewhat soothed by his words. After a while, he turned his attention to Court matters at hand and forgot about the dream completely.

The following day, Harjol gave premature birth to the Emperor's eighth son. He was overcome with joy and announced that he would grant a general amnesty when his son was one month old, as a token of gratitude to Buddha. As the infant was very weak at birth, the finest Court physicians were ordered to take daily care of the baby until he showed more strength. They fed it soup made with birds' nest on a daily basis until the bluish color of the little body disappeared.

On his first month's birthday, the baby looked underweight but otherwise healthy enough. Swaddled in embroidered yellow velvet, he nestled peacefully in the arms of his radiant mother, who paraded him with pride around the Banquet Hall where the grand feast was held in his honor. No grander feast had ever been held for any of the Emperor's sons on their first-month birthdays. Choicest pieces of roasted lamb shoulders and pork shanks, on top of delicacy dishes cooked in Chinese style, and barrels and barrels of barley and rice wine were served throughout the day. Entertainment included Chinese dancing, acrobatic and opera performances, which had taken one month to rehearse, day and night, and couldn't have been more spectacular. The feast was to continue into the next day.

In the Imperial edict that granted general amnesty, the Emperor referred to his newborn son as the "royal heir". This was the first time that the Emperor had ever used the words "royal heir" in any official Court document. Having been informed about Manggusi's death after his son's birth, he now granted his late father-in-law the posthumous title of Prince of the First Rank in another edict. He apparently did this out of love for Harjol more than for anyone else.

On this day, cartloads and cartloads of congratulatory gifts arrived from the Borjigit clan in Mongolia. Big feasts were also being held on the clan's home turf in the southern steppe. The birth of this royal heir signified the permanent strengthening of bonds between the Khorchin Mongols and the Manchus. Words could not express the pride that the tribesmen felt for this "fair-faced daughter" for performing her duty well.

Bumbutai had known she was with child before her sister gave birth to hers, but thought she would withhold the news for a little while so as not to steal the show. When she returned to her

Palace from the feast, she disclosed it to Sumalagu. The maid was beside herself with joy for her mistress, having actually dreamed the previous night that her Bumbutai was carrying an infant boy.

But the mistress was in a different mood. She couldn't feel any joy. All she could envision was scene after scene of sibling rivalry and perpetual hatred in the struggle for the throne. She could never forget what had happened that fateful night at the Throne Hall when Daisan had read out Nurhaci's will. If she were to bear a son, she couldn't see how she could avoid being drawn into the political vortex. The memory of what had happened to Lady Abahai still sent chills into her bones.

She called to mind one particular unhappy face she had seen at the royal heir's birthday feast. It belonged to the Emperor's eldest son, Hooge. He was born of Lady Ulanara, the Emperor's deceased first wife. Though not the Emperor's favorite son, Hooge was a young valiant warrior who often boasted of his military trophies. Pomposity and arrogance were his weaknesses that made his father dislike him, but that didn't discourage him from having an eye on the status of Crown Prince. Jealousy was written all over his face when the Imperial edict was being read out, referring to Harjol's son as "royal heir."

Empathetic as she was towards the Emperor, Bumbutai couldn't help but feel that Dorgon was the one on whom gross injustice had been inflicted. If it weren't for Hong Taiji's maneuvers, Dorgon would have become the Emperor rather than he, and in her opinion, Dorgon could have been just as good an Emperor as Hong Taiji. But then again, maybe things would have worked out differently, that circumstances might have deposited poisonous residue in Dorgon's soul and hardened his heart. It was impossible to say. But now that she was carrying Hong Taiji's fourth child, she felt ashamed of her used body and the fact that she had been unable to give herself to Dorgon. Then she paused. Perhaps her current circumstances allowed her to give him what he deserved, and desired.

She wrote a note and asked Sumalagu to take it to Dorgon at the feast. In the note she asked him to come to her Palace the next evening under the guise of a Court physician, at the same time as the previous meeting. The feast was due to continue into the next night, and there would be hordes of people coming and going and it would be easy for him to slip in and out.

Once he was seated in the lounge, Bumbutai appeared in a jade green half-sleeved silk waistcoat adorned with butterfly buttons and a pleated silk skirt of the same color. Quietly she offered him rice wine and then began twirling around in a seductive butterfly dance that she had specially rehearsed for him. She had learned the dance from Siu Mui and Siu Fa, who had learned it in their childhood. Before it came to a finish, Dorgon could wait no longer and got up from the couch. In one swift brush, he swept her into his arms and carried her into her bed chamber.

He slowly removed her waistcoat first, then her skirt, then her undergarments. Savoring every inch of her milky skin, he teased her with his rousing caresses. "You look so lovely in green," he whispered in her ear. Their eyes locked, as they entered each other's souls. Each saw in the other their younger selves joyfully riding across the Mongolian steppe. In her watery eyes, he saw an inflamed yearning. She was blushing like the girl he had known back then. His guts burned. Her mesmerizing scent made his heart throb. She opened herself to him uninhibitedly, like a lotus flower.

The star-studded sky on that enchanting night and his boyish smile flashed through her mind. How she wished she could stop time.

The next day, Bumbutai summoned the real Court physician named Sima. He gave her the good news that she already knew and she bade him to announce it to the Emperor, which he gladly did. The Emperor promptly rewarded him with five gold bars for delivering such a pleasing message. He had a feeling that she would bear him a son this time and decided that he would love both these sons equally. He was proud of the fact that these sons were of royal Mongolian and Manchu parentage, believing that they would possess the best traits of both races.

TEN

WHEN PHYSICIAN SIMA was leaving the Emperor's Residence, a eunuch from Guansui Palace approached him and took him to see Consort Chen, Bumbutai's sister. She questioned him as to what information he had just revealed to the Emperor. Seeing the look of concern on her face, the physician promptly told the truth. He was then asked when would be his next appointment with Consort Zhuang. The eunuch beside him whispered something into his ear, and the physician's face turned a pale shade of grey instantly. He cowered and bowed his way out.

In the middle of the following month, Sima went again to see Bumbutai. He was a man of morals with an innate good heart, and he had to speak.

"Venerable," he said in a choked-up voice, "I was instructed by Consort Chen's eunuch to prescribe some vile herbs for you, which would cause a miscarriage if taken. I am a physician and I could never do such a thing. In order to escape the consequences of disobeying Consort Chen, I have decided to take early retirement and return to my home town. I will ask another trusted physician to take care of you in my place."

Bumbutai shuddered. She had never imagined that her sister would do anything to harm her. She thanked the physician repeatedly for saving her unborn child's life and asked Sumalagu to give him a piece of jewelry from her jewelry box to help with his future livelihood.

She recalled that Harjol had once told her that a man's love was everything to her. But couldn't she understand that the Emperor was under no obligation to be loyal to her? A consort would always be one of many consorts, no matter how beautiful or intelligent she was. But perhaps having a son could provide the mother with a more secure status. In the Manchu culture, mothers had a higher status even than wives. Harjol should be content that she had a son that was favored by the Emperor. Her status would never be questioned for that alone. Bumbutai's wish now was that she was carrying a boy, who would be able to protect her when he grew up. As for Harjol's seeming heartlessness, she was ready to forgive her sister. She believed that there must be some sensible reason behind the desperate action. Sumalagu volunteered to find out.

The maid came back and told her that Harjol's infant son had been ill for some time and all the best Court physicians had been consulted to no avail. She had been to a temple just outside the city to light incense and to pray for her son's quick recovery. While at the temple, a Taoist monk had told her that her younger sister was carrying a male infant inside her womb who would become the true heir. Fits of depression and jealousy had driven her to the awful act. According to her maid, she had since shown remorse and had in fact sent a message to Sima on the day of his visit to Bumbutai, retracting her order. Sima had found it on his return. Harjol had sighed with relief when she learned of Sima's honorable act and urged him to stay on in his Court post.

After hearing out Sumalagu's report, Bumbutai went over to the Guansui Palace to pay her sister a visit. As soon as she entered the lounge, Harjol came up to embrace her.

"My sister," she sobbed, "I am so ashamed of myself for what I did. I didn't mean to harm you or your unborn child, Bumbutai. You have to believe me. I honestly don't know what came over me. I beg you to forgive me. "

Her crescent-moon eyes were doused in a morose gloom as she spoke.

"There's nothing to forgive, dear Harjol. We all make silly mistakes when under unbearable pressure. I understand how you feel. You must have been devastated by your son's illness. How is he now? Shall we go and see him?" Bumbutai put her arms round Harjol's shoulders and stroked her back tenderly.

"He's been really ill, and none of the Court physicians can do him any good. I'm so worried! Let's walk over to the Nursery." She held Bumbutai's hand tightly and led her out.

The Royal Nursery was right next to Qingning Palace and just a short walk across from Guansui Palace. Anguish had piled years on Harjol's youthful face. A few dull grey strands had intruded into her once shiny black mane, and her beautiful eyes had lost their usual luster. Bumbutai's heart ached for her sister.

They found the baby sleeping fitfully in a hanging cot. His face was wrinkled like an old man's, and his bony frame was the size of a cat. He was twitching in spasms underneath the quilted cover. Bumbutai's eyes brimmed with tears when she saw her infant nephew. She quickly looked the other way lest she should make Harjol cry too. Her heart went all out to her sister.

"Let us go outside and pray together to Eternal Blue Sky in the garden," She said. For the Mongols, in situations where human effort is apparently futile, the last spiritual refuge would always be Eternal Blue Sky.

The sisters knelt on low padded stools and prayed earnestly until the sun descended into the mellow depths of darkness. The twilight emitted an evil blood red glitter. Bumbutai then gave Harjol the Borjigit jade seal that Manggusi had passed to her, saying it was for her son and that she hoped it would bring him good luck. Sadly though, where life and death were concerned,

Eternal Blue Sky seemed to have an iron will that no human had the power to bend.

By order of Empress Jere, festive activities for Chinese New Year at the Imperial Palaces were cut to a minimum due to the lingering sickness of the royal heir. No one dared mention that the eighth son of the Emperor had yet to have a name bestowed on him, as he had relapsed into ill health many times since his birth. On the first day of the New Year, the Emperor and Harjol went together, in separate royal sedans, to the Buddhist temple that stood on a small hill just outside the palatial district. They offered their prayers to Buddha and to the Goddess of Mercy, asking for good health to be restored to their beloved son.

Two days before the end of the first lunar month, a screech of agony tore through the Guansui Palace. Consort Chen went berserk with grief and was inconsolable. After her son's bluish corpse had been wrested from her clutches, she seized her own hair with both hands and tried to pull with all her might, giving out blood-curdling shrill wails. All her maids were terrified and took flight. Her chief eunuch scrambled out and ran towards the Yongfu Palace to look for Consort Zhuang, who was very near the time of delivery for her own child.

Bumbutai made her way as fast as her heavily pregnant body could manage to the Guansui Palace. She saw her sister curled up in a prostrate position, groaning ceaselessly. Her hair was a tangled mass and she looked like a cadaver, with sunken eyes and sallow skin. She had no tears left. Bumbutai knelt beside her sister and put her arms round her. She knew that by custom she should not be visiting her bereaved sister, as the deep grief might bring bad fortune to her unborn infant. But she had never had a second thought about coming. She rocked her sister like a small child and said to her softly:

"Harjol, it's alright to cry. Cry, my precious, cry out loud.

You'll feel better."

There was no response. Harjol stared at her bulging belly for a long time and then at her face in a visionless gaze. Then her repressed tears erupted like a violent flash flood. Bumbutai continued to soothe her, rubbing warmth into her hands and saying tenderly:

"You're still young. You'll conceive again easily. Don't be sad, don't be sad."

That night, Harjol had a high fever. Bumbutai stayed at her bedside throughout the night, bringing her fresh wet cloths to put on her forehead to cool her down. She heard her sister murmuring something to the effect that she was being punished by the gods for the evil she had done. To soothe her, she hummed a childhood song about fair-faced daughters. She stayed until the early hours of the morning, when Sumalagu came to relieve her.

The Emperor refused to see anyone after he received news of the baby's death. The next day, he did not attend Court proceedings, nor did he take any food. The entire Imperial Complex was shrouded in a thick aura of grief.

On the following day, Bumbutai gave birth to a healthy male infant. She bade Sumalagu to deliver the news as quietly as possible to the Emperor. She also gave strict orders to the eunuchs, maids and servants that no celebration of any sort was to take place.

When the baby was one month old, she went to the Emperor's Residence Palace and asked that her son be given a name. The Emperor decreed that his ninth royal son should be named Fulin, which meant the arrival of good fortune. She immediately wrote to her parents about the birth and the royally-decreed name.

Like other royal Princes and Princesses before him, Fulin was taken to the Royal Nursery to be breast-fed by a wet nurse. When he grew older, he would be placed in the care of Empress Jere, who would be his foster mother. The idea behind this practice was that Princes and Princesses had to be brought up according to a stringent set of etiquette and strict disciplines, without the pampering of their birth mothers. They would then be educated by specially appointed teachers and tutors. Bumbutai split her time between taking care of her sick sister and visiting her infant son on a daily basis. She also prayed daily to Eternal Blue Sky asking for the continued good health of her son.

When the Emperor was done grieving for his lost son, he focused his attention on the biggest prize yet of his dreams, which was Ming China. The Ming Court was now in its final stages of decay. Empty coffers, rampant corruption, a pestilence called smallpox and widespread mob uprisings constantly weakened the Empire. The Chongzhen Emperor had earlier succeeded in suppressing the subversive eunuch faction which under his brother's reign had grown out of control. But that effort was just a drop in the ocean. Being an extremely insecure and paranoid person, he knew no better than to rely on his favorite eunuch for information about his Court officials. This only served to spawn yet another conniving eunuch network. Without the Emperor's trust, the Court officials found it easier to please and collude with the eunuchs than to function dutifully. Corruption thrived once again.

Hong Taiji's gut told him that the time was ripe for another attack. He foresaw the significance of these imminent battles, victories which would lift the reputation and status of all those involved. Hence he carefully circumvented Ajige, Dorgon and Dodo in his selection of commanding generals, and instead chose Hooge and Jirgalang. Hooge, for all his foibles, would still be the first choice to succeed him as Banner Chief for both the Plain and Border Yellow Banners. Bumbutai's son was still only an infant.

Since the death of the Ming General Yuan Chonghuan, the

Ming army had not changed its defensive strategy in the fortress towns of Jinzhou and Songshan along the Shanhai Pass corridor which protected the Great Wall of China. These towns were vital to the Manchu Army because they would be the key relay points in their supply lines. As of now, military supplies had to be looped through inhospitable Mongolian desert regions. Without these towns, it was also hard to have the loot from raids on Chinese border towns safely returned to Mukden.

After the victorious Battle of Dalinghe, the Manchu army had improved their mastery of artillery thanks to advice from Ming generals who had surrendered to them. The Manchu Emperor planned to replicate his Dalinghe siege tactics in the attacks on Jinzhou and Songshan.

Hong Chengchou was a patriotic military commander of Ming China who, like Yuan Chonghuan, was a strategic thinker with a strong faith in the use of European cannons in artillery warfare. In the twelfth year of Chongzhen Emperor's reign, the Ming commander had successfully put down an uprising mob in southern China led by a desperado named Li Zicheng, After that, he was transferred to the north to fight against the invading Manchus.

In the early autumn of Chongzhen's fifteenth year of reign, which was Hong Taiji's fifteenth as ruler of the Manchu Empire, Ming general Zu Dashou was in charge of defending Jinzhou. He had pretended to be a turncoat earlier in the Battle of Dalinghe and had surrendered to the Manchu army, offering to take Jinzhou for them. But when the fortress town had come under his control, he had changed sides again and defended the town for the Ming army, pushing out the Manchus. Now Jirgalang's troops lay siege to the town, under the command of Hong Taiji. The small Jinzhou garrison was in an untenable position and Zu Dashou immediately wrote to Beijing asking for rescue forces to be sent.

In response, the Chongzhen Emperor appointed Hong Chengchou as the commanding general to lead 130,000 troops to liberate Jinzhou from the siege.

Geographically, Songshan and two other flanking mountainous towns formed a natural protective triangle for Jinzhou. If the Ming army could take up a defense position in those hilly towns before the Manchu forces reached them, then Zu Dashou could have a chance to break out of the siege. So Hong Chengchou brought his troops right into Songshan and stationed them there. Hong Taiji, meanwhile, led his Manchu and Mongolian Eight Banner cavalry of 80,000 to meet the enemy midway between Songshan and Jinzhou. In the first battle, the Manchu army suffered a terrible setback.

As Hong Taiji's troops were outnumbered, he thought it best to use small-scale attack tactics with the aim of exhausting the enemy. He then asked some of his soldiers to scatter fear-mongering pamphlets in the battlefield, stressing the brutality of the Manchu cavalrymen towards captured enemy soldiers. Just when the Ming forces were least expecting it, he launched a sudden full-scale attack, employing cannons that had been produced based on the design of the Ming army's Portuguese-made cannons. Many of the unsuspecting Ming infantry soldiers had arms and legs blown to pieces. They had never previously experienced the violent body-mangling power of the new cannons. Bone-chilling cries of agony made the surviving Ming soldiers cower in terror.

As the Ming army was trying to retreat from the front line, Hong Taiji ordered his cavalrymen to slaughter the retreating soldiers and to mutilate their bodies, creating pandemonium, and to raid the Ming camps' supplies. Hong Chengchou lost 80,000 of his men and most of his military and food supplies. At last, he had no alternative but to withdraw into the Songshan fortress with only 10,000 men left.

Over at Jinzhou, which was surrounded tightly by Jirgalang's troops, Zu Dashou's men were getting restless as the hope of breaking out faded, while food supplies had long been depleted. Talk of eating corpses started to run wild among the starving soldiers.

Inside the Manchu Chief Commander's camp, Jirgalang reported to Hong Taiji about the Jinzhou situation, while Hooge suggested an immediate siege of Songshan. The Chief Commander questioned the prudence of an immediate siege, pointing to the exhaustion of the cavalrymen after the strenuous battle. Just as the discussion was going on, a sentry guard came in to report a post-horse heading towards the camp.

A moment later, a dust-covered courier entered, knelt on one knee and bowed before the Emperor. One of the Emperor's guards inspected the envelope that the courier handed him, then submitted it to the Emperor. He noticed there was a burned corner of the envelope and immediately felt an ominous unease. There was only one sentence in the letter: "The Court physician attending to Consort Chen said she is dying."

His heart sank to the floor on reading the message. Without hesitation, he handed over the Chief Commander's seal to Hooge and ordered three Imperial Guards to accompany him on a ride the next morning back to Mukden, brushing aside all requests for him to reconsider. The only image that filled his head was that of a smiling Harjol waving to him.

The four riders rode on day and night without rest. On the third night of the journey, they took a rest at a post-horse station, where they got news that Consort Chen could be gone any moment now. On hearing that, the Emperor fell down on his knees in tears and begged Buddha and the Goddess of Mercy to spare his beloved.

Two days later, Hong Taiji rode his black stallion through the Imperial pathway right up to the entrance of Guansui Palace. He jumped off his horse and scrambled into Harjol's bed chamber. On her bed she lay peacefully, freshly made up and dressed in her bridal garment. In tears, Jere, Bumbutai and Sumalagu were kneeling beside the death bed. Eunuchs and maids were weeping aloud. Oblivious to the people and surroundings, Hong Taiji dashed forth and threw himself over the corpse in an outburst of tears and groans. He embraced the stiff body and madly kissed the stone-cold face. No one dared to try to stop him.

When Bumbutai saw this, she broke into sobs all over again. Perhaps she had been wrong about Hong Taiji. His love for Harjol was genuine after all.

Elven

As the highest tribute that could be granted to any deceased Imperial clan member, the Emperor ordered that his Consort be given a state funeral and mandated a one-year mourning period.

Five days after giving the order, the Emperor was found lying unconscious on the floor of his bed chambers. A Court physician told Empress Jere and Bumbutai that the Emperor had been suffering too much grief which had caused a sudden stroke. Bumbutai suggested that Buddhist monks be called to perform a psalm chanting ritual for the reincarnation of the dead Consort in order to pacify the Emperor. Empress Jere nodded in agreement. She also ordered that all Court banquets and all entertainments be banned in the Inner Palaces during the mourning period.

On the last day of the ninth lunar month, the Emperor led the whole Aisin Gioro clan in paying respects to the late Consort in a memorial rite. After the rite, the jeweled casket containing the embalmed body was carried in a white-silk-curtained palanquin, escorted by Princes dressed in white mourning garment. The cortege headed towards the Imperial mausoleum beyond the city walls. Heading the funeral procession were cavalrymen carrying white banners atop horses draped in white cloth, followed by clansmen and Court ministers. Behind the hearse trailed Princesses, Consorts and Concubines, all clothed in white hemp robes.

In the following month, the Emperor granted a posthumous

title to his beloved Consort, naming her as his "First Consort". The title carried in its prefix four bestowed characters that symbolized wisdom, geniality, modesty and graciousness. The title granting ceremony was attended by Jaisang and his wife who had come all the way from Inner Mongolia to mourn their daughter. In memory of his late wife, the Emperor bestowed the titles of Prince and Princess of the First Rank on Bumbutai's aging parents. Bumbutai was thrilled to see them, especially her mother, but only wished the reunion were under happier circumstances. She was also glad that they had a chance to visit their grandson Fulin, who was now almost four years old. For the old couple, the experience of their short visit was a mix of bitter and sweet.

Sadly, all the rites and rituals could not console the Emperor over his tragic loss. He was losing stamina and increasingly avoiding Court attendance. No one close to him could ever have foreseen that a fierce leader such as he would abandon himself so utterly to grief over a deceased Consort.

By the second lunar month of the sixteenth year of Hong Taiji's reign, with the Emperor not yet prepared to go back into the battlefield, Hooge decided to lay siege to Songshan, having successfully intercepted Ming rescue forces sent from Beijing. Hong Chengchou was facing a desperate situation similar to that of Zu Dashou in Jinzhou. Soldiers were starving and morale in the army was plunging. He tried to break out with his small number of men twice, but failed both times.

One of his subordinates surnamed Xia lost his nerve and one starless night sneaked out of the camp and, holding a white flag, waded across the moat. He crawled his way through the heavily-guarded barricade in the dark. A Manchu sentinel guard seized him on sight and took him to the Chief Commander.After telling Hooge the exact state of the forces inside the fortress, Xia offered to secretly open the fortress gate to let in the Manchu troops the following night, in exchange for his life and freedom. He would shoot a burning arrow as the signal. Being anxious to claim victory, Hooge readily agreed. Xia snaked his way unnoticed back into the fortress.

When daylight began to recede the next evening, Hooge ordered his troops to stand by and wait for the signal. A full-scale escalade attack on the fortress was in the offing with as many scaling ladders as were available. Hooge figured that his forces outnumbered those of his enemy by a wide margin and thus a concerted and sudden attack would ensure victory. Half of his men would engage in the scaling of the battlements, while the other half would be on horseback and charge straight through the opened gate.

Hong Chengchou and his half-starved men were startled out of their sleep when they heard the outburst of thunderous noises outside the crenellated walls. Hardly did they have time to absorb the first shock when they watched with dropped jaws the heavy metal gate swinging open and hordes of cavalrymen flooding in through the lowered drawbridge. Up on the fortress terrace, machete-wielding Manchu soldiers who had climbed up ladders were swarming in and cutting down stunned sentry guards like melons. On the ground, other soldiers fell under the horse hoofs and drawn swords of the invaders.

Xia saw a good friend of his having his head chopped off, and he ran over shrieking, wracked with guilt and remorse. With one hand he picked up the head, with the other he thrust his sword into the horse carrying the killer. The beast screeched in agony and fell on its side while the cavalryman slumped to the ground. Xia went forward and chopped off the man's head in a fit of frenzy. A group of cavalrymen rode up and surrounded Xia. One of them slashed his throat, another cut off his right arm, and a third finished him off by sticking a sword through his heart.

The remaining Ming soldiers were too fear-stricken to fight on. They had no option but to surrender. Hong Chengchou and his three generals were captured alive and brought back to Hooge's camp, where the three generals were executed on the spot.

As soon as news of victory at Songshan reached Jirgalang, he ordered an all-out attack on Jinzhou, an attack which also ended in victory. General Zu Dashou was captured. Under strict orders from the Emperor Hong Taiji, Hong Chengchou and Zu Dashou were kept alive and promptly brought back to Mukden, as the Emperor insisted on persuading them to defect to his rule.

After the victorious Battles of Songshan and Jinzhou, all other smaller fortress towns outside the Great Wall of China fell under Manchu control and this paved the way for their penetration into China proper through the Shanhai Pass. The Pass was defended by a gallant Ming general named Wu Sangui who had survived the Battle of Songshan but had not retreated into the fortress with Hong Chengchou. Instead, he had fled back to Beijing. He would later become an enabling pawn in the Manchus' successful incursion through Shanhai Pass.

At Mukden, all the surrendering Ming generals were treated to a grand feast held in their honor and were granted gifts of silver and gold bars. Though unable to attend the feast, the Emperor Hong Taiji sent a special envoy to represent him. The envoy courteously explained to the Chinese generals that the Emperor was still in mourning over the death of his late Consort, and the generals were all touched by the warm and sincere treatment afforded them. All, that is, except for Hong Chengchou who disdainfully declined to attend the feast and rejected all gifts. He impudently declared with that he would welcome immediate execution.

Hearing this, the Emperor ordered that he be accommodated in a luxuriously decorated mansion and waited on by a team of servants and maids. The proud general was adamant in his refusal of food and clothing, preferring to appear unkempt and woeful in the presence of visiting Manchu officials. No one was able to persuade him to change his stance.

Then the Emperor sent Scholar Fan to meet with him. Before the meeting, Scholar Fan promised to only talk to him about Chinese history and nothing else. In response, Hong cleaned himself up a bit and had his hair combed out of respect for the Scholar. During the meeting, specks of dust from the beams landed on Hong's sleeve and he reflexively flicked them off. At the end of the meeting, though, Hong's determination did not appear to have wavered in the least.

Scholar Fan reported on the meeting to the Emperor at the daily morning session of Chinese history and literature lessons, which had resumed at Bumbutai's request a little while ago, after a pause of some years at Harjol's insistence. When Bumbutai heard about how General Hong had flicked off specks of dust, she told the Emperor not to be concerned.

"Your Imperial Highness, you don't have to worry about Hong Chengchou. He will soon come round to doing your bidding. He cares too much about trifles to want to give up life so easily. I am certain Your Imperial Highness was having the same thought."

"You have a sharp mind as always, Bumbutai. I happen to think you're right. What would you suggest that I do now?"Bumbutai's comment had given a healthy jolt to the Emperor's lethargic mind, but was also understated enough to preserve his pride.

"It may be worthwhile for Your Imperial Highness to pay General Hong a personal visit. That would make him feel special and respected. If it suits Your Imperial Highness, showing him a little kindness can help," she added with confidence.

With that suggestion, the Emperor went to Hong's abode. He was careful to leave his Imperial Guards behind, allowing only his chief eunuch to accompany him.

General Hong greeted the Emperor with courtesy, feeling important and honored. After tea was served, they sat down to chat like two old friends, with the Emperor seeking Hong's views on subjects like interracial marriages and tax exemption for the Chinese farmers.

It was springtime in Mukden. The previous day had been unseasonably warm but a cold breeze was now blowing outside, whirling fallen plum blossom petals like a snowstorm in the garden. The Emperor saw that Hong was dressed only in a flimsy robe made of cotton cloth and was shivering from the cold.

"It seems you are not yet used to the fickle Mukden weather," he said and, without a thought, he took off his fur cape and put it over Hong's shoulders. Hong gazed at the Emperor's face in amazement for a long time, incongruous images of the brutal execution of General Yuan Chonghuan suddenly scurrying across his mind.

"Kindness makes for a ruler! Long live my Emperor!" he tearfully exclaimed. Rising from his seat and falling to his knees, he made obeisance to the Emperor for the very first time.

The next day, the Emperor invited General Hong to the Banquet Hall for a feast held in his honor. Later he granted him and his family a huge mansion in Mukden and appointed him to head the Han Border Blue Banner of the newly-created Han Eight Banners. He would go on to become one of the most valued military advisers for the Manchus' Qing Empire during the succeeding reign.

When news of Hong's defection spread, some of the

noblemen in the Manchu Eight Banners began to grumble about the Emperor's apparent favoritism shown towards this Chinese general. To them, the Emperor posed this question:

"Why do you think Nurhaci led us into battle after battle?"

"To ultimately conquer China," they answered unequivocally.

"So what is more valuable than having a good guide to show us the way into unknown territory?"

To that last question, no answer came forth.

During the sixteenth and seventeenth year of his reign, Emperor Hong Taiji let Dorgon lead his forces to stir unrest in some of the Chinese border towns inside the Great Wall, taking the opportunity to demonstrate the military strength of the Manchu Army. The Ming Dynasty of China, meanwhile, was by now threatened by mob uprisings led by the notorious rebel leader Li Zicheng. The Manchus were counting the days to a final showdown with Ming China. Meanwhile, Hong Taiji established the policy of not only welcoming defections of Ming officials, generals and scholars from conquered towns, but actually rewarding such defectors by placing them in official posts and granting them gifts. In explaining such policy to his clansmen, he said:

"Material possessions only have limited value, but talent is priceless. The Qing Empire is growing and is in great need of talent. The exchange could not be more beneficial to us. Besides, only benevolent gestures can win hearts. Remember this: we have not truly conquered a nation until we've conquered its people's hearts. I urge you all to follow this policy for the benefit of our Empire."

In the sixteenth year of the Chongzhen Emperor, Li Zicheng captured the cities of Luoyang, Kaifeng and Xiangyang and in the historic capital of so many dynasties, Xi'an, declared himself as "Emperor of the Shun Dynasty".

Li had lowly beginnings as a shepherd, and at the age of twenty had learned horse riding and archery. During his youth, his hometown in the Shaanxi region of north China had suffered a famine and the peasants had harbored chronic grudges against the Ming government. He joined a rebel group to ambush and murder Ming officials and subsequently became leader of a rebel army of 20,000, a force that eventually grew to a million-strong. The rebel army's slogan was "equal land distribution and no grain tax". They had the fervent support of most peasants. Wherever Li's army went, they seized land from the rich landlords and distributed it among the tenant farmers. At the same time, another rebel leader Zhang Xianzhong was stirring up unrest in other parts of China. After losing to Li's army in the battles for Luoyang and Kaifeng, the Ming government showed itself totally powerless in the face of peasant rebellions, especially as it was so busy fighting the Manchus in the north.

Following the death of Harjol, Bumbutai and Dorgon no longer dared to meet in the Yongfu Palace, Bumbutai's residence, as there was always a chance of the Emperor calling on her or summoning her to his Residence. Dorgon grew restless and one day sent Bumbutai a letter, which said:

My Love,

I have lived life yearning daily for your scent, your sweet lips, your fragrant hair, your soft skin. I cannot go on like this any more. The more I pine for you, the more I hate Hong Taiji. He is the reason for our endless suffering. I cannot but rejoice that he has lost the love of his life and is made to suffer. But his suffering is nowhere close to the hell that I have been through. I can never forgive him for killing my mother and purloining all that should have belonged to me. I swear I will make him pay.

I have to do something to end this waiting.

Yours forever,
Dorgon

After reading the letter, Bumbutai became very agitated and nervous, distressed by what might be festering in Dorgon's mind. At the same time, what her father had said to her during her parents' visit to see Fulin came back to haunt her: "My dear daughter, you are a Borjigit princess and you must never forget that. You owe it to the Khorchin Mongols to make Fulin the Crown Prince. The future glory of our homeland and our tribe now depends on Fulin, You must take over Harjol's role and win Hong Taiji's heart."

Her father's words spun around in Bumbutai's head and weighed her down like a lump of lead.

A year had passed since Hooge won the Battle of Songshan and he kept as low a profile as possible and took every care not to indulge in his old habit of boasting. But he couldn't let his glory go unsung. Daisan was still the most respected Aisin Gioro clansman and could help in pressing his case, he thought. Now that the greatest obstacle - the "royal heir" - was out of the way, he was determined to grasp the opportunity and quietly push forward his own campaign for the status of Crown Prince. He knew full well that his great competitors would be the Fulin mother-son team, backed by the Borjigits, Dorgon and his full brothers. He had to think of a way of getting his hands on the old man's Plain and Border Yellow Banners. After all, he had earned his right to them. If he was refused, he would have no alternative but to …

With that last thought, Hooge entered the lounge of Daisan's mansion one late summer day. When Daisan came out to greet him, he told his uncle straight away that it was going to be a very private conversation. Daisan immediately dismissed his servants and guards.

"Uncle, I desperately need your advice and help regarding my future. No doubt you can see that the Emperor is growing weaker by the day. Yet he doesn't seem to realize the absolute necessity of picking his heir before his health further deteriorates. I think we must do something before it is too late."

"Nephew, of course I see the urgency of the issue here. The thought has lately been troubling me a lot too. There are still big battles to be won and strife in our Court is the last thing I wish to see."

Daisan spoke earnestly, not betraying the least shred of his own scheme – that he had already given his support to Dorgon's plan to usurp the throne in concert with Jirgalang.

His support for Hong Taiji had from the start always been superficial. He would not have endorsed Hong Taiji's ascent to the throne had he not feared his underhanded tricks. He now saw a way to play one camp against the other and stir up more rivalry. Should the Hooge camp and the Dorgon camp face off with each other, then his own sons might benefit from the confrontation and choose the winning camp to side with or even to master.

"You know about our long siege of Songshan and Jinzhou and our final victory, in which I played a pivotal role," Hooge continued. "I know that His Imperial Highness does not approve of my audacity and so I have not formally claimed any credit. I was hoping that you might try to put in a good word for me to the Emperor ..."

"Of course I will do that for you, Nephew! I will even suggest to the Emperor that you could take over the command of both the Plain and Border Yellow Banners. The way I see it, it's time for him to pass on the Banners to you."

"That is very kind of you, Uncle. You have my gratitude and

I won't forget it."

"But I have a feeling that the Emperor will be giving Dorgon the Plain Blue Banner, to reward him for his many victories in the battles in Inner Mongolia, the war against Korea as well as the various conquests of Chinese border towns," Daisan added, trying to kindle some jealousy in Hooge.

"That is bad news," Hooge said, surprised. "If that really comes to pass and the three brothers team up with Jirgalang's Border Blue, they will form an ironclad alliance. That's what brings me to my next request, Uncle. Assuming I have command of the Plain and Border Yellow and there is an all-out confrontation with the Dorgon-Jirgalang team, would you support my claim to the throne with your two Red Banners?"

"I assure you that my two Banners will be at your service. You are the eldest son of Hong Taiji .... you have a legitimate claim.... I will certainly support you, Nephew," Daisan faltered and his eyes looked down unconsciously. But Hooge was too full of his dreams to notice.

Two days after that meeting, Hooge received an Imperial edict from the Emperor making him Chief of the two Yellow Banners. He wasn't aware, though, that the idea came voluntarily from the Emperor himself without any persuasion on Daisan's part.

Twelve

After having convinced Hong Chengchou to defect, the Emperor again relapsed into inertia and depression. His health deteriorated. Bumbutai knew there was little she could do to mend his heart, but she still tried to nurse him and fed him precious herbal supplements. In order to lift his spirits, she arranged for Siu Mui, Siu Fa and other beautiful Chinese dancers to perform all kinds of exotic dances for him, sometimes even taking part in them herself. She was pleased when the Emperor summoned Siu Fa, who was the prettier of the two sisters, to his bed chamber for three nights in a row. Under the Manchu code, emperors were only to bed Manchu or Mongolian women, but obviously exceptions were sometimes made for the prettiest of young Chinese maidens

One early autumn evening in the eighth lunar month, the Emperor summoned Bumbutai to his Residential Palace.

"I appreciate all that you've done for me," he told her. "You have such intelligent maids. Siu Fa is good company. Did you teach them Chinese history?"

"Thank you, Your Imperial Highness. I'm glad that Siu Fa served you well. I did teach my maids a bit of Chinese literature, but the Han sisters basically learned their history from their own parents in childhood."

"How is Fulin doing with his lessons?"

"Very well, Your Imperial Highness. Scholar Fan is doing a

great job teaching him Chinese history and literature. Sumalagu is teaching him Jurchen history. I myself will see to it that he learns Mongolian history as well. He has a good memory and is a fast learner. He seems to have a special interest in Han Chinese culture."

"That is good. Don't forget to make him practice horse riding and archery and tell him stories from the journal about Genghis Khan."

"I won't forget, Your Imperial Highness."

"I just wish he'd grow up fast. I'm afraid that my end is not far away, Bumbutai."

He signaled for her to come closer to him and he held both her hands in his clasp and sighed a sorrowful sigh.

"I beg Your Imperial Highness not to say such things," she exclaimed in anguish. "You can't leave me. You still have a long life ahead." She burst into tears.

"Bumbutai, listen very carefully to what I have to say. I know I'm not going to recover and I must tell you what is on my mind before it's too late."

His brows wrinkled into a deep frown, and he continued.

"I want Fulin to inherit my throne, but since he is only a child, he has need of Regents to assist him. In order that there is an appropriate power balance, I will give Dorgon the Plain Blue Banner. Hooge already has my Plain and Border Yellow. Daisan and his sons will continue to control the two Red Banners. Ajige, Dodo and Jirgalang will still respectively command the Plain White, Border White and Border Blue. The Empire will be safer if there is a balance of power among the clansmen."

"Your Imperial Highness," she said solemnly. "I will do whatever that you want me to do and I will protect Fulin with all my power for the sake of the Empire."

"Fulin has Mongolian and Manchu blood in him. I'm sure

he has your wisdom and my determination. If you give him the right education, he will grow up to be a good emperor and will bring glory to the Empire. The important task of mentoring him will fall on you."

Hearing those words, Bumbutai's eyes turned red again. Fulin would be her protector once Hong Taiji was gone. But Fulin was only a five-year old child. She could already envision her future path strewn with deadly traps.

"I believe Dorgon will not intentionally harm you," Hong Taiji continued. "Daisan is basically a coward who will go with whichever side is on the ascendant while Jirgalang will be loyal. The only real danger is likely to come from Hooge. He is rash and witless and thinks he's entitled to the throne. But I am sure that he would be a poor emperor. So, if you can get Dorgon, Jirgalang and Daisan all on side, then you will be quite safe as Empress Dowager. I will require that you and Fulin complete the grand scheme of conquering China, and to do so you will need their help. But I am sure that you will find a way to get their cooperation, Bumbutai. If all the Banner Chiefs agree, Dorgon and Jirgalang can be elected as Regents."

"I am taking your words to heart and will do my best, Your Imperial Highness. Please do not worry."

She was silently asking herself if she really had a choice.

Having completed what he needed to say, Hong Taiji appeared to shrink on his seat.

"I am feeling very tired," he said. "I must lie down to rest now."

She gently helped her ailing husband to the bed and sat by the bedside until he fell asleep.

Then she returned to the Yongfu Palace and wrote a long letter to Dorgon:

"My Beloved Dorgon,

I have received your letter and read it with alarm. I hope reason will restrain you from doing anything you will regret. If we lose patience and take one false step, all will be lost. Please do nothing without first consulting me. I love you, Dorgon, and want only the best for you. You have to trust me.

Hong Taiji has just spoken to me. He wants balance of power among the clansmen, to which I agree. It is for the good of all and for stability. He also intends for Fulin to be his heir, to be assisted by Regents.

I understand that you have always felt that you were robbed of the right to rule. But I am sure you will agree that Hong Taiji has proven himself to be a fair, capable, respectable and benevolent leader who has given his all in leading the Manchus and Mongols into an unprecedented era of solidarity and prosperity. The way he treats the conquered Han Chinese is also most admirable.

I can assure you that Hong Taiji deeply regrets having taken your mother's life. Please believe me that it was deep insecurities and not depravity that drove him to commit that act. He has since tried in his own way to make amends to you. He is a man who is now in his last days. I beseech you with all my heart to put down the burden of hatred and to forgive and forget.

Fulin is only a five-year-old child. Without your help and the cooperation of the other clansmen after Hong Taiji passes, my son and I will be exposed to great threats and perils, the likes of which I dare not even imagine. What, for instance, if some impudent clansman proposes that I follow in Lady Abahai's footsteps?

I am praying to Eternal Blue Sky that you have not yet done anything harmful that cannot be reversed. And I hope you will find it in your heart to forgive your brother.

Yours forever,

Bumbutai"

When she finished writing, she asked Sumalagu to deliver the letter to Dorgon in person the next day.

In the town of Gusu in Jiangsu Province, there was a beautiful orphan girl named Chen Yuanyuan who had been brought up by her aunt. Being a peasant widow, the aunt was living in abject poverty and had no choice but to sell Yuanyuan to a brothel. She was then re-sold as a maid to a wealthy family surnamed Zhou. Old Master Zhou happened to be the father of the Ming Empress who, it transpired, was plagued by jealousy over Chongzhen Emperor's favoritism towards one of his Consorts, named Tian. The Empress found it expedient to present Yuanyuan to the Emperor in an attempt to distract him. But her plan did not work as the Emperor showed no interest in the girl. Even worse, Yuanyuan's exquisite beauty aroused envy and animosity in Consort Tian. The jealous Consort first had the girl whipped and expelled from the Palace, then given as a concubine to her father, Old Master Tian.

General Wu Sangui was a good friend of the very rich Tian family. One day he paid Old Master Tian a visit and Yuanyuan appeared to serve him tea. Wu's eyes would have been glued to her if it weren't for propriety's sake. But Old Master Tian caught General Wu's sidelong and leering glances in the directions of the girl and thereupon came up with a mutually beneficial arrangement. Now more than ever, the Tian family's vast land and property holdings needed protection from peasant rebels' random marauding, and General Wu's soldiers could readily provide that protection. On Yuanyuan's part, she secretly admired the general's gallantry and could imagine no better future for a low-born woman such as herself. It was thus that she ended up in General Wu's household as his favorite concubine.

Both General Wu and Yuanyuan had grown up in Jiangsu Province and their early childhood memories bonded them. He installed her in a courtyard house in Beijing and lavished jewelry, silk garments and perfumes on her. He never even looked at another concubine or any other woman. Although for a time they would enjoy each other's love, Yuanyuan's tragic destiny would land her in yet more infamy and disgrace. She was also to become, ironically, the pivotal figure behind the Manchu Empire's defeat of the Ming Dynasty.

The rebel leader Li Zicheng's peasant army was growing from strength to strength and his next target was the Forbidden City in the heart of Beijing. Li had heard tell of General Wu's beautiful concubine from his underlings, and he couldn't get her off his mind. One of his deputies saw an opportunity and proposed a plan to him to force General Wu to defect to Li's forces. They would abduct Yuanyuan and other members of Wu's family and hold them as hostages.

Inside the lounge of Dorgon's mansion, Ajige and Dorgon were in deep discussion, devising a plot. Sumalagu arrived at the entrance gate in the early afternoon and Dorgon's personal guards on duty refused her entry. She waited for a while, aware of how important the letter was, but in the end had no alternative but to leave the envelope with one of the guards. She implored him repeatedly to hand it to the Beile as soon as possible.

Inside, unaware of Sumalagu's presence outside the door, Dorgon was immersed in the conversation with Ajige.

"I have recently been in contact with Daisan and Jirgalang and they both agree to cooperate," he said. "The chance is finally presenting itself. Hong Taiji's health is on the edge of total collapse and he doesn't have a successor named. Our first step is to seize control of the Plain Blue Banner."

"That should be easy, because the soldiers under that Banner never specifically pledged loyalty to Hong Taiji when he grabbed it from Manggultai," Ajige replied with confidence. "You can personally address them and seek their allegiance."

Ajige and Dodo had for a long time tried to persuade Dorgon to claim the throne for himself, but Dorgon had always rejected the idea. He had thought that their military power was inadequate to support such a move.

"I plan to make a formal speech on the eighth day of the eighth lunar month, that being an auspicious day. But first I will visit the soldiers to find out what they are thinking."

"That's a good idea. With Daisan's and Jirgalang's support, we don't have to worry about a confrontation with Hooge. Dodo and I have waited so long for you to come round to making this decision. It's time to remove Hong Taiji from the face of the earth altogether," Ajige couldn't hide his excitement as he bellowed.

"We must do this quietly," Dorgon warned.

"Yes! Then on the ninth day we can send Hong Taiji on his last journey. We can at last avenge our mother! I know a herbalist and I can get some arsenic powder for you. You must use your most trusted servant." Ajige spoke feverishly, his face flushed. He then whispered details of his plan into Dorgon's ear.

For Dorgon, the thought of taking Bumbutai for himself had been the constant spur to take this fate-changing step. The time had come for him to claim his due.

Ajige didn't leave Dorgon's mansion until dusk, by which time the guard with the envelope had already gone off duty and stepped into a nearby tavern. As was his habit, the guard got drunk and had to be carried home. His wife undressed him and put him to bed, dropping the letter to the floor without noticing it. Her toddler child picked it up, played with it and tore it to pieces. It would never be known whether Dorgon would have changed his mind had he read Bumbutai's long letter.

Sumalagu did not realize that her mission had failed, and Bumbutai was still snug in the belief that her letter had reached

Dorgon. On the eighth day of the eighth lunar month it suddenly dawned on her that the Emperor hadn't put anything down in writing about the succession. She was on her way to his Residence to remind him when a maid from the Royal Nursery rushed towards her with news that Fulin had contracted a fever, so she hurried over to see her son instead.

The following night, a maid from the Emperor's Residence took two bowls of sweet almond soup from the royal kitchen to the lounge where Bumbutai was telling the Emperor about Fulin's condition. It was luckily nothing serious, she told him. On a side table, she began grinding an ink slab on a stone plate.

The Emperor was taking the sweet almond soup from his personal bowl, using a porcelain spoon. Bumbutai stepped from the side table to sit down beside him at the main table. She had just picked up her own bowl when, out of the corner of her eye, she noticed the maid trembling like a leaf. An uneasy feeling crept up on her. But before she could act, Hong Taiji had already emptied the bowl in three gulps. She was too late.

In a few heartbeats, he was clutching at his throat and went into convulsions. A thunderbolt struck her and her mind started whirring. She struggled to keep herself calm.

"The Emperor has a headache and needs to retire early," she declared. She and the maid helped him to the bed, and as he lay down, he had another seizure and passed out, foaming at the mouth. Without a word she wiped his mouth clean and let down the bed curtains.

Then she sent the Emperor's eunuch to get Sumalagu and then signaled for all the maids to leave except for the ashen-faced one. When she lifted the curtains to look at the Emperor again, he had already stopped breathing, his face a morbid pallor. She put her ear on his chest and heard no heartbeat.

The maid couldn't stop her violent shaking. She eventually

dropped to her knees to beg for her life. On Bumbutai's questioning, she revealed that Beile Dorgon's manservant was her beau and had persuaded her to do the deed, giving her a jade bracelet and promising to take her away to his hometown afterwards. Just then, Sumalagu appeared. Bumbutai whispered to her what had happened. Then she turned to the maid.

"Do you understand the gravity of this crime and what punishment awaits you and your beau?" she asked. The maid bobbed her head in answer. "Now listen carefully. I'm going to give both of you an alternative to a death sentence. You are to convince your lover to leave with you permanently for a place outside the borders, never to return in your lifetime. I will give you five gold bars to sustain you both for the remainder of your lives. You have to give me your answer right now."

Bumbutai's instinct told her that the maid was not evil-hearted, and so took a chance with her. The stricken maid fell to her knees and banged her head on the floor three times, uttering between sobs, "May the Goddess of Mercy bless you. We owe you our lives. I swear on my life that we will leave Mukden immediately and will stay away forever."

Having taken the bowls and spoons from the table, Sumalagu stepped forward to help the maid rise. On their way out, Bumbutai bade Sumalagu fetch Dorgon and Physician Sima immediately.

Dorgon soon arrived. Bumbutai gazed at him, her face white as marble and imbued with a mixed emotion of deep pain and anguish. The only word she could utter from her dry throat after a long silence was: "Why?"

"You know very well the reason," he answered with indignation.

"Dorgon, there was no need for this. He was going to pass soon any way. You could have laid down the burden of hatred and been a free man. But now you have blood on your conscience, just as Hong Taiji had blood on his. This is not going to bring back your mother."

"He took so much from me!" He spluttered. "He deserved this!" Then he cast a sidelong glance at the deathbed and realized she was right. This wouldn't bring back his mother. He was hit by an unexpected wave of remorse.

"He was going to give you the Plain Blue Banner, and was going to write a will making Fulin his heir, to be assisted by a number of Regents including you. Now that he has passed without leaving anything in writing, I don't know what's going to happen. I am so, so sad that my letter had absolutely no effect on you."

"What letter?" he asked, puzzled.

"It is no longer important. The most urgent thing is to cover your tracks. I've already dealt with the maid and your servant. I trust Physician Sima could help us."

Even as she spoke, the eunuch announced Physician Sima's arrival. He approached her respectfully.

"The Emperor had a sudden and violent stroke just before going to bed and lost consciousness," she told him. "His last breath came while you were being summoned. Please record the circumstances to pass on to the Banner Chiefs."

Physician Sima made a cursory examination of the dead body.

"The likely cause of death was a heart stroke," he said carefully. "The Emperor has previously had bad strokes."

He then wrote down the time and cause of death on a piece of paper.

After the physician left, Dorgon grabbed Bumbutai by the waist and kissed her passionately. She put up a little resistance at first and then relented. Then she pushed him away.

"Fulin and I are in great danger now," she said. "You must

promise me that you will support his enthronement and that you will agree to be a Regent."

"I will do whatever you wish me to do," Dorgon replied. "All I ask is that after the throne succession issue is settled, you will marry me and live with me." His heart was on fire.

"But according to Chinese customs, such a marriage would be considered immoral," she replied.

"Bumbutai, you are a Mongol and I am a Manchu!" he exclaimed. "In both our cultures, it is natural for a brother to marry his widowed sister-in-law. Are you trying to fabricate excuses to reject me?" His face twisted in pain as he spoke.

"No, no, Dorgon. I just want you to know what is on my mind. I am afraid that our Han officials might not take it well. I am thinking of the honor of the Imperial clan. I promised you I would offer you both my body and my soul and I intend to keep my promise. Besides, both Fulin and I need you to protect us from harm." She was keenly aware as she spoke of the dangers that lay ahead.

"Bumbutai, are you sorry that Hong Taiji is dead? I need to know the truth."

"Dorgon, what do you expect me to say? He was my husband for eighteen years and I have children by him. Even though I never felt any love for him, I believe he truly cared for me. This .... this is a great shock for me. I thought you had read my letter... " She paused, blinking away a tear before she continued. "I don't think he deserved such an end. As I said before, this needn't have happened. Now you and I will carry the guilt with us for the rest of our lives. If you still doubt my heart .... "

"But he didn't seem to be bothered by his cold-blooded murder of my mother. This is only an eye for an eye."

"You're wrong. He was weighed down with remorse every day. He knew he had committed the gravest mistake of his life out of cowardice. Fearing the wrath from you and your brothers was his daily curse and punishment."

Dorgon looked at her for a long time, a pained expression on his face. "It seems you cared a great deal about him," he said finally. "Please try to understand me, Dorgon. First and foremost I care about our Empire and its subjects, including my own clan and tribe, and I always will. I have a duty and interest in giving them my very best. But I have always had only one true love and friend, and I think you know that." She spoke with a naked honesty that he found at once compelling and endearing. For a long while he could find no words. The dewy mist in her eyes dissolved his heart, like the random sprays of spring showers thawing away piles of winter snow.

"I know it's senseless of me to be jealous of a dead man," he said. "I promise I will help you in whatever way you need, Bumbutai."

"I will forever be indebted to you, my love."

"You must understand that it is for your sake that I will agree to be a Regent instead of claiming the throne myself, although I also think such an arrangement is best for the stability of the Empire."

Guilt was pricking his conscience and acted to mollify him.

"Yes, I understand," she said, relieved. "I only hope Hooge won't try any tricks to upset our plans."

"Leave everything to me. I will call a meeting of the Private Council in Dazheng Hall first thing in the morning and will summon all men under the two White and two Blue Banners to gather in the Square just in case. Jirgalang gave me his word that he would side with me."

"I will get the eunuch to make the death announcement to Daisan and Hooge," She responded.

He hugged her one more time before leaving the chamber. As

soon as he was out of sight, Bumbutai drew a deep breath. She didn't know where she had drawn the courage from, but both Fulin's life and hers were at stake. Either act or die.

She told the eunuch to summon Jirgalang.

Thirteen

When dawn broke, mourning bugles blasted to the four corners of the Imperial Palace. Huge white lanterns had been hung round all the porticos of the Imperial Residence and Dazheng Hall in the early morning hours. In the middle of the Residence lounge, a casket draped in white silk cloth was placed on a lacquered bier, surrounded by burning white candles. The corpse had been dressed in a golden Imperial robe embroidered with dragons and a gold-rimmed red velvet crown. White-robed male mourners knelt in rows in front of the casket while female mourners in white veils and robes grouped on both sides, all kneeling and wailing loudly.

Moments later, troops from the Manchu Eight Banners marched in through the Main Gate and stood at attention in the Square in front of Dazheng Hall, while the Imperial Guards lined both sides of the grand pathway, instantly creating an atmosphere of hostility and tension.

Inside the Hall, the Banner Chiefs were all present wearing white mourning robes over their plated armors and seated by order of Banner rank on the right and left, a little distance from the throne dais. Hooge and Daisan took their seats respectively on the right and left closest to the dais. Next to Hooge sat Dorgon, with Jirgalang next in line; on the other side were Daisan, Ajige and Dodo.

The late Emperor's chief eunuch read out the eulogy which

had been prepared by the Minister of Documents. As the late Emperor had left no written will, by custom of the Aisin Gioro Clan, the successor to the throne had to be decided by consensus reached by the Banner Chiefs.

The previous night, after his meeting with Bumbutai, Dorgon had a big argument with Ajige, but finally Dorgon succeeded in convincing his elder brother of the prudence of taking a regency role rather than trying for the throne. Dodo had also agreed.

When the reading of the eulogy was complete, Hooge rose to his feet and addressed the Banner Chiefs.

"As the late Emperor's eldest male offspring and as Chief of the two Yellow Banners, I think you will all agree that I have a legitimate claim to the throne. However, it is not my intention to lay such a claim. I would rather leave it to my Uncle Daisan, who is the most venerable member of our clan, to name a suitable candidate."

He was thinking that by acting modest and calm, he would get what he wanted. He was certain of Daisan's support.

Daisan stood to speak.

"It is the tradition of the Aisin Gioro Clan to choose the most capable and valiant warrior to be the leader of our Empire. In terms of warfare merits, I would have to say that Dorgon and Jirgalang are unrivalled."

Hooge glanced over at him, startled. Savage fury enveloped him and he jumped to his feet.

"My late father never liked Dorgon," he thundered. "His decision to pass to me the two Yellow Banners is proof enough that he wanted no one but me to inherit his throne. Please do not forget that he also made me Chief of the Imperial Guards."

It was a threat that would have been better not made, and Dorgon stood to address him.

"Be calm, Hooge," he said. "I declare here that I have no

interest in taking the throne. I would urge all Banner Chiefs to consider and support a decision that would ensure stability in our Empire."

Hearing that his arch-rival was withdrawing from the race, Hooge was momentarily taken aback, and hesitated for a second. Then he spoke:

"I will submit to whatever decision the Banner Chiefs make by consensus and I will abstain from voting."

Hooge then strode away from the meeting in feigned indifference.

Daisan addressed the gathering again:

"I am sure that the last thing our late Emperor would have wanted to see is infighting and bloodshed among our clansmen. We are all well aware that the allegiance of the Bannermen under the two Yellows to Hooge is not necessarily total, while on the other hand, Dorgon, Jirgalang and Ajige are all respected military leaders of their respective Banners. The problem is that there is only one throne. If any Banner Chief has any suggestion by way of a solution, kindly speak out."

Jirgalang jumped to his feet.

"I would urge all Chiefs to bear in mind the unprecedented success and glory that our late Emperor brought to our Empire with his visionary and valiant leadership. We would not be where we are today were it not for his great efforts and dedication. I was formally informed by Consort Zhuang of the last wishes of our late Emperor, which are for his son Fulin to succeed him on the throne, to be assisted by Regents. I suggest that we respect those wishes."

There was a murmur in the Hall. After a moment, Daisan proposed that all Banner Chiefs vote on Jirgalang's suggestion, and there was unanimity in favor of acceptance. Dodo was sent to inform Hooge of the meeting's decision.

On hearing the news, Hooge lost all control of his emotions and ordered a siege of Dazheng Hall with his Imperial Guards. The Guards shoved their way through the packed Square to just beneath the flight of marble steps leading up to the Hall.

Some of the soldiers of the Blue and White Banners in the Square drew their swords and moved to obstruct the Guards from proceeding up the steps, and a bitter altercation broke out between one irate Plain White Bannerman and one of the Imperial Guards. Blood was spilled as the Guard got stabbed in the arm. Angry shouting and clanging of swords followed. More scuffles. An all-out clash was on the verge of breaking out. Dodo dashed back into the Hall to report and all the Banner Chiefs inside could hear the commotion outside. Dorgon went and shut and locked the tall brass gates of the Hall.

After a brief discussion among those at the meeting, Ajige went out on Dorgon's bidding through a narrow opening in the gate to command the White Bannermen to stand down. He then negotiated with Hooge on the marble terrace. They finally reached agreement whereby the Bannermen of the two Yellows would vote on the meeting's decision by a show of hands. Many of those Bannermen had been ultra loyal followers of Hong Taiji and about three-quarters voted in favor of Fulin acceding to the throne. Hooge then had no alternative but to acquiesce. He ordered the Imperial Guards to move back and left the Imperial Palace on horseback in a belligerent mood.

Inside the Hall, the meeting continued to deliberate on the choice of Regents. Daisan now had a good sense of where things were going and promptly proposed that Dorgon and Jirgalang be appointed co-Regents. The proposal met with full approval from the meeting and the two swore an oath of allegiance on the spot to Fulin, a five-and-a-half year old child, and to his mother, the new Empress Dowager.

Bumbutai, dressed in full mourning garments, was pacing in the Yongfu Palace garden in a state of angst. She had sent Sumalagu to find out the latest news from the meeting hall. After what seemed like an eternity, her maid appeared. Her heart froze as she imagined the worst, her knees knocking with fear. Everything was in flux and nothing was certain. She remembered the initial shock on Jirgalang's face the previous night when he had learned of Hong Taiji's sudden death. If he had doubted her words in the least, it would tip the balance against her. It was only when she detected a smile on Sumalagu's face that she was able to breathe easily.

Her long-time confidante curtsied playfully before her.

"Venerable Empress Dowager," she said.

Hardly had Bumbutai recovered her composure than she started worrying about the inevitable separation from her beloved son that would result from this change. She was not fooling herself. The title of Empress Dowager was purely for show. Dorgon would want to marry her as soon as possible, and once she became his Wife, she would not even be able to protect herself, let alone her son. She had to try and delay the marriage ceremony for as long as she could. The one excuse that Dorgon would not object to would probably be that the goal of conquering China should take priority, as that was his most cherished dream.

Even with the succession issue now settled, Dorgon could not be at ease. He was fearful that Hooge might be plotting subversion and in the following months he progressively purged Hooge's loyal followers from the two Yellow Banners. The remainder, who had voted for Fulin, were happy to respect the co-regency. Next, he set his mind to planning the crossing of the Shanhai Pass and an all-out assault on China proper.

In the third lunar month of the eighteenth year of Chongzhen's reign, the rebel leader Li Zicheng kidnapped the concubine Chen Yuanyuan and General Wu Sangui's father and thirty-eight of his other family members. Li's rebel forces were a million-strong and were itching to lay siege to the Forbidden City, the Imperial Palace in the heart of Beijing. By mid-month, Li's forces had reached the outskirts of the capital and on the twenty-third day he sent an envoy to seek the surrender of the Chongzhen Emperor. The latter stoically refused. The next day, Li led his rebel army in a full-scale attack on the Forbidden City. Two days later, the Chongzhen Emperor stood on the terrace of his bed chambers and watched in despair as the Palace was ransacked and set on fire. He fell to his knees and wailed: "I am a disgrace to our ancestors. I've failed to protect my subjects and my Court. The Ming Dynasty has perished in my hands. I am a shame to our clan!"

In a frantic fit, he took his gilded sword from the scabbard hanging on the bedpost and stumbled his way into the Consorts' Palace. Blinded by frenzy, he slashed madly at any woman who came into his path.

"I cannot allow the rebels to defile you!" he screamed. "Accept your fate!" His sword whirled around him, killing and maiming as it went. Screams and mass hysteria enveloped the ornate chambers. The Empress Zhou had already hanged herself in her bed chamber with a white silk rope.

This happened to be the wedding day for the young Princess Changping. In the maelstrom, still dressed in her bridal garment, her left arm was sheared off. But she survived and would later be rescued and, under orders from the first Manchu Emperor installed within Chinese borders, be wedded to the groom to whom she had been betrothed, only to commit suicide along with him a year later, as a patriotic gesture to the fallen Ming Dynasty.

As for Chen Yuanyuan, fate played with her too. Her earlier expulsion from the Imperial Palace ironically spared her from this slaughter. But her enviable beauty landed her right in the lecherous clutches of the rebel leader, Li Zicheng.

When the Chongzhen Emperor thought he had accomplished his last mission, he hurried to Prospect Hill, behind the Imperial Gardens, carrying with him a long rope. There on the crest of the Hill, witnessed by no one except Mother Earth, he hanged himself from one of the trees.

He probably had no idea at that moment that the fatal blunder of his reign had been the killing of the patriot, General Yuan Chonghuan.

At this time, General Wu Sangui was stationed with a garrison at Shanhai Pass. When a courier from Beijing brought him news of the abduction of his father and his Concubine, he flew into a rage. Around the middle of the third month, he led his troops on a rescue mission to the Forbidden City on earlier orders from the Chongzhen Emperor. But on the way, he received news that the City had already fallen into the hands of the rebels, so he decided to head back to his base in Shanhai Pass.

By the fourth month, after looting and wrecking many of the Beijing Palaces, Li Zicheng turned his attention to his nemesis, Wu Sangui. Outraged by the latter's rebuff to his invitation to join forces against the Ming Army, Li spitefully retaliated by torturing Wu's father and then decapitating him. He even had his head spiked on a stake in the capital's execution ground.

Before leading his army of 100,000 towards Shanhai Pass, Li had killed all thirty-eight members of Wu's household whom he had earlier abducted. Chen Yuanyuan, however, was kept alive to serve him as a courtesan.

Though deeply tormented by the news about his family, Wu still managed to keep calm. His survival instinct told him not to submit to Li without putting up a fight. He was certain that Li, being a depraved character, would not let him live even if he did surrender. With around 100,000 men under his command, half of them soldiers and half untrained civilians, he felt that his chances for victory would be much enhanced if he could enlist Manchu help. Consumed by a desire for vengeance, he wrote a letter to Dorgon pleading for military assistance.

Dorgon received Wu's plea for help. At this time, the Manchu Army was already on its way to Shanhai Pass under the dual command of Ajige and Dodo, with Dorgon as the Chief Commander. With the encouragement of Scholar Fan and General Hong Chengchou, Dorgon had spent much time studying maps and preparing the Banner troops for the assault beyond the Wall on the Ming forces.

Ajige and Dodo each led a cavalry of 10,000 on the right and left flanks while Dorgon was in charge of the main column of 30,000 in the middle. Wu's letter fitted in exactly with what Dorgon had been hoping for, and he immediately sent a reply encouraging Wu to defect. By the latter part of the fourth lunar month, Dorgon's forces were only eight kilometers from the Shanhai Pass. That night the Manchu soldiers slept in their armor for only a few hours until being woken by their commanders shortly after midnight and ordered to press ahead.

In the early dawn, the Manchu Army reached the gates of Shanhai Pass, where Dorgon accepted Wu's formal surrender. With the conscious motive of personal survival as much as anything else, Wu opened the gates and welcomed the Manchu forces into China, an act that would change Chinese history in a monumental way.

That afternoon, Wu deployed his troops in the vanguard to attack Li's rebel army near the Sha River, west of the Shanhai Pass fortifications. The clash caused heavy casualties to Wu's army as Li's men, although in some disarray, were fierce and experienced fighters and the attack failed to break the frontline of Li's forces. By late afternoon, it looked like total defeat was imminent for Wu, and Dorgon decided to act.

"Ajige, Dodo, tell your men to stay put," he shouted to his right and left-wing commanders. "Don't make any move until I give the signal!"

Since dawn, his troops had been perched on a small hill near the central gate of Shanhai Pass, from where he had a clear view of the battlefield. Beyond, he suddenly spied dark yellow clouds twisting over the horizon, hurtling directly towards the embroiled armies. His heart leapt for joy - sign of help from the heavens.

Before long, a violent sandstorm blasted out of the plains, gales churning with desert sands creating a thick yellow veil over the battlefield that reduced visibility to almost nothing. At this critical moment, Dorgon raised the flag in his hand, signaling to his two commanders, and shouted "Charge!"

The cavalry under Ajige and Dodo barreled downhill in an explosive headlong gallop and swerved around the right flank of Wu's army to charge into Li's left flank in full force. In less time than it takes for a joss stick to burn down half way, the left flank was shattered. Dorgon's central column then ploughed into the rebel army's right flank at lightening speed. The calvarymen were used to fighting battles in desert conditions and the sandstorm was of little concern to them. Wu had earlier ordered his men to wear a band of white cloth on their right arm so the Manchu warriors could distinguish them clearly from Li's rebel soldiers. Li's troops were flabbergasted to see the ferocious cavalrymen with shaved foreheads thundering towards them like wild beasts bursting from the earth. Fear on top of near-blindness occasioned by the sandstorm sent them into a catastrophic retreat, during which tens of thousands of the rebels were massacred. Li fled back to Beijing with the handful of survivors.

The next day, Wu gave orders for his surviving soldiers to shave their foreheads and join with the Manchu forces. Dorgon put Wu in charge of pursuing Li and the remnants of his army and also of chasing and neutralizing the Ming Imperial family and loyalists as they tried to escape.

Beijing residents, relieved to see the back of the fleeing bandits, welcomed the triumphant troops into the capital. But they were baffled to see General Wu Sangui with the Manchu Army instead of with the Ming heir apparent.

Before his departure, Li had set fire to many of the Palaces and Halls in the Forbidden City, leaving only the Wuying Hall in the Outer Court intact. Dorgon decided to set up his temporary Court there so that he could receive surrendering Ming generals and Court officials. He gave strict orders to his Banner troops forbidding looting and violent acts against civilians, in order to allow for the transition of sovereignty to proceed smoothly.

A profound sense of pride surged inside him as Dorgon seated himself on a dais in the Wuying Hall. He later wrote a letter to Bumbutai sharing the moment with her:

"The Aisin Gioro clan's cherished dream has come true. Ming China is finally defeated. Five centuries ago, the Jurchens under the Wanyan Clan of the Great Jin Dynasty only occupied and ruled the northern portion of China. Now the whole of China will come under our Manchu Empire. I am the ruler of the three races. I hope you will rejoice with me over this hard won victory. I now look forward in earnest to the day of our formal nuptials."

PART 2

Heartache

Fourteen

On the second day after the Ming Court's collapse and submission to the new Qing Empire, Dorgon issued an order for all Han Chinese in Beijing and other areas under Manchu rule to shave their foreheads and wear queues in the Manchu style. Scholar Fan objected to this order, but Dorgon brushed him aside.

"The Han are now a conquered race," he shouted at him. "They have an obligation to follow our Manchu customs. This will be a good way to find out whether they have true respect for us."

To his mortification, though, he soon realized that the Chinese were very resistant to the order and many would sooner spill blood than have their hair cut in the Manchu way. Faced with an imminent full-blown uprising, Dorgon sulkily repealed it.

The new Regent had never been a true believer in his late half-brother's idea of benevolent rule. On the contrary, he believed strongly in using the tactic of luring Ming officials, military commanders and scholars with rewards of status and wealth into converting to Manchu customs and then coercing them to press their fellow countrymen into doing the same.

During one Court session, Scholar Fan tried to offer him some relevant lessons from Chinese history, but Dorgon eyed him askance and said huffily:

"Perhaps if you give me a Manchu version, I may read it. I don't have the time or patience to learn the Han language."

Yet Dorgon also understood that in order to assert effective control over this vast population, there was merit in allowing the Ming model of governance to continue.

"I am prepared to let the Ming government structure remain as it is, except that all government officials must speak the Manchu language," he told Scholar Fan. "I trust you to take charge of the civil examination body. We need the organ to select administrative talent for our new Court."

To quell the dissatisfaction with heavy taxes levied by the former Ming government, Dorgon granted a big tax reduction for the peasants. But this meek effort was more than offset by land grabs by greedy Manchu Bannermen and their enslavement of Chinese peasants to work on their newly appropriated estates. Dorgon gave tacit approval to the land grabs and enforced slavery as a reward to the Bannermen for their efforts in achieving victory.

He decreed that the vast swaths of land surrounding the Forbidden City in the center of Beijing be divided into four quadrants: the North portion to the Yellow Banners, the East to the Red Banners, the West to the Whites and the South to the Blues. Walls were built to enclose these areas to form what was to become the Imperial City, in which only the Aisin Gioro clansmen and the Manchu Bannermen and their families had the right to reside. This decree naturally bought Dorgon the loyalty and support he needed from the Manchu noble groups. But on the other hand, the consequence was also seething anger among the displaced Han Chinese, both nobles and commoners alike. There was not even any proper channel for lodging complaints for the loss of their homes and lands, let alone any decent compensation.

For Dorgon as much as for Hong Taiji before him, China had been the single most coveted prize of all targets of conquest. But Hong Taiji had appreciated not only the vast tracts of fertile land

and beautiful landscapes but also the long and rich history and cultural heritage. Dorgon, however, appreciated only the former.

He had had a chance to study the layout of the Forbidden City while helping in the planning of the Imperial Palace in Mukden, and one fine day soon after the occupation of Beijing was compete, he rode out to take a tour of this architectural wonder. Its vastness alone he found overwhelming. His memory informed him that from the Meridian Gate to the south to the Gate of Divine Might in the north was a distance of over three thousand feet, while the east-west span was about three-quarters of the north-south axis. He saw that the layout was exactly as it was on the drawings he had once studied. Behind the double-winged Meridian Gate stood the imposing Gate of Supreme Harmony, the sentinel gate guarding the Outer Court to the south.

The central stone-slab path traversing the palaces was entirely composed of elaborate and symbolic bas-relief carvings leading from the Meridian Gate right up to the Gate of Divine Might, forming the Imperial Way. This north-south pathway included a single-slab ramp carved with nine dragons that connected the Outer Court with the Inner Court. By decree, the Imperial Way was for the exclusive use by the Emperor's Imperial carriage or litter and his entourage.

Having passed through the Gate of Supreme Harmony, Dorgon was unable to resist the temptation and trotted audaciously along the central regal pathway. He dismounted from his horse and ascended the three tiers of white marble steps to inspect the three main Halls of the Outer Court. All these Halls had multi-inclined, yellow glazed-tile roofs and scarlet walls and pillars. Standing majestically on the glistening white terrace, these Halls represented the apex of power and prestige. The oblong Hall of Supreme Harmony, which had witnessed countless coronations and Imperial weddings was perched in front, the square-shaped, pyramidal-roofed Hall of Central Harmony snuggled in the middle, and the rectangular Hall of Preserving Harmony where the imperial examinations were held, lay at the back. He couldn't help marveling at the fastidious craftsmanship of the exterior sculpted eaves. The plush interiors awed him just as much, especially the cerulean painted glass ceilings and the glittering golden-brick flooring. He wondered how much labor, time and artistic skill had gone into the embellishment process.

In the Inner Court, he found on the central axis the three most luxuriant Palaces. Greeting him first was the ornate double-eaved Palace of Heavenly Purity, roosting on a single-tiered white marble platform. This was where the Emperor would reside and hold Court. Next appeared the demure Hall of Union, where the Imperial seals were kept. The Palace of Earthly Tranquility, which served as the Empress's abode, lounged at the back. All these Palaces were finished to an opulent standard.

Looking out from the balustrade-fenced marble platform, he saw six dainty Palaces symmetrically lining the east and west wings. He knew these were lodgings for Consorts, Princes and Princesses. Further north at a distance, nestled between the Inner Court and the Gate of Divine Might, a vista that looked like a silk kerchief embroidered in emerald, violet and pink caught his wandering eyes. That was the Imperial Garden, manicured to perfection with rare plants.

Though he did not like to admit it, he knew that no matter how closely the Mukden Palaces resembled the Forbidden City, it was at best a bland replica with no glorious past to boast of. And the Forbidden City's history could be traced back to the Kublai Khan era of the Mongol Dynasty, four hundred years before. Bumbutai had once told him of it.

"At that time, the Mongolian Imperial clan created a miniature steppe within a tightly guarded walled compound in the middle of the city. It was thus that the ruling clan and families could preserve their culture of communal living in *gers,* away from the prying eyes of the Han Chinese. That is where the name 'Forbidden City' comes from."

She had shared the tidbits gleefully.

"In the Mongolian culture, as you know, the *gers* are the women's property and domain. They can move or dispose of the *gers* as and when they like, or as the circumstances dictate, because the men are always engaged in hunting or fighting wars."

When the Chinese expelled the Mongols with the start of the Ming dynasty, the capital was first placed in the city of Nanjing, far to the south. But the draw of Beijing was strong, and before long, the Ming rulers moved their capital back there, replacing the the *gers* with the web of Palaces now laid out before him.

While strolling on foot around the Inner Court Palaces, many of which had been defaced by the plundering rebels, he was overwhelmed by a taunting thought. In terms of power and prestige, no one in the Manchu leadership surpassed him now. He was the *de facto* ruler. The boy Fulin, who had been given the imperial title of Shunzhi, was only a puppet and would remain as such for some time to come. Yet it was also clear that he, the all-powerful Regent, was not the true master of these Halls and Palaces, and never would be. For better or for worse, he was bound to the bargain he had made with Bumbutai. But then, who would dare stop him if he chose to build a residence that resembled the Palace of Heavenly Purity, both in exterior design and interior trimmings?

Thus musing, he laid eyes on the spacious Palace of Earthly Tranquility, the very name of which evoked the spirit of Mother Earth. An idea dawned on him. With Shamanism being the predominant religion for the Manchus, what could be more fitting than to set up a Shamanist Temple within this Nature-inspired Palace? This would be the best way for the victorious Manchus to etch their cultural imprint on China. At that thought, he almost wanted to jump to action at once, but checked his impulse. His immediate task was to get the Hall of Supreme Harmony quickly repaired so that the new Qing Emperor could be formally received into the Forbidden City.

Having finished inspecting the walled-in maze of regal buildings, he rode out to the West Park beside the Forbidden City. Almost immediately he found himself within the embrace of a scented forest of pine sprinkled with crystal-clear lakes fringed by willows. Elegant terraces and dainty pavilions randomly dotted the immense Park.

Splendid as this Park was, it was too artificial for his taste. What he really fancied was a sprawling piece of virgin land that could be used for hunting, and he had a good idea where he wanted it set up. At the end of the tour, he felt much pleased that he had earlier assigned the West quadrant, which lay just beyond this landscape of delight, to the White Bannermen as a reward for their loyalty to him and to his brothers.

Unlike Hong Taiji, Dorgon was not a willing listener to Bumbutai's advice, especially now that she was going to become his wife. She had been trying to dissuade him from forcing Manchu customs on the Hans, but he would always find a way to avoid being drawn into dscussion with her.

Bumbutai was not surprised by such a reaction, as she had always known about his chauvinistic attachment to Manchu traditions and culture, not least from his doting wife Little Jade, who was her younger half-sister. By arrangement between Hong Taiji and Manggusi, Little Jade had been given to Dorgon in marriage around the time Bumbutai gave birth to her first child.

She could still remember vividly how much her heart ached when news of this had broken.

Little Jade had loved Dorgon at first sight and had been trying to win his heart all these years, knowing, not without a tinge of jealousy, that she could never compete with Bumbutai in this domain. In order to win his approval of her, she had even given up her belief in Buddhism and taken up Shamanism.

Every day, seated in front of her bronze mirror for hours, she would docilely let her maid dress her hair meticulously in the classic Manchu hairstyle – two knots of hair piled up on top of the head – and decorate it with the same pair of pearl hairpins that Dorgon had given her at their wedding. She would always choose to wear Manchu-styled wide-sleeved robes with bright-colored silk appliqué and decorated apron, and high-heeled Manchu shoes.

Each evening, she would have Dorgon's favorite dishes set out in her lounge and wait patiently for him to appear. Nine out of ten times, though, she would end up eating alone. Knowing one of his favorite pastimes was falcon hunting, she went so far as to take falconry lessons even though she had a natural dislike for strenuous activities. To her great disappointment, her eager efforts to please usually met with nothing but a stone-cold face.

Sumalagu fed Bumbutai regular reports of such gossip, gathered from maids in Dorgon's household, saying on one occasion: "Your half-sister is a piteous soul. She'll die of heartbreak one day."

Five months after the decisive Battle of Shanhai Pass was won, one cool autumn day the Qing Imperial procession marched through the citadel gates of Shanhai Pass and started out on the journey west towards the Meridian Gate of the Forbidden City in the center of Beijing. Leading the procession were Jirgalang and the Manchu Eight Banner cavalry. Next in line was the Imperial carriage drawn by four stallions draped in golden satin, in which sat a nervous Shunzhi Emperor, in the company of his regally-attired mother, now Empress Dowager Xiaozhuang. The carriage was followed by the Mongolian Eight Banner cavalry and the Chinese Eight Banner infantry in horse-drawn wagons. Manchu clansmen and Court ministers trailed behind in ceremonial carriages.

Waiting at the Meridian Gate was Dorgon in full shining armor atop his brawny black stallion, surrounded by Ming generals and court officials who had defected, also on horseback. On the approach of the Imperial carriage, the receiving company, with the exception of Dorgon, promptly dismounted to make obeisance to the new Emperor. The Imperial cortege then rumbled along the Imperial Way towards the Hall of Supreme Harmony, with the rest of the cavalcade clanging along on the right and left flanks.

Upon entering the Hall, the Emperor's eunuch helped the six-year-old boy to be seated on the golden dragon Throne Seat in the middle of the raised dais of white marble, while Empress Dowager Xiaozhuang - Bumbutai - stepped up and seated herself on his right on a winged chair with the back sculpted in the shape of a phoenix. A Ming Minister of Protocol knelt in front of the dais, holding the Imperial Jade Seal that had belonged to the Chongzhen Emperor. After bowing three times, he raised the Seal above his head in an offering gesture. The eunuch took it from him and handed it to the Qing Emperor.

Then he read out an Imperial edict which declared that the primary purpose of the new Qing dynasty's assumption of sovereignty was to avenge the Chongzhen Emperor, quell rebellions and restore peace and order. The edict had been carefully worded by Scholar Fan on Dorgon's orders, with Bumbutai's advice. She had said to him: "The last thing we want is to have the Hans see us as alien usurpers of the Ming throne. We must back our claim with noble motives."

When the ceremony concluded, the Shunzhi Emperor and the Empress Dowager retired to Wuying Hall, which had been turned into temporary living quarters for them, as the Inner Court Palaces were still being restored to their original state.

On a bright day of the tenth month, the young Emperor led a Shamanist ritual in the Square in front of the Hall of Supreme Harmony to give offerings to the Heavens and to seek blessings for the new Dynasty. The new reign would carry the official name of "Qing" and the new Emperor would be titled Shunzhi of the Aisin Gioro clan. Beijing was declared as the Empire's capital, and Mukden as its secondary capital. When the ritual ended, the clansmen, Banner Chiefs and Court ministers filed into the Hall, where the formal Regent appointment ceremony was to take place.

The child Emperor, with a custom-made gold-rimmed red velvet Imperial crown sitting on his head and dressed in an Imperial golden robe embroidered with dragons, received the full Court's tribute of obeisance and good wishes.

At the Emperor's bidding, his eunuch then read out an Imperial edict bestowing on Dorgon the official title of "Uncle Prince Regent" and on Jirgalang the official title of "Prince Regent." The Shunzhi Emperor, on his mother's prompt, climbed down from his Dragon Throne and stood in front of the audience. He was trembling. The eunuch handed him a sheathed sword with a gem-studded hilt and scabbard, a symbol of regency power, and invited Uncle Prince Regent to come forward.

Dorgon knelt with one knee on the ground and the other half-bent and accepted the sword with a smirk on his face. Shunzhi's eyes darted away instinctively to avoid his uncle's baleful glare. Dorgon then spoke..

"I will serve the Qing Empire and Your Imperial Highness with all my heart," he made his declaration, the disdain in his voice plain for all to hear. "To this I swear."

Then Jirgalang's name was announced, and he came forward to receive the same type of sword, kneeling with both his knees on the ground in deference and taking the same oath.

Three days later, Dorgon issued an Imperial edict in the capacity of Uncle Prince Regent, changing Jirgalang's title from "Prince Regent" to "Assistant Uncle Prince Regent". If Jirgalang was in any way displeased with this, he did not let it show. Since being elected a co-Regent, Dorgon had been behaving as though he was the sole Regent. He had thirsted for absolute power for too long to care about anything now. His turn had at long last come to impose his own will. Jirgalang had always understood that Dorgon would never be content with anything less than absolute power. Soon after the Manchu Army's victorious entry into Beijing, on Dorgon's hint, Jirgalang had already voluntarily ceded all his power over state affairs to him. Dorgon now had both the government and the military in his clutches.

The following spring, the Chinese general Wu Sangui had successfully chased the rebel Li Zicheng out of his redoubt in Xi'an. Li's army was shrinking by the day and those remaining were fast losing their faith in him. Some of them formed a group which secretly decided to surrender to Wu's army and to take the concubine Chen Yuanyuan to him as proof of good faith. One night, after Li fell asleep, they took Yuanyuan, put her on a horse and rode with her to Wu's camp. Each rider held up a white flag as they approached.

When Wu saw his beloved woman, he was beside himself with joy and immediately ordered his deputies to reward the surrendering rebels with a feast and silver bars. Yuanyuan fell to her knees in a wail, wrapping her arms around Wu's legs: "My master, I thought I would never see you again!" Aware of her own wretched condition, she clambered up and on impulse, tried to grab a dagger from one of the soldiers. Wu sprang forward to stop her just in time. She struggled and cried: "Please let me end my miserable life. I am not worthy of you." It was only when Wu held her tightly in his embrace that she let the dagger drop from her hand.

After the initial thrill of reunion started to wane, Wu had second thoughts about taking her back as his concubine. He gazed at her for a while, searching in her pale face for traces of their happier past. In the end, he gave in to his instinct. The image of vulgar peasants violating her proved to be beyond his capacity to endure.

Yuanyuan on her part had never harbored unrealistic expectations, knowing it would be hard for any man to look past her stigmatized condition. After a long and painful silence, she begged Wu to allow her to retire to a Taoist nunnery where she could spend the rest of her life in reclusion. He didn't even pretend to dissuade her. For Yuanyuan, Wu was the love of her life, and his all-too-eager acquiescence to her request cut her heart to pieces. But she knew tears would only make her look pathetic. So, with a deep sigh, she walked out of the camp in a steady gait and her head held up high, never looking back. She forced herself to picture a new life in the Temple of the Three Sages, in the city of Kunming.

Several months later, Li Zicheng was stabbed to death in his sleep by one of his deputies, and the rebel army disintegrated.

As soon as Xi'an was taken, the Qing army began forging their way into the region of Jiangnan, south of the Lower Yangtze River, where the Ming loyalists had made a home base with their capital in Nanjing. Bloody battles were fought in many regions, with a particularly hideous slaughter in the town of Yangzhou in

Jiangsu Province.

In the fifth month of the second year of Shunzhi's reign, the Manchu forces laid siege to Yangzhou for seven days. The Ming loyalists were led by a man named Shi Kefa who had been trying with all his might to defend what was left of the old empire. Before the siege, Dorgon had written to Shi pleading for his surrender, to which Shi had written an eloquent reply in a tone that was neither arrogant nor self-humbling, rejecting the proposal. But to Dorgon's egocentric self, the letter was an impertinent and insulting rebuff.

On the 24th day, with Yangzhou running out of ammunition and food supplies, the Qing army led by Prince Dodo began a heavy bombardment of the walls with cannons. With no rescue forces in sight, the town finally fell in the evening. Shi Kefa botched an attempt to slit his own throat and begged his foster son to kill him instead. But to his chagrin, the youngster cowered and fled. Shi was captured and later executed because he flatly rejected all entreaties for his defection. Dodo, who was angry at the heavy casualties in his army incurred by Shi's recalcitrance, ordered a massacre of all the residents of Yangzhou.

Inside the town, houses with thatched roofs were targeted by archers who shot balls of burning straw at them. Slow-moving old people were choked by the dense smoke and burned to death. Those who managed to escape the fires were trampled under horse hoofs or cut down by the machete-wielding Qing soldiers. Defenseless women and children were rounded up like animals, tied together with ropes and bludgeoned to death. Cobble-stoned streets were turned into rivers of blood and charred corpses piled up everywhere, spilling into the canals. The wail of agonized screams from those still alive rent through the whole town, sending ghoulish echoes up to heaven and down to hell.

The massacre went on for ten days and it was said that a total of 800,000 people were killed. On the surface, it was Dodo who willed the slaughter to take place. But in reality, it was Dorgon, anxious to assert rule over southern China, who had given the order. He had told Dodo: "There are still so many Jiangnan towns resisting our rule. It will take forever to subdue southern China. Let us make Yangzhou an example with a message for all to see."

Soon after the massacre, pamphlets describing the atrocities were disseminated through the towns of the region. As expected, the technique worked, as it had worked for Genghis Khan across Asia. In the following month, Nanjing surrendered without putting up much of a fight. Then Hangzhou and Suzhou also surrendered. The Ming loyalists were pushed south of the Qiantang River and would remain inactive for a long while. Although much of southern China was now under Qing control, beneath the apparent calm there lurked deep resentments against the new rulers. Strategically shrewd as he was, Dorgon had a blind spot, which only Bumbutai was able to identify and raise with him. At the end of a victory celebration feast, she initiated what became a heated argument, as she voiced her concerns.

"Why are you doing this to the Hans?" she asked. "You know violence is not the solution. It never is. Why did you insist on such mass murders?" Her eyes were shrouded in a vapor of deep angst.

"My love, you don't understand warfare," Dorgon replied patronizingly. "Creating terror amongst the enemy is a tried and proven military strategy. It is the fastest way to overpowering them." He looked calm but he was a little taken aback by her effrontery.

"But this will just exacerbate the antagonism!" she cried. "Once the vindictive mood spreads, it will be hard to contain, let alone reverse. Cruelty can never earn allegiance. Ask any survivor from Yangzhou, if there is one, if he truly respects the

Qing Empire. And even if, out of fear, he declares respect, he will still have hatred rooted deep in his heart."

"We have come a long way to getting where we are today," he countered. "China is our great enterprise and our work is not yet done. How can we let the Ming loyalists gather strength in the South and be a persistent threat to our sovereignty?"

Bumbutai had no ready answer. But she knew that violence would only sow the seeds of enmity.

"Don't you remember what Hong Taiji used to say?" she said breathlessly. "Winning the hearts and minds of the conquered is the ultimate way to rule. What you're doing now will only alienate them. There must be better ways."

On the mention of his deceased half-brother, Dorgon's face crinkled into a glower.

"Hong Taiji is hardly a model for me," he shot back. "You should know that. I don't care what he said. I'll do things my way." Fumes of anger lit up his eyes.

"He had his flaws," she agreed. "But in terms of ruling compassionately, he was not wrong..." before she could finish, he raised his hand to stop her.

"That's enough. It's better that we don't discuss such matters. I know what I'm doing. An important end always justifies the means, any means. My focus is on the end alone. Besides, some of the Hans are selfish and depraved. I am going to use that trait to my advantage."

Bumbutai was surprised to hear from him the familiar comment *the end justifies the means*. It seemed ironic that Dorgon, for all his opposition to Hong Taiji's ways, shared what had been an early belief of Hong Taiji's. She could see that his military successes and the idolization of his army subordinates were feeding him a lethal dose of hubris and had given him a sense of infallibility. There was little she could do now to make him change his approach – his enemy forever was Hong Taiji and whatever he had publicly advocated.

Dorgon had not given up his desire to re-impose the shaved-head order, which he had reluctantly repealed soon after the occupation of Beijing and northern China. He knew that such an order was a symbol of oppression, and he therefore made it a rule to use former Ming generals of the Han race to implement the order, so that any resulting wrath from the populace would be directed at them rather than at the Manchus. One such Han general was Li Chengdong from Jiading in the rich lands just south of the mouth of the Yangtze River. Dorgon knew him to be a venal character who would do the vilest things in exchange for status and wealth.

The region around Jiading, including the tiny fishing town of Shanghai, was one of the places where resistance to the order was fiercest, especially among the scholar class who felt it was a defilement of their Confucian tradition of filial piety. Shortly after Dorgon's shaved-head edict was announced in July of the following year, Li Chengdong led a heavily-armed troop of bandits on boats to Jiading under the Qing banner.

Li had no qualms about using any evil means to get what he wanted. He allowed his soldiers to rob and rape to their hearts' content, provided they offered him a cut. After he and his men had their fill of looting and debauchery, they stashed their spoils on board their boats moored on the canals nearby, left some soldiers to guard them, then went off to plunder other neighboring towns, under the pretense of implementing the shaved-head order. While they were gone, the Jiading villagers armed themselves up and launched a surprise attack on the bandits on the boats, killing a few and burning the boats. Among those killed was Li's brother. When Li returned and found his brother's charred body, he went berserk and ordered his troops to bombard the small walled town day and night with cannons borrowed from the Qing army. The town's fortifications gave way the following night amidst a tempestuous downpour. Li ordered his soldiers to kill every inhabitant of the town who could not offer up valuables. Many of the scholars who had volunteered as defenders thereupon committed suicide.

After three days of killings, the town's canals overflowed with corpses. Yet there were still many survivors who managed to escape the massacre and hid themselves in the vicinity of the town. When Li's army left the town, the surviving villagers gathered together and took control of Jiading town again. News of this reached Li and he ordered his underlings to suppress the resisting villagers, resulting in another slaughter.

About ten days later, a band of Ming loyalists entered the town in an attempt to wrest control back from Li's men. The two groups fought ferociously for several days, but finally Li gained the upper-hand and a third slaughter ensued. By the end of this, not a single living soul could be found in the Jiading district. Ming army and civilian deaths in this area and those close by were said to be in the hundreds of thousands.

Dorgon rewarded Li as he had promised by making him a Han Banner Chief, but secretly despising his baseness, granted him no fiefdom.

Towards the end of the second year of Shunzhi's reign, Hooge was getting restless and, with the help of one of his military deputies, devised a plot to overthrow Dorgon's Regency.

The deputy had, during one of the military campaigns, spent time with one of Dorgon's five closest personal guards. He had learned from the guard that Dorgon had a habit of taking a stroll in the garden of his residence after dinner each evening alone with only that guard. At other times he would be surrounded by the whole team of five. The deputy told Hooge that the guard had a great appetite for beautiful women.

To buy the service of the guard, Hooge sought to entice him with a Mongolian beauty from amongst his many concubines. Treating him to a sumptuous feast, Hooge bade the concubine perform an erotic dance. The guard, drunk on rice wine, begged to be granted the woman. After being under her bewitchment for some time, he began to entertain the thought of switching masters, and Hooge bribed him with twenty gold bars to assist in staging an ambush on the Regent.

Two days before the ambush was to take place, Hooge met Dodo in a tavern. As was his habit, he binged on alcohol but got so drunk that, bleary-eyed, he mistook Dodo for his deputy and unwittingly blurted out some details of his scheme. Fatally, he also revealed the name of the bribed guard. His few incoherent words were enough to make Dodo understand the danger, and he wasted no time in heading to Dorgon's residence, where he passed on all he had just heard.

Dorgon immediately had his guard seized and tortured with burning iron rods until he disclosed the plot and the mastermind behind it. He then had Hooge and his deputy arrested and imprisoned. After a trial, the deputy was executed while Hooge was stripped of his title of Imperial Prince and incarcerated for life. Some months later, he was found dead inside his heavily-guarded prison under suspicious circumstances.

FIFTEEN

BUMBUTAI SUGGESTED A delay to the date of her wedding ceremony, and while Dorgon had agreed to this, it didn't mean he was happy about her apparent hesitation. To show his displeasure, he decided to hold a lavish feast to celebrate his wedding with Hooge's primary wife, whom he had taken into custody after Hooge's death. She happened to be a beautiful young cousin of Bumbutai's from the Borjigit clan. Dorgon had first seen this Lady Borjigit at one of the Court banquets and had been arrested by her charming presence.

Lady Borjigit, being the youngest and most beautiful of her Mongolian noble clan, undoubtedly gave a boost to his ego. But in his position now, he could take any number of young beautiful virgins he desired. It was obvious that she, now a widow, was more a pawn in his wile. He made sure that the wedding was ostentatious and ordered that wedding invitations be sent to all the Aisin Gioro and Borjigit clansmen and clanswomen.

Appearing unannounced in the Cining Palace where Bumbutai resided, he swaggered through unannounced into Bumbutai's inner chambers. With a smug grin on his face, he waved the gold-embossed invitation card at her.

"I would have liked the bride's name on the card to be yours," he said. "Unfortunately that was not to be. My patience is wearing thin and I need a woman's comfort. Would you honor me with your presence at my wedding?"

"Venerable Highness, you shouldn't have troubled yourself to deliver the invitation," she replied with a forced smile, her lips twitching with unease. "May I offer you my congratulations? Why, I cannot wait to share your joy. Your bride is a renowned beauty in our clan."

"I take that as a promise. You must come early, so you won't miss anything. Your cousin has been rehearsing a dance for the occasion." He let out a raucous laugh, as if he had just won a bet.

The banquet was held in the large courtyard in front of the main wing of Dorgon's opulent residence. Flaming torches had been put up at close intervals all around the courtyard to light the whole scene up like day. When dishes were being served to guests, Dorgon, seated at the head table, gave a signal to his chief bondservant. A moment later, his new concubine and a male dance partner appeared on horseback, as fiddle music started to float through the scented night air. Horses' hooves hit on the cobbled ground rhythmically in time with the folk song being played and the dancers moved their horses in rehearsed cadence.

Bumbutai noticed that her cousin was dressed in a Mongolian-style dancing costume, just like the way she had dressed while performing the same waltz in her homeland years ago. Her face looked dewy fresh as lilies and her body as supple as an eel. A stab of envy stultified her as she shifted in her chair. When she stole a glance in Dorgon's direction, her eyes unexpectedly caught his fervid gaze, which was riveted on her. She understood at once what all this meant. Instinctively she turned her face aside to hide her misty eyes.

As Dorgon claimed more and more victories in battles in the conquest of the remaining territories of China, he did not forget Bumbutai's promise to wed him. He thought it was now time she made good her side of the bargain. His position of Regent would only be secure if he became the husband of the Empress

Dowager and step-father of the Emperor. Therefore, a formal tying of the knot was not only the consummation of a life-long desire, but actually a necessary step in consolidating his position. Once he became the Emperor's step-father, no one would be or could be above him. Not even the joint forces of Daisan and Jirgalang could oust him from power then.

One balmy night in the spring of the third year of Shunzhi's reign, Bumbutai had just taken a bath and was getting ready to retire to bed when Dorgon barged into her bed chamber. She was startled by his sudden appearance. They hadn't seen each other since his wedding feast. His eyes were fixated on her silky black tresses cascading down her shoulders and back. Her white silk robe, tied at the waist, draped fluidly over her body and gave accent to its curves. The sight stoked a latent flame in him. He stepped closer to run his hand through her hair, drinking in its delicate fragrance with closed eyes.

His unexpected gesture set her pulse racing and she winced.

"Venerable Prince Regent, I beg you to stop! My maids may walk in on us."

"I didn't mean to startle you. I have come to seek your approval on our wedding date. Yesterday I consulted Scholar Fan on an auspicious date, and he suggested a day which is three months from today." Ignoring her plea, he drew her closer and continued to play with her hair.

"Do you think three months is enough to make preparations?" She couldn't hide her surprise.

"All I need to do is to set the date," he pressed on. "I will leave the rest to the Board of Rites. So do I have your agreement?" He was determined not to let her wriggle her way out this time.

"I am sure Scholar Fan has warned you about the possible negative reaction from the Han Ministers. Dorgon, perhaps we could opt for a small quiet ceremony."

She was looking intensely at him, searching obsessively for the boyish warmth on his face that she had been so irresistibly drawn to on that day of their first encounter. But what met her gaze now were frosty eyes, deeply set in a still very handsome though weathered face, from which she could scarcely read any feelings, save for raw desire.

"I wouldn't mind a small ceremony, but you would have to live with me in my residence. I don't like it at all that you and Fulin stay so close together. It will turn him into a spoiled child."

Bumbutai had been dreading the day when she and her son would be forced apart. Now that day was almost upon her. She must be careful not to annoy Dorgon, otherwise she could even be robbed of the chance of ever seeing Fulin again.

"I don't like living in the Palaces anyway, and I can't wait for us to start our new life together, Dorgon," she replied, her tone softening. "Please go ahead with the arrangement." She let him run his hands over her lithe body with no resistance, remembering what Sumalagu had revealed to her.

She was trying to relive those dreamy moments that they had shared on those two most memorable days of her life in her homeland. But just as soon as she wanted to let go her feelings, twinges of guilt started to spike her like punishing thorns. Her dark phoenix eyes began to swim in tears. With a fluttering of her long lashes, a big drop rolled down her hot cheeks. She gently pushed Dorgon away, averting his burning gaze, and tried to change the subject.

"Dorgon, have you ever considered retracting your shaved-head order? There is so much rancor in the Han society…"

The edict had decreed a death sentence for any Han Chinese who disobeyed the shaved-head order and Manchu dress code. Bumbutai was well aware she was fighting a lost cause, knowing that he had already rejected Scholar Fan's advice to delay the order, but she felt the need to still make one more attempt.

"I don't see any need to do that," he said imperiously. "It's the only way to pick out the troublemakers. For stability to take root, we must first eliminate those who will not yield."

Not even her tears would be allowed to change his mind.

"But oppressive rule will only alienate the Hans further. The trauma of the Yangzhou killings has already left deep, open wounds on them. Peace might prove to be an elusive goal for us. There's much to learn from our own history and from their history too, Dorgon. Hatred only begets more hatred. We must show good faith and respect for the Han culture if we want them to trust us as rulers."

He shook his head. "I would hear no more of that, Bumbutai. I'm not Hong Taiji and I will do things my way. Even Genghis Khan didn't tolerate those who dared stand in his way." He hated it when she brought up Chinese history, which he had always loathed.

"But Genghis only fought those who resisted," she pointed out, "he didn't oppress the defenseless. In Han culture, a person's hair is considered sacred because it was given to them at birth by their parents. It would be against filial piety to have one's hair shaved for no good reason. If you force the Manchu hairstyle and dress code on the Hans, it will only exacerbate their ill feelings."

"But if the Hans will not follow our customs, it means they are not willing to submit to our rule," he said stubbornly. "Until they do, we are not truly the master of China." There was a pause, and he stared into her eyes. The naked candor they revealed mollified him and he relaxed somewhat. At length he said:

"You know how much I love the way you look in Han clothes..... Alright, I will exempt the Hans from the Manchu dress code, excepting Court officials. But all Han males must still shave their heads and wear queues like us."

Bumbutai had not expected that he would make any concession at all, and was secretly pleased. Outwardly though, she displayed no emotion.

"Dorgon, we did pledge to restore peace to Han society at the sovereignty handover ceremony, remember?"

"That is precisely what I'm trying to do. Divide and conquer is the quickest and most effective way to establish our authority and to restore peace and order." He adamantly refused to budge. Intuition told her that his approach was short-sighted and callous and would never win the Hans over, but she knew that locking horns with him further now would serve no purpose. She could only pray he would somehow come to his senses.

"It's very late, and I'm tired," she said. "… Isn't your young concubine waiting for you?" She had not forgotten how her heart had been stung.

"I was hoping I would make you jealous," he said with a touch of triumph in his voice. "So you *are* jealous? Don't you want me?" He tightened his grip on her waist.

"I do … But it wouldn't be proper for you to stay here the night. Fulin usually comes in to see me in the early mornings." She lowered her eyes in a deep blush, satisfied that he was still under her spell.

"He'll learn about us soon enough. I'll go if you say you want me to. Just so you know, you can dance far better than your cousin," he pressed against her body and cupped her breasts, feeling their softness under the flimsy silk. Before he could loosen the string that held her robe, she wriggled out of his embrace.

"Please, Dorgon, go for my sake, I beg you," she pleaded. "We only have to wait a few more months …"

"I've changed my orders just to please you, and this is how you reward me? It's you who are pushing me to my new concubine tonight…." He laughed shortly, and strode out.

In the early dawn on the day before her wedding, she went into Fulin's bed chamber in the Palace of Heavenly Purity to talk to him. He was still in bed when she entered.

"Fulin, there's something I wanted to talk to you about."

"What is it, Mother?" The boy said, yawning, still half asleep and flushed pink from his deep slumber. "Master Fan will be coming to give me Chinese history lessons later."

The child knew by instinct that the mere mention of Master Fan would please his mother.

"I know," she replied with a smile. "It won't take very long, my precious child."

She took both Fulin's little chubby hands in her own and gazed tenderly into his face, in which she noticed for the first time an amazing likeness to Hong Taiji, only without his fierceness. She paused for a moment, then continued.

"Starting from tomorrow, I will be living in your Uncle Dorgon's house, but you will continue to live here. Your grandaunt Jere will still be looking after you as usual."

"Then I won't see you everyday like now?" His dark round eyes dilated in surprise.

"Don't worry. Sumalagu will be visiting you every morning. You have to be a good boy and learn well your Manchu script from her. You also have to study hard and be a good student to Master Fan. Do you remember the reason for that?"

"Yes, because I have to learn how to be a good Emperor, like my father," his answer almost came on reflex. Sensing a tension in this conversation, he couldn't help blurting out: "But I want to see you every day, Mother!" He withdrew his little hands and puckered his lips, his eyes reddening.

"My precious boy, I will try to come to see you whenever I can. If you miss me, you can always write me letters. Then I will know how good you're getting at it. Will you write me letters?

In Chinese?"

"Yes, I will. But why do you have to live in Uncle Dorgon's house?"

"Because your Uncle Dorgon will take care of me and protect me, like your father did when he was alive. If you're good and do as your uncle says, he will let me see you."

"I think I understand," he said. But he couldn't hide his sadness and was trying very hard to hold back his tears.

When Bumbutai saw this, she felt like her heart had been ripped apart. She put her arms round her child in a tight embrace and kissed his forehead over and over again as big teardrops slid down her cheeks. She turned her face away and wiped off her tears with her hand.

"Now let's have our morning meal together," she said coaxingly. "Sumalagu has made you your favorite dumplings. Will you promise me that you will remember to put on warm clothes when it gets cold?"

"Yes, Mother, I promise."

To facilitate his daily trips to and from the Forbidden City, Dorgon had chosen to locate his new residence to the immediate south of the Meridian Gate. It had five lavishly furnished buildings perched on three sides of an expansive courtyard. The sumptuous residence provided ample lodging for his entire household consisting of six wives, four concubines and a large team of guards and house servants. He called this the "Prince Regent Mansion".

In anticipation of Bumbutai joining his household, he had recently taken another grand mansion nearby with a medium-sized courtyard, being well aware of the importance that she attached to open space. This mansion had earlier belonged to Dodo, who had generously offered it to Dorgon as a wedding gift. He had also given orders to his house servants to have the courtyard landscaped exactly like Bumbutai's Yongfu Palace garden in Mukden, complete with lavender lilies, willow trees and a pond filled with large white lotuses.

By this time, Dorgon had already upgraded his own title from "Uncle Prince Regent" to "Imperial Uncle Prince Regent". He was now in the habit of abstaining from the prostrating posture of obeisance when he came into Shunzhi's presence in the Audience Hall. Gradually, Dorgon began holding Court and receiving Ministers inside his own Mansion, instead of at the Emperor's Audience Hall. He also pointedly kept the Imperial Jade Seal inside his residence. The Emperor, though still at a tender age, could discern the snub but said nothing.

The wedding was held at Cining Palace after the Emperor had issued an edict, on the advice of the Board of Rites, giving his blessings to the ceremony. Cining Palace, which Bumbutai had picked as her residence, was one of the smaller and modestly furnished Palaces situated in the quiet north-west corner of the Inner Court. Bright red lanterns had been hung round the porches of the Palace the previous night. Auspicious couplets written in black ink on red silk vertical scrolls adorned the two entrance pillars.

A scrumptious feast was served to guests seated in the main lounge at round tables draped in red satin. Dishes of roasted geese and piglets, grilled deer, lamb shank hotpot, steamed sturgeon and numerous Chinese delicacies including birds' nest soup, along with copious quantities of mare's milk wine, kept the guests' palates happy.

The bride and groom had earlier performed the ritual of tea-offering to Empress Dowager Jere, Prince Daisan, Prince Jirgalang, Prince Ajige and Prince Dodo. The bride's hair was piled up in a chignon at the back of her head and dressed in a Han-style pearl-studded wedding headdress with a veil of pearly strands.

She donned a Han-style silver- and gold-thread brocaded satin jacket, embroidered on the front with two phoenixes, and a full-length red silk pleated skirt hemmed with silvery tassels.

When she moved about, the tassels would sway in sync with her steps, emitting a rustling sound like she was treading on sun-scorched sands. The sound reminded her of the dunes in which she and her horse Jirgal used to frolic. Closing her eyes, she prayed silently to her guardian spirit, the sand fox, for blessings on her beloved Jirgal, now ten years gone.

The bridal garment was an elegant work of art to which Sumalagu had devoted two months of toil. That evening, when the loyal maid saw how radiant the bride looked in her exquisite garb, she felt unspeakably proud, her eyes becoming all red and misty.

The feast was not one of the grandest wedding feasts, but was nonetheless one which thoroughly delighted the guests' taste buds. The Board of Rites had taken the precaution to exclude all Han Ministers from the invitation list and to keep the number of guests small.

When all the guests had departed, Dorgon took his new bride in his carriage back to their new home just outside the Forbidden City. As she sat quietly beside her husband, Bumbutai felt mixed emotions of measured joy and lurking fear. Scene after scene of the hurdles that had been strewn on their path to love flickered across the vista of her mind.

She was at last joined with the man she loved with all her heart. At the same time, she couldn't help but dwell on how the birth of Fulin had changed everything between them. Her life-long desire had now been gratified, yet in the far recesses of her mind there stirred an ominous foreboding. The man sitting next to her was a very different person from the warm and guileless lad she had met on the Mongolian steppe. His thoughts were like a fathomless black pit that defied light. Meanwhile, a voice in her head kept saying: *You have a duty to protect your son. You owe this duty to your tribe and clan. Your son has Mongolian blood and is the anointed one who will eventually bring peace to the three peoples. You have to help him.*

A few days after the wedding, Dorgon issued an Imperial edict requiring with immediate effect that all Court documents should address him as "Imperial Father Prince Regent". He also gave strict orders to Scholar Fan to stop giving Chinese lessons to Shunzhi Emperor. Jirgalang, who had been coaching him on horse riding and archery, was also ordered to cease the training. Bumbutai was naturally distressed by these measures and did not hide her displeasure. One evening after dinner, she implored Dorgon to change his mind.

"Venerable Prince Regent, would you be kind enough to hear me speak? It is about your recent orders to stop all Fulin's lessons."

"I know what you're going to say," he said shortly. "Nothing will make me change my mind."

"Dorgon, I made Hong Taiji a solemn promise, and that promise was to educate Fulin properly. Now you are making me break that promise. We owe this much to Hong Taiji."

After a long pause, he spoke again, more softly.

"Fulin is just a child and he doesn't need to be encumbered yet with serious studies. He has plenty of time ahead of him. Now then, instead of retracting my order, I will allow you one concession. I will issue an edict in Fulin's name to permit interracial marriages between Han commoners and Manchu Banner women. The purpose of this edict is to ease the current racial tensions, and Fulin will earn the praise for initiating it. Would that please you?"

Bumbutai knew Dorgon was aware that knowledge could be

a powerful tool for a fledgling Emperor and was thus bent on robbing Fulin of access to it. Keeping Fulin ignorant was a way of exerting permanent control over him. It reflected Dorgon's deep insecurities and also his naked ambition to become a true Emperor himself. But she felt she had no better option now than to acquiesce to the deal.

Nothing pained Bumbutai more than helplessly watching Dorgon's precipitous descent into the trap of power addiction. Tell-tale signs, large or small, didn't escape her. Jirgalang had always behaved in a deferential manner towards Dorgon, but that was not enough to put him at ease. Before long, Dorgon stripped Jirgalang of all Imperial titles and Regency powers, letting him retain only his position as the Border Blue Banner Chief.

As Dorgon was amassing power in his hands, he was at the same time indulging his lust for beauties. Not satisfied with the number of his wives and concubines, he pressed the Banner Chiefs to select the most beautiful girls from their clans and to offer them to him as new concubines for his harem.

On one of his hunting trips to Inner Mongolia, he paid a visit to the Chakhar Mongol state, which was now a vassal territory and its tribal chief a vassal king. That day, he had brought along a hunting entourage of fifty cavalrymen, each carrying a trained Altai hunting gyrfalcon, the largest of the falcon species. After a whole day of game hunting with the skilled birds of prey on the rolling steppes, the hunters took their rest in tents erected near the vassal king's village of *gers,* the portable tents of the steppe.

The vassal king had a nephew who had just taken a bride. The couple had been married just that afternoon. At dusk, the hunters gathered outside their tents and lit bonfires to roast the game they had caught earlier, and they invited the vassal king, his nephew and the new bride to join their merry-making.

Dorgon and his men had already had several rounds of mare's milk wine when the nephew and his bride joined the party. The moment Dorgon laid eyes on the bride, he was startled by her striking likeness to the adolescent Bumbutai. Then alcohol did the trick of drowning him in a pool of fantasy. "I want a virgin," he was heard slurring. The surroundings transformed in his mind into Bumbutai's family compound, the star-studded sky as it had been when he first saw her dance. His personal guard, seeing the flame of desire in his eyes, went over to the vassal king and whispered something into his ear.

The vassal king was later seen talking to his nephew in a corner and stuffing gold bars into his hand. When the eating and merry-making was over, the nephew was nowhere to be found and his bride was left all on her own. Watching her retire alone to her *ger*, Dorgon, wobbling drunkenly, followed. The next day, he asked his guard to give the girl five gold bars before summoning his hunting group to take leave of their host.

When the story traveled and fell on Bumbutai's ears, she didn't know how to feel. She couldn't help but wonder if she had played a part in pushing Dorgon over the cliff of wanton arrogance.

SIXTEEN

IN THE SPRING OF the fifth year of the Manchu conquest of China, Dorgon led his army to Shanxi Province to put an end to an uprising incited by the remnants of Li Zicheng's rebels. In the midst of the battle, news reached him that his little brother Dodo was dying from smallpox. He immediately relegated his Chief Commander's duties to his deputy and headed back to Beijing with just a couple of guards.

While on the way, he received news that Dodo had just died on his sickbed. He was thunderstruck and broke into a deluge of tears. He had always doted on this brother and the unexpected news of his death cut him to the core. Without uttering a word to anyone, he dismounted and walked his horse to the nearest post-horse station, with his guards trailing mutely behind him. At the station he discarded his armor and tore out two strips of cloth from his white undergarment. He tied the narrower piece of white cloth round the crown of his head and the wider piece around his waist. Dazedly he mounted his horse again and galloped without stopping until he reached Dodo's residence.

At his deathbed, Dorgon became inconsolably stricken with grief, shouting down servants who wanted to access the bed in order to embalm the corpse. He remained in a kneeling position by the bed throughout the night. For the following two days he couldn't sleep or eat. When he finally recovered a little from his rending grief a couple of months later, he adopted Dodo's fifth son Dorbo as his own heir, as he was still childless after all these years.

In the country south of Beijing lay a sweeping terrain of forested hills and rolling lowlands with rivers snaking through them. Dorgon had ordered for the scenic area to be fenced off and turned into an Imperial hunting park. It was given the name "South Park". On the hilly northern side of the Park, he kept nearly a thousand gyrfalcons in a huge aviary. They were trained to hunt by a special team of falcon trainers. On the lowland side of the Park lived a herd of special deer named elaphures with huge antlers, slender legs and large hoofs. Apart from the falcons and elaphures, the Park teemed with all sorts of wild game fit for hunting. This land of natural wonder became Dorgon's favorite haunt and Bumbutai's spiritual sanctum.

Little Jade was an occasional visitor to South Park since taking up falconry lessons from one of the trainers. But her nature had always been of the sedentary kind and she had never taken a liking to the sport. For the last month, she had been sick and bedridden, but this bright early summer day she wanted to ride to the Park to take in the fresh air and visit the tame and mild-mannered elaphures. On her request, Bumbutai rode along to keep her company.

Little Jade was Bumbutai's half-sister by a mistress of Jaisang's. They had not grown up in the same household together, so they had never had a chance to become close before their respective marriages. It was only after Bumbutai moved into Dorgon's mansion that the two sisters came to know each other better. Having once been abandoned to solitude herself, she felt compassion for her half-sister on learning how Dorgon had been mistreating her.

The sisters were riding towards a scenic spot beside a river which emanated from a waterfall tucked deep in a gorge and meandered downwards toward the densely wooded valley on the other side. It was here that the forest wardens kept the domesticated elaphures inside a ranch.

On reaching the spot, they dismounted and tied their horses to one of the poplars that lined both sides of the gurgling river, then started to stroll downstream. At places where protruding rocks blocked its flow, the river hissed, eddying in ripples and foams, and then wrested its way forward with renewed rigor. For a while Bumbutai stood still, enchanted by the struggling brook, her spirits lifted and were imbued with a refreshing sense of hope. Mother Earth's healing hand could always do wonders to a world-wearied soul.

"Oh, look, there are deer coming out from those wild rose bushes!" she exclaimed. "Look at those antlers! They almost seem too heavy for their heads to hold." Bumbutai couldn't hide her excitement at the sight of those meek and slow-moving animals. Her heart went out to the vulnerable fawns when she saw their doleful eyes. How captivity could sap an animal of all spirits! Her thought then turned to her favorite daughter Shuhui, who had chosen to live freely as a commoner in Mongolia with her husband. The thought of their leading a simple and happy life gave her great comfort.

Little Jade turned in the direction that Bumbutai was indicating and her face lit up for a moment, but the light soon gave way to nuances of gloom.

"They are so like me," she said. "Clumsy and ugly."

"Oh, don't say that, Little Jade. You are beautiful and clever. You've been unwell for a long time and that has drained your spirit and energy. The sweet air here will do you good, I'm sure."

Bumbutai wanted so much to impart her sense of joy to Little Jade as she drank in the free spirit of Nature. The green-clad mountains were in idle conversation with the demure blue sky, interrupted now and then by impish white clouds. The scene spontaneously harkened back to her happy, care-free girlhood days on the Mongolian steppe. Little Jade looked over at her.

"How I wish I could be more like you, Bumbutai," she said. "You're so brave, clever and full of life. No wonder you have the love of both Hong Taiji and Dorgon. You are so blessed."

"Little Jade, sometimes things are not as they appear. The love of Hong Taiji's life was Harjol, not me. He might have been infatuated with me at one time, but the thing is, he didn't realize until he met her that what he felt for me was not love. You might call it a desire to possess, but it was not love. In return, I could only give him my affection out of duty."

She paused to meditate for a while, before continuing.

"As for Dorgon and me, life has played a joke on us both," she murmured, almost to herself. "How I wish he and I were not born Prince and Princess."

She recalled the secret that Sumalagu had previously divulged to her, how Dorgon had been injured in the Battle of Songshan, three years after Shunzhi's birth an injury that had made him permanently sterile. It was that revelation which had removed her hesitation about marrying Dorgon. Being the mother of the Emperor, she could not and would not bring shame on Fulin by bearing Dorgon's child. She couldn't help feeling ashamed of her calculating approach, though. But this was one secret that she didn't think prudent to share with Little Jade.

Little Jade was taken aback by Bumbutai's words. She had always imagined Bumbutai to be the most fortunate woman on earth, possessed of the all-consuming love of the two most valiant Manchu Princes in history.

"I just don't understand why Dorgon keeps collecting more women when he already has a slew of exquisite beauties pining to serve him at home," Little Jade said in a low voice, afraid of being overheard criticizing her husband. "I'm sure I'm not the only one that he never deigns to touch."

"Perhaps that's a way of creating a semblance of virility," Bumbutai suggested. "He probably believes that virility is equal to power. But the irony is that the obsession with power has drained him mentally, and his body in turn has weakened due to too much stress. As a man's health deteriorates, he can become paranoid and feel even more compelled to prove his potency. So amassing women has become Dorgon's way of combating his own fear. He just can't help himself."

Lately he had not been near her bed chamber either.

"That may be true too, Bumbutai. But I think the main reason for his disinterest in his women is that he doesn't feel any love for any of them. I believe that in his heart, there has always been just one single woman."

"In my view, Little Jade, you deserve Dorgon's love more than anyone else." Bumbutai tried to divert Little Jade's focus, "You give of yourself to him so selflessly that it puts me to shame. But my destiny was written at birth. Mongolian Princesses have only one purpose in life, and that is to serve the interests of their clan and their tribe. Little Jade, I'm so looking forward to the next life, because I believe only there can couples share pure love, like Blue Grey Wolf and Beautiful Red Doe do."

Bumbutai sighed. She had bared her soul to her innocent half-sister, who appeared baffled by what she heard.

"But aren't you and Dorgon already like Blue Grey Wolf and Beautiful Red Doe now?"

"I wish we were. What I owe him, I can only repay in my next life."

"If you were to choose to save either one of Fulin and Dorgon from death, whom would you choose?"

Bumbutai was stumped by this piquant question coming

from one apparently so naïve. Her brow wrinkled into a frown and after a short pause, she gave an answer of which she herself seemed unconvinced:

"I think I would be left with no choice but to save Fulin, for the Borjigits' and Khorchin Mongols' sake."

As they talked, they were making their way slowly through the verdant valley. All varieties of trees abounded – elms, maples, oaks, magnolias, birches, pines, poplars and mulberry trees. In the shady depths of these sprawling lowlands, azure-winged magpies sang with abandon and iridescent butterflies danced in ethereal grace. The serene silence was otherwise only disturbed by the curious chirps of cicadas and the sleepy croaks of frogs. These little creatures liked the shades and had a habit of hiding in the marshes where the sun could not cleave through the thick foliage.

As they threaded their way through drier patches, the sun's gentle rays traversed the swaying boughs and threw a soft filtered light on their complexions, making both of them look radiant and young. The refreshing scent of pine mixed with subtle flowery fragrances was as inebriating as a draft of fine wine. The younger woman's face, however, was clouded by a sickly tinge that not even the mellow light could gloss over.

A sudden gust of cool wind caught Little Jade off guard and she started coughing. Bumbutai untied the cord of her cape and put it over Little Jade's shoulders. When her cough had eased somewhat, Little Jade stretched out her hand to hold Bumbutai's firmly. They strolled slowly back upstream along the riverbank and chose a smooth rock on which to sit. Gazing at the river, they caught sight of a school of grey carp slithering along with the current. On the opposite bank, two forest wardens were throwing fishing lines into the water.

"I think I am not far from my end," Little Jade said wistfully as she stared at the vibrant shoal. "I'm not afraid of dying. Humans or fish, we all come to our own end somehow, sooner or later. But I worry about Dorgon. He's such a poor solitary soul."

"Oh Little Jade, don't say that. You only have to take better care of your health, that's all, and everything is going to be fine. As for Dorgon, you know that together we shall keep him in good shape."

"Of course we shall, Bumbutai. I'm so silly. Please don't mind me."

The two sisters sat in silence for a while longer, watching the wardens catching their dinner.

"We should be riding back before it gets dark. You need to rest up," Bumbutai said soothingly.

The landscape was now washed in the oblique rays of the sinking orange globe which spread a golden gauze on the water. Astride their mounts, the two sisters cantered back to their separate homes in the Imperial City.

A couple of months later, Little Jade passed away from a bout of smallpox. As much as Dorgon had kept a cool distance from his first wife, he had been far more affected than he let on by her unalloyed devotion to him. On her death, he fell into another prolonged fit of depression, having barely recovered from the loss of Dodo.

Bumbutai's heart ached when she saw his face knotted in pain. It reminded her of the young angry lad in the Throne Hall in Mukden when he had heard of his mother's forced suicide. He was now in such a sorry state that she was really worried and she took it upon herself to take personal care of him, nursing him day and night at his bedside for three months.

One day during his recuperation, Dorgon motioned for her to sit on his bed and he clasped her hand tightly in his.

"I always knew you were right," he said. "You can conquer

on horseback, but can never rule on horseback. I was only trying to finish what we had started. As soon as the south is under our control, that will be the day for us to put away our weapons and let peace and order take hold." He paused. "You know that there is nothing I wouldn't do for you, right? You are my sweet green phoenix."

She scanned his stolid pale face for a long while. The contours still outlined a proud visage, although weariness had scored his brow. When she peered deeper into his brooding eyes, she seemed to perceive the young lad in him anew, a glimpse of unguarded tenderness. She leaned over and kissed him passionately on the lips, saying repeatedly: "I love you, Dorgon, so much."

She prayed hard that it was not too late to mend the damages already inflicted on the Hans.

Dorgon felt he owed Little Jade a debt of gratitude. As soon as he was well enough to go back to his duties, he issued an edict granting her a posthumous title of "First Consort" with a prefix of four bestowed characters, in the same way Hong Taiji had honored Harjol. As his health improved, he resumed his old habit of going on regular hunting trips, now always taking with him the gyrfalcon that Little Jade had personally trained.

In the summer of the seventh year of Shunzhi's reign, a Korean foreign minister came to pay obeisance to the Prince Regent and submitted a request for financial assistance for the purpose of building an extensive wall of defense on Korea's borders. Dorgon seized the opportunity to strike a bargain. In exchange for granting loans to the Korean vassal king, he demanded that his daughter Princess Yi Ae-suk be given to him in marriage. He was thinking that the Princess could be held as hostage against any possible disloyalty on the part of the new tributary state.

On top of that, he imposed an additional condition that Korea should hold a beauty contest to select a couple of the most beautiful virgins and offer them to him as concubines. The condition was meant as a test of the Korean court's loyalty to the Qing. He was aware that Korean society had long held Manchu culture in contempt, regarding it as barbaric and inferior to the Han Chinese culture. But the Korea foreign minister felt he could not return home empty-handed and he finally agreed to Dorgon's terms.

It was arranged for Dorgon and his hunting entourage to meet Princess Yi and the two newly-selected Korean beauties in the autumn at the Mukden Imperial Palaces, which now served as an Imperial Retreat for the Aisin Gioro clan. Dorgon sent orders for the Emperor's Residence, Yongfu Palace and some of the service buildings to be made ready for temporary use.

King Injo, who had been humiliated in public by Hong Taiji, was a Ming loyalist and was a fervent believer in Confucian thinking and values. When the Korean Crown Prince dared to contradict him by expressing his love of European culture and support for the Manchu's Qing Dynasty, King Injo was so incensed that he picked up an ink slab from his writing table and smashed his son's skull with it, killing him instantly. He then disposed of the body by burying it in the imperial garden. The Crown Prince's wife harbored suspicions about her husband's disappearance. When she started to ask questions around Court, King Injo became paranoid and ordered for her to be executed.

The tyrannical King then fell seriously ill and died in 1649. He was succeeded by King Hyojong who was prudent enough to start extending a friendly hand to the Qing Empire, at least in gesture.

When King Hyojong learned about Dorgon's terms for granting the building loan, an idea dawned on him. He thought that if Princess Yi could be impregnated by a Korean prince's seed before she was sent to the Qing Prince Regent, then any male heir thus "produced" would carry Korean royal blood. There was a chance that Dorgon's heir might accede to the Qing throne. If that happened, Korea would be able to rule the Qing Empire without shedding one drop of blood. It was a bet that seemed worth taking. What King Hyojong could never have guessed was that Dorgon was sterile and any child that the Korean Princess might carry after bedding him would expose the ploy.

King Hyojong talked his idea over with his ministers and they applauded their King's clever idea as they were supposed to. As planned, a young and robust royal prince deflowered Princess Yi a couple of months before her departure for Mukden. After a Court physician verified that she was with child, she was sent forth with emissaries and the two Korean beauty contest winners.

Seventeen

Upon arrival at the Imperial Palaces at Mukden, Dorgon took a tour around the Complex in a nostalgic mood. The empty and cobweb-infested Dazheng Hall looked dreary and maudlin. Trees in the square were shedding big teardrops of dead leaves, which echoed the gloominess. The forlorn surroundings plunged him into the abyss of his painful past.

He had been the golden boy of Nurhaci and Lady Abahai, destined for the throne, and he had won the innocent love of a sparkling Mongolian Princess. But Hong Taiji had brutally murdered his mother and had schemed to snatch the throne and the love of his life from him. True, his mother's death had been avenged. But what about the Qing throne? What about Bumbutai? The Empire should have belonged to him and his descendants! He had sweated in battle more than anyone else in the clan. He and Bumbutai should have had a blissful union and the joy of breeding and raising an heir - *his* heir. A spasm of agony surged through him and he stomped away from the ghostly hall.

His wandering legs took him to a stop at the garden gate of the Yongfu Palace, and he went inside and sat on the stone bench underneath one of the two weeping willows. He fell into a trance and went down memory lane to the time when he had first laid eyes on the girl Bumbutai. Fumbling in the pockets of his surcoat, he took out a pink package, untied the purple ribbon knot and unfolded a letter with fraying edges, exposing a lock of hair. He held the hair in one hand and the letter in the other, reading it hungrily as if he wanted to devour every word in it. Then he carefully folded it up, putting the lock of hair back inside, wrapped it up in the pink silk kerchief and tied the package neatly again. Unaware of what he was doing, he fingered the blue swallow embroidery, and his eyes turned misty.

Then his thoughts leapt to the time Bumbutai had danced a butterfly dance for him right inside this Palace. His pulse raced as he vicariously relived that night of torrid passion. Every fiber in her had yearned for him. How he had hungered for her too.

In a flash, the image of Fulin appeared to him, twisting and twirling like a vicious tsunami, and tore to shreds the raft of daydreams to which was tied his very existence. His face wrenched itself into a scowl. Fraught with despair, he silently moaned as he fumbled his way out of the garden.

The following day, Princess Yi and her entourage arrived at the Imperial Palaces. The noblewoman and the other two Korean beauties settled in the Yongfu Palace, as previously arranged. The wedding was to be held the next day at the Emperor's Residence main hall. Dorgon had deliberately chosen the Mukden Palaces to hold this wedding, as he felt that he could really feel and act like an emperor here, away from the Qing Court in Beijing and all its cumbersome protocol. Also, he would not be under Bumbutai's watchful scrutiny.

He had heard of Korean women's submissiveness to men and was intent on them pandering to his whims. At the wedding feast, he bade his servants serve jug after jug of mare's milk wine to all his guards and soldiers and the Korean male guests, and a slew of the most sumptuous dishes. Half way through the drinking and eating, on his clap of hands, a group of scantily clad dancers including the Korean women came into the hall to perform a ribbon dance.

When the dancing was over, the half-nude dancers were made to sit with the male guests and feed them like infants. The sodden men became more and more rowdy and abandoned themselves to debauchery.

It was well past midnight when the feast finally came to an end. Struck by an onslaught of ennui, Dorgon had earlier left the scene, his initial interest in the Korean girls gone. Before leaving, he had whispered to a young Border White bannerman that he could enjoy Princess Yi for the night.

The Princess and the two other Korean women were escorted back to Yongfu Palace by two of Dorgon's bodyguards, who were rewarded with a night with the two courtesans.

Princess Yi had never expected to be treated with such degradation, although she was not proud of what her countrymen had done to her either. The next morning, exhausted from crying, she sat alone on her bed after the bannerman had left. However, she did feel a bit relieved now, because even when her pregnancy became known, her hosts would only believe the child to be by the bannerman and would never suspect it to have a Korean father. She was only glad that she didn't have to bed Dorgon, who she now came to suspect was impotent. But if her child turned out to be a boy, she would still have some difficult explaining to do to her Korean king. She was thus praying with all her heart that the child she was carrying was a girl. Then no one would care to ask any questions.

When Dorgon got tired of Mukden, he took Princess Yi and the two Korean courtesans back to his Mansion in Beijng. He bestowed the title of primary spouse on Princess Yi and made the other two his concubines. Then he never set eyes on them again.

Around this time, in Guangdong Province far to the south, another Ming defector and self-seeker called Shang Kexi committed the same odious crime as Li Chengdong against his fellow Hans. Shang led a Han Chinese Border Blue Banner army to lay siege to the city of Guangzhou in order to enforce the shaved-head order. Historically, the southerners in the coastal regions had always been obstinate opponents of despotic rule, perhaps due to their long contact with the outside world through trade. The siege lasted for ten months before the town's defense finally began to crumble.

In the eleventh month, the Qing army used a combination of Dutch cannons and an escalade invasion technique to breach Guangzhou's fortress towers and ramparts. Once the incursion started, Shang gave his soldiers explicit permission to mass rape the women as a reward for their ten-month hardship during the siege. He also encouraged them to loot the houses and keep whatever valuables they could find. Lastly, he ordered them to "cleanse" the town by killing as many males as they could, including children.

The bedlam of blood-curdling shrieks grated the air like the tortured wail of ghosts in every corner of the town. The soldiers raped and killed until utter exhaustion blunted their beastly instincts. Corpses piled up in columns as high as the houses and the streets were flooded in a crimson red. The massacre lasted eleven days and resulted in the deaths of as many as a hundred thousand.

After Guangzhou's defeat, only small groups of loyal Ming scholars survived and these went underground to live as hermits. For his atrocious treatment of his fellow Hans, turncoat Shang gained a fiefdom in Guangdong and was installed as provincial governor.

By this time, the Manchu conquest of China was almost complete except for sporadic small-scale uprisings here and there. Bumbutai's unceasing pleas at last convinced Dorgon to send Hong Chengchou, the favorite Han general of Hong Taiji, as the Regent's envoy to pacify the residents of southern China. Hong brought relief funds to help them rebuild their lives, and clamped down on the abuses of power by self-seekers like Li Chengdong and Shang Kexi. He was empowered to execute plunderers and rapists on the spot. This eventually brought back order of some sort, but such peace would prove to be short-lived. Shang Kexi's son would later attempt to rebel in concert with Wu Sangui against the Manchu's Qing Empire during the next Emperor's reign.

Following the death of Little Jade, Bumbutai had for several months wallowed in melancholy. She missed Fulin terribly, as Dorgon had forbidden her from visiting the boy. He had sent a middle-aged palace maid named Ah Lan to keep a watchful eye on her And Bumbutai now had no one to talk to except Siu Mui. She greatly regretted having given Siu Fa to Hong Taiji, because under the Inner Court rules, as a childless widowed Consort, Siu Fa had to live in seclusion in the Imperial retreat house until death. She only hoped one day she would be in a position to rescue Siu Fa from that ghastly place, where its inhabitants were treated like lepers.

One day in the twelfth month, a teary-faced Siu Mui came into the lounge where Bumbutai was sitting doing needlework.

"Mistress, our uncle and aunt and all our cousins in Guangzhou have been killed," she sobbed. "Their neighbors who fled the town have just delivered the news."

"Oh Siu Mui, that's so terrible! What happened to them?"

"Guangzhou resisted the shave-head order and so a Ming defector general led an army to attack the town. They killed everyone they could. I don't understand why some Hans can do unspeakable things to their fellow men like that. They are so evil. Our uncle's family were our only relatives left. Now Siu Fa and

I only have each other." The maid couldn't control her flood of tears as she spluttered out the news.

"I've heard what happened there, it is a big tragedy," said Bumbutai. "General Hong Chengchou is doing all he can to salvage the situation. Don't be sad, Siu Mui. You have me. I have always treated you like a sister, haven't I?" A pang of guilt jabbed at her. She wondered if she could have used her influence on Dorgon more persistently and sooner.

"Yes, Venerable Empress Dowager, Siu Fa and I will always be indebted to you. We can never thank you enough for your kindness." She used her sleeve to wipe away her tears.

"Do you want to take a trip to Guangzhou to pay your respects?"

"Yes, I think I want to at least try and find their bodies and give them a proper burial."

"I understand. You should go and pack at once then. I will ask General Hong to send a guard to take you in a carriage and protect you on the way. It's too bad Siu Fa can't go with you."

Bumbutai put down her needlework and went into her bed chamber, then returned holding a jewelry box. She took two green jade bracelets from it and gave them to Siu Mui, who dropped to her knees and bobbed her head a few times. The valuable jewels were more than enough to pay for the travel and burial expenses.

"Take all the time you need, Siu Mui. But as soon as you've done what you need to do, come back. Scholar Lin has agreed to take you as his concubine. I'll soon start planning for your wedding."

Scholar Lin was a favorite student of Scholar Fan's and a Minister of Documents. She had met Lin a few times at the regular tea talks that she hosted for the Han literati, and had thought the middle-aged Scholar and Siu Mui would make a fine pair.

"Venerable, I would rather stay here to serve you until I die.

You are my family now. I don't want to marry anyone." Siu Mui plonked herself down on her knees again, drowning in tears.

"Oh, Siu Mui, I would hate to see you leave me. But just think. You will have a much higher social status and a more comfortable life. Scholar Lin is a learned and kind man and he will treat you well...." Tears choked her too at the thought of having to let go of this second twin as well as the one already lost.

Then Siu Mui remembered she had something important to tell her mistress. She looked around to make sure that Ah Lan was not nearby, then took from her sleeve a crumpled piece of paper and handed it to Bumbutai. It was one of the secret letters written in Chinese that Fulin wrote to his mother. Mother and son had been keeping in touch through letters which the maid furtively couriered between Dorgon's mansion and Sumalagu's quarters inside the Forbidden City. Sumalagu was responsible for serving Fulin breakfast each morning in his bed chamber.

From Fulin's letters, Bumbutai had read between the lines his deep-seated rage and bitterness towards Dorgon. In her replies, she would always try to coax him to lie low and pretend to care nothing about Court matters. She even encouraged him to pass the time in playing chess and indulging in sports like horse riding and archery. She told him that for his own safety, he must never do anything to provoke Uncle Dorgon, lest it would give him an excuse to usurp the throne by force. To her great consolation, Fulin seemed to understand well enough what she meant. On the surface at least, he kept his head down.

When news of the capture of Guangzhou reached Dorgon, he was thinking of going on a trip to Kharahotun, his favorite hunting ground northeast of Beijing in the mountainous Province of Jehol, with its copious stash of wild life. He had set his heart on building a luxurious mountain retreat there. It was in a region with steep cliffs, plateaus, gorges, lakes and a large river running through the center, and because of its high altitude, summers were much more pleasant than in Beijing. But its winters could be brutal with erratic and severe snowstorms.

Since his return from the Mukden wedding, Dorgon had been feeling unwell, but would not admit it to himself. But news of the Guangzhou victory was reason enough for a hunting celebration and he invited his brother Ajige to accompany him to Kharahotun with his favorite Plain White cavalrymen. Feeling in better spirits than he had for a very long time, he also extended an invitation to several of his favorite Han advisers, students of Scholar Fan. He wanted to show these weakling bookworms what gyrfalcon hunting was like. One of these advisers happened to be Scholar Lin.

After several days of travel, the hunting expedition finally arrived late one afternoon at the camping grounds on a wide plateau naturally screened on all sides by high pine-covered hills. As it was already early winter and the mountain air was icy cold, they started bonfires to keep warm. In an instant, the dark evening sky morphed into an ominous pitch black. A violent blizzard began to howl and soon thrashed out several of the bonfires. It was with great effort that the hunters managed to set up their tents amidst the violent gusts. The agitated horses and gyrfalcons had to be pacified for a long time before they would settle down. The gales and sleet continued all night, and before dawn broke, a sudden monstrous hail shower pounded the tents with ice pellets, making a deafening noise.

During the night, Dorgon had broken into a wheezing cough as the biting-cold mountain gales whipped through narrow openings in the tent walls. By morning, the sleet had changed into a heavy downpour of freezing rain. His cough became more sporadic.

By midday, the rain finally stopped and the sun peered out

timorously from behind thick blankets of leaden clouds. Buoyed by the clement break, the group buzzed with excitement and started to saddle up their horses and equip themselves with bows and arrows and gyrfalcons. Seasoned hunters filed out in front, followed by the scholars and the acolytes.

Within these lush mountains thrived all sorts of wild game birds including pheasants, partridges, grouses and quail. There was no lack of mammal quarry either. Foxes, sables, beavers, elks, argali, deer, boars, rabbits, coneys, moles, squirrels and marmots all flourished in abundance. The hunters were eagerly looking forward to a dinner of roasted rabbits, quail and partridges and planned to hunt for furs on another day.

In fine weather, the rocky slopes would present no challenge to such skillful riders as the Manchu and Mongol cavalrymen. But the blizzard of the night and the freezing rain in the early morning had rendered the terrain treacherous even for the most nimble of riders. Thus the group headed out into the mountain forests in a slow and cautious manner.

After a while, though, the snail-paced movement was getting on Dorgon's nerves and, against Ajige's advice, he charged forward alone and soon disappeared from sight. Then the hunters and company began to scatter, some in pairs and some in groups of four or six, each going their own way, happy to have some space in their search for quarry.

By sunset, most hunters and their attendants had returned to the camping ground and were preparing for a roasting feast. There was a steady buzz of conversation as the hunters bragged to each other about their day's catch.

When the last rays of twilight were about to disappear, Dorgon was still nowhere to be seen. Ajige was beginning to feel anxious and, tired of waiting, he took two of his cavalrymen and started out to look for his brother.

Bright stars populated the dark vaulted sky and an eerie feeling overcame the hunters as in the moonlight, Ajige's team could be seen at a distance, heads drooping, returning slowly to camp. As they came nearer, Scholar Lin saw Dorgon on the back of one horse, bloodied and bruised, unconscious and prostrate. When Ajige had found him, he was lying unconscious in a dark pool of blood. The spot was on the steep incline of a fiendish crag. He had fallen from his horse, hitting his temple on the sharp edge of a jagged boulder.

The scholar, who happened to have brought along some medicinal herbs for dressing bleeding cuts and scrapes, was immediately called by Ajige to tend to Dorgon's wounds. There was a three-inch long deep gash just above his right eye. Scholar Lin pressed a handful of herbal powder onto the bone-revealing gash, covered it with a clean cloth pad and ran a strip of rag around his head to hold the pad in place. The cloth pad soon turned soggy with blood and had to be replaced.

Lin fed Dorgon ginger tea, but it failed to return any color to his ashen white face. His sporadic groans indicated that he was suffering searing pain from the gash. Lin touched his forehead again and found he had a scalding fever.

Ajige declared he would keep close vigil on his brother through the night. He then gave orders for the group to pack up and get ready to return to Beijing the next morning. When Lin last set eyes on Dorgon, his face was of a lifeless grey, and he was clutching a pink bundle in his trembling hand. A little after midnight, in his dying breath, Dorgon spoke his last words to Ajige. Moments later, Ajige was heard breaking into a loud wail. He then came out of his tent to call the group to attention, and with a solemn face announced Dorgon's death. A loud gasp emitted from the group.

Scholar Lin, who was in a tent right next to Ajige's, was able to catch part of a conversation between Ajige and his personal guard: "We must take them by surprise if we're to succeed. We'll head straight to the Forbidden City and take Fulin. Once we have him, everything is set….."

Lin heard enough to make him sense grave danger taking shape and knew he must make a move ahead of Ajige in order to arrive in Beijing first. So before dawn, he quietly left the camping ground with Suksaha, a close friend of Jirgalang's who had always disliked Ajige. Lin confided in him as to what he had heard. Suksaha had originally pledged allegiance to Dorgon under the Plain White Banner, but had later become irked by his self-indulgence and had turned into a sympathizer of Jirgalang. The scholar had met Suksaha at several of Bumbutai's tea gatherings. Morning broke with an evil shroud of fog on what was the ninth day of the twelfth lunar month. A tense atmosphere permeated the camping ground as the group prepared for departure with Dorgon's body.

Scholar Lin and Suksaha appeared panting at Bumbutai's door to pass on the news of Dorgon's death and the plot against her son, and the news hit her like a thunderstroke. She crumpled into a heap and the two men had to prop her up as a numbing chill encompassed her entire body. But she had no time for thinking, only for action. Ajige's usurping army would be at the gate of the Forbidden City any moment now. Still disoriented but without a second thought, she rode with Suksaha and Scholar Lin to Jirgalang's residence to consult with him.

All she could think of was that her life and her son's life were now hanging by a thread. Daisan and Empress Dowager Jere had both passed on the previous year. There was now no authority figure in the Aisin Gioro clan except herself. She was still Shunzhi Emperor 's birth mother and the Empress Dowager. She could only pray that she would be able to command sufficient respect.

As soon as Jirgalang heard what was happening, he addressed Bumbutai.

"Venerable Highness," he said in a firm tone, "you have to issue two edicts as Empress Dowager at once. The first is to announce the death of Dorgon and to denounce Ajige as the traitor and usurper. The second is to command the Imperial Guards and the Seven Banner cavalrymen to gather inside Forbidden City to protect the Emperor and yourself."

He then turned to the scholar.

"Scholar Lin, would you kindly start working on the edicts? My men will help with the posting. Then we must all head to the Forbidden City. As soon as our cavalrymen arrive, we will lock all the gates. I will personally direct my Border Blue men to waylay Ajige and his men near the Outer City gates."

Jirgalang showed himself to be an effective strategist and Bumbutai's trembling started to ease a little. In her confusion, she was still able to discern that Jirgalang's proposition was the best option. She was only glad that she had always kept on good terms with Jirgalang, Suksaha and Scholar Lin.

As her nerves calmed, the full force of Dorgon's untimely death finally struck her. She was left all alone now, no one to share intimate thoughts with any more. For all his faults, he had truly cared for her and taken her interests to heart. There was no denying that her heart had been firmly grafted onto his from the day of their first fateful encounter.

Inwardly she upbraided herself for her hypocrisy in front of Little Jade that day in South Park, sounding all pompous and detached. Fulin was a duty imposed upon her, but Dorgon was the one who had lit up her life and had kept her going through the darkest hours. His abrupt departure was sending everything crumbling around her, the whole Qing Empire crashing down onto her shoulders. She just wished she could follow Dorgon into that other world, where she would not have to face all these mundane worries. Before she could further indulge in her reverie, Scholar Lin's voice propelled her back to the stark present."Venerable Empress Dowager, would you kindly take a look at the wording to see if it is acceptable?"

"I trust you, Master Lin," she said weakly, taking up a brush pen to put her name on the edicts. As she wrote, Scholar Lin said absent-mindedly, as if to himself:

"When I last saw the Venerable Prince Regent, he was clutching something like a letter wrapped in a piece of pink kerchief. It must have meant something to him."

Bumbutai's face blushed deep pink and her heart throbbed wildly, as if someone had caught her pilfering. She couldn't believe that after all these years, Dorgon had still held onto her first love letter! Her eyes tinged red with emotion and hot tears escaped her. She quickly turned aside her face to hide it. It was with great difficulty that she managed to find words for a reply.

"It must have belonged to Little Jade," she said nonchalantly. She pretended to have a final look over the edicts, then handed them over to Jirgalang.

"We must not waste any more time," he urged impatiently. "I will get my men to make as many copies as possible and post all over the Inner City. Let's all leave at once."

Eighteen

Jirgalang had known that Ajige's men would be coming down the main thoroughfare of the Outer City, as it was the only access route to the Inner City. There was a stretch on this road that was most tightly flanked by houses on both sides and archers had taken up position on the rooftops. When their quarry came into view and at Jirgalang's chirping signal, the arrows rained down on them, trapping the blindsided cavalrymen. A chaotic melee ensued, in the midst of which Ajige's horse was hit by an arrow, throwing him to the ground. Seizing the chance, Jirgalang bolted forward with two of his men and seized him. After a short but intense fight, all the riders, roughly equal in number to the ambush group but badly stung by surprise, were subdued and put in chains.

A month later, in the Emperor's Audience Hall, the young Shunzhi sat on his dragon throne seat with a stern look on his face, with Empress Dowager Xiaozhuang seated to his right. The Banner Chiefs and the Six Ministers made obeisance and stood in two lines in front of the marble throne dais. On the Emperor's summons, announced by a eunuch, Jirgalang entered the Hall, bringing with him a defiant Ajige in chains.

Shunzhi, who had earlier rehearsed his speech with the help of his mother, addressed the Banner Chiefs and the Ministers, briefing them on Dorgon's accidental death and the subsequent treasonous act committed by Ajige. He then sought advice from the Court as to what should be done with the chief traitor and the other insurgents. After deliberation, they gave their unanimous consent to having Ajige placed under permanent house arrest, with all the others being sentenced to immediate execution by beheading.

Having taken the Court's advice, Shunzhi issued an Imperial edict with the express endorsement of Empress Dowager Xiaozhuang, declaring the immediate transfer to the Emperor of control of the two Yellow Banners and the Plain White Banner, now to be called the "Upper Three Banners". Jirgalang had earlier secured the support of two generals, Oboi of the Border Yellow Banner and Suksaha from the Plain White Banner. In return for their allegiance to Shunzhi Emperor, Jirgalang allowed them to join the Emperor's Private Council. As instructed by his mother, Shunzhi ordered that Dorgon be granted a state funeral and the posthumous title of "Righteous Emperor" in order to pacify his loyal followers.

Six days later, in the first lunar month of the year, just a few days before Shunzhi's thirteenth birthday, an extravagant ceremony was held at the Hall of Supreme Harmony to officially bestow on him full Imperial ruling powers, thus bringing a formal end to Dorgon's Regency.

Less than a month after the Emperor's grant of the posthumous title to Dorgon, the generals Oboi and Suksaha requested an audience with the Emperor for the purpose of presenting to him evidence of Dorgon's traitorous intentions before his death. He had acted, they said, like an Emperor himself, using the Imperial Jade Seal on Court documents without the Emperor's knowledge; that he had murdered Hooge and taken his wife; that he had built an Imperial palace for his own use; that he had appropriated an Imperial golden robe embroidered with five dragons; and that he had not prostrated before the Emperor as he should have.

With the consent of the Court, Shunzhi therefore ordered that Dorgon's corpse be exhumed and flogged in public, that he be stripped of all Imperial titles, that all his property be confiscated and that his adopted heir be stripped of the right of inheritance. Without Shunzhi's explicit instruction but with his full knowledge, Oboi went ahead and ordered the corpse to be decapitated, cut to pieces and fed to the vultures.

Shunzhi had long harbored a deep dislike of his hubristic uncle, who had slighted him, the true Emperor, in every possible way. The news of the corpse mutilation gave him visceral delight and assuaged his long bottled-up resentment towards Dorgon. He used Oboi's argument that the Emperor's authority must be manifested at every opportunity as an excuse to purge all Dorgon's followers.

When news of this reached Bumbutai's ears, she was heartbroken, but thought it best not to interfere. She was well aware that there was a need for the fledgling Emperor to consolidate power in his hands at this critical moment. She was also still suffering under the crushing weight of a sense of guilt towards Shunzhi over his father's unnatural death. Desolation pushed her to find refuge in solitude in South Park. Her only solace was that when she attended to the embalming of Dorgon's corpse, she had found the pink bundle still firmly ensconced in his stiff cold hand. In her solitary moments in the Park, she would recall that scene again and again as if she were indulging in a guilty pleasure.

That day, alone with the corpse, she had the luxury of draining her repressed tears as she washed and embalmed the huge lifeless body with incense and white cloth. Alternate pangs of remorse and deep grief jabbed at her heart like serrated blades. She wanted to scream out her pain but the sound had lodged itself in her throat.

With a trembling hand, she had carefully removed the pink packet which was glued by congealed blood to his icy hand. A weeping candle lit the morbid chamber and kept her company. It gave her an idea…

Watching the letter and the lock of hair disintegrate slowly in the flame, she had a strange sensation that part of her was turning to cinders and melding with the smoke, wafting into the underworld to join her Dorgon. She then stopped weeping and murmured to herself: "Forgive me, my love. My empty shell must carry on. The subjects of Qing need it to work for them."

On leaving the mortuary, she had the pink kerchief with her. The kerchief with Dorgon's blood on it.

With the help of Oboi and Suksaha, Shunzhi spent most of the next two years persecuting Dorgon's favorite Court Ministers, military followers and supporters until no remnant of his influence remained. Oboi had been a loyal follower of Hong Taiji's and had in secret always resented Dorgon's rule. To reward Oboi for his help, Shunzhi appointed him Chief Commander of the Imperial Guards. Emboldened by this appointment, Oboi went on a vendetta to eliminate those who had ruffled him in Dorgon's days.

As Oboi gained more of Shunzhi's trust, he saw fit to get rid of Scholar Lin, a rival who had been a favorite Minister of Dorgon's and had wielded great influence on policies in Court. Being an impetuous person, Shunzhi decided to trust Oboi's judgment and without consulting his mother ordered the execution of Scholar Lin. By the time Bumbutai heard the news, it was too late. Less than six months after her wedding, Siu Mui became widowed. Bumbutai couldn't but feel desolate about her maid's tragic fate. She had wanted so much to give her a happy life, but Eternal Blue Sky had other plans.

Towards the end of the eighth year of his reign, Shunzhi let Oboi persuade him that Ajige had to be taken out in order to quash any hope of a usurpation of power by his followers. He assigned this unpleasant job to Jirgalang.

One afternoon in the tenth lunar month, Jirgalang visited Ajige in his prison residence. When Ajige saw his uncle, he thought that Shunzhi had at last found it in his heart to release him. But Jirgalang had stashed inside one of his sleeves a small vial filled with arsenic-laced wine. On entering the lounge, he stuttered in an awkward way:

"It has been a while since you and I had a good meal together… Let's eat, drink and chat." He signaled for the manservant who had followed him into the lounge to lay out a sumptuous meal. As the dishes were being put on the table, Jirgalang couldn't help fidgeting as he was not used to such playacting.

"Yes, Uncle, it has been a while," said Ajige. "It's good of you to come. I was hoping you might have some good news for me …" Had he been a more observant man, he would have detected Jirgalang's flitting eyes as he spoke. The latter avoided giving an answer and turned his eyes to the dishes.

Jirgalang was glad that the aroma of the hot dishes distracted them both for a while. On his signal, the manservant poured more wine into Ajige's goblet. In the next while, they were able to enjoy the food. When they were half-way through, Ajige casually said:

"Did you come on your own, or did someone send you here, Uncle?"

"I, … I came on my own…. Have this tender piece of stewed pork, it's been cooked to perfection." As he put the piece of pork into Ajige's bowl, he poured him more wine. The two continued to eat and drink, while reminiscing about the old days on the battlefield.

At the end of the meal, Jirgalang nervously pulled the vial from his sleeve and placed it on the table. In a blink, Ajige realized what was up, His eyes dilated, hegave out a beastly growl and jumped up from his seat.

"Damn them!" he shouted. "How dare they?" He knew it was the Shunzhi Emperor and the Empress Dowager who were behind this. Jirgalang called in his four burly guards who had been standing vigil outside the lounge. They pounced on Ajige and subdued him.

"Ajige, either you drink it peacefully, or I will have to force it down," said his uncle. "It's your choice. Try to understand that it's all over for you. I promise you that I will take care of your household ….."

Before Jirgalang could finish, Ajige wrested free from the guards' grip, grabbed the table with both hands and overturned it, sending porcelain dishes, bowls and goblets crashing onto the floor. The vial somersaulted a few times before rolling to a stop, unbroken. The guards rushed forward and pinned the frenzied prince to the floor. Jirgalang walked over and picked up the vial and removed the lid. As the guards pried their prisoner's mouth open with a spoon, Jirgalang poured the venomous liquid into it. Ajige choked, his temple ridged with pulsing blue veins. There was a pause, then he went into a violent convulsion, foaming at the mouth. Another moment and his body was rigid, his dead eyes wide open.

With Ajige gone, Jirgalang was expecting to be able to resume his Regent status, if only to reward him for all the help he had given to the Shunzhi Emperor and his mother. But the Empress Dowager had a different plan. She was afraid that Jirgalang would only follow in Dorgon's overbearing footsteps were he to become Regent again. On her instructions, Shunzhi issued an edict commanding all Court Ministers and the Chiefs of the

Upper Three Banners to henceforth report to the Emperor direct, entirely bypassing Jirgalang's authority.

A little later, the Empress Dowager found an occasion to reassure Jirgalang in private. She looked him in the eyes and said gently:

"The Emperor is still too young and inexperienced. I need you to be my eyes and ears about State affairs. No doubt you understand that the Private Council is meant as a check to Shunzhi's powers, and I rely on you in particular to apply that check. Jirgalang, know this: you are the only one in Court I completely trust. You will not fail me, will you?"

At one stroke, she dispelled any hard feeling he might have felt and made him a loyal ally who would remain faithful to her until his death. Bumbutai knew that in order for Shunzhi's authority to be undisputed, it was important to arrange a marriage for him, whereby he would be seen to have attained true adulthood. She had always set her heart on her brother Wukeshan's youngest daughter as her first choice of daughter-in-law candidates. As a Mongolian Princess from the Borjigit clan, she had the duty to see to it that the Qing Imperial lineage would continue to evince the close bond between her Mongolian Borjigit clan and the Manchu Aisin Gioro clan.

Wukeshan had always known this to be his sister's cherished wish. With that in mind, when it was just a few months into Shunzhi's reign as a real Emperor, he chaperoned his daughter all the way from Inner Mongolia to Beijing, just as he had accompanied Bumbutai and Harjol to Mukden all those years ago.

When Shunzhi set eyes on this cousin of his, he was rather charmed by her fair complexion and pleasant disposition. But one little incident took place which would turn his attraction to distaste.

On the day the welcoming banquet was held, a maid-in-waiting unintentionally spilled a little wine onto the honored guest's sleeve while pouring it into her chalice. Thereupon, the Empress-to-be flew into a fit of nasty temper and shrieked out a peremptory demand: "I want the maid flogged right this moment. Pain will teach her to know her proper place and to be more careful next time."

The Empress Dowager tried to calm her down by ordering the maid to retire at once. But her niece was too used to being pampered to let her request go ignored. She continued to throw her tantrum in full public view. It was only when she saw Shunzhi's expression of distaste that she quietened down.

After that, Shunzhi purposely delayed the wedding and focused instead on the more urgent Court matters at hand. He would not allow his Court officials or his mother to cajole him into changing his mind. Knowing full well that this was a political marriage, he saw he had little option but to comply with his mother's wish in the end. Still, he thought it a good idea to humble his bride-to-be a little bit by making her wait. He also hoped the delay would send his mother this message: "I am no longer just a puppet. I am a true adult Emperor capable of setting my priorities. You see how dedicated I am to State affairs."

In fact, the young Emperor had such a lot to grasp that he actually couldn't afford to lose any time in catching up with his learning. In the first days of his reign, he felt completely overwhelmed by the load of Court documents, many of which were written in Chinese. To ensure he could understand them he spent his leisure time studying Chinese books on history and governance. He also developed a voracious appetite for Confucius's *Analects* and his philosophical teachings, as well as for Chinese classical literature.

He developed the habit of reading all afternoon and evening, and well into the early morning hours before retiring to bed. Surrounding himself with young, well-read scholars, he drew pleasure from leisurely discourse with them about Chinese art and literature.Well aware of her son's learning efforts, Bumbutai showed her encouragement by occasionally dropping in on his literary gatherings as an observer. At the end of one such session, she said casually: "Fulin, I'm very pleased with the remarkable progress you have made in your Chinese lessons. Are you as proficient in the Jurchen and Mongolian languages these days?" That hint, ever so gently put, was enough to remind Shunzhi of his origins.

One of his first efforts to make his mark was to proclaim a fight against corruption in officialdom. He knew this was a major cause of the Ming dynasty's collapse. Believing that harsh rules and stiff penalties for offenders would be the best medicine for the ailment, he lost no time in promulgating rules and penalties to support his new policy. But well-intentioned as it was, the campaign was executed selectively, thereby deepening factional strife and stoked the back-stabbing in Court. Manchu Bannermen and the Han literati whom he had come to favor formed into two main rival camps.

Shunzhi found himself relying more and more on his favorite eunuch Wu Liangfu for gossip about the activities of the various factions. He knew there were pitfalls in relying on such information, but could think of no better way. Ironically, he had earlier declared a strict ban on eunuchs meddling in Court affairs.

In Bumbutai's eyes, his life was as yet a book of blank pages in which much was to be written, be it good or bad. In trying to guide him onto the right path, she had to strike a balance between respecting his status and keeping a watch over him.

That summer, Bumbutai had barely recovered from her

grieving over the loss of Dorgon. Her son's decision to delay his wedding annoyed her a bit at first, but she came to understand her son's intentions. She was delighted to see that he was maturing and was proving to be an industrious and open-minded Emperor.

One evening, Shunzhi came to visit her in Dorgon's mansion. She was in the garden reading the *Spring and Autumn Annals* when he entered through the gate, unaccompanied by guards or eunuchs.

"Mother, I have come to pay obeisance to you. How is your health? Are you eating well and sleeping sound?"

"Fulin, I'm so happy to see you!" she exclaimed. Bumbutai's face lit up the moment she saw her son. "I haven't seen you for two months. Why, you've grown even taller. Let me take a good look at you, my handsome boy." She urged him to sit beside her on the stone bench, her gaze never leaving his face, flushed from the hurried walk over to her.

"Mother, I have ordered for Cining Palace to be completely renovated. It's going to take a couple of years. Then you'll be able to move back in and we will be close to each other like before."

"I would love to live closer to you, my son. But I don't want any lavish trimmings for my residence. Just some repainting work would be good enough. Don't put a strain on the Court's coffers, because such resources can serve as a lifeline for our subjects in times of deprivation."

"You are the Empress Dowager. Your Palace should at least be properly furnished. I will try to be thrifty about expenses."

He stood up. "Mother, I have come to ask for your advice on picking an adviser for myself at Court. Do you have any suggestions?"

"Fulin, have you thought of promoting the Jesuit, Schall von Bell? The Director of the Imperial Observatory. He seems to be an intelligent and learned man. I have heard of him making accurate predictions about sun and moon eclipses with his new calendar. Knowledge is a powerful tool, never forget that. And it is important that we are receptive towards new knowledge and foreign cultures. This priest is also noted, I am told, for his moral principles of humility and compassion. He could be a good teacher for you."

"Mother, you always have wise counsel for me. I have also heard many good things about this foreign priest's work. I am sure I can learn much from him."

She smiled. "I know you have been enjoying reading Chinese literature and history. Have you ever considered having the Chinese Four Books and Five Classics translated into Manchu, so that our Manchu subjects will be able to read them too?"

"Mother, that is an excellent idea! Thank you for suggesting it. I will get that done as soon as I can. It's a good way to promote cross-cultural understanding. I think Manchus and Mongols should learn well The Analects of Confucius too."

"I agree with most of the teachings in The Analects, especially those about the virtuous qualities that a ruler should cultivate. The problem is that self-seeking rulers try to twist those well-meant teachings into tyrannical tools to oppress their subjects. I am also inclined to disagree with the grading of people as Confucius proposes, but I suppose the imposition of some kind of hierarchical order is necessary for a nation as immense and diverse as China."

"Yes, Mother, as a ruler, I need a means to manage our subjects. Confucius's ideas of filial piety, loyalty to senior ranks and submission to authority help us a lot in our governance."

"Son, authority is not about foisting your will on our subjects. It's about earning their respect and trust through your candid words and benevolent actions. You must remember that you are first and foremost a human being like any other person, and as such, you are not infallible, and you must be humble enough to admit it and to open your ears to your Court. The greatest wisdom of Confucius's teachings is in this advice: do not do unto others what you do not want done unto yourself."

"I will learn to be humble, I assure you, Mother."

"It is unfortunate that prejudices misguided your Uncle Dorgon, and some of his actions caused the Hans to suffer unspeakable afflictions. You must now try to make amends at all costs and put them on equal footing with the Manchus and Mongols."

"Mother, I understand what you mean and I will do my best."

"So when are you going to have your wedding? I don't mean to pressure you. But don't you want some company at night time, my son?" She patted him tenderly on the back of his hand as she posed the question casually.

"I was actually going to ask for your approval for a date one month from now…."

"Oh, that will make me so happy, Fulin. I'm giving you my blessing right now. I must admit that I need an auspicious occasion to cheer me up. Now I have my precious son's wedding to look forward to." She couldn't help but give her son a motherly hug. She had an urge to kiss him on the cheeks too, but feared that it might be too unbecoming and so restrained herself.

"Mother, I wanted to say that I am so sorry about the awful things that were done to Uncle Dorgon's corpse. Oboi acted without my permission…."

"Son, you don't have to apologize. I know it's not your fault. I had been aware of the animosity between you and your uncle when he was alive. He had his reasons and you had yours. Now that he's gone forever, Fulin, all hatred must end."

"Yes, I know that, Mother."

The wedding went ahead smoothly as planned in the lunar month of August. It was the most imposing of Imperial weddings ever held by the Aisin Gioro clan. The Hall of Preserving Harmony was chosen as the venue with its spacious main hall because the guest list was a long one and included many Mongolians from the Borjigit clan who came all the way from Inner Mongolia just to attend the wedding.

Among the vast quantity of valuable wedding gifts received were thousands of Mongolian horses from the clan. The bridal garment took a team of fifty seamstresses a full month of day-and-night work to finish on time. The outer full-length vest was made entirely of gold-thread brocaded satin with two phoenixes on the front, while the inner wide-sleeved gown was of crimson silk richly embroidered in floral pattern. The bridal headdress was of golden silk fabric studded with gemstones and golden tasseled hairpins. It was the most elaborate and ornate bridal garment ever made for an Imperial bride. The wedding feast and the Empress titling ceremony straddled three days, during which the largest number of guests ever entertained passed through the Hall of Preserving Harmony.

After the wedding, the Shunzhi Emperor returned to his busy routine of attending to Court matters. He seldom called for the Empress's service and never visited her at her Residence. Less than a year after the grand ceremony, he had already become so bored with his life that he had to make a personal request on one of his visits to his mother.

"Mother, I have just one small wish that I hope you will approve of. May I order for a selection of Imperial Concubines?"

"You are the Emperor now, Fulin. You can do whatever that you deem suitable. I have no objection to that. But you will still respect your Empress, won't you?"

"Yes, Mother, I will respect her as long as she knows her place and follows the rules and etiquette of the Inner Palaces."

There was a barb in his words that reminded Bumbutai of the domineering way that Hong Taiji used to treat her. She was quite startled at how closely Fulin had come to take after his father in exhibiting an imperious attitude towards women, even at his young age.

It also appeared to her that he had a weakness for women. In this respect his indulgence surpassed even that of his father. But Bumbutai concluded that if her son was unhappy with his cousin, he might as well find some distraction with other women, although she had an uneasy feeling that as he began to revel in his power, he could become over-indulgent in pleasure-seeking. At this point, the thought of Siu Fa suddenly came up, and she took the opportunity to implore her son:

"Son, I also have a small wish that I was hoping you might be able to make come true. Siu Fa, one of your father's Consorts, used to be my maid for many years. Being a widow, she is leading an ascetic life in the Imperial retreat house, which, for her young age, is hard. I would like to take her back into my residence, if you would approve."

"Mother, it would give me pleasure to grant that." The Emperor was now in such a buoyant mood that he would grant anything she asked.

On the Emperor's orders, his eunuch Wu Liangfu arranged through the Board of Rites for a selection of Bannermen clan maidens to join the junior rank of Imperial Concubines in the Inner Palaces.

As prescribed by etiquette, the Empress Dowager would preside as an observer over the final round of selection. In order to show her support for her new daughter-in-law, Bumbutai decided to let the new Empress take her role in the final selection of Imperial Concubines. Twenty maidens - twelve Manchus, five

Mongolians and three Hans - had been shortlisted from three hundred to go to the final contest, from which ten would be picked.

After attendants had touched up their hair, faces and lips, the twenty teenage girls presented themselves in two horizontal rows in the plaza in front of the Empress's Residence, each holding a small tray that contained a name card with the written side face-down.

The Empress, rather than graciously accepting the Empress Dowager's invitation to take up her role, had felt it a demeaning task. She knew the choices would in truth all be the Emperor's own and she would have no say at all. So she decided that she would show up late to exhibit her disdain for the process. Shunzhi was infuriated at the Empress's deliberate tardiness and after waiting for a while, grumpily signaled for the presentation to start without her.

When the eunuch announced the name of a maiden, she would come forward and let the Emperor take a good look at her face and her figure, and then step back. If the Emperor liked her, he would turn the name card face-up; if not, he would not touch the card.

By the time the Empress arrived, Shunzhi was picking his fifth favorite. The Empress sat on her seat inside the lounge, playing with the tassels of her elaborate headdress. At last, the Emperor turned the last name card, and all ten Imperial Concubines were chosen. Five of those were Manchus, three were Mongols and two Hans.

That night, Shunzhi told Wu that he wanted the youngest Han Imperial Concubine, who was a pretty thirteen-year-old daughter of a Chinese Plain White Bannerman, to serve him. Her surname was Tong and her father was a Han Court Minister whose family had lived in Manchuria for generations. The next day, she was promoted to the rank of Consort. Later, her clan would be granted the Manchu clan name of Tunggiya and she would bear Shunzhi's third son, Xuanye.

NINETEEN

BEFORE THIS SELECTION of Imperial Concubines, Shunzhi had endorsed his mother's choices of two Noble Consorts and three Consorts shortly after his wedding. These noble women had failed to please him.

With the fresh young girls now added to his harem, all handpicked by him, he was having such a frolicking time that the Empress was pushed right out of his mind. He was already thinking of getting Eunuch Wu to arrange another selection of maidens the following year, even though the tradition was to have such selection only once every three years.

Wu, on his part, was happy to pander to his master's wishes, as these maiden selections were a good opportunity for him to extort bribes from parents eager to send their daughters into the Forbidden City. It was also not uncommon for Imperial Concubines, Consorts and Noble Consorts who wanted to be called to the Emperor's bed chambers to offer his eunuch big bribes in the form of precious jewels. Wu was the only one charged with presenting name cards for the Emperor to choose from each night and he benefited accordingly.

The young Empress, spoiled by her upbringing, had little interest in anything other than luxurious clothing and jewels. Her garments were made of the finest satins and embroidered silk with pearls and sequins sewn on. Bracelets, necklaces, earrings, brooches and other jewelry made of green jade, white jade, pink pearls, rubies, emeralds, sapphires and corals filled ten lacquered jewel caskets. All of her quilt covers and bed curtains were made of fine silk. All her personal eating utensils were custom-made in solid gold. Freshly-cut flowers were brought into her lounge and bed chambers every day to perfume the air.

Favored eunuch as he was, Wu Liangfu had a deadly rival in Court. He was Wang, Chief of Staff in the Imperial Household Department, who had come from the Dorgon clique. Wang now found it expedient to curry favor with the new Empress, and he made every effort to pander to her unending extravagant whims.

Used to having her way, the Empress was annoyed by Shunzhi's cold-shouldering of her. What she wanted now was a way to avenge her hurt pride. From Eunuch Wu, she gleaned the information that the Emperor's most favored woman was Consort Ningyi from a Manchu clan, deemed the most beautiful of his entire harem, and that she had the good fortune to bed the Emperor once every two or three nights. The Empress chose her as the target for unleashing her vengeance.

One winter's night, the Empress summoned Wu to her lounge and asked him who the Emperor's bed partner was that night. He replied that it was Consort Ningyi. She bade the eunuch to come closer and stealthily placed a packet of whitish powder and a green jade bracelet into his hand, then whispered a few words in his ear.

Having unrolled the naked Consort Ningyi from the quilt onto the Emperor's bed, Wu and another eunuch retreated quickly into the antechamber. The Consort was petrified to suddenly find an eruption of a blistery rash all over her body. She started to scratch her limbs uncontrollably.

Shunzhi, on approaching his bed, was shocked by the sight. He shouted for Wu to take the Consort away immediately and bade him summon a Court physician to take care of her. Wu at this point began to come to his senses. He realized that his true master was the Emperor and not the Empress, and fearing that he might be blamed himself, he fell to his knees and confessed everything to the Emperor. Shunzhi had always had a soft spot for Eunuch Wu, who had been one of his only playmates in his boyhood days. Having heard the whole story, the Emperor immediately pardoned Wu, but became even more disaffected with his jealous Empress. But he said nothing to her and the arrogant Empress mistook the Emperor's silence for an apologetic gesture for neglecting her. She continued with her malicious tricks on any Consort whom he took a liking to. In one instance, she tried to poison a Manchu Imperial Concubine who was a lissome dancer and a new favorite of the Emperor's. She ordered a maid to take a dish of sweet meats laced with hemlock, which would rupture the intestines, to the Concubine, but at the last minute, the maid alerted the victim and saved her life, only to be flogged to death by order of the Empress. The incident terrified all the maids who served her. News of this incident spread through the Inner Court and finally landed in the ears of the Emperor.

Wu was fully aware that by admitting his crime to the Emperor, he risked antagonizing the Empress, who was also in a position to do him harm. Lurking danger pushed him to mull on a plan that would serve a dual purpose. He knew that the Empress Dowager had been urging the Emperor to cut household extravagances, and that the Empress, egged on by Wang, knew no bounds where her lavish whims were concerned. Also within his knowledge was the fact that his master was deep in a campaign to root out corruption. Perhaps his plan could, in one stroke, strike out Wang and undercut the Empress.

For Wu, dealing with Wang was a relatively easy task, because the latter's record of having served Dorgon was itself a deadly original sin. If evidence could be found that he was corrupt, then he would be doomed. And if the Empress were to be found implicated in a corrupt act of Wang's, then the battle would be won. First he would bribe a maid in Wang's household as well as a maid in the Empress's Residence, which was an easy enough task. These maids would be his informants.

Wang, meanwhile, had fallen into thinking he had found a safe harbor with the Empress, as she was under the protection of the Empress Dowager. Emboldened by the Empress's apparent support and protection, he abandoned himself to the fantasy that he was the king of the Imperial Household Department. He would go so far as ignore requests from Consorts for silk fabric, reserving the best for the Empress's sole use. Maids from the Consorts' Palaces coming to ask for tea leaves, sweet meats or household supplies would get an acerbic scolding from him for no reason,. He made it a rule to refuse dispensation of such items unless a bribe was paid by the Consort.

Having control over food provisions also meant that he could extend his power to the Imperial kitchens. He arranged coarse fare to the Consorts and ensured that the Empress was served nothing but gourmet dishes.

Since becoming Empress Dowager, Bumbutai had formed a habit of declining birthday presents, and these ended up in the custody of Wang. Some of the presents were valuable jewelry and expensive sculptures, which should have been registered by Wang's department and then sent to the Court's Treasury for storage. But Wang never registered them nor sent them to the Treasury.

Over time, he accumulated many exquisite sculptures made of jade or ivory, as well as a collection of the finest jewelry of green and purple jades, rubies and emeralds, filling several lacquered caskets which he kept in a sandalwood chest beside his bed. He had a fondness for all jewelry, but it was the beautiful pink jade antique sculptures that captured his heart. Being aware of the Empress's love of jewelry, he developed a plan to secure her permanent trust.

One summer's day, learning from the Empress's maid that her mistress was in a good mood, Wang took two caskets of jewelry and two ivory sculptures from his sandalwood chest, put them all carefully inside a black velvet bag and headed to the Empress's Residence.

"Venerable Highness, I have come to make obeisance and offer my very best wishes for your health," he said, flopping down on all fours as soon as he entered the lounge in the most obsequious way.

The Empress did not even glance down at him. "Wang, you may stand and speak," she said. "I was going to send orders to you to change the flowers in my lounge twice a day, to make the air fresher." Her gaze was fixed on her nail-guards which one of her maids was painting. "What have you come to see me about?"

"If I may ask to be heard in confidence...."

The Empress shot an inquiring look at Wang, and then grouchily waved all her maids to retreat.

"So what is it that you deem so important?"

"Venerable Highness, I believe you have never laid eyes on the birthday presents that the Venerable Empress Dowager has received over the years and thought that these might interest you."

He stepped forward, untied the black velvet bag and took out the contents one by one, placing them on the marble-top side table next to the Empress's couch. As he opened the jewel caskets, his sideways glance caught the Empress's eyes dilating with greed.

"What beautiful pieces these are!" she exclaimed. She picked up the jewelry pieces one by one to examine them, paying no attention to the sculptures.

"I was thinking that Your Venerable Highness might like to keep these, perhaps. It seems such a waste for them to idle in my chest…"

"Well, I don't mind adding these to my collection. I must say, you did the right thing, Wang. You may keep the ivory sculptures as your reward." Her eyes as she spoke were glued to the sparkling jewels.

"I can't thank you enough, Venerable Highness. It is so very generous of you." Wang prostrated himself fawningly in front of the Empress again and kowtowed three times. Then, looking up, he added slyly:

"If it pleases your Venerable Highness, this will be just between you and me …."

"Don't worry. No one else will know about it. Now if you will show yourself out, I'm going to take a nap."

During this conversation, a maid had been hidden behind a richly-embroidered silk screen, eavesdropping. When Wang left, she quietly slipped out after him and went straight to Wu.

Earlier, Wu's informant at Wang's house had already confirmed that there was a sandalwood chest full of treasures that he kept beside his bed. Having subsequently found out from Sumalagu about where the Empress Dowager's birthday presents had been sent, and now in possession of the latest bit of information, Wu could piece together the whole picture. He lost no time in making a full report to his master.

The next day, the Emperor sent a team of his Imperial Guards to make a surprise raid on Wang's quarters and seize the sandalwood chest. Wang was arrested and thrown into jail, waiting the Emperor's decision as to his sentence.

Shunzhi personally went to the Empress's Residence, and brought Sumalagu along to identify the jewels. Sumalagu had been responsible for recording details of all the Empress Dowager's birthday presents and had kept a written record of them all before sending them over to the Imperial Household Department. The Emperor growled with rage.

"Bring me those two jewel caskets right this moment!" he shouted, his face white with fury.

The Empress's face drained of blood and her hands shook uncontrollably as she handed the caskets over to the Emperor. Sumalagu checked all the contents against her records and affirmed that they were the Empress Dowager's birthday presents.

The Emperor, who had never before visited the Empress Residence, couldn't help noticing the gaudy opulence of its décor and furnishings. He left in disgust without saying one more word. Later, Sumalagu verified the contents of Wang's chest to be the remainder of the presents.

Shunzhi had not forgotten what Wang had done in Dorgon's times. Wang had then been eager to please Dorgon and had trimmed Shunzhi's daily meals to exclude all the sweetmeats he had loved so much as a child. But he was determined to pass a just sentence based only on the evidence of his corrupt crimes, which mounted by the day as his investigators did their work with the eager help of the Consorts and their maids. He thought this to be a good opportunity to clean up Dorgon's lingering influence.

His Court officials, after deliberating on the case for a while, unanimously recommended a death sentence for Wang. Shunzhi was inwardly pleased but, in a deliberate show of leniency, he ordered the confiscation of all Wang's assets and sentenced him to permanent exile. In Wang's place, Shunzhi appointed, on his mother's recommendation, one of his trusted Ministers, Sonin, who was from the Plain Yellow Banner and was fluent in all three languages, Chinese, Manchu and Mongolian. Bumbutai had known him to be a man of integrity from the days of Hong Taiji.

When Wu heard the news of Wang's exile, he couldn't help but smile.He could never forget how Wang had once humiliated him and called him a bitch when he had been serving the child Emperor during Dorgon's rule.

In the eighth month, Shunzhi paid a visit to his mother, who had just moved back into Cining Palace. He looked unhappy. In response to gentle questioning , he told his mother how he could no longer tolerate the Empress for her petty jealousy, her spitefulness, her lavish indulgences and her general unfitness to be head of the Inner Palaces.

"Mother, I have tried my best to be patient with her, hoping that she would come round to taking her role seriously," he said. "But she has disappointed me in every way possible. I know you won't take this well, since she is your beloved niece. I beseech you to consider my view too, for the benefit of the Empire."

Bumbutai had long known this day would come. She couldn't argue against the points her son had made, as she knew very well how spoiled her niece had always been as a child.

"Son, this is a matter over which you have total authority as the master of your household. If you have made a decision about her, I believe you have good reasons. What do you plan to do with her?"

"I intend to demote her to the position of Consort and let her live out her life in one of the smaller Palaces. But I was hoping that I could do so with your approval." From Empress to Consort was a three-step plummet through the ranks.

"Demoting an Empress may stir up dissent in your Court, especially among the Han Ministers with their strict adherence to Imperial rites," she added. "But if there is to be any opposition to your will, you can rest assured that it will not be from me. I understand your situation, Son."

"I appreciate your support so much, Mother. I will take this matter into my own hands."

As his mother had predicted, several of his Court Ministers signed a petition imploring him to reconsider the demotion, claiming that such a dramatic move might impair the Imperial Household's honor. To these dissenters, he asked a scathing question:

"What is wrong with demoting someone from a position that she has shown herself to be unworthy of?"

Realizing that the Emperor's mind was determinedly set in this matter, they finally acquiesced to his wishes.

At the end of that month, the Empress moved out of the Palace of Earthly Tranquility into a small West Palace, to the delight of all maids in her former Residence. Within a couple of months, she was quietly sent back in a carriage to her homeland in Inner Mongolia, in stinging contrast to the spectacular reception of her bridal procession into Beijing and the dazzling pomp of her wedding day.

In the middle of the following year, another wedding was held for sixteen-year-old Shunzhi in the Hall of Preserving Harmony. This time, his new Empress, three years younger than he, was a grandniece of Bumbutai, the daughter of her second elder brother's son, which meant that she was also from the Borjigit clan. Shunzhi feared that the demotion of his first Empress might hurt the feelings of his Mongolian relatives and hence affect the Manchu-Mongolian bond that her mother had tried so hard to nurture. He thus agreed to his mother's proposal of making another Borjigit Princess, actually a young niece of his, his new Empress.

By this time, his harem had already grown to twenty-five Consorts and Concubines, so it didn't matter to him that he had no feelings for his new Empress. He was well aware that the marriage was purely a political matter. That he found her clumsy and stupid was just another excuse for never showing up in the Palace of Earthly Tranquility.

Shortly after this second wedding, Wu saw his master become quite downcast from his heavy workload and considered how to raise his spirits. He told him of the Han maidens in the Jiangnan region of China to the south and their reputation for delicate beauty, slimness of figure and superb dancing skills. Showing him paintings of some of the famous courtesans of Hangzhou and Suzhou, he piqued his master's interest.

Unable to control his desires, Shunzhi ordered Wu to go south to select Han maidens on his behalf. They were to serve in name as special maids-in-waiting, when in reality they would be objects of his lust. When news of this reached the region, parents of many young girls rushed to betroth them to boys of other families. In protest, a district official made a daring petition to Shunzhi pleading against the maiden harvest. Shunzhi could do nothing but deny the allegation, and out of pride, he dismissed the petitioning official from his post and exiled him to a remote and derelict village.

When the Empress Dowager heard about this, she was furious and gave her son a severe tongue-lashing for the first time since he had assumed power.

"Son, I have let you have free rein over your private life, as I always thought I could trust you to use your sense and discretion. But I am so disappointed. Distressing your subjects to satisfy your desires is bad enough. To punish a forthright official, whose only crime was to speak the truth is pure cowardice. How do you think the people of Jiangnan will hold you in their regard now?"

Her stern eyes bored into him, as he stood fidgeting in front of her in the garden of Cining Palace. She resumed the watering of her lavender lilies while waiting for his response.

"Mother, please forgive me. I have made a mistake. I am just overwhelmed by work," he stuttered with his eyes cast down.

"Overwhelmed by work? Surely there are more refined ways to deal with such a problem. Was this Wu Liangfu's idea?" She knew the answer before posing the question, but wanted to test him.

"No, the idea was mine. He only did as I told him. Mother, I will make amends for the wrong I've done, I promise."

"You don't have to promise me anything, son. I only ask that you always respect your privileged position as an Emperor." Her tone softened as she took comfort in discovering that her son at least had the courage to answer for his own actions.

Later that same day, he granted a pardon to the petitioning official and reinstated him in his former post. He returned to his studies and developed a passion for painting and calligraphy. His talent in the arts was visible through the vast quantity of works that he produced in this period.

Shunzhi's weakness for the fairer sex did not prevent him from building an effective administration. He issued a decree demanding that all district government administrators pass a public examination once every three years. This applied to both Manchu and Han officials alike. Those who failed to pass would be demoted or dismissed. In the first year, a total of nine hundred and sixty-nine administrators failed the exam and were either demoted or dismissed on the grounds of incompetence.

Meanwhile, Shunzhi re-established the Ming institution, the Hanlin Academy, which scholars used as a stepping stone to a Court career.He sent special investigating envoys to all provincial governments to investigate complaints of official corruption. Before their departure, Shunzhi personally lectured them on the principles of integrity and fair play.

But many of the envoys abused the special powers endowed in them and colluded with local corrupt officials to gain personal benefits while falsifying reports against honest ones. In one case, an official who had planned to make a corruption complaint against his superior was arrested by an envoy on fabricated charges and tortured. The official committed suicide by slashing his own throat.

When the news reached Shunzhi, he flew into a rage and ordered the incarceration of the envoy involved. He personally conducted the interrogation of the prisoner and after sentencing him to death by beheading, he also punished those who had recommended him to the post. Then he sentenced to exile a large group of local officials who had colluded with the envoy in corruption crimes.

For all his weaknesses, Shunzhi set a good example of fighting corruption that would be followed by later Emperors of the Qing dynasty.

Despite his good intentions, his favoritism towards the Han literati backfired. Many of the Manchu Bannermen officials in his Court were jealous of the rapid rise to important posts of Han scholars.

Shunzhi befriended one such scholar, Chen Mingxia, whom he admired for his knowledge of Chinese literature and art. When Chen made an ill-timed proposal allowing Han Court Officials to revert to Ming-style hair and attire, the Manchu faction used it as an excuse to force the Emperor to execute him. In other matters where the Manchu clansmen's special privileges were at stake, such as their right to enslave Chinese peasants, Shunzhi was pressured into protecting the interests of the Manchu nobility.

On his mother's advice, Shunzhi had, since taking power, begun placing trust in Schall von Bell's advice on matters of administration. Bumbutai had earlier befriended the German priest when he had cured her niece, the first Empress, of a grave illness soon after her arrival in Beijing.

In time, Shunzhi came to respect the priest so much that he would go out of the Palaces to visit him at his home, often talking with him for long periods of time. In offering his advice, the priest was consistently honest and unpretentious, always taking the welfare of the people to heart and persuading the Emperor to act with generosity and mercy, and Shunzhi appreciated this. The priest regularly submitted petitions to the Emperor containing ideas or suggestions for solutions to problems, and over time, the Emperor formed a habit of placing the priest's petitions on a special bookshelf in his library. Whenever he went on a hunting trip, he would always pick several of those petitions and bring them along to read.

On one occasion, the priest heard of a sentence of exile being passed on five Han officials in a district government who had been caught flouting the Manchu attire code while at work, and he immediately went to the Emperor's Residence to plead on their behalf for leniency. The Emperor asked for his reason and the priest simply answered with a question: "Your Imperial Highness, do you not feel in your heart that the sentence is disproportionately harsh?" After pondering this for a while, Shunzhi granted a full pardon to the five prisoners, and ordered their immediate release.

By this time, the Emperor held the priest in such high esteem that he addressed him as *Mafa* (Grandpa), with Bumbutai's express approval. He was allowed to enter the Emperor's Residence at any time and was even exempt from the prostrating posture when he came into the Emperor's presence.

Twenty

At the start of the thirteenth year of Shunzhi's reign, the Empress held a modest banquet at the Hall of Union to celebrate the lunar New Year, to which she invited all the Aisin Gioro clansmen and their spouses. Among the guests, one graceful young woman caught Shunzhi's eyes. She was Lady Bombogor, wife of Prince Bombogor, the only son of Noble Consort Namuzhong (a widow of Hong Taiji's) and a half-brother of Shunzhi's. The Lady was the daughter of a Court Minister under the Plain White Banner who was born in Liaoning Province and whose wife was Han Chinese. In her maiden days, she had been known for her affecting beauty and exceptional talent in reading and needlework.

This day, she looked especially ravishing in a pale blue Manchu-style wide-sleeved robe embroidered in floral pattern and with dark blue borders, worn over a white pleated skirt. On her head she wore a dark blue pearl-studded headdress with long tassels hanging down both sides of her face. She had the most beguiling smile on her face.

When Bumbutai first laid eyes on her, she was awestruck at the likeness she bore to Harjol: the same heart-shape face and the same crescent-moon eyes. Only she had eyebrows like willow leaflets while Harjol's eyebrows were arched. Bumbutai became quite speechless when the young noblewoman presented herself and made obeisance to her. The next thing she noticed was that Lady Bombogor's face effortlessly arrested her son's previously wandering eyes, which never strayed again for the rest of the evening.

When the young woman realized that she was the object of a constant stare from the Emperor, she became quite nervous and tried to pretend she was unaware of it. But like any young woman who attracts the steady attention of a young man, she couldn't resist the temptation to throw back a surreptitious glance. Out of the corner of her eye, she saw a florid face defined by a square jaw-line, with ebony dark eyes and a straight nose. She blushed a deep pink, her heart galloping like an untamed mare. She took a quick sip of wine from her chalice in an attempt to regain her composure.

A couple of months after the Court banquet, Lady Bombogor received an invitation from the Empress to a cherry blossom viewing in the Imperial Garden. When she arrived at the appointed time, she was surprised to find no one there except two maids-in-waiting and the Emperor, who was working on a painting inside a pavilion. When Shunzhi saw her, he put down his brush and motioned her to enter. She approached and made obeisance timidly, just outside the pavilion:

"Your Imperial Highness, may I offer my best wishes for your pristine health."

"Please rise, Lady Bombogor. Let us do away with the formalities, shall we? Come in and take a look at my work." The painting in front of him was a landscape painting with, in the background, a distant vista of steep cliffs covered with old pine trees, and in the foreground, a snaking river with three fishermen idling away on a midstream islet.

"It would be my honor, Your Imperial Highness," she said softly as she stepped lightly inside the pavilion. She looked at the painting and exclaimed:

"This picture brings to life the poem *Immortals by the River,* by the Ming poet Yang Shen!"

"That's right!" he replied. "I knew I had read that poem before! It was at the tip of my tongue but I couldn't recall the title. When I was painting it, the image just rose up in my mind. You are indeed well read in Chinese poetry!"

He clasped her hand in his ecstatically. This embarrassed her beyond words and her face glowed a deep pink. But she did not try to withdraw her hand.

"How would you like to do me the honor of penning the poem on the painting?" he asked. "I have heard that you are skillful at calligraphy. I won't accept a refusal. Come, don't be shy." He cajoled her like a child, while signaling for his maids to grind more ink.

"The honor would be all mine, Your Imperial Highness."

She sat down on a porcelain stool and picked up a brush pen confidently. Steadily focusing her attention on the tip, she began writing the verse in a firm but delicate hand, occasionally dipping the brush into the ink dish. Her exquisite craft put a delightful finishing touch on the Emperor's spontaneous work of art. The poem went like this:

On and on to the east rolls the Great Yangtze,
Burying in its current hordes of gallant men.
Right or wrong, shame or glory, all comes to naught.
Only the green hills linger, after many a glowing sunset.
White-haired men by the river, mind the seasons not;
All they care of is in the bottle, and meeting with old friends.
Stories new and old, come alive in their witty repartee.

Shunzhi carefully held up the scroll of paper to admire the new addition, nodding his head approvingly. The two then went on to discuss Tang and Song poetry. By the time they had extricated themselves from that world, the lukewarm sun was bidding farewell on the horizon. Spontaneously he held her hand and led her to the cherry blossoms garden, the blissful sight of which made her heart jump. Like a troupe of ethereal dancers clad in pink tassels, the trees seemed to sidle forth in lissome gait to welcome the approaching admirers.

"Oh, Your Imperial Highness, I've never seen such beauty in all my life," she said softly, a little short of breath. A rosy luster slipped onto her face, tinted gold by the oblique rays of the setting sun. The falling petals of the blossoms were like tiny snowy nymphs sent from the heavens, frolicking in the sprightly breeze. Light as feathers, as fleeting as Zephyr, one moment they breathed pink, the next they faded. Cherry blossoms were as much an inspiration for beautiful verse as they were a reminder of life's fickleness, she thought.

Shunzhi couldn't take his eyes off her impeccably featured complexion, now lit up by her serene meditation. As he walked by her side, he was besotted by the delicate scent wafting from her. Was it from her hair, or from her body? He couldn't stop wondering.

That night, he could not close his eyes without recalling the image of Lady Bombogor and her fragrance. He did not call for any Consort or Concubine, content to wallow all night in his lonely thoughts. His strange behavior troubled his eunuch.

The next morning, Wu fussed over his master, trying to find out what was wrong with him. He was about to call in a Court physician, when Shunzhi waved his hand dismissively. By the time he had finished eating his morning meal, he could restrain himself no longer and he sat down at his writing table to pen a personal invitation to Lady Bombogor, requesting her company for dinner in his Residence. When Wu was ordered to deliver the invitation, he understood.

By the time the lovers had had their fourth secretive meeting, gossip about the liaisons reached Prince Bombogor's ears. Having the Chakhar Mongolian blood of his mother in his veins, and being a fearless warrior with a passion for honor, he did not take his wife's indiscretions well. But his adoration for her, as well as the power of the Emperor, held him back from confronting her. His silent resentment festered inside.

Lady Bombogor had never been attracted to her husband, being married to him at the age of thirteen. She had never tasted what love was until she met Shunzhi. Since meeting him, she could not put him out of her mind. The gentle touch of his hand, his artistic flair and his mild manner haunted her day and night. She felt she understood him well. From the painting she gleaned the fact that he was pining for a life that would be forever beyond his reach. Though she knew her acceptance of his love was breaking all moral codes, yet she lacked the strength to resist the forbidden fruit.

On the day they met for their sixth liaison, they were walking amongst rose bushes in a quiet corner of the Imperial Garden. The path was a narrow one. Lady Bombogor's body scent intoxicated him and he put his arms round her and kissed her mouth passionately. She was flustered by his move but did not resist. He started to move his hands over her body when Prince Bombogor, Shunzhi's half-brother, suddenly bolted out of nowhere. The abashed Emperor was at a loss for words and Lady Bombogor gasped in terror, her face turning ashen white.

The agitated husband stared Shunzhi in the face without saying a word, his face a rancorous scowl. His glare didn't budge even when Shunzhi cast down his eyes. Shunzhi's reaction was to view the stare as an insolent challenge to his supreme authority and he became incensed. He raised his hand to slap the Prince's cheek and regretted the move almost at the same instant. The

Prince howled like a wounded beast and would have jumped upon the Emperor had not Lady Bombogor pulled him back with all her might.

Just then, a maid came up to offer tea to the guests and, seeing the strange expressions, scrambled away as quickly as she could. This interruption put a check on the tensions and the humiliated husband and his teary wife made for the Gate of Divine Might, mounted the carriage in which he had come and departed.

That night, a loud scream tore through the nocturnal silence of the Prince's residence. One of the housemaids found the Prince hanging from a beam in his bed chamber. By the time he was untied, all signs of life had gone.

In the summer of that year, the seventeen-year-old Lady Bombogor was admitted into the Inner Palaces as Consort Donggo with the permission of Empress Dowager Xiaozhuang, and installed in the East Palace. Having seen the way her son looked at Donggo at the Court banquet, Bumbutai had been convinced that he would pursue her with the same zeal that his father had pursued Harjol. She understood that the Lady's hold on her son was not simply due to her physical beauty. They were attracted to each other by a deeper connection, one that was more spiritual than corporal. As things turned out, she was right. Her only worry was that the Emperor's favoritism towards the Lady might spur her latent ambition, if any existed. So before giving permission for Lady Bombogor to join the harem, Bumbutai had held a private meeting with her.

"Venerable Empress Dowager, may I offer you my best wishes for your pristine health," Lady Bombogor began, timidly making obeisance in Cining Palace.

"Rise, my dear child, you may stand and speak," Bumbutai said in a motherly tone. "I hear that you are well versed in the Chinese classic *The Legend of Honorable Women*. Presumably you know that your loyalty towards the Emperor as his woman shall always take precedence over any personal concerns?"

"Yes, Venerable, I do know that and would never dare to forget it for one moment."

"As one of his Consorts, you know that your first duty is to serve him well with all your heart and that you have to respect your senior sisters in the Inner Palaces?"

"Yes, Venerable, I have read the Inner Palaces book of etiquette and rites and will abide by them faithfully."

"If the Emperor were to offer to make you his Empress, what would you do?"

Not expecting such a question to come from the Empress Dowager, the Lady appeared disconcerted for a moment, and, after mulling for a little while, she replied:

"Venerable, I would ask His Imperial Highness to punish me, because I must have done something wrong to make him commit such a grave mistake," she said this with humility. Bumbutai could find no fault with her words.

"Will you take an oath that you will never pursue the position of Empress?

"Venerable, I vow on my life that I will never dare harbor the thought."

Bumbutai had been satisfied with the meeting. The Lady's docile nature meant that she would not be a source of trouble for the Emperor.

A little more than a month later, Shunzhi issued an edict promoting Consort Donggo to the prestigious rank of Imperial Noble Consort, bypassing the Noble Consort rank. A lavish title-granting ceremony was held in the Hall of Central Harmony one fine day in the twelfth lunar month. On the same day, the happy Emperor granted a general pardon to all criminals. Under the Imperial rites, there could only be one Imperial Noble Consort, and the rank was second only to that of the Empress.

Imperial Noble Consort Donggo, for her part, felt like she was daily walking on thin ice. Being the recipient of so much honor and glory in such a short period of time, she was the target of acidic envy in the Inner Palaces, and would take only one false step to have all the other Consorts gang up on her. Snide gossip about her disgracing the Bombogor household increased the precariousness of her position. She knew she had to make every effort to win over hearts and made a point of never having dinner with the Emperor, purposely letting other Consorts enjoy some time with him. Emulating the Empress Dowager, she set an example of leading a frugal life. She insisted on only having two maids and never ordered clothes of expensive silk and satin fabrics. Her meals were the same as those of the other Consorts. She took every opportunity to take personal care of any Consort who was sick.

On one occasion, Bumbutai was at the receiving end of this tender nursing care and her guard finally came down and she began to love her new daughter-in-law. She was pleased that her son had finally found a woman of virtue to be his true spouse.

One day the following spring, the Imperial Noble Consort told the Emperor that she was with child. The news invigorated him with uninhibited joy. He kissed every inch of her body and ordered Wu to send three extra palace maids to serve the pregnant Consort. Then he began insidiously to complain about the Empress not being attentive enough to the Empress Dowager's health. Using that as an excuse, he ordered the Board of Rites to stop sending copies of Court Ministers' congratulatory messages on ceremonial or festive occasions to the Empress (an Empress was entitled by decree to read such messages). The staff of the Board of Rites, as well as Donggo, knew that this was a precursor to the demotion of the Empress, paving the way for the Imperial

Noble Consort to take her place.

Much alarmed by the Emperor's apparent plans, Donggo fell to her knees when the Emperor came one evening on his daily visit.

"Your Imperial Highness," she pleaded, "I beg you never to think of demoting the Empress. It would hurt your mother's heart to the core! I will not rise unless you give me your word!"

"You mustn't hurt your knees, my love, you're three months pregnant," Shunzhi said agitatedly, trying to lift her up. But she was determined not to rise.

"Please give me your word first. I mean it."

"But the fact is that you are already taking care of all the affairs of the Inner Palaces," he pointed out. "The Empress has shown herself to be indolent and incapable. I just want to be fair."

"I know you've been good to me, and I am forever indebted to you and to the Empress Dowager," she said. "No one has loved me like you have. I know how blessed I am. It is exactly because I owe you so much that I cannot let you upset your Inner Palaces. Any anomaly will only bring chaos and will break your mother's heart. It would be too great a sin for me if I let that happen. I am a woman of humble birth, and I could never be worthy of the Empress title. Please, please, Your Imperial Highness, I would rather die...." tears gushed forth as she implored him.

When Shunzhi saw her face streaked with tears, he could stand it no longer. "Alright," he said, falling to his knees beside her. "It will be as you say." He had never cared so much about any of his other Consorts' pregnancies. Three years earlier, Consort Tunggiya had given birth to his third son, Xuanye, and one year prior to that, Consort Ningyi had delivered his second son, Fuquan. His first son had died in infancy. Shunzhi had seldom bothered to visit the mothers during their respective pregnancies. With the issue of her status cleared away, the young couple was able to enjoy each other's company and further strengthen their bond.

As satisfying as his emotional life was, Shunzhi's heavy responsibilities as head of state exhausted both his mind and body. He was desperately seeking a relief valve. At this time, through an introduction from the eunuch Wu, he came to know several Zen Buddhist monks, whose lectures filled him with a spiritual urge to search further for the ultimate peace of mind. He paid a visit to a Zen Buddhist Temple and began to develop a keen interest in Zen Buddhism, which preaches deep meditation as the way to connect with one's inner self. When Bumbutai learned of her son's latest interest, she grew concerned that he might be lost on such an escapist path.

In the tenth lunar month, to the immense pride and joy of the Emperor, Imperial Noble Consort Donggo gave birth to his fourth son. His pride and his joy were not only visible on his face, but also expressed through his reference to the newborn child as "his first-born son" in his conversations with Court Ministers. It was thus that news spread that the Emperor intended for this child to be his heir and successor.

As Han scholars at Court busied themselves with the search for an appropriate name for the Crown Prince, Shunzhi began to fall under the influence of a Buddhist monk named Mu, who was extremely well versed in the theory of Zen as well as in Chinese literature and calligraphy. The Emperor would often be absorbed in talks with the monk in the evenings until well into the night, in the company of his beloved Donggo.

It was a common belief that if a couple was blessed with too much happiness, disaster would follow. And as it happened, ill fate did await the happy Imperial couple. After a brisk journey of just one hundred and four days on the wearisome earth, Shunzhi's newborn son returned quietly to dust.

On that gloomy, rain-drenched morning, the wet-nurse went into the child's chamber to offer her tits to his little hungry mouth, only to find in the hanging cot a bluish, lifeless bundle. When she touched the little body with her hand, she was shocked to feel the icy coldness. She put a finger under his nostrils, and could feel no breath. Scared stiff from the discovery, she turned and ran like mad all the way to the neighboring East Palace to deliver the news.

The child's young mother was brushing her hair when the wet-nurse dashed into her bed chambers dripping wet, jabbering incoherently. When she made out what the wet-nurse was trying to say, the brush dropped from her hand. The full force of the message hit her like a rock and she would have slumped onto the floor had the wet-nurse not caught her in time. In trembling distress she asked a maid to get Physician Sima to come at once to take a look at her son. Her legs trembled uncontrollably as she staggered to the Princes' Residence with the wet-nurse supporting her.

Sumalagu, who had now moved back into Cining Palace along with Siu Fa, was the first one to learn the terrible news. She had been at the Princes' Residence giving the princes Xuanye and Fuquan their Manchu lessons in the chamber next to the newborn's nursery, and she had heard the scream. She had raced back to Cining Palace to deliver the news to her mistress. Thus Bumbutai arrived at the scene only a moment after Donggo.

She was lying prostrate on the floor, screaming hysterically, all sense of self-control gone. She tore at her hair, she crawled on all fours, she laughed like a madman. It was a heartrending, and an all-too familiar sight for Bumbutai. She had seen it before in Mukden twenty years earlier, two days before Fulin's birth when Harjol had lost her first and only son. Sometimes Eternal Blue Sky had strange ways of suddenly changing people's fate that would confound the wisest of men. She was twenty years older now, with silvery strands making their rude appearance, but she was none the wiser on the matter of life and death.

She winced at the thought of how hard a blow the newborn's death would deal the Emperor.

"Why does Fulin have to go through the same agony as his father?" she wondered silently. "How come they both had to lose their precious infants born of their most beloved?" She would never have an answer and it would be futile to dwell on such questions. But she also was keenly aware of the deep irony. If Harjol's son had survived, what would have happened to her and to Fulin? She dared not even think about the possibilities. But in matters of life and death, Eternal Blue Sky was not to be argued with. Experience told her this much.

Returning to the present scene, she was a little consoled by the thought that Fulin still had two other sons. Besides, Donggo was still young and would be able to conceive again. With that last thought, Bumbutai stepped forward to take the stricken mother into her embrace, soothing and coaxing her like she had done Harjol. But a sense of foreboding brushed over her when she looked at the girl's haggard face, hollow eyes staring into empty space.

Twenty-one

Donggo was so shattered by the death of her son that she was bedridden for some time. Soon after the tragedy, Shunzhi granted a prestigious posthumous title of "First Glorious Prince" to his beloved son, whom he had not even had the chance to name. He ordered a special mausoleum to be built for the little corpse at the foothills right next to the Imperial Mausoleum, and he personally wrote a lengthy and emotional epitaph for him.

But such exceptional honors for her dead child failed to stanch Donggo's tears. Shunzhi paid regular visits to her and tried his best to distract her by giving her Zen lectures and chanting prayers together with her, which seemed to calm her down a bit. He gave her a manual of Zen Buddhism, so that she could practice meditation and seek peace from it. To his consolation, she showed a marked uplift in spirits after starting on the meditation ritual. One day when she was feeling a little better, she spoke with Shunzhi.

"Your Imperial Highness, I know how much you had wished to make our son the Crown Prince," she said in a feeble voice as her eyes brimmed with tears, "But I urge you to stop fretting over this unfulfilled wish, because sadness and remorse will harm your health, and I do not want our beloved son to be the cause of ill-being to you."

"I will do whatever you say, my love," he replied. "But please, you must not shed another tear. We have to get you back to full health again." He couldn't control his tears any better than she. Instinctively, he held her in a tight embrace and patted her back tenderly.

"Yes, yes, my love, we have to…."

He gently put her head down on her pillow and bade her to rest up, keeping a close watch on her until she fell asleep.

Although she was far from feeling well, she insisted on not making known her continuing sickness to the Empress Dowager, lest it should upset her. She struggled every morning to do her hair and put rouge on her cheeks to cover her sickly pallor, and to walk with the other Consorts to Cining Palace to make obeisance. Her frailty and visage of faked health, though, could not escape the eyes of Bumbutai whose heart ached silently for her.

Since losing his son, Shunzhi's leanings towards Zen Buddhism became more pronounced. He would often travel to the South Park where the monk Mu was staying as a guest, to hold long talks with him. Mu, with his profound knowledge of Chinese literature and Zen Buddhism, became his spiritual guide and Shunzhi got so carried away that he played with the idea of becoming a monk himself. But Mu staunchly advised against the idea, saying that his station in life was his predetermined fate, and he must not shirk his position or the attendant responsibilities.

The Emperor seemed receptive to the monk's argument that he could do more good to all under heaven and to the cause of Buddhism as a ruler rather than serving Buddha in a monastery. After staying as a guest for eight months, Mu bade the Emperor farewell. As a farewell gift, Shunzhi gave several of his painting scrolls to Mu, who was a great admirer of the Emperor's works. In return, Mu gave the Emperor several scrolls of his calligraphy, which he adored.

Another monk, Yu Lin, soon appeared to keep Shunzhi company. Yu Lin was a well-traveled but world-weary intellectual from Kunming and his philosophical concepts found an attentive audience in the Emperor, who felt burned out and attracted to the monk's Taoist idea of passivity. Like Mu, however, Yu Lin advised strongly against the Emperor retreating to a monastery.

By the middle of the fifteenth year of Shunzhi's reign, the Ming loyalists based in the far south had rebuilt their strength under the Ming Pretender Yongli and the military leadership of General Zheng Chenggong (also known as Koxinga). Zheng had lived in Japan in his childhood, being born to a Japanese mother and a Chinese merchant father, but when he was seven years old, his father brought him back to China to receive a Confucian education and to serve the Ming loyalists. In 1645, his mother left Japan and joined her husband and son but during a raid on the town of Quanzhou in Fujian Province, the Manchu forces captured her and forced her to commit suicide, while his father defected to the Qing Empire. Zheng swore in a Confucian temple that he would avenge his mother and fight the Manchus to his death.

He took the port city of Xiamen and Jinmen Island nearby as his base, assembling supplies and Ming loyalists, and pledged his allegiance to Pretender Yongli. Shunzhi on several occasions tried to persuade Zheng to surrender, but he refused. By the summer, Zheng controlled large parts of eastern China and early the following year, his army of over 100,000 was closing in on the city of Nanjing.

News that Zheng's fleet was sailing up the Yangtze River to attack Nanjing was announced by the Minister of Defense in the Emperor's Audience Hall during a morning session of Court in Beijing. Shunzhi immediately broke down in a fit of panic-stricken hysteria and he leaped from his Throne, shouting:

"If Nanjing falls, it will be the end of us! What shall we do? What shall we do?"

The Ministers present were more astonished by the Emperor's reaction than by the news itself and they looked at one another in bewilderment. Since Dorgon's death, this was the first time that alarming battle news of this kind had been heard in Court.

Jirgalang, seeing that matters were in a state of flux, advised the Emperor to adjourn the Court session to a meeting of the Private Council in Cining Palace, at which the Empress Dowager could preside. To this suggestion, the Emperor readily agreed. The Private Council now consisted of Jirgalang, Sonin, Suksaha, Oboi and Ebilun.

Once inside the meeting lounge in Cining Palace, Jirgalang apprised the Empress Dowager of the precarious situation in Nanjing. Bumbutai listened intently but made no comment. Her silence made Shunzhi even more anxious and he yelled:

"We have to leave Beijing and retreat to Mukden at once. We'll be safe in Mukden. Yes, that's what we should do...."

The Private Council members murmured their disapproval. Then Bumbutai, in a grim face and stern voice, spoke.

"So we are going to desert Beijing and China, and leave our trusting Han subjects to fend for themselves against the self-serving rebels?" she said slowly and loudly.

His mother's admonition pierced Shunzhi's pride.

"Of course not!" he shouted. "I am not a coward. The Empire needs me... As a worthy ruler of the Hans, Manchus and Mongols, I will personally lead the Army against them!" He snatched a sword from Oboi, who was the only one allowed to carry a weapon inside the Inner Court.

The Councilors all shook their heads at this outrageous idea and fearing her son might become even more irrational, Bumbutai quietly sent Sumalagu to summon Shunzhi's wet nurse and the German priest Schall von Bell.

Shunzhi looked at the disapproving faces around him, and

snarled: "I am determined to head the Army and defend Nanjing to my death. If anyone dares oppose me, I will slash his throat, like this!" He raised the sword and in one clean stroke, cut the armrest of his chair in two.

Silence fell on the lounge.

"I have heard," Bumbutai said gently, "of a brilliant captain named Zuo who has won many battles in the South. Prince Jirgalang, can you not tell me whether my memory still serves me well?"

"You are certainly right, Venerable Empress Dowager," replied Jirgalang. "He is the captain of a naval fleet under the Green Standard Army."

"Can he be trusted to lead a counterattack on Zheng?"

"In my humble opinion, there's no better choice for a naval commander," he replied, the relief clear in his tone. "All we need to do is to back him up with artillery, ammunition and men."

"How fast can reinforcements reach Nanjing?"

"I would say at most ten days. Our men and supplies in Nanjing are adequate for the city to hold out for longer than that without reinforcements in the event of a siege."

She turned to her son. "Would Your Imperial Highness see fit to reconsider your options?"

Shunzhi, though pleased that his mother had found a solution to the dilemma, still insisted on taking the role of Chief Commander, lest he should be mocked for backing down. At this moment, the wet nurse threw herself down on her knees in front of him, begging him between sobs not to risk his life. Shunzhi had always loved his wet nurse, but he knew how ludicrous it was for such a lowly woman to interrupt discussions of grave matters of state and, his nerves already frayed, he raised his sword threateningly, scaring the poor woman into scrambling her way out of the lounge.

Then Schall von Bell entered the lounge and made obeisance to the Emperor and the Empress Dowager. He had been briefed by Sumalagu about the situation, and when Shunzhi saw the kindly priest, his nerves calmed. In a tired voice, he asked for von Bell's opinion on the present debate. After ruminating for a while, the priest looked straight at the Emperor and responded in fluent Chinese:

"Your Imperial Highness, you are the supreme head of the Qing Empire and as such, you have an obligation to your subjects. That obligation is in the form of their expectations for you to keep safe in times of turmoil so that you can be an effective leader providing guidance and instructions from the capital. I dare say they would be very disappointed if they were to see you risk your life unnecessarily." He paused for a moment and, seeing the Emperor listening intently, continued.

"Looking at the matter from another viewpoint, I should congratulate Your Imperial Highness on having so many valiant and loyal generals who would readily give up their lives to protect you, the Empress Dowager, and the entire Empire. Why not, then, allow them to fulfill their patriotic duty, so that you can at the same time show your subjects that the state is in good hands at all levels?"

With those wise words from the Jesuit, Shunzhi was able to climb down from his untenable position without embarrassment. He issued an edict appointing Zuo as Naval Commander and Jirgalang as Chief Commander to defend Nanjing and to mount a counterattack against Zheng Chenggong.

Bumbutai breathed a sigh of relief. When the meeting was all over and all Councillors and Shunzhi were gone, she went over to the German priest who, at her request, had stayed behind.

"Father," she said with a grateful smile, "I wish to thank you on behalf of the Emperor and of the Empire."

"Venerable Highness, I beg you not to mention it," replied the humble priest. "I was merely speaking the truth. In reality, I owe you and the Emperor a heavy debt of gratitude for your continuous support of the Jesuit mission in your esteemed Empire, which I can never hope to repay. There is nothing I wish for other than the Empire's continued stability and prosperity."

"I have always admired your wisdom and am so glad that you have had such a positive influence on the Emperor. He has not been quite himself since the death of his fourth son. Added to his sorrow is the constant worry about the protracted illness of the boy's mother. This inauspicious news of insurgence in the South is just too much for him at this time." Bumbutai talked unreservedly as to an old friend.

"I can indeed empathize with the Emperor over his unfortunate loss," the priest replied. "I will pray for His Imperial Highness, for the soul of his lost son and for the sick mother."

"Thank you, Father, for your kindness. We appreciate your help so much. You will always be my son's *Mafa*, and if there's anything we could do to help your mission, please do let us know."

"May God bless you for your kind heart, Venerable Highness."

By the early part of the eighth month, the Qing forces had laid a long sturdy iron chain across the lower Yangtze River, fortified with wooden rafts to form a barricade to protect the riverside towns, but Zheng's fleet of two hundred and ninety warships and 100,000 men breached it by axing the chain and setting fire to the wooden rafts, and seized several forts. Their next target would be Nanjing, a short distance further upstream.

At this juncture, opinions diverged among Zheng's generals as to whether to stage a siege or mount an outright attack. Zheng himself was in favor of an attack to keep up the momentum, but his plans were upset when a fierce storm blew up, killing eight thousand of his men, sinking forty of his warships and causing severe damage to many others. Also, the strong winds made it impossible for his fleet to sail upstream. His men raced to repair their ships and hauled them along the riverbanks. It took a half a month more for the fleet to reach its destination, which provided ample time for Jirgalang's reinforcements to quietly reach Nanjing in the interim.

Towards the end of the month, in a ruse to give Zheng a wrong impression, Commander Zuo sent a letter to Zheng saying that Nanjing would be able to hold on for about a month and would then have to surrender. So Zheng and his men, exhausted from their battle with the elements, were content to maintain their blockade. Commander Zuo infiltrated a few of his men into the enemy's ships, and on the eighth day of the ninth month, a major sortie was made from within Nanjing via a secret passage through the city walls and inflicted heavy casualties on Zheng's forces. The next day, another attack was mounted just as Zuo's agents ignited explosives on board many of Zheng's ships. Mayhem ensued and Zuo's men launched an all-out attack which forced Zheng's ships to retreat down the river and ultimately flee to Taiwan. It was thus that the Qing Empire's last great enemy was defeated. The last Pretender to the Ming throne, Yongli, fled to Burma after the Battle of Nanjing, and was finally captured by Wu Sangui four years later and executed.

When the news of victory reached Beijing, Bumbutai instructed that a portion of her birthday presents be taken out from the Court's treasury chest and exchanged for silver. In the Emperor's name, she distributed the proceeds as rewards to all soldiers who had fought in the Battle of Nanjing.

Previously, she had already donated her own funds on several occasions as relief to help peasants who had fallen victims either to floods or drought in various provinces. She would, as a habit, have general items around her repaired rather than replaced, and would ordinarily only wear clothes made of cotton and hemp. Silk and satin were reserved only for ceremonial occasions. Thus she could always put aside some of her monthly stipends for other purposes. Consort Donggo had always been a fervent follower of hers in leading a frugal life, which was one of the reasons that Bumbutai cared for her so much.

Donggo's illness took a turn for the worse in the autumn of the following year. She was now permanently bedridden and was unable to do the daily rituals of obeisance at Cining Palace. Her absence caused Bumbutai much anguish.

Shunzhi had long been depressed over Donggo's sickness and could only find solace by escaping into the world of Zen through chanting and endless conversations with monks. One day, during his daily visit to her, Donggo said to him in a barely audible voice:

"Your Imperial Highness, I wish to thank you with all my heart for the love you have given to me, a woman so unworthy of you. If I may, I would like to ask you to do me one favor after I am gone. Please do not let them dress me in luxurious garments or put any jewelry in my coffin. A simple hemp dress is all I need." She paused to take a deep breath, and then took Shunzhi's hands in hers.

"Please promise me that you won't grieve after I'm gone," she continued. "You would not want to let your mother worry about you, and the affairs of state need all your attention..... If you love me, I would ask that you also grant me this wish.... that you will show mercy on criminals sentenced to death......" She paused again briefly before carrying on:

"When the Ministers and Court Officials send in funeral offerings, please donate them to the poor peasants. It is the least that I can do to help them."

"I promise that I will do as you wish.... Only I cannot bear to be without you." Shunzhi's effort to hold back his tears failed, and he wept uncontrollably. His tears had a contagious effect on Donggo, hitherto calm and collected, and she too melted in tears.

"My dearest, you must not feel sad," she implored him. "I am only going to a place where I can be with our son. I will be so happy to see him again." A faint smile appeared on her tear-scored face and having finished what she had to say, she leaned weakly on Shunzhi's shoulder and wearily closed her eyes.

On the nineteenth day of the eighth lunar month, at the age of twenty-one, Imperial Noble Consort Donggo departed from the world in peace. Pain-stricken, Shunzhi's whole frame shook as he watched the last flicker of life extinguished from her emaciated face. In a fit of illusion, he saw Donggo dressed in her favorite pale blue floral robe with dark blue borders and a white skirt floating through the air towards him, holding in her arms their son swaddled in yellow cloth. He stepped forward and stretched out his arms to embrace them, but they dissipated without a trace. Forced back to the real world, he broke down, wailing.

On the third day after her death, still in a state of torpor, Shunzhi issued an edict to bestow the posthumous title of Empress on the Imperial Noble Consort. This obviously went against the Imperial rites, as there was already an Empress alive and well. But no one dared to point this out to the Emperor, who had abstained from attending Court for three days in a row. For the following four months, he used blue ink instead of black to mark Court documents as a sign of mourning for the Consort, something traditionally only applied to the passing of Empress Dowagers with a duration of usually one month.

TWENTY-TWO

BUMBUTAI TOO WAS devastated by the death of this beloved daughter-in-law, whom she had treated like her own daughter. She had been counting on her being a constructive influence on Shunzhi, as well as his emotional prop. But with that hope dashed, she didn't dare to guess if her son, hardly recovered from mourning his own son's death, could survive the blow. Eternal Blue Sky sometimes could be so brutal, but its doings were not to be argued with. With this train of thought, she went over to the Princes' Residence to visit seven-year-old Fuquan and six-year-old Xuanye.

When she entered the garden, she found Xuanye playing hide-and-seek with Fuquan. As soon as he spotted her, he scampered over with a big smile on his face. He was always happy to see his Nana and loved to have her tell him stories. He stretched out his little hand to hold his Nana's and led her into his study to show her his Chinese calligraphy.

Looking at his little roundish face dotted with pockmarks and his endearing big dark eyes, she couldn't but be smitten with him. She had always tried to show affections equally to the two boys, but in her heart, she couldn't deny that Xuanye was the one she preferred. He had such a prodigious memory that by now he could already answer most questions posed to him on The Analects, and he could recite scores of Tang poems.

When his Nana had visited him last time, she had told him

about the secret journal of Genghis Khan and he had nagged her to let him read the book in the Manchu script as she had agreed.

"Nana, did you bring me the secret journal?" he eagerly asked in his childish lisp.

"What do you think?" She teased him lightly. "Do you think Nana has a bad memory?" She recalled, looking at his face, how terrified she had been when he had fallen ill with smallpox the previous year.

"I know Nana never forgets things," he replied, swinging her hand to and fro with excitement.

"But you have to answer a question first. If your answer is correct, the journal will be yours to keep. But if it's wrong, you won't have it this time. What do you say?"

"Ask away, Nana!"

"Who was the best archer in the Borjigit family in the times of Temujin?"

"Hmm... Oh, I know! It's Khasar. Nana, you told me he was Temujin's brother and our ancestor." The child never missed a thing that he heard from his Nana. His mind was a sponge, absorbing everything it came into contact with, and Mongolian stories always caught his fancy.

"And what did his family call him?

"*Habutu Khasar*! I want to be a *Habutu* too!"

"You've answered very well, Xuanye. Here's your reward." Bumbutai retrieved the booklet from her sleeve and handed it to the child. Her heart, which had been sorrow-laden, found comfort in just talking with her beloved grandson.

"Nana, yesterday I played lasso on horseback with Fuquan. Can you guess who won the game?"

"No doubt it was you, Xuanye. You always win. But you have to remember to be considerate to your brother too. "

"I know, Nana. Sometimes, I let him win."

"How are your Mongolian language lessons coming along? You're proficient in Chinese and Manchu, but don't neglect Mongolian." Bumbutai had insisted on the appointment of reputable Chinese scholars to give literature and history lessons to her grandchildren, while letting Sumalagu teach them Manchu.

"My Mongolian teacher always falls asleep while giving lessons," Xuanye replied. "So I'm only learning very slowly."

"Would you like Nana to help you, then?"

"Yes, yes, Nana. I love to hear your stories."

"Alright. What story did you want me to tell you today?"

"The story of how Temujin made Jamuka his brother! Please don't begin yet, Nana. I'll get Fuquan to come and listen too."

"After I've told you the story, you two will have to practice writing the Mongolian script."

Bumbutai spent the rest of the afternoon telling her grandsons stories that she had heard from her grandfather when she was a child, and also teaching them the Mongolian language. It was a much needed distraction for her.

As promised, the monk Yu Lin sent his favorite disciple, Mao, to stay at the Emperor's South Park Retreat. He arrived just a few days before Donggo passed away and Shunzhi gave orders for Mao to conduct a Land and Sea Spiritual Valediction ritual in which he would lead a group of one hundred and eight monks in an incantation meant to bid farewell to the Consort's soul and to send it on its way to the other world.

The casket had earlier been carried to a temporary sepulcher on Prospect Hill, just beyond the Gate of Divine Might, the main northern entrance to the Imperial Palace. The pall bearers were all high-ranked Ministers and Bannermen.

On the day of the ritual, one group of twelve psalm-chanting monks circled round and round the white silk-draped casket laid on a bier near the sepulcher, while eight other groups stood in rows on each side, waiting their turns. Large quantities of paper offerings and incense were burnt in an open furnace. Mao stood behind an altar placed next to the bier, on which were placed burning joss-sticks and candles. Chanting unceasingly, he occasionally picked up a small brass bell and tapped it, creating a penetrating tone that was supposed to call forth the soul of the dead so that the incantations could lead it to that mythical place where it could be reincarnated.

On the twenty-first day after Donggo's passing, just a few days after the Valediction ritual, the casket and bier were to be cremated in accordance with Manchu traditions. On this day, Shunzhi was present at the ritual, accompanied by Schall von Bell. The Emperor had barely slept for the past fortnight, and his body was stiff with pain and distress, his face haggard and sallow. Mao and the other monks began the ritual with chants, after which Mao threw a burning torch onto the bier which was covered with dry brushwood. Watching the conflagration, the Emperor was suddenly beset with a paroxysm of hysteria. He sobbed and laughed, he shouted that Consort Donggo would need maids and other underlings to serve her, and ordered thirty maids and eunuchs to be sent on their way with the Consort. Mao dropped on his knees before the Emperor and begged him to retract the order, saying it would be a grave sin. The German priest also stepped forward and joined Mao in trying to restrain the Emperor from his impulsive act.

At this time, Xuanye, on his Nana's prompt, came before his father and handed him the scroll of the painting on which Donggo had penned a poem on that day they had viewed the cherry blossoms together. As if waking up from a nightmare, Shunzhi embraced the scroll and wept aloud, heaving a cathartic groan. His repressed sorrow relieved, he finally recovered himself and expressed remorse over his momentary madness. Everyone present drew a deep breath of relief.

Shunzhi spent the following month writing a four-thousand-word eulogy for his beloved Consort, in which he described in emotional detail all her virtuous qualities, substantiated by intimate anecdotes. He even ordered Court officials under the Ministry of Documents to write an official memoir for the Consort and to keep it with the Court's historical records. With such an order, he was setting yet another precedent in Chinese Imperial history.

When Bumbutai read the touching and candid eulogy, in which her son poured out his heart, she could not hold back her tears. As a mother, she could feel the depth of pain he suffered. There was not a day from then on when she didn't fear that her son might collapse under the weight of inconsolable grief. She knew better than anyone else that her son's sensitive fibers were not made to withstand such brutal torment.

One night in the gloomy and rainy time of early winter, as the darkness of the night was about to give way to the first pale gleams of dawn, Shunzhi had a dream while in a state of semi-slumber. In the dream, he saw a chained Donggo being dragged along a long and dimly-lit path by a group of rough guards wearing grotesque masks shaped as cow heads and horse' heads. They were heading towards a patch of white light and she was entreating them in a hoarse voice to help her find her son.

"There is no way that you can see your son now," one of the horse-headed guards told her. "You are condemned to reincarnation as a deer, and your son will become a child born to a hunting family. He is destined to kill you when he is five years' old, after which you can attain rebirth as a human."

"But is there no way I can meet my son now? I miss him so very much," she sobbed.

"No. He has been taken to the Bridge of Rebirth, where he awaits his turn to be reborn."

"I beg you, Master, please have mercy on me! I had so little time with my son. Could you please let us be sent together on the same route, either to be humans or to be animals?" She begged and begged with all her strength.

"Both your destinies were fixed by the Emperor of the Ghosts and there is nothing we can do about it. This is how you atone for the wrong you did to him in your previous lives."

"Please, let me petition the Emperor of the Ghosts!" she pleaded desperately.

"No. I cannot help you," snorted the horse-head guard, and he began shoving Donggo along. She gave out a ear-splitting shriek as she was pushed closer to the white light.

It was the shriek that jolted Shunzhi out of his dream. Cold sweat covered his forehead and his back.

That afternoon, he summoned the monk Mao to his Residence and asked him about the strange dream. The monk told him it was just a delayed reaction to his recent loss.

"You had the dream because you miss Empress Donggo so much. It is not uncommon for troubled dreams to include such grotesque images."

Shunzhi was unconvinced by this theory. He kept murmuring to himself that he must go and argue the issue with the Emperor of the Ghosts.

A couple of days later, General Oboi requested a private audience with Shunzhi to raise the issue of the corruption of the chief eunuch, Wu Liangfu. Oboi had long been jealous of Wu's closeness to the Emperor and he detested his arrogance. Wu, for his part, had nothing but disdain for Oboi, who he saw as a brutish, witless and self-important bodyguard. He would pay dearly for his contempt.

Oboi had painstakingly gathered evidence of Wu' regular solicitation of bribes from suppliers of tea leaves to the Imperial Household Department. The head of the Department, Sonin, had known about the eunuch's corruption but had kept quiet about it, not wanting to stir up trouble. He was glad that Oboi had taken it upon himself to speak out and readily provided him with evidence. Apart from his flagrant acceptance of bribes, Wu had also formed alliance with Han Court Ministers to oppose the Manchu faction on policies regarding land seizures by Manchu Bannermen. It was in fact this action that irked Oboi the most, as he was one of the most aggressive land hoarders.

By involving himself in Court matters and in corruption, Wu was guilty of serious breaches of the Rules Governing Eunuchs' Conduct, a code of law that Shunzhi had ordered to be engraved on an iron plaque and placed at the entrance to the Bureau of Eunuchs. Such crimes, under those Rules, would be punishable by death by a thousand cuts.

Shunzhi asked Wu to retreat to the antechamber, and received Oboi in his study. After Oboi had presented the case, the Emperor was silent for a long while. He knew the gravity of the case, but he was not one to betray his closest friends. Wu had been his playmate in childhood and a companion in adulthood who had always looked out for his interests. Besides, it could be said that Wu was supporting the Emperor by aligning himself with the Han Ministers, and as for corruption, his acts had hardly caused the Imperial Household or the common people any loss. But Oboi was a cunning wolf and would some day find a way to get Wu. Shunzhi made up his mind to protect Wu. The next step was to deal with Oboi.

"About the bribery," he said in a deliberately brusque and dismissive voice. "I will talk to Sonin to change tea leaf suppliers. As for Wu meddling in Court matters, I will personally see to it that he won't have the chance to do it again. Is there anything else that you wished to speak to me about?"

Oboi was astute enough to be able to read between the lines. He saw there was no point in pressing the case further, and made his obeisances.

After Oboi departed, Shunzhi called for Wu and said to him:

"Liangfu, how many years have you served me?"

"Over twenty years, Your Imperial Highness," Wu said with a flush on his face, fearing for the worst.

"I am exhausted and I feel depressed. You are the only one who understands me," the Emperor said and motioned for Wu to rise.

"Your Imperial Highness, would you like to take a ride to South Park for some fresh air? I know your heart still aches for the Imperial Noble Consort, no… the Empress. But it will do your health no good if you let this sadness get to you. I used to be able to make you laugh, but I no longer have that power….."

"I know you care about me, Liangfu. I care about you too. I have to ask you to agree to one thing: retire to a monastery and live out the rest of your life there. This is for your own good and safety. I know I don't have much time left, and before I go, I want to witness your ordination ceremony." Shunzhi tone was melancholy and his eyes were misty with tears.

"Please forgive me my crimes, Your Imperial Highness," Wu said quietly. "You are so kind to save me from punishment. I know I am not worthy to serve you. I owe my life to you. Do what you please with it."

Wu threw himself down on his knees and hugged Shunzhi's legs, as rivulets of tears slid down his cheeks.

"I will ask Mao to take you under his wing. I only hope you will have a peaceful life and live to a ripe old age," Shunzhi was choked with emotion, and waved for Wu to retreat.

Over the years, the Chinese General Wu Sangui, who had let the Manchu forces enter China through the Shanhai Pass, had subsequently vanquished Li Zicheng's rebel army and then helped the Qing Empire to put down many peasant uprisings in southwestern China. To reward him for his numerous victories, Shunzhi had granted him a fiefdom in Yunnan Province and had provided him with abundant military supplies and financial resources. General Wu had thus been able to build up a strong army of his own. At the same time, Shunzhi had also granted respective fiefdoms to two other Chinese warlords—Shang Kexi in Guangdong and Geng Jingzhong in Fujian. These three would later become a source of great trouble for the next Qing Emperor.

Following the fligtht of the last Ming Pretender to Burma, Wu had total control of the provinces of Yunnan and Guizhou and lived like an emperor. He levied taxes on the peasants which he never passed on to the Qing government, he built mansions and retreats for his own use. He monopolized the salt supplies and mineral sources of the region and used the wealth created to hire yet more soldiers and buy more weapons.

Bumbutai was throughout suspicious of the three Lords, in particular Wu Sangui. She had purposely arranged for a Qing Princess, a daughter of Hong Taiji's, to wed Wu's eldest son, Wu Yingxiong, but in reality, the son was kept as a hostage within the Qing Palaces to discourage Wu Sangui from turning against the Qing Empire.

Once comfortably settled in Yunnan, Wu recalled his former love Chen Yuanyuan, who had left him soon after the Manchu victory to go to Kunming. Fifteen years of ceaseless warfare had made him yearn for a peaceful life, with his beloved woman by his side. After months of searching, he found her at last in the Temple of the Three Sages, hidden deep in the hills beyond Kunming, where she lived as a Taoist disciple taking lessons from the monk

Yu Lin. The day they met, he begged her in tears to return to live with him in his Palace. She refused him out of hand, which only made him pine for her even more. He could see that she still had a fresh complexion and a slender figure, and for three days, he visited and begged her to relent. Moved by his dogged persistence, she finally let her woman's heart persuade her to give in. But Wu had not anticipated that his first wife would be so obstructive on this matter. Jealous by nature and uneducated, she was soured by the younger woman's elegance, beauty and cultured air. Upon Yuanyuan's joining Wu's household, she used every opportunity to bad-mouth her among relatives and house servants. She made sure everyone knew about her lowly birth and former prostitute status. She never acknowledged her greetings and forbade Yuanyuan from joining her for meals whenever Wu was not at home, and instructed maids that she be served only vegetables and rice in her own chamber.

For nearly a year, Yuanyuan tried to maintain her patience and tolerate the woman's meanness. But at last, dignity drove her to beg leave of Wu to return to the Temple, much to Wu's dismay. By this time, she had become completely disillusioned with secular life and, after having a long talk with Yu Lin, she made up her mind to have her hair shaved and become a nun, taking on the Taoist name of Yu An.

In her honor and perhaps out of guilt for having mistreated her, Wu Sangui built a large landscaped garden with a retreat house and a beautiful lotus pond in the northern part of Kunming and named it "Anfu Garden". Yuanyuan would spend the rest of her life as a Taoist nun inside this retreat house.

Shunzhi was unable to shake off the depression that beset him. On a cold and windy day, he went out in a carriage to the South Park Retreat to visit Mao. On Bumbutai's instructions, Eunuch Wu Liangfu kept a close watch on his master, following the carriage on horseback.

During his talk with Mao, Shunzhi entreated him to take Eunuch Wu as his disciple and to ordain him as a monk at the Lunar New Year. The monk gave his consent and Shunzhi addressed him again in an earnest tone.

"I now beseech you, Master Mao," he said, "to shave my head and ordain me as a monk. I am determined to put my secular life behind me and begin a new life in the monastery. I know I must have sinned gravely in my previous life and I want to make amend. This is the only way you can help me find peace of mind.

"I don't know what to say, Your Imperial Highness," Mao replied, shocked and discomfited by Shunzhi's request. "This is not a small matter. I think I would have to consult Master Yu Lin before I do anything….."

"Master Mao, you of all people will understand the pain that I have been going through. Can you not find it in your heart to do me this deed of kindness?"He began to weep like a child.

Eunuch Wu, who had been eavesdropping on the conversation, was stunned by his master's request, and without a second thought, he mounted his horse and raced back to Cining Palace to report the news to Shunzhi's mother. Bumbutai immediately sent an urgent message to the monk Yu Lin, Mao's teacher, asking him to go to the South Park Retreat to prevent the ordination if at all possible.

By the time Yu Lin arrived, Mao had already shaven off all the Emperor's hair. After making obeisance, Yu Lin entreated Shunzhi to reconsider his decision.

"Your Imperial Highness," he said, "have you thought for one moment how this action might hurt the Venerable Empress Dowager's heart, and how your subjects might be affected by it?"

Shunzhi closed his eyes, refusing to listen. Yu Lin continued nonetheless.

"Your status as an Emperor is a huge blessing. You alone are in a position to use your status to improve the livelihood of your subjects, while at the same time championing the cause of Buddha. By practicing the religion in your esteemed position, you can be the savior of the secular world. If you give up the position, chaos could result and nothing would be gained."

Shunzhi seemed a little more receptive, but remained stubbornly reticent. Yu Lin turned to Mao.

"You have committed a grave breach of our monastery's rules," he declared. "You have no authority to ordain monks but you misled the Emperor into believing that you do. It is a double crime and the penalty is death by fire."

Mao was aware that Yu Lin was creating a story to mollify the Emperor and he prudently played along with it, faking remorse, kneeling down before Yu Lin, pleading for mercy.

"No, no, Mao did not mislead me!" Shunzhi interjected, horrified. "I ordered him to do it!"

"Even so, he has no right to shave or ordain anyone. He has to be burned alive for his presumptuous act as a grave warning to other monks."

"You mustn't condemn him on my account, I beg you! I will give up the idea of becoming a monk and will let my hair grow back. Will that allow you to absolve him?"

"You have the most generous of hearts, Your Imperial Highness," Yu Lin replied. "That would certainly clear him."

Twenty-three

Panting heavily, Sumalagu rushed into the garden of Cining Palace to report the latest news to her mistress. She found Bumbutai waiting anxiously on one of the four stone benches, with Siu Fa keeping her company.

The aging maid took a moment to catch her breath.

"He's on his way back to .... the Palace," she gasped. "He has a shaved head. though...." Bumbutai gasped in shock.

"No, no!" the maid quickly added. "He hasn't been ordained. He says he has given up the idea, for now. Yu Lin will be here shortly to make a full report to you." She was exhausted, but managed to give a summary of Yu Lin's ruse, and Shunzhi's reaction. Bumbutai heaved a sigh of great relief, but her face still betrayed her concerns.

"My poor boy," she said. "He has a good heart, but a weak will and a volatile temperament. I only pray that Eternal Blue Sky will have mercy on him."

"Venerable, I know Buddha will keep His Imperial Highness in good health," Siu Fa said soothingly.

"He has been under so much stress, and, lately more than a fair share of emotional pain. I can't blame him for toying with silly thoughts now and then. He is only human. What worries me most is his frailty these last months. He seems to have lost all appetite and always appears tired."

"Perhaps I could bring him birds' nest soup everyday to keep up his strength," Sumalagu suggested. She had always been the one most concerned with Shunzhi's well being apart from Bumbutai.

"That is a good idea, Suma. Thank you for offering to do that. I don't know how I could ever live without you."

Yu Lin arrived, and Bumbutai listened keenly to his every word. He concluded reassuringly: "The Emperor has definitely given up the idea of entering the monkhood."

On the second day of Lunar New Year, Shunzhi attended Eunuch Wu Liangfu's ordination ceremony at a Buddhist temple on the outskirts of Beijing, conducted jointly by Mao and Yu Lin. In his heart he felt happy for Wu, whose life would now be free from the shackles of wants and desires. He could see the inarticulate joy reflected on Wu's serene face.

The monks' chanting during the ceremony sounded very much like a children's song, almost lulling him to sleep. It reminded him of the magical lullaby that Wu used to sing to him at bedtime. He would always be asleep before the song ended. His eyelids were now so heavy that he wished a bed was near at hand. Then he realized he had a fever and started to feel nauseous. He bade Wu farewell and left the ceremony to return to the Palace.

That night, when the young eunuchs were helping him undress to take a bath, he noticed with concern that red sores had appeared all over his body. His fever had gotten worse and he was feeling dizzy.

Several days earlier, he had noticed a few blemishes on his face and arms and had thought they were from mosquito bites. Now the rashes had turned into ugly pustules. After a short moment of deep shock, he quickly resigned himself to the reality that he had contracted smallpox. The shock turned into a strange, calm feeling of acceptance, and the eternal crushing load on his chest seemed to be lifting. He ordered a eunuch to go and fetch Schall von Bell and another to invite the Empress Dowager to come. He felt so enervated that he wanted nothing more than to lie still in bed.

Bumbutai was just getting ready for bed when the eunuch conveyed the Emperor's urgent invitation. An ominous feeling gripped her and she threw a cape over her shoulders and hurried to her son's Residence. When she saw Shunzhi's flushed and speckled face, she burst into tears. The worst of her fears had finally come to pass. Her whole body convulsed and she threw herself to the ground beside the bed, crying:

"My precious, why isn't the Court physician here? We have to get a physician…"

"Mother, please calm down. No physician can help me now. There are important things that we have to discuss…. before my time is up. You have to help me…."

"Son, you know you can always count on me. But first, how are you feeling? Are you in pain?" She felt his forehead and recoiled at its raging heat.

"No, Mother, I'm fine. Don't worry. I want to ask you, was Xuanye the one who had smallpox?"

"Yes, he was lucky to have survived. Fuquan has never had the disease."

Just then, the German priest entered the chamber. As soon as he saw Shunzhi's face, he knew that he was nearing death. He bade Bumbutai wash her hands immediately with vinegar and to not touch her son again, due to the highly contagious nature of smallpox. Bumbutai did so.

"Father," she said, "Xuanye had smallpox last year and recovered. Is there a chance…. that the Emperor too can get over this?" She knew in her heart she was wishing for the impossible.

"Venerable Empress Dowager, I have to be honest with you. From my experience, I think the Emperor's infection is already in a late stage, and the chances that he will live… are not good."

Shunzhi signalled for the priest to come closer.

"*Mafa*, I know I'm dying," he whispered. "The reason I asked for you to come is that I want you to tell me whether Fuquan is likely to ever catch the disease."

"Your Imperial Highness, I have to say that there is a likelihood that he will, and no one can tell whether he will be as lucky as Xuanye."

"Having had the disease once, is Xuanye guarded against another infection?"

"Yes, he has acquired immunity from it."

Shunzhi turned to look at Bumbutai.

"Mother, it is Eternal Blue Sky's will. I will appoint Xuanye as successor to the throne. I know this is what you would want too. When I feel up to it, I will send for someone from the Hanlin Academy to write down my will. Xuanye is only seven and we will have to appoint a Regent to help him. Who would you suggest?"

"Son, what I want most is for you to get well. Don't give up fighting. But I have to say that you have made a prudent choice as far as your heir is concerned. As for regency, assuming Xuanye comes to the throne, perhaps a number of regents would be better than a single one? I was thinking that shared power would be preferable to absolute power." She couldn't help reminding herself of Dorgon's hubris and tyranny during his Regency.

"I can see the wisdom in that, Venerable Empress Dowager, if I may offer my humble view," the priest respectfully interjected.

"My mother is the wisest woman in the whole world, *Mafa*!" exclaimed Shunzhi, speaking from his heart. He was well aware of how much his beloved mother had helped him with her quiet support and timely hints throughout his reign. He agreed with the idea of having a Council of Regents, and having taken his mother's cue, as always.

"I will appoint Sonin, Suksaha, Ebilun and Oboi as the Four

Regents for Xuanye, as they have served me well on the Private Council,"he said. "I have left out Jirgalang, as I think he will prefer a well-deserved retirement."

The priest expressed his full and sincere support, and then, seeing the Emperor was already quite worn out, made his farewell.

After the priest left, Bumbutai pulled up the quilt and tucked her son in.

"Mother, please promise me not to feel sad when I'm gone. I haven't felt this peaceful and calm for a long long time. You know, I can't wait to meet my Donggo and my son...."

"I know, Son, I know," she said, swallowing her tears. "You mustn't talk any more. You have to get some rest now." Choked with repressed emotion and unexpressed love, she now yearned more than ever to cradle her son in her arms and kiss his cheeks, but his infection barred her from doing so.

Looking tenderly into his face, she could see the dreamy youth who had been crushed by the heavy load that his destiny had imposed upon him. She had done her best to mold him into a perfect head of state. But his delicate nature had limited her success. But he had given his best. And if it was eternal peace that he sought so passionately, who would have the heart to ask any more of him? She certainly did not. Together, mother and son had come a long way since Hong Taiji had left them behind. They had won some battles, and lost others, but better than anyone else, she knew how hard he had tried to do good for his subjects.

Above all, the mother-son link between them had always been strong. She had Eternal Blue Sky to thank for preserving that bond, and for giving her Xuanye as her grandson, now her son's heir. Already the child was showing clear traits of superior qualities. Her mission, ultimately a Mongolian mission, would continue.

Five days later, Shunzhi summoned Scholar Wang Xi from the Hanlin Academy to his bed chambers to write his will in which he appointed his third son Xuanye as successor to the throne, to be assisted by Sonin, Suksaha, Ebilun and Oboi as his Four Great Regents. He specifically made Sonin the senior of the Four Regents, while leaving Oboi in the last position. Then he instructed that the new Emperor and his Regents should continue the implementation of his policies to lower taxes and levies, fight corruption, recruit more Han scholars to the Court and provide equal treatment for Han and Manchu Court officials.

When the will was finished, Shunzhi told Scholar Wang to take it to the Empress Dowager to provide her formal endorsement and signature. As Wang was walking down the marble steps of the Palace, he was accosted by Oboi, who roughly snatched the scroll from Wang's hands. Terrified of the armed warrior before him, Wang just cowered and put up no resistance. After reading the scroll, Oboi took from his sleeve an identical scroll and handed it to Wang, ordering him to go back into the Palace to put the Imperial Seal on it. Fearing for his life, Wang meekly obeyed.

The next day, the Shunzhi Emperor passed away in peace, just a month and a few days before his twenty-third birthday.

When Bumbutai heard her son's will being read out by the Minister of Rites to the full Court the following day, she was puzzled. The appointments were exactly as Shunzhi had commanded, but the sections that followed, which had a self-accusatory tone to them, were perplexing. They almost completely negated the policies that he had himself instituted, and sounded almost apologetic for his admiration of Han Chinese culture and for his favoritism towards Han Court officials. It declared an immediate return to Manchu systems and traditions.

She had heard of Oboi's efforts to plant his spies and functionaries all over the Court and in the Palaces, even at the level of the Provincial governments. She suspected that one of Shunzhi's new eunuchs might have overheard the Emperor's conversation with her and the German priest and snitched to Oboi. Oboi was the only one who could have the audacity to tamper with the Emperor's will. A return to the full Manchu system meant reinstating and entrenching the privileges that Manchu Bannermen used to enjoy, and endorsing the oppression of the Hans. She alerted herself to be more vigilant. She now had a new child Emperor and the Qing Empire to protect.

Oboi had risen through the ranks rapidly mainly due to his military prowess during the numerous battles against the Ming forces both in the days of Hong Taiji and Dorgon's Regency. Dorgon had once tried to sentence him to death for insubordination, but the sentence was not implemented due to his substantial war credit, largely relating to the killing of the Ming rebel leader Zhang Xianzhong, who ranked second in viciousness only to Li Zicheng. After Dorgon's death, he gradually gained Shunzhi's trust by helping him purge the late Regent's followers and with his rise in status, he showed himself to be a ruthless statesman thirsty for power as well as for blood. During the purge of Dorgon's followers, he had perosnally executed dozens of people who had previously rubbed him the wrong way. He had employed the cruelest punishment of all—dismemberment. Bumbutai had a presentiment that a dark cloud was lurking on the horizon.

Out of respect for Shunzhi's fervent Buddhism beliefs, Bumbutai asked Mao to conduct a Buddhist funeral for the late Emperor, to be followed by a cremation ritual in accordance with Manchu traditions.

During the cremation, Xuanye, as the chosen heir, offered incense at the altar and performed various rites under the direction of Mao. The child's teary eyes, cast in bewilderment until they found Bumbutai, and he was instantly calmed. He had been feeling distraught since his father's passing. But young though he was, he had some idea of what was expected of him. In a couple of months, he would be enthroned in the Hall of Supreme Harmony. He knew it was a serious and grown-up duty, and that the only way to live up to the challenge was to acquire knowledge through study. The prospect was as frightening as it was perplexing. He had only learned a little from the books he had read so far about what an emperor was supposed to be and to do, and he was curious to know more.

All he knew was that from now on he would be treated differently from his brother, Fuquan. He had so many questions that he wanted to ask his Nana, who he knew was smart and always had ready answers. More importantly, she was the one who could always soothe his fears and calm his nerves. He loved his own mother, too, but he couldn't talk to her in the same way he could with Nana. Remembering one of her tricks—reciting poems silently to calm fears—he now began to recite one of his favorite Tang poems.

At the end of the ritual, Bumbutai instructed Mao and Sumalagu that the urn containing her son's ashes should be buried next to Consort Donggo's in the Shunzhi Imperial Mausoleum. Then she went over to Xuanye and Fuquan and held their little hands in hers and led them back to the Princes' Residence.

On the way, she secretly said prayers to Eternal Blue Sky asking it to help reunite and give eternal blessings to the deceased family of three, and to help Xuanye fulfill his duties as a righteous and benevolent ruler. Looking at the bright young face of the new Emperor, she felt hope and consolation, making all her previous trials and heartbreaks worthwhile.

PART 3

Pride

Twenty-Four

After being ordained a monk, Wu Liangfu lived a quiet and sheltered life in the temple on the outskirts of Beijing. Following Shunzhi's death, he unfailingly chanted prayers for him first thing every morning, fingering as he did so the chanting beads his deceased master had given him as a keepsake. For ten days in a row after he received the awful news, he was unable to suppress his tears during the morning ritual. He knew he could not have had a kinder master than Shunzhi and he sorely missed him. Other novice monks, some of them teenagers and some just small kids, teased him when they saw him shedding tears. The bubbly faces reminded him of the child Emperor and the happy times he had spent with him, which just increased his sense of loss.

One chilly day about a month after Shunzhi's passing, a teenage novice came running into the monastery, announcing breathlessly that several Manchu soldiers on horseback were riding up the hill. It was a big surprise for them all, as the temple was isolated and rarely visited by worshippers. The last event that had drawn a crowd was Wu's ordination ceremony, following which the temple had sunk back into its normal state of tranquility. The more senior monks herded the noisy novices into the backyard and informed the head monk of the visitors.

Having dismounted, the six armored riders, all armed with swords sheathed at their sides, tromped up to the head monk, who was standing in the front courtyard to welcome them. Their leader demanded in an imperious voice to see Wu Liangfu immediately. The head monk enquired as to the purpose, but the leader's deputy dismissed the enquiry.

"You have no business to know, bald head!" he shouted in stilted Chinese. At this, the head monk, flanked by four well-built monks, addressed the leader of the visitors in a steady voice:

"I hope you will understand that this is the house of Buddha and whoever enters it needs to comply with the Rules. No man may carry any weapons within these peaceful grounds. This is Rule number one. If you would be so kind as to disarm yourselves, I would appreciate it."

"We will do nothing of the sort!" the deputy shouted. "Who do you think you are to give us orders? You had better get Wu Liangfu to come out at once, or else….."

His superior checked him with a flick of his hand.

"Please excuse us, Master," he said apologetically but firmly. "We are just soldiers and are quite ignorant of temple rules. If you will kindly ask Wu to come out to the gate, we will leave the temple grounds at once. We are under orders from General Oboi to summon the eunuch."

The head monk hesitated, bound by his solemn promise to the late Emperor to ensure Wu's safety, and he suspected the intentions of the armed intruders. Oboi's name especially rang an alarm bell. He himself and four other senior monks had trained in Shaolin martial arts and would be a close match for the six armed cavalrymen, but he was aware that a confrontation might provoke more hostility from Regent Oboi's men. Well-versed in Sun Tzu's *The Art of War,* he knew that stalling and avoidance were the best stratagems in this situation.

"Venerable," he said. "Unfortunately Liangfu has been sick for the last few days and is still bedridden today. May I trouble you to come back in, say, three days? I believe he will have recovered by then."

The group leader appeared a little annoyed by the head monk's subterfuge, but he kept his temper in check. After a short pause, he cursorily apologized for the intrusion and ordered his men to withdraw.

When the riders were out of sight, the head monk hurried to the rear courtyard to find Wu and told him of what had transpired. He urged Wu to pack a few things and head straight for the Bamboo Temple in Kunming.

"It is time for you to seek shelter under Master Mao," he said. "The Master promised the late Emperor to protect you. My temple is no longer a safe place for you."

He then went into his chamber to fetch five silver bars and gave them to Wu, telling him that the late Emperor had left the funds there for him in case of emergency. Wu fell on his knees and bowed three times to the head monk to thank him for saving his life. The monk advised him to take advantage of the cover of night to start his journey.

Feelings of despair and isolation bore in on Wu like an invisible noose, and his thoughts reeled back to his early childhood and that fateful night when his destitute parents had sold him for two silver bars to the Bureau of Eunuchs. He had been pinned on a long table, stripped of his pants… the waxen faces staring down at him… the brutal tying up of his genitals... the cold glint of the hideous knife… the singeing pain… the callous gagging of his screams… the three-day water deprivation. Rivulets of cold sweat ran down his face.

When night fell, Wu threw a packed cloth sack on the back of the donkey that the head monk had given him, bade farewell to his fellow monks and led the animal out into the dark freezing unknown. A sterile half-moon dawdling in the sky provided the only light to the winding path leading from the temple down to the main carriageway. On both sides of the path rose tall pine trees hugged by a low spread of entangling bushes, throwing out eerie shadows.

Not a single other soul was on the dirt path. Dead silence stretched out its ensnaring arms as if ready to trap anything that came within its reach. Only an occasional daring chirp of a cicada punctuated the unrelenting quiet.

Wu, who was scared of the dark, thought it best to walk on foot with the donkey by his side. He badly needed the illusion of having a companion with him. The donkey seemed as though it could sense its master's fear and gave out a low grunt now and then to calm his nerves.

Man and beast stumbled onwards, bracing themselves against the biting night frost. Wu tried humming a folk tune for distraction. As they were about to negotiate the last turn in the path before the main carriageway, a rustling sound gave Wu a start. Then there was a flicker of silvery light, and three dark figures jumped out and blocked his way. The riders had stayed behind on their leader's orders, laying in wait for him. Wu was gagged and strong-armed away by the riders while the donkey paced helplessly backwards and forwards, bleating piteously.

A couple of days later, back in Beijing, Wu was charged with corruption and criminal meddling in state affairs. He was sentenced to death by slicing on the direct orders of Oboi.

When Sumalagu broke the news to Bumbutai, she was devastated, knowing as she did that Wu had in truth committed the crimes that he was accused of. The punishment, though unspeakably awful, was in accordance with the code. There was a small consolation when she found out that the executioner had been a beneficiary a few years earlier of her largesse—drought relief donations to Sichuan—and she immediately wrote to him, appealing for Wu to be given a quick death with the first cut, discreetly slashing the throat, thereby killing him instantly. The executioner received the letter in time and willingly did as he was asked. Later, he secretly cremated Wu's remains and took the urn containing his ashes to the head monk of the temple for a proper burial in the temple's rear courtyard.

Two months after the Imperial funeral, seven-year-old Xuanye was formally enthroned as the Kangxi Emperor in the Hall of Supreme Harmony, and Bumbutai took the title Grand Empress Dowager. In the following year, she issued an edict formally appointing Sonin, Suksaha, Ebilun and Oboi as the Four Regents to Kangxi, with Sonin as the Chief Regent. She knew in her heart that she would have to play the balancing game from then on.

As soon as the Four Regents were formally installed, Oboi began to show his true colors. He had always coveted the White Bannermen's Western quadrant of land in the Imperial City, which was the fertile and lush green area that abutted West Park. At the first meeting of the Regents, he didn't bother to hide his covetousness and made a proposal to exchange the Yellow Banners' more arid Northern portion for the White Banners' Western lands. Ebilun, like Oboi from the Border Yellow, and who always followed his lead tacitly supported the proposal. But Suksaha of the Plain White objected in the face of Oboi's greed and argued that all White Bannermen had already been settled in the Western section for a long time and it was beyond reason to upset their lives now.

The Chief Regent Sonin, though senile and ailing, was shrewd enough to discern Oboi's proposal as nothing than a ploy to seize more land for personal gain. While he could have put his foot down, he was unwilling to make an enemy of Oboi and cannily suggested that the issue be referred to the Ministry of Revenue for a deliberation. The Minister of Revenue and other senior officials from the Ministry were clear on Oboi's rapacious intent and unanimously rejected his proposal.

Undeterred by this setback, at another meeting of the Regents Oboi mooted the abolition of the Hanlin Academy, the institution revived during the Shunzhi reign for the purpose of nurturing Han scholars to be Court officials. He called for a significant reduction in the number of Han scholars in civil recruitment, and as the other Regents had no strong opinion about these matters, Oboi took silence for approval and went ahead with the implementation. He also dismantled the Bureau of Eunuchs, which had been a power hub under Shunzhi's reign, with Wu Liangfu as its head.

What Bumbutai had feared was now coming to pass. Oboi became more and more brazen, not even deigning to show courtesy for the Kangxi emperor, much less allowing him to participate in any matters of state discussions. He attended Court only when it pleased him. Court memorials were to be sent direct to his residence, and he made decisions on urgent issues without consulting the other Regents. His followers formed a wide web throughout the Court, the military and all levels of government. They took orders from no one but him.

Suksaha, with the two powerful White Banners behind him, was the only one who still had the nerve to challenge Oboi in Court. In cases of serious disputes, Suksaha would report to the Grand Empress Dowager, and only when the latter decisively interfered would Oboi grudgingly back down.

Oboi did not deal kindly with dissenters, and he was not lenient with those who had thwarted his land exchange plan. In order to preempt Suksaha seeking help from the Grand Empress Dowager, he played cunningly to keep him isolated as he set in motion his plans for reprisal.

Having been the Chief of the Imperial Guards under Shunzhi's reign, he had enough loyal followers to form his own personal guard force. One day, a troop of Imperial Guards marched into the residence of the Minister of Revenue, chained him in front of his family, took him away and dumped him in jail. On the same day, a provincial governor and an investigation envoy directly under him, both of whom had voiced their objection to Oboi's land exchange proposal, were also imprisoned. All three were tortured into confessing to corruption charges, obviously trumped up. The next day, they were beheaded.

The next few years would see Oboi and his cronies embark on a forced land exchange and land grabbing spree. Many Hans who had hitherto lived peacefully around Beijing, were forcibly evicted from their properties. At a time when Han society was beginning to heal from the endless battles and rebellions and accept Manchu hegemony, the Oboi regency reversed everything that Shunzhi had done to harmonize the relationship between Manchus and Hans.

Earlier, right after Kangxi was enthroned, a Han scholar named Zhou from Jiangnan had petitioned for the Grand Empress Dowager to take up the regency herself, as she was much-loved and respected by all the Qing subjects. Much as she appreciated the petitioner's good intentions, Bumbutai loved freedom too much to want to wield such power over others.

"My only mission is to bring peace to all and to help my Xuanye make a mark on history as a truly benevolent Emperor," she said. By accomplishing that mission, she would fulfill her Mongolian obligation as well as her promise to Hong Taiji, and would have no regrets. One secret dream that she had never shared with anyone was her longing for the day when she could return to her homeland.

While she kept a low profile, Bumbutai did not let matters of governance escape her sight. She had the foresight to see what Oboi was up to. For the time being, while Kangxi was still a minor, she knew she had to exercise the greatest restraint. Protocol ruled that he could only acquire full imperial power at the age of fifteen, but she was contemplating how to nudge that date forward.

Meanwhile, she did all she could to encourage Kangxi, who had been living with her in Cining Palace since his enthronement, to learn well the Chinese Four Books and Five Classics, as well as Chinese, Mongolian and Manchu history. She was secretly pleased that she had nothing to worry about in this respect, as the child Emperor was industrious and extremely intelligent, and had a natural affinity with Chinese literature and history. He was tall, well-built and well-proportioned, and was interested in all kinds of physical activity, with a particular bent for hunting and archery.

For Bumbutai, it was an immeasurable joy to be living under the same roof as her favorite grandson and watching him grow. This was a joy of which she had sadly been deprived with her son. She made herself a solemn promise to dedicate all her attention to cultivating Xuanye's moral character as well as his intellect.

In order to set him on the right track, she wrote on a parchment her special advice to him and bade him read it once each day.

Every morning, before getting out of bed, he would quietly read what was on the parchment, which he kept in a small lacquered box placed next to his pillow. The text read thus:

"The ancients once said: 'An Emperor's work is the hardest of all work. Why? Because he, as a supreme leader, has his subjects to take care of. The subjects are like his children, who look to him for provident care.' Your grandfather used to say: that if you can win the hearts of your subjects, then you will truly win the nation. You will do well to contemplate these words. In short, it is your natural duty to strive

hard to give your subjects a good life, which they can extend to their future generations, and you are not to rest until this is achieved. If you can nurture a generous and kind heart, be gentle and respectful, be cautious in your behavior and words, be diligent and be mindful of your ancestors' teachings, you will have no regrets in your life."

In the spring of the following year, Kangxi's birth mother, Consort Tunggiya, contracted an illness and passed away. In accordance with Inner Court rules, Kangxi had been brought up not by his birth mother but by Shunzhi's second Empress (Bumbutai's grandniece, now the Empress Dowager) who had no child of her own. As a consequence, Kangxi had since infanthood developed a deeper bond of affection with his foster mother. It was Bumbutai who had willed this, as her grandniece was a purebred Borjigit with aristocratic Mongolian blood. Shortly after Kangxi's birth, she had said in private to her grandniece:

"I know Shunzhi has neglected you, but Eternal Blue Sky is kind to you and has given you Xuanye to bring up. I trust you to teach him to love Mother Nature like all Mongols. Only such love can purify and strengthen our souls. Take him to the South Park Retreat as often as you can and teach him to ride and shoot when he is old enough. Love him as if he were your own."

The young Kangxi appreciated all that his foster mother had taught him, and never ceased looking up to his Nana as a pillar of strength and trust. But he was always proud of his mother's Chinese influence, which cultivated in him a soft spot for the Chinese language and culture. His natural aptitudes were further honed by the education he received from prominent Han scholars, whom Nana meticulously selected as his teachers.

When the funeral rituals were over, nine-year-old Kangxi sat at the writing table in his bed chambers and personally wrote an edict under Nana's guidance, granting Consort Tunggiya the posthumous title of Empress Dowager. While comforting her grandson, Bumbutai gave instructions to the Board of Rites to have the late Consort buried alongside Shunzhi and Donggo in the Imperial Mausoleum.

Since Shunzhi's death, Father Schall von Bell was rarely called to the Imperial Palaces. One of his subordinates, surnamed Yang, was a xenophobic self-styled astronomer who believed in the faulty Mohammedan version of calendar. He used every occasion to vilify the priest's version which was based on astronomical calculations, while harboring a deep grudge against him for winning the late Emperor's special favor. Ignorance, jealousy and presumption superseded reason. Now, seeing the priest falling out of imperial favor, he launched a full-scale attack. Not even the priest's poor health was enough to hold back his malevolence.

On a gloomy autumn day three years after Shunzhi's death, the Jesuit priest and other Christian missionaries living in Beijing were chained and thrown into prison on charges of high treason and propagation of an evil religion. The conservative Regents, in particular Oboi, were pleased to see the Christians' influence on society vitiated, because foreign spiritual influence was always something to be wary of.

When Donggo's infant son died, the German priest had supposedly been asked to select a propitious date for the burial rite. It was now alleged that he had selected an unlucky date, which had subsequently jinxed the Emperor's favorite Consort and led to her untimely death. Schall von Bell was unable to answer the charges himself due to his illness, so his fellow Jesuit priest Ferdinand Verbiest was present at the various trial hearings to speak on his behalf. After further investigation, it was discovered that Schall von Bell had never been asked to pick the date, which fact thus invalidated this charge. But the Court

Magistrate still pressed on with the other allegation, that the priest had leveraged his Court appointment to propagate an evil religion. To this charge, Father Verbiest replied that Schall von Bell had never desired his appointment as Director of the Board of Mathematics, and that the late Emperor had bestowed it on him against his wishes. In the end, the Minister of Punishments, who, together with the Court Magistrate, was in fact answerable to the anti-Christian Regents, delivered a guilty verdict on this charge.

In the fourth month of the following year, Schall von Bell was condemned to death by slicing and beheading. In the late morning of the fifteenth day of the fourth month, the sky was raven black with blood-red streaks. Crows cawed non-stop, frogs leapt out of their swampy abodes in large numbers, snakes woke from their deep slumber and slithered everywhere. A deafening clap of thunder followed a blinding spark of lightening. Then a monstrous spurt of black rain cleaved open the bowels of the sky.

The old German priest was inside a wooden cage on a wheeled cart, which was rumbling along a muddied cobblestoned street toward the execution ground. His fellow missionaries and Christian followers braved the noxious weather to follow the procession, chanting prayers in a low murmur, their faces glistening and stoic. The square was packed with spectators. Well-dressed merchants carrying their abacuses, trades people with their toolbags slung over their shoulders, maids with straw baskets looped through their forearms, peddlers laden with their wares, market hawkers… They were a hardhearted bunch who never tired of gawking at others' tragedies. The sudden downpour sent them all scrambling to find shelter.

Oboi had been careful to keep Bumbutai entirely ignorant of news regarding the priest. Around noon on this day she was in discussion with Sumalagu and Siu Fa about her intended choice of a bride for Kangxi, who was nearing the age of eleven.

"I have heard that Sonin's granddaughter is about one year older than Xuanye. Is that the case?" she asked of the old maid, almost a sage to her eyes.

"Venerable, you are correct. She is a little beauty too, and very well read." Sumalagu always understood her mistress well and replied with confidence, having earlier gathered all the available information regarding the girl. Her father Gabula, Sonin's eldest son, had recently replaced Oboi as the Chief of the Imperial Guards.

"But Venerable, don't you want to have a Borjigit Princess to be the bride?" asked Siu Fa. Her mind was not as sharp as the older maid's.

"Siu Fa, the Grand Empress Dowager has her reasons," said Sumalagu. "There is a need to curb those who are too powerful...."

"I know that Oboi has plans to propose his niece to become Empress," said Bumbutai with a sigh. "He is so presumptuous! But what I have in mind is not going to please him."

Looking up, she was stunned to see through the latticed screen window an eerie blood red sky that was darkening in shade with every passing second. A chill ran down her spine.

"Is there an execution in the square today?" she asked.

"I'll send Ah Tak at once to find out," said the vigilant Sumalagu. Ah Tak was a young Han bondservant serving in Cining Palace who had become the maid's protégé and her eyes and ears.

As Ah Tak galloped toward the execution ground, all the forces of Nature seemed to have converged with deafening roars of thunder smothering a ferocious downpour of pebble-size hailstones. The horse was startled and reared up on its hind legs several times, almost throwing the servant to the ground. The young man braced himself against the hailstorm and forged his way forward. Peering out from under his black hood, he saw a meteorite with a shiny tail shooting across the crimson sky. The premonition of something bizarre about to happen made his skin crawl, but he had no time to reflect and, with a whack of the whip, pressed his horse to race ahead.

As he approached the square, he craned his neck and got a glimpse of the execution scaffold with a white-haired figure being tied to a pole. Then in the blink of an eye, the earth itself split open and caved in. The violent earthquake sent the scaffold crashing on one side and mayhem ensued in the crowd, people scattering in all directions, like mercury spilt on the ground.

The Jesuit priests and the Christians stayed where they were and were miraculously untouched. One of them, whom Ah Tak recognized as Father Verbiest, jumped onto the half-collapsed scaffold to untie the elderly priest from the pole and carried him off. Too frightened to put the old man back in chains, the cowering guards made no move to stop them.

Elsewhere, a flash of lightening hit the roof of the Court Magistrate's workplace, where the death sentence for Schall von Bell had been deliberated and passed. Half the roof caved in, turning the building into a heap of debris. At the time, the Magistrate was inside his work chamber and came within an inch of being hit by falling beams.

TWENTY-FIVE

WHEN BUMBUTAI HEARD Ah Tak's report, she bolted from her seat and began pacing the lounge in agitation. She had never expected Oboi to have the nerve to seize and torture one of her closest allies. But she was grateful to Eternal Blue Sky for preserving Fulin's *Mafa*, and she cringed in visualizing what would have otherwise happened. She realized that unless she took a stand, Oboi would walk all over her, and for that matter, the Emperor too.

After a moment of contemplation, she sat down to write an edict in her own hand. She then she summoned the Minister of Punishments to her Palace and questioned him on the causes and events surrounding the case of the German priest. When all her questions had been answered, she glowered at the Minister in anger.

"As far as I can see, there is absolutely no case against Father Schall von Bell," she said.

"The priest was tried by the Provincial and Court Magistrates and they passed the guilty verdict," the Minister replied, trying to shirk the blame.

"But on what grounds? I know for a fact that the Court appointment was against the priest's wishes, and that he had the late Emperor's explicit permission to preach the Christian faith wherever he wanted. So, where is the guilt?"

The Minister was unable to come up with an answer and kept

his head bowed in reply.

"Who gave you the authority to impose such a totally ridiculous sentence on him?" she demanded. "Were you not aware that Father Schall von Bell was the late Emperor's *Mafa*?"

The Minister realized he was in deep trouble, and he threw himself on his knees.

"It was… it was Regent Oboi," he stammered. "No! It was the Four Regents…."

"Listen to me carefully!" she said, cutting him off. "I now order you to immediately annul the sentence, rescind the guilty verdict and release the priest. If anyone questions your action, show him this edict." She handed him the scroll. "You are dismissed," she added with a wave of her hand.

As soon as he was gone, Bumbutai summoned the Minister of Civil Office and ordered him to dismiss the Minister of Punishments with immediate effect and replace him with a cousin of the late Shunzhi named Mingju, a member of the aristocratic Nalan clan and one of the most trusted Senior Imperial Guards from the Plain Yellow Banner.

Her mind was also now made up about Kangxi's bride. Sonin's Heseri clan was a powerful and trusted clan. Both his sons, Gabula and Songgoto, were valiant generals under the Plain Yellow and both served as Senior Imperial Guards, with Gabula as the Chief. In order to build a strong alliance to resist Oboi, she would need the help of the Heseri clan. Thus Gabula's twelve-year-old daughter would be a perfect match for eleven-year-old Kangxi.

Early the following month, Schall von Bell was allowed to return to his house and resume his missionary practice. But due to the ill treatment he suffered in prison, the life in him was ebbing away and he would die a year later.

Bumbutai felt a strong sense of urgency in establishing

Kangxi's adulthood and wanted an Empress by his side without further delay. In the late summer, she asked the Minister of Rites to announce the Emperor's betrothal to Regent Sonin's granddaughter and to fix the date of the ceremony.

When Oboi heard the news, he stormed into Cining Palace unannounced to confront Bumbutai. The Dowager Empress, fully expecting such a move, was sitting calmly in her lounge reading Chinese poetry.

"Venerable Highness," he shouted with only a veneer of courtesy visible, "I have heard that Sonin wants to make an Empress of his infant granddaughter. Is there any truth to this rumor?"

"You may have it wrong. The idea was mine and not Sonin's. I wonder why that would make you so unhappy?" Bumbutai said in a glacial tone, not bothering to look up from her book.

".....But why Sonin's granddaughter?"

"And why not? Are you questioning my choice of a granddaughter-in-law?"

"I don't mean to be impertinent. I am just wondering... why... there is such a rush. His Imperial Highness is still just a boy...." he stuttered, taken aback by Bumbutai's curt response.

"Xuanye is a grown adult physically and mentally, as the Empress Dowager can readily attest to. Besides, the Emperor's marriage is entirely a family matter. I don't see why it should concern anyone outside the family," she continued in a dispassionate voice.

"Venerable ...I...I apologize for ... disturbing you. Please forgive me." He realized he had gone too far.

"I have known for some time that your beautiful niece has reached marriageable age," Bumbutai added. "If you trust my judgment, I would be happy to make a suitable match for her. I do have several candidates in mind."

"That would be our family's honor, Venerable. The girl's parents would be very grateful for your kind assistance. But I must not take any more of your time."

Oboi left Cining Palace in a sour mood.

The Imperial wedding went smoothly as planned. On the wedding night, Kangxi was delighted to find that his bride was a charming and genteel girl. What pleased him most was that she also happened to be a lover of Chinese poetry and literature like himself. He chatted with her all night long and the two youngsters became good friends instantly.

Palace etiquette would ordinarily require that the Emperor move into the Palace of Heavenly Purity after his Imperial wedding, with his Empress installed in the Palace of Earthly Tranquility. Since the Imperial Residence was undergoing major refurbishing, an alternative was necessary and the Imperial Household Department arranged for Kangxi to live temporarily in Wuying Hall in the Outer Court.

Bumbutai was sad to see her grandson move out of Cining Palace, but accepted the fact that her Xuanye was now a grown lad. Besides, she and Xuanye had an important plan up their sleeves. Wuying Hall was ideal as a training ground for young *buku* (wrestling) guards, as it was located in a quiet and unfrequented corner of the Outer Court. Songgoto, a virtuoso in *buku* and now the Emperor's uncle-in-law, was appointed as the chief coach.

After being spurned by the Grand Empress Dowager, and knowing that he could not stop the betrothal, Oboi diverted his attention to more material issues. He issued edicts in his capacity as Regent to squeeze tax revenue from Han peasants and landowners alike and to impose harsh punishments for tax delinquents. This was done in parallel with the enforcement of the involuntary land exchange, which was used as a cover to seize more land from the Hans.

Oboi had always loathed Chinese values and culture and he desired a return of all the special privileges for the Manchu Bannermen that Shunzhi had done away with. His egregious example instigated rampant corruption within the Manchu aristocracy, while at the same time exacerbating the Hans' resentment toward the rulers.

In one extreme case, one of Oboi's cronies who, being frustrated with a Han landowner's inability to pay his tax arrears, abducted his young daughter and forced her to be his concubine. When he tried to violate her, she grabbed a pair of scissors and stabbed herself to death. The news enraged her mother who forced her way into the Manchu aristocrat's residence, swinging a kitchen cleaver at him and badly wounding him. She was killed by the aristocrat's guards. Later, the husband reported the case to the local magistrate, who happened to be another in Oboi's network. He was thrown into jail and subsequently committed suicide.

In eighteen cases, tax delinquents were arrested and beheaded after long trials. In numerous other cases, the offenders were thrown into jail without proper trial. The luckier ones were those who had relatives willing to pay up on their behalf and they were released. Those who lacked any means were left to rot to death in prison. Complaints were useless because many of the senior district official and magistrate posts were occupied by Oboi's people. Apart from the Yangzhou and Jiangnan tragedies, these were the darkest times for the Hans since the Manchu invasion of China twenty-one years before.

Following his move into Wuying Hall, Kangxi made a habit of going over to Cining Palace every morning to make obeisance to his Nana. On his Nana's birthday, he rose earlier than usual and took a scroll of his recent calligraphy with him. He made a detour to the Imperial Garden to pick a bunch of lavender lilies, which he placed in a dainty porcelain vase. With bounding steps, he entered the garden of Nana's Palace and found her seated on a stone bench reading. As he approached her, he hid the scroll and vase of flowers behind his back.

When Bumbutai saw him, she was all smiles as usual. Noticing he was hiding something, she said teasingly:

"Have you got dirty finger nails, Xuanye?"

"Nana, I wish you a happy life like the East Ocean, and longevity like the South Mountain!" he said cheerfully, and knelt on the ground and presented the scroll and lilies to her.

Enraptured and flustered like a young girl, she gazed with misty eyes on him. The sight of the lilies and of her grandson, who bore a strong likeness to Dorgon, transported her back to that magical night under a spangled Mongolian sky. For a flitting moment, she was again that vivacious girl of eleven on horseback. That was forty-two years ago. It took a while for her to collect herself. When she settled down, she unfurled the scroll.

"Xuanye!" she exclaimed in amazement. "Your calligraphy is beautiful. You must have put in a lot of effort. Nana is so proud of you. And you're such a thoughtful child. I am so very happy. Come and sit close to me."

"Nana, I remember you told me that Granduncle Dorgon had once given you a drawing of mountain lilies. You still like lilies, don't you?"

"Yes, yes, I still love them, and I still have that drawing. They have a special meaning for me. Thank you so much for the flowers, Xuanye. So, tell me, how are your *buku* lessons going?"

"Oh, I love them! I love wrestling with the young guards. I'm smaller than they are, but I often win more points in matches with them."

"Don't forget that the guards are being trained for a purpose."

"No, I won't forget. They have a special duty to protect

you, the Venerable Empress Dowager, my Empress and myself. When the time comes, Uncle Songgoto will assign them a secret mission….." he glanced around to make sure no one was within earshot. Then he whispered something into her ear.

"I'm so glad you have a good grasp of our plans," she said.

"I know that Regent Oboi is not a good person and that he is doing harm to our Empire. Sometimes I feel frustrated that he is able to do so many wrong things, levying high taxes on the Hans and seizing their lands. I wish I could stop him. It's not right to make them suffer. They will only hate us."

"Where did you hear all this from, Xuanye?" She was surprised that he seemed to be abreast of what was happening.

"Oh, I have my eyes and ears," he said with a smug look on his face. Bumbutai could guess where he got his information from. The Imperial Household Department was right next to Wuying Hall, and according to Sumalagu's report, Kangxi liked to spend time around there and chat with Ah Tak and other maids and bondservants with whom he was friendly.

"I must say I am very pleased to see that you have compassion and a keen sense of justice. You must have learned your *Analects* well," she said.

"Nana, I have just been reading a book called *Extended Meaning of The Great Learning*, which is an excellent practical guide for good governance. I need to study the book well."

"That is excellent, Xuanye. The book was written in the Southern Song Dynasty by Scholar Chen Te-hsiu to expound on *The Great Learning*. It is a useful guide for emperors. I am so glad you're studying it."

"The essence of the book is that in order for an emperor to be fit to rule, he must first cultivate his own person with sincerity, restrain his self-indulgent desires and expose himself to knowledge. It is very inspiring."

"Those indeed are the golden rules!" Bumbutai exclaimed. "It is a good practical handbook. I wish there were a Manchu translation of it so that our clansmen and Court officials could read it too." She did not expect her grandson to take her comment to heart.

"Oh, Nana, I wanted to tell you that I plan to issue an edict banning the practice of foot-binding. It puzzles me as to how such a barbarous custom could be allowed to thrive for so long among the Hans. I pity the Han women."

"Xuanye, I feel much the same way as you. Traditional dogma is a terrible thing, especially when it does obvious harm to people. You have your Nana's complete support on this."

Looking at the young lad's effervescent face, she could perceive an amalgam of Hong Taiji's brawny audacity, Shunzhi's agile wit, his mother's poetic nature and her own equine free spirit. He was the epitome of the finest traits of the three cultures and for the first time she saw in him a glinting ray of hope for a better and more harmonious future for Manchus, Hans and Mongolians alike. It filled her with a pride that she had never felt before. She now could also see more clearly her own role, standing beside her grandson.

In the summer of the fifth year after Shunzhi's death, Bumbutai decided she must make a move to allow Kangxi to acquire his full imperial powers. She summoned Hung Chili, a Han scholar from the Hanlin Academy and Kangxi's Chinese teacher, and requested him to draft a memorial proclaiming that on reaching the age of thirteen the following year, Kangxi should follow the precedent set by the late Shunzhi Emperor and be vested with full ruling powers. She specifically instructed him not to mention when the regency should end, so as not to ruffle Oboi. Hung was skilful with words and the memorial was approved by all Four Regents without adverse comment.

The following spring, Sonin's health deteriorated and one day in late summer, he lost his battle against chronic illness and passed away. Just nine days later, Bumbutai called a meeting of the remaining three Regents together with Kangxi in Cining Palace to discuss the transition of power. Kangxi spoke first.

"On the day before he died, Sonin instructed me with his last breath to prepare myself to take the full powers of Emperor. I have since consulted with the Venerable Grand Empress Dowager, and she has given her approval. As each of you have indicated your consent to the memorial on this topic, I am now seeking your confirmation so that the proper rituals can be arranged."

Suksaha, who had become tired of the constant dueling with Oboi, was only too glad to support Kangxi.

"Your Imperial Highness," he said. "I have been waiting impatiently for this day to come for a long time. You have been married now for two years, and I see no reason for further delay."

Oboi was silent for a long while. Then he snarled: "If that is Your Imperial Highness's wish, so be it."

His curt declaration was echoed by Ebilun, who was over all a cautious man. Bumbutai then added a note of caution:

"The Kangxi Emperor is still an inexperienced youth," she said. "He will need the assistance of all of you."

To that remark, the three Regents vowed to give whatever support and advice was needed. Grasping that as a cue, Bumbutai immediately summoned Hung Chili, and when he appeared invited him to select an auspicious day for the ceremony to mark Kangxi's assuming full reigning powers.

Having been well prepared and feeling confident in the presence of the Grand Empress Dowager, he promptly named the day four days hence. Oboi, teeth clenched, made no comment.

On the appointed day, thirteen-year-old Kangxi was bestowed

with full imperial power in an elaborate ceremony held in the Hall of Supreme Harmony, in the presence of the Grand Empress Dowager, the Empress Dowager, the three Regents, the full Court, the Eight Manchu, Mongol and Han Banner Chiefs and the Aisin Gioro clansmen. With that accomplished, Suksaha immediately wrote a letter to the Emperor begging to be allowed to retire to his hometown due to ill health. With Sonin, his only ally, gone, he thought it best to withdraw from the Court battlefield. But in a twist of fate, his letter fell into the hands of one of Oboi's spies planted in Suksaha's residence.

Oboi had long hated Suksaha because of his opposition to the land exchange policy. With Suksaha's injudicious letter now in hand, he was ready to fabricate charges against his enemy, using the Privy Council to give the semblance of legality to the proceedings. He ordered the Privy Council members to conduct an investigation into Suksaha's "motives" for requesting retirement, and in the end, they came up with twenty four criminal charges, including the treasonous charges of "breaching the trust of the late Emperor" and "being contemptuous of the young Emperor". The Council found Suksaha guilty on all twenty four charges and recommended that both he and his son and heir be executed by slicing, while his other sons and grandson should be beheaded. It also recommended that their respective family members be enslaved and to have the Imperial Guards under Suksaha demoted to the ranks.

In the Audience Hall, the Privy Council presented its findings and recommendations on Suksaha's case to Kangxi. And so the young Emperor found himself facing his first test in Court politics.

With his keen eyes, he could easily see through Oboi's tricks. Yet he was stumped when the Privy Council claimed the charges were substantiated by so-called witnesses, who undoubtedly belonged in Oboi's venal cabal. At his tender age, he had never encountered anyone more vicious than Oboi. Inexperience made him hesitate, but all eyes were on him and he had to make a decision.

"Suksaha has served me well as a Regent," he said "He does not deserve to die."

Oboi responded with a contemptuous smirk.

"Your Imperial Highness is too young to know right from wrong," he shouted. "You should respect the decision of your Privy Council."

The young Emperor leapt from his dragon throne, rage at Oboi's impertinence inflaming his face.

"I am the Emperor!" he shouted. "You will do as I say. I find Suksaha not guilty of any of the charges brought against him. That is all!" He strode angrily out of the hall and back to his temporary residence in Wuying Hall.

Oboi grinned slyly. The Imperial Jade Seal was still with him, and he had control over many of the Banner troops and had allies at all levels of government. The Emperor had no power over him. With no hesitation, he issued an edict in Kangxi's name affirming the Privy Council's guilty verdict and sentences. In order to make the edict look more like it had come from the Emperor, he added a clause of mercy commuting the sentence from death by slicing to death by strangulation. But whatever the method of execution, Suksaha and his male heirs perished, and his followers under the Plain White were ruthlessly purged.

When Kangxi heard of what had happened, remorse and guilt roiled inside him. He knew he had acted too impetuously in the Audience Hall. Crushed by his error, he now called to mind his Nana's written advice: *"Be cautious in your behavior and words"*. By losing his temper, he had caused unjustified deaths and suffering. For the first time, he felt the massive weight of responsibility that came with the throne .

Having thus learned a harsh lesson in Court politics, he swore to himself that he would from now on move as cautiously as a steppe wolf. He remembered reading in Genghis Khan's journal that "*Victory does not come to the one who plays by the rules; it comes to the one who makes the rules and imposes them on his enemy*". He was going to defeat Oboi his own way.

The following year, the Emperor's Residence in the Palace of Heavenly Purity was ready for occupation and Kangxi moved back into it. By now Songgoto's team of young guards, whose first duty was to protect the Emperor from any possible action that Oboi might initiate, were trained to perfection in agility and physical prowess. In order to allow Oboi to become accustomed to the presence of the young guards, Kangxi purposely arranged for them to practice *buku* inside the Audience Hall on a daily basis, even when Court meetings were in session. He would often join in the practice, which was made to look like a sportive game for youngsters. Oboi's initial circumspection gradually gave way to cynical dismissal, regarding them as a bunch of frisky kids indulging in mindless romps.

Twenty-six

Bumbutai knew there was deep dissatisfaction amongst Han officials with Oboi, as he had tried his utmost to limit their influence and cut their numbers in Court.

In one of their early morning meetings in her garden, Bumbutai listened to Kangxi's lament over the deaths of Suksaha and his family, and she posed him a question.

"Xuanye, you know very well who your enemy is. But do you know who your friends are?"

"I don't feel like I have any friends, Nana. Sometimes I feel very alone. It seems everybody is afraid of speaking up in Court." The young Emperor was dejected, his brow wrinkled.

"My dear child, you always have Nana right behind you. I will always be your best friend. There is no reason to feel alone. Have you forgotten that your enemy himself has many enemies? His enemies cannot but be your friends." She patted his hand lightly.

"You mean the Han officials in Court?"

"Yes. All they need is your tacit support and they will rally to you. Trust me, they have been longing to be your friend and ally. But unless you take the initiative, they will never dare to show their devotion, lest you should rebuff them. They are not without influence on judicial and administration matters."

"How come I never thought of that before! Nana, you are a life saver! And on the military side, I have Gabula, Songgoto,

Mingju and Tuhai, who are all very loyal to me."

Kangxi's eyes glittered with excitement, his self confidence beginning to bounce back.

Bumbutai then suggested he call on Father Verbiest to conduct a full investigation into Father Schall von Bell's case in order to exonerate the latter, so that Shunzhi's *Mafa* could be given a proper state funeral. Such an investigation, apart from being justified, could also be a cover for a counter-attack against Oboi's allies.

"This is all for the purpose of laying the ground work, Xuanye. Ultimately, our single most important objective is to bring down Oboi. He and his clique hang over us like a dagger."

"I know, Nana. I'm only waiting for the right moment."

"When the need arises, don't hesitate to use his own dirty tricks on him. If he can plant spies, so can you, Xuanye," she said, lightly sowing the idea in his mind.

In the months that followed, Kangxi quietly gave orders to Scholar Hung from the Grand Secretariat to gather evidence of Oboi's corruption, his rigging of bureaucracy appointments, his interception of memorials to the Emperor and his organization of a private clique to deliberate on state matters. He was to write a memorial listing all of Oboi's crimes, elaborating on how such crimes had led to a demoralized and non-functioning Court, and suggesting sweeping reforms.

When the memorial was read out in Court, Oboi appeared unfazed.

"Your Imperial Highness, who was it that wrote this memorial?" he asked in his usual condescending manner.

"It was Scholar Hung from the Grand Secretariat."

"I request that Your Imperial Highness order the immediate execution of this insolent character, " Oboi shouted, his eyes smoldering with fury. "How dare he insult me and smear my name thus? I once saved your grandfather's life on the battlefield and risked my own in numerous battles. Have you forgotten that? Is this how you treat an old loyal servant?"

"Calm down, Regent Oboi," said Kangxi in a flat tone, "The memorial is substantiated by evidence and witnesses. As for executing Scholar Hung, it is out of the question. He has done nothing but speak the truth."

"Then are you going to throw me into jail?" Oboi bellowed.

"I wish the Court to deliberate on this and present a decision." He looked over at the Court officials. "Have you come to any conclusion?"

No one dared to utter a word. Silence sailed from the four walls. But Kangxi knew better than press the issue at that moment. He had intended to use the memorial to test the waters and now he had the answer. Shrewdly, he adjourned the meeting to a future date.

He then convened a secret meeting with all the Han Ministers and Court Officials who, in the absence of Oboi, all expressed earnest approval of the memorial.

The Verbiest investigation, on the other hand, which had the full backing of a commission whose members Kangxi had hand-picked, went ahead smoothly. The Court Magistrate who had presided in the case and those who had backed him were found guilty of falsifying charges against Schall von Bell, and were sentenced to imprisonment or exile. Schall von Bell was exonerated. But apart from causing Oboi some slight embarrassment, this did nothing to restrict his power one bit. By that time, Schall von Bell had already been dead for over two years. On Bumbutai's recommendation, Kangxi ordered that he be given a belated grand funeral, and he personally wrote a long epitaph for his tomb eulogizing his contributions to the Qing Empire.

While Court matters were not all going smoothly, the young Kangxi did not let the setbacks dishearten him. In his free time he would go hunting in South Park, or read Chinese poetry with his Empress. After all, he still possessed the magic of youth and was in robust health. Lively as he was, thoughts of posterity were a constant source of vexation. His Empress of almost four years had not yet given him a son.

It had always been his secret regret that there had been no strong male figure in his life to look up to. He had hardly known his own father, and his only elder brother, Fuquan, was too pampered to be a good role model for him. Fathering a large family of his own thus became almost an obsession. Often he would fantasize about how he would select from his sons the most talented ones and personally mentor them. They could be his loyal friends and could assist him in his imperial duties. In time, he would groom the best to be the heir… Such were his cherished dreams.

Not long after his wedding, he had fallen for a beautiful woman from his harem, Concubine Hui from the Manchu Nalan clan. She was Mingju's niece and a cousin of Mingju's son Xingde, a talented poet. Her alluring beauty and dancing skills cast a spell on Kangx.

It was a lovely early spring evening, the air buoyant with the trilling of birds as they darted back and forth from their nests. Kangxi strolled from his Residence, feeling relieved after having completed a hard day's work. His thoughts strayed to Concubine Hui and he quickened his steps toward the West Palace where she resided. As he approached the front garden, he heard a male voice conversing with his Concubine. Kangxi strode in and Xingde jumped up from a bench, startled. He had been sitting side-by-side with Concubine Hui. His face turned crimson and, after making quick obeisance, scurried away.

Kangxi knew Xingde to be a very shy man but was still surprised by his precipitous retreat.

"What were you two talking about?" he asked casually.

"…. Nothing much… just poetry," the Concubine stammered a little, apparently discomfited by Kangxi's unexpected appearance. He was suspicious now, but didn't want to reveal it on his face. Then he noticed a white kerchief with some writing on it lying on the stone garden table beside them. He picked it up and saw it was a love poem written in seven-character regular verse, eight lines in total. Concubine Hui's face turned ashen and she dropped on her knees.

"Your Imperial Highness, there is nothing between Xingde and me," she half-pleaded, half-sobbed. "You have to believe me!"

"I know you two were close in your childhood," he replied, beset by a wave of jealousy. He threw the kerchief down on the table.

"Since becoming your concubine, I have laid down the past and have never given a thought to him. I promise you that I will never allow him to enter this Palace again."

Her shaky but earnest voice had an effect on him.

"I know I can trust you, Hui'er. But can I trust him?" Kangxi was struggling between a sense of inviolable male vanity and a sense of fair judgment. But unable to put his doubts aside, he chose not to stay the night with her as he had planned. He left Concubine Hui and headed to the Palace of Earthly Tranquility to look for comfort in his Empress.

A month later, having mulled the situation with a cool head, Kangxi decided that Xingde was an honorable man, albeit lovelorn, and that he had no cause to doubt either him or Concubine Hui. Yet it didn't escape him that Xingde was an acclaimed poet and literary talent, aside from being very handsome. One night Kangxi summoned Concubine Hui to his bed chambers. As soon as the lovemaking was over, he presented her with a seven-character quatrain that he had earlier written in Chinese, expressing his affections for her. The short verse was simple in style and form, unpretentious in tone.

Reading it over and over as if it had cast a spell on her, she was speechless for a long while. Savoring the sentiment that Kangxi had poured into the writing, she silently cried. He gazed into her unshielded eyes and knew for certain that his suspicions had been unnecessary. They held hands throughout the night, their love bond renewed. Meanwhile, he secretly vowed that he would appoint the best Han scholars to be his teachers to help him master Chinese language and literature.

Early the following year, both his Empress and Concubine Hui would each deliver him a son. But to his desolation, both would die in their infancy. The sad events would reinforce for him the notion of having an expanded harem, not for pleasure, but for reproduction's sake.

Events at at Court were also moving, albeit slowly, and the air was thick with a sense of foreboding. One early summer day, Oboi wrote a message to Kangxi asking for permission to be excused from attending Court for an indefinite period, citing ill health. His intention was to test how Kangxi would react. Three days later on a sunny afternoon, having given a day's advance notice, Kangxi appeared at Oboi's residence with three bodyguards. He was paying the ill Regent a compassionate visit. True to form, the healthy-looking Oboi did not bother to rise from his bed to make obeisance to the Emperor. Kangxi didn't let this snub discomfit him the slightest. He approached the bed, and courteously conveyed his get-well wishes. Then, seating himself on a stool a few steps from the bed, he started chatting about trivial things.

While they were talking, one of Kangxi's bodyguards

suddenly jumped forward.

"It's a blade!" he shouted, pointing to the end of the bed where a pile of quilts lay. One of the other two guards dashed forward and fished out a dagger with a gilded hilt, inscribed with Oboi's name.

The commotion jolted the supine Oboi into an upright position. He knew he could be immediately arrested for an attempted assassination of the Emperor. The three guards would have pounced on him, had Kangxi not ordered them to stand down.

"I apologize for my guards' ignorance," he said soothingly with a smile. "They should know that it is the habit of every Manchu warrior to carry a weapon at all times. There is no call for alarm."

Even so, it took some time for the Regent to calm himself after this stunning drama. He was confused. He had a habit of stashing a couple of daggers in his bed, one under his pillow and one under the quilts, but he thought he had removed them the previous day in anticipation of the Emperor's visit. All his house servants and maids had strict orders never to touch his daggers. It was also true, though, that lately his memory sometimes played tricks on him.

In a much more polite tone now, he assured the Emperor that it was his grave oversight to let a weapon lie about on the day of his visit.

"Let's not dwell on this triviality," Kangxi replied. "The reason I have come to see you is actually to try and persuade you to attend Court as soon as you feel a little better, because there are a couple of urgent matters that I need your expert advice on." Kangxi's tone was steady and he watched Oboi's face closely.

"Your Imperial Highness, I am always at your service. My physician will be coming later to check on me. But no matter what he says about my condition, my duties always come first. I will make every effort to attend Court the day after tomorrow."

With this, the Emperor and his guards left the mansion. Once inside his carriage, Kangxi's lips curved in a faint smile.

Oboi appeared in the Audience Hall as he had promised. He tramped over the golden brick flooring with his usual swagger, his sheathed sword dangling by his side. Nothing was out of the ordinary. The usual bunch of rowdy kids were wrestling with each other in the flanking sections of the hall. The usual wave of somber Court-attired officials occupied the middle section. The Emperor appeared stiff in his sitting posture.

The throne is obviously too large for this lanky kid, Oboi thought contemptuously. *The Ministers will never take him seriously. The Qing Empire needs a resolute leader, not a naïve suckling.*

He almost pitied the poor lad and stifled a chuckle rising in him.

But sometimes things were not as they seemed.

He waded as usual through the throng of blue-robed Courtiers, who moved quickly to let him pass. When he got to his reserved spot right in front of the marble steps leading up to the dais, he heard three loud handclaps and wondered where they came from. Just then, five of the wrestling kids lunged at him like a pack of wolves, three from one side and two from the other. Before he had time to figure out what was happening, they had pinioned him, and the Courtiers were scampering away from the brawl.

One robust lad snatched the sword from Oboi's belt and flung it far away. Oboi tried with brute force to shake off the four brawny wrestlers clutching each of his limbs. Even at his advanced age, he had the feral energy of two hardy warriors. But the *buku* kids were well-trained and just as ferocious in muscular strength. They yanked him down, pinning him hard on the floor and with lightening speed and practiced agility, they tied his hands behind his back and bound his feet with thick ropes.

"How dare you? Who are these kids?" he rasped. "Release me at once!"

Kangxi, wearing a grave expression, said loudly:

"If you must know, they are my bodyguards. Regent Oboi, you are under arrest on thirty counts of charges, seven of them treasonous."

"What treasonous crimes are you accusing me of? I have served the Empire all my life and I was loyal to the two late Emperors. How dare you say such ungrateful things to me?"

He was yellng with the full force of his lungs, his forehead throbbing with blue veins.

"Your most nefarious crimes include a brazen assassination attempt on my life only two days ago, the murder of Regent Suksaha and his family in my name, the private execution out of vengeance of the former Minister of Revenue and his subordinates for having opposed your land exchange proposal and the operation of a clique aimed at overriding my imperial power," said Kangxi in a calm voice. "These are in addition to all the crimes listed in the memorial prepared by Scholar Hung."

The Emperor turned to Mingju, the Minister of Punishments.

"Minister Mingju, will you please read out the list of charges against Oboi, the list of his accomplices and......"

Before he could finish his sentence, Oboi erupted in a raucous laugh.

"Ahh, so you've learned my trick!" He snorted. "I see you are a good imitator...."

Oboi had no doubt that Kangxi had planted spies in his residence.

Mingju ignored Oboi and did as he was told. When he had finished reading the list, Kangxi turned to the full Court.

"Ministers, I now ask you to be judge. Do you find Oboi guilty or not guilty of the said charges?"

"Guilty!" the previously quiet audience gave out a roar.

"Does he deserve a death sentence?"

"Yes, he does! Yes, he does!" the even-louder roar ricocheting from the walls.

"I hear you. But in order to give Oboi and his fourteen principal accomplices a fair trial, I will delegate the responsibility to the Privy Council and allow them to consider the verdicts and recommend the appropriate sentences. Upon their guidance, I will then make the final decision. Songgoto," Kangxi added in an authoritative voice, "take the prisoner to jail and arrest his accomplices."

He was certain that the Privy Council would now switch allegiance back to himself. But as a safety measure, he would have Mingju preside every Council meeting and oversee all the trial procedures.

Bumbutai had all this time been behind the painted partition at the back of the throne, listening intently to the whole proceedings. When the session adjourned and Kangxi retired to the rear chambers, she gave him a tight, congratulatory embrace. He became emotional and cried on her shoulder in cathartic relief. When he had settled down, she said gently to him:

"You are a marvel, Xuanye. We've finally done it. But we must not relax as there are still many loose ends to tie up. There's a lot of damage to be repaired."

"Nana, I couldn't have done this without your sagacious advice and support. You are my goddess," he said modestly as he wiped away his tears, still shaken by the traumatic experience.

"When you consider the sentencing, you should bear in mind that Oboi did serve your father and grandfather well as a loyal Bannerman," she said. "As for his accomplices, try not to turn the purge into a bloodbath. Where forgiveness is possible, forgive. The strongest of men are the ones who can forgive, Xuanye. A kind ruler is an invincible ruler."

His grandmother's advice agreed with his instincts perfectly. Though he believed in severe punishment for heinous crimes, he was generally disposed to the idea of rehabilitating criminals.

After twelve days of deliberation, the Privy Council recommended that Oboi, Ebilun and all fourteen of the principal accomplices named and ten other senior clique members be sentenced to death, with their property and assets confiscated and their women and children enslaved.

After consideration, Kangxi commuted many of the sentences. He decreed that Oboi be incarcerated for life, Ebilun be reprieved but censured for aiding Oboi, nine principal accomplices who were of ministerial rank be put to death because of their reckless murder of innocents, with the remaining offenders each sentenced to a hundred lashes. Their families would all be spared. Thereafter, Kangxi granted a general amnesty for all those who had been involved in Oboi's clique and its affairs. Due to his magnanimity, a great number of Oboi's followers thereupon welcomed the young Emperor into their hearts.

In the following couple of years, Kangxi acted swiftly to address cases of social injustice, including harsh penalties for tax evasion and illegal land grabs. He also moved to implement equal emoluments for Manchu and Han government officials who occupied the same rank. Then he issued an imperial edict banning Manchu aristocrats from seizing Han farmers' land. He reinstated the civil service examinations which Shunzhi had put in place but which the Oboi regency had obviated. He also revived the Hanlin Academy and made Scholar Hung Chili its head.

On the administrative side, he was cautious to only promote

those in whom he had the most trust. Songgoto was made Grand Secretary, Mingju, Chief of the Imperial Household Department and Tuhai, Minister of Revenue. These three Manchu aristocrats had all been his loyal Senior Imperial Guards. To reward Scholar Hung for writing the anti-Oboi memorial, he appointed him Minister of Rites.

Despite his efforts to show himself to be a benevolent ruler to the largely Han society, Kangxi could not but sense that many Han scholars had been so ill-treated by the Manchus during the Dorgon and Oboi Regencies that they still resented the Qing rulers, let alone having any desire to serve as Court officials. To remedy this, he initiated a project documenting the Ming dynastic history, in the hope of enticing Ming scholars to engage in a positive way. He hoped that such a project would be viewed as a gesture of respect for Han society.

Not forgetting his grandmother's comment about the need for a Manchu version of *Extended Meaning of The Great Learning*, he assigned the Bureau of Translators under the Hanlin Academy to translate the book into Manchu. He wanted the translated book to be read by all Manchu Princes and officials.

To inculcate Confucian values throughout society, he issued a Sacred Edict containing sixteen maxims based on Confucian ideology, to be studied and observed by all subjects. The Sacred Edict was widely distributed in the form of posters to all towns and villages. Twice a month, local officials would read aloud and explain the sixteen maxims at a public audience.

When the Bureau of Translators presented Kangxi with a Manchu edition of his favorite book, he ordered a leather-bound copy to be made immediately. One day a month later, in the early hours of dawn, he took the beautifully-bound copy with him to Cining Palace. Words could not describe her joy when Bumbutai saw the book.

"My dear Xuanye, my dear dear child," she said emotionally, taking his hands in hers. "Words fail me…. This book is of such great value, and now because of your initiative, it can nourish the minds of our Manchu subjects. I am so proud of you. I will reward the translators with a thousand silver bars for their invaluable work. You, my dear grandson, as always and ever, have my unalloyed love and adoration!"

Twenty-seven

Soon after the removal of his formidable enemy, a second crisis surfaced in Kangxi's young life. He began to feel the lurking threat of the three powerful warlords who occupied the fertile regions of south and southwestern China. The Lords were Wu Sangui in Yunnan, Shang Kexi in Guangdong and Geng Jingzhong in Fujian.

These fiefdoms had for a long time been a terrible drain on the Empire's coffers as the upkeep of their armies required constant state funding, and now amounted to almost half of all state revenue. In return, though, the Lords had neither the obligation nor the desire to contribute anything to the Empire. They had virtually a free rein to squander all the taxes they legally or illegally collected. For commoners who lived under them, it meant neither peace nor a decent life. Widespread corruption and tyranny were the order of the day. The Lords served nothing but their own self-interest.

Of the three, Wu Sangui was the most avaricious and belligerent, having built up a strong army of seventy thousand men. He monopolized his fiefdom's salt fields and copper mines and levied heavy taxes on farmers. The wealth he extracted from these sources enabled him to live like an emperor and also allowed him to lure bandits from Li Zicheng's disbanded rebel army to join his ever-growing military force. As his wealth and military power grew by the day, he became more and more contemptuous of the Qing Empire.

Early in the twelfth year of Kangxi's reign, Shang Kexi, the Ming defector who had overseen the massacre in Guangdong under Dorgon's regency, was ailing and becoming senile. He petitioned Kangxi for permission to retire to the Liaodong peninsula to the east of Beijing, allowing his son Shang Zhixin to inherit his title of Feudal Lord. Kangxi, on receiving the petition, considered it for a long while and decided it was a golden opportunity to start the process of dealing with the three fiefdoms.

His mind made up, he broached the issue for discussion at a meeting of the Privy Council. Most members of the Council, including Songgoto, were opposed to the idea of terminating the fiefdom, while Mingju was one of the few who supported it. Kangxi went as usual to his Nana for counsel.

After hearing him out, Bumbutai said meditatively: "We tried our best to tolerate the Feudal Lords as we needed them to maintain some sort of order in those remote regions. But it was always to be just an interim measure. Our rule is never complete until we have south and southwest China under our total control. Besides, these Lords have shown themselves to be nothing but self-serving predators. There will never be true peace if they are allowed to continue to fleece our subjects. It is about time we did something."

"That is exactly how I view the situation, Nana. We cannot sleep well until this long-standing problem is resolved once and for all." He was truly glad that Nana and he were always of the same opinion.

"Xuanye, of the three Lords, the old fox Wu Sangui is the most cunning and you must be especially vigilant in dealing with him. If circumstances demand it, don't hesitate to kill the hostage Wu Yingxiong in order to rein him in."

Kangxi took heed of his Nana's words as always and, emboldened by her support, he went ahead and approved Shang's petition in a highly visible manner, hoping the approval would induce the other two Lords to follow suit.

By summer, Wu wanted to test out Kangxi's real intentions, and he petitioned to retire to Manchuria. Kangxi again consulted his Privy Council on how to handle Wu's request, and the majority of the Council took the view that Wu was only playing a game and had no real intention to retire. They believed there was a good chance that he would rise in rebellion once the retirement arrangement was agreed. After long deliberation, Kangxi made his decision.

"Wu has been planning to rebel against our Empire for a long time," he declared. "Even if we allowed his fiefdom to remain in place, it would be naïve of us to think we could tame him. But if we act first and take him by surprise, we may well prevail."

In the early autumn, the Kangxi Emperor issued an order for Wu Sangui to resettle to Manchuria and sent a Court envoy to Yunnan with the order. When Wu received the order, he flew into a rage, cursing Kangxi in the foulest language. The next thing he did was to have the Court envoy beheaded and sent the severed head in a gift box back to Kangxi by courier. Then he wrote letters to Shang Kexi and Shang Zhixin in Guangdong and Geng Jingzhong in Fujian inciting them to rise up against the Manchus in concert with him.

At this time, Wu Sangui's former concubine, Chen Yuanyuan was living a secluded life with the Taoist name of Yu An, in a garden retreat he had built especially for her on the northern outskirts of Kunming. Wu still paid her a visit whenever he was troubled and she was always able to soothe his soul by talking to him about the Taoist Three Treasures (compassion, frugality and modesty) that Yu Lin had taught her. For him, Anfu Garden and

Chen Yuanyuan were like a spiritual refuge. But he still had an innate proclivity for power and worldly treasures and pleasures.

After Yuanyuan had left him the second time, he had moved his wife Madam Zhang out of his Palace into a small mansion so that he could install a harem of young and pretty concubines for his carnal pleasure. He spent an average day drinking and feasting himself into a torpor and watching his concubines perform erotic dances naked.

The villa that Yuanyuan resided in was nestled in an expansive landscaped garden filled with flowering trees, rose hedges and jasmine shrubs, and adorned by small creeks, wooden footbridges and pagodas. In front of the villa's main south-facing entrance was a large pond with gigantic pink and white lotus flowers floating atop wavy green leaves. On the farther side of the pond stood several willow trees, beneath which were placed four stone benches around a stone table. The garden's main gate opened on the east side. The landscaped garden area lay to the west, with a pebble-stone path leading to it.

The main lounge of the villa had been turned into a Taoist shrine where Taoist nuns gathered from time to time to chant and perform rituals. Yuanyuan's private residence, which she shared with two novice nuns, was discreetly tucked away at the back, fronting a small backyard where they grew fruit and vegetables.

One day, a crisp fine day in autumn, Wu appeared in Anfu Garden, drunk and haggard. He had had several sleepless nights, struggling with the risky decision that he had taken. It was true that he had huge prestige and immense wealth. Yet there were always more riches and more glory to be had. Nothing would ever be gained if no risk was taken, he knew.

He found Yuanyuan sitting serenely on one of the stone benches, reciting her daily Taoist prayers. She was dressed in a simple light-grey hemp robe with a dark-blue vest on top, and in her soft white hands she held a string of black prayer beads. On her shaved head she wore a light grey cloth cap that framed her smooth forehead. Her eyes were as clear as water and had a starry glint in them.

He sat himself on the bench next to her.

"I'm going to lead my men to war again," he blurted out. "This time, we'll be fighting the Qing dogs…"

Yuanyuan gasped in shock. She had had a bad feeling the whole morning. So this was it. She fixed her gaze on Wu.

"Do you know you are making a big mistake?" she said with great seriousness. "The Qing Empire has always been generous to you. How can you even think of doing such a thing?"

".....I am a Han and not a Manchu. It is my duty to fight them," he replied.

"But you chose to side with the Manchus long ago. You said the Ming Empire was corrupt to the core and its demise was justified."

He puckered his lips in a show of displeasure, as he hated to be reminded of his defection. "I owe my loyalty to Ming," he persisted. "I'm going to resurrect the Empire…."

"The Qing Empire appreciated the help you gave them and rewarded you most lavishly. Isn't that true?" Her gaze never faltered.

"You have too simple a mind to understand the complexities," he said, irritated. "They now want to withdraw my fiefdom and resettle me to Manchuria. Those ungrateful Qing dogs…."

"The fiefdoms were never meant to be permanent," she said patiently. "There can't be several kingdoms in existence at one time. The Qing Empire naturally would want to assume control sooner or later." She tried to talk some sense into her old friend and the love of her secular life, whom she could now only regard with pity and compassion.

"They could have left my fiefdom alone...."

"Resettlement is not such a bad idea after all. Shang Kexi has agreed."

"You don't understand, woman! Why do you think I built up such a strong army? I want you right here where you belong. I know you are happy here and I can protect you...."

"But I could follow you to Manchuria...."

"The truth is, I can't live..... with lessened power. They're going to divest me of my power once I have resettled. But if I fight now, there's still a chance I can hold on to what I have. With a little luck, I might even become the *Emperor*...." He finally exposed his deepest and best-guarded thought. Yuanyuan was the only person in the world he could bare his soul to.

On hearing his confession, Yuanyuan no longer harbored any hope of convincing him to change his mind. Unbridled ambition was his curse and there was nothing she could do to remove the curse. She knew he was doomed.

"I see that there is no way I can persuade you to change your mind. But can you at least promise me one thing?" she said.

"If I can do it, of course."

"If you don't survive this war, I won't want to live either. Can you leave instructions for us to be buried together?"

He raised his eyes to meet hers and saw the glint that lit up her beautiful placid face. The happy years they had spent together came rushing back in a tide of euphoria. His weary eyes reddened.

"Don't be silly," he replied. "I will live to a ripe old age, and so will you." He held her tight in his arms.

Early the following year, Wu's army, carrying white banners emblazoned with the slogan "Overthrow Qing and Restore Ming", marched out of Yunnan and stormed into the provinces of Hunan and Sichuan. The weak and lazy Qing Bannermen were no match for the well-trained and well-equipped rebel army, and the two provinces were captured with surprising ease and speed.

The Manchu and Mongolian cavalrymen had been steadily losing their agility and efficacy, having grown fat and indolent from an easy lifestyle. Even in Dorgon's days, they had been surpassed by the Chinese Eight Banners, which had since been transformed into the formidable Green Standard Army. It was the Green Standard Army that had helped Shunzhi win the Battle of Nanjing. Kangxi witnessed the floundering of the Manchu Eight Banners in their shameful defeat in Hunan and Sichuan.

Meanwhile, Geng Jingzhong in Fujian was emboldened by the supporting army of 150,000 that crossed the Taiwan Strait to join the Fujian rebellion. The army was led by Zheng Jing, eldest son of Zheng Chenggong, the Ming loyalist who had fled to Taiwan after losing the Battle of Nanjing. He had helped his father drive the Dutch colonists from the island and had built the Kingdom of Tungning there.

In Guangdong, Shang Zhixin also looked set to respond to Wu Sangui's call to rise up against the Qing Empire, and one of Wu's followers, Wang Fushen, led an uprising in the provinces of Guangxi and Shaanxi. Instantly, half of China was plunged once again into bloody warfare. For the Qing rulers, the only saving grace was that most of the Chinese commoners were not sympathetic with the rebel armies, because it was clear that these plundering warlords had no plans other than their own rapacity. Kangxi knew well that the commoners would bear the brunt of brutality if the fighting was allowed to drag on.

He could not but feel that he was treading a thin line. It was the most dangerous situation he had ever found himself in. One false step and he would see his Empire and the Aisin Gioro clan of which he was head pulverized into dust. Cold sweat gathered on his forehead as he contemplated how all that his forefathers had sweated to achieve could so easily slip from his grasp.

As if there was not already enough on his plate, the Chakhar Mongols in Inner Mongolia under the leadership of Abunai and his son Borni chose this moment to become restive, eager to join the empire-wide rebellion. Abunai had earlier been put under house arrest under Kangxi's orders, as he had tried to renege on his predecessor's vow of allegiance to the Qing Empire. In Hong Taiji's time, intermarriage had been used as a means of keeping peace in this region, but now the marital bonds were losing their magic touch.

Bumbutai was being briefed on a daily basis on the situation. One day before dawn broke, she went to Kangxi's bed chambers in the Palace of Heavenly Purity to speak with him. Intuition fed her fears as she felt her grandson's despair at the turmoil he faced. As she arrived, he was already up and about to leave for Cining Palace. They sat down together in the main reception room.

"Xuanye, I've received news that Abunai and Borni are planning on taking Mukden. Mukden is our secondary capital and we must make it our priority to protect it."

"I know, Nana. But our forces are already spread thin to deal with the rebellions...." He was obviously stymied for a solution.

"I would suggest you send Tuhai to lead a team to deal with them. His family used to live in Mukden and he spent his childhood and youth there. So he knows the territory well."

"Oh, I hadn't thought of him. Yes, he should be the right choice."

"I will urge my Khorchin Mongol relatives to assist him. Have you ordered the execution of Wu Sangui's son yet?"

"Not yet. I will do that today." He was still feeling overwhelmed by his sense of responsibility and fear of failure.

"That should help to curb Wu Sangui's arrogance," she added, hoping to inject a dose of confidence into her grandson. "I wonder if we should appoint Han commanders for our Banner forces in the south and the southwest to replace Manchu commanders? It is clear that we cannot rely on them. I think the Green Standard Army would perform better under Han command. This is no time for pride."

Bumbutai had been mulling this for a long time and she surmised that Kangxi's inaction with regard to military command was due to resistance from his Privy Council.

"Nana, thank you. I did propose this idea again to the Council. They were not receptive when I raised it before."

"Go ahead and issue the orders and I'll try to convince the Council members in private. I will also write to my clansmen to seek their help."

As if chancing upon a glitter of light in a pitch-dark tunnel, Kangxi could now at least find his bearings.

The severed head of Wu's son, Wu Yingxiong, was prominently displayed in the execution ground of Beijing. When the news reached Wu Sangui, he broke down in grief, effectively bringing the war to a short halt. Then Kangxi offered Wu and his family amnesty if he agreed to surrender. Wu flatly turned down the offer.

In the spring of the fourteenth year of the Kangxi reign, Borni led an armed force of three thousand Chakhars into Mukden and released Abunai from imprisonment. Tuhai had put together a motley team of untrained Bannermen and household bondservants and managed somehow to put up an effective defense, with discreet help from Khorchin Mongols.

One day, word came to Tuhai's camp that Borni had been stabbed to death by a Khorchin cavalryman inside his own camp. Within days, Tuhai's men captured Abunai and drove the Chakhars out of Mukden. Thereupon, Kangxi ordered that

Abunai and all Chakhar royal males be executed and their royal females and children enslaved with the exception of Manchu Princesses. The Chakhar Mongols were henceforth put under the Qing Empire's direct control.

In the midst of this turmoil, Kangxi's beloved Empress passed away at the age of twenty-one, while giving birth to her second son. By this time, five of his sons had died in infancy and only one, born of Concubine Hui, had survived. Her death devastated him. Their intimate bond had been sentimental as much as spiritual, and the premature death of her first-born a couple of years earlier had already broken his heart.

Severely depressed, he went to visit his newborn son several days after his Empress had passed away. Watching the vulnerable tiny bundle flailing its limbs happily in its cot, he placed his little finger in its tiny hand and felt the needy infantile grip. A paternal flame lit up his heart, and made him feel that all he wanted was to shower all his love and attention on the little being who had just lost his mother.

"I will protect you and love you, little one," he whispered as he bent down to kiss the infant's forehead. "There's nothing for you to fear."

He couldn't wait for the boy to grow up so he could teach him all of his skills and life's lessons. In the following year, he made this infant son, Yinreng, the Crown Prince. It was a way of showing gratitude to his late Empress.

But after the mourning period was over, Kangxi had to plunge right back into the battle with the Feudal Lords which had long been stalemated. Kangxi began writing messages in his own hand openly reprimanding the Manchu Bannermen for their inferior performance and lavishing praise on the Han Green Standard Army for their valor. He ordered the execution of one Manchu general for desertion. Then the warlord in Fujian

Province, Shang Zhixin, who had been sitting on the fence and now seeing the Qing forces in such a bind, decided to jump in. Kangxi despaired. Morale in the Qing Army was at its lowest ebb. There were even posters pasted on walls in many towns criticizing the Emperor.

Then, the winds of war began to shift. Internal strife started to infect Wu's rebel army as incessant fighting wore down the rebels' spirits. Many started to question their allegiance to Wu. Then Wu's lieutenant Wang Fushen decided it was expedient to change sides and Kangxi immediately appointed him as a Green Standard Commander charged him with crushing Wu's army. He also spread the word that rebel soldiers who surrendered would be spared punishment and be assimilated into the Green Standard Army. This enticed a great number of the beleaguered rebels to defect. The change of heart had a rippling effect.

Then Geng Jingzhong in Fujian surrendered a few months later, followed by Shang Zhixin. Zheng Jing, the son of Zheng Chenggong, retreated back to Taiwan.

In the case of Geng and Shang, Kangxi renegedon his promise of leniency. Geng was executed by slicing and Shang was forced to commit suicide in return for having his family spared. Kangxi felt certain that most of his Han subjects despised these two outlaws and would applaud his decision. They did.

After four years of gruesome fighting, the Qing forces finally managed to shift from the defensive to the offensive and moved to recover many towns. Kangxi could now concentrate his forces on Wu Sangui. Before long, Wu saw that his venture was nearing total ruin, but rather than admit to defeat, he instead declared himself emperor of the newly-established Great Zhou dynasty in Hengzhou in Hunan Province.

TWENTY-EIGHT

WITH THE FEUDAL LORD situation generally under control, Kangxi could at long last spare a little time to attend to his harem. Since the death of his first Empress, the prestigious post had been left unfilled. Now, after consulting his grandmother, he issued an edict bestowing the title of Empress on Ebilun's daughter from the Niohuru clan. Bumbutai and Kangxi concurred that there was a need to reinforce this powerful clan's support for the Emperor. The edict also granted titles to eight Concubines.

Under the edict, Concubine Tunggiya, his first cousin and daughter of his birth mother's full brother, was the only one granted the title of Noble Consort, while the other seven, including Concubine Hui, were granted the title of Imperial Concubine, which was one rank below the title of Consort. From this edict, it was clear that Noble Consort Tunggiya had a special place in Kangxi's heart and also had the approval of the Grand Empress Dowager.

As Kangxi matured into a man, he began to realize that infatuation with physical beauty was a fragile sentiment, too shaky a foundation for a lasting bond. His once-flaming love for Concubine Hui dimmed to a mere flicker. But he still sought a spiritual bond with another woman. Unfortunately, he could find no such spark in his relationship with his second Empress and his heart was for a couple of years enveloped in wistful solitude. As destiny dictated, that situation would change when he was reunited with his childhood playmate and first cousin, Hexian from the Tunggiya clan.

One day the previous autumn, Kangxi's maternal uncle, who was the Minister of Defense, brought his daughter Hexian and her younger brother Longkodo to the Forbidden City to attend a birthday celebration for the Empress Dowager. The three cousins had been playmates from the days when Kangxi was a toddler, although he had not seen these two cousins for several years. When he saw Hexian this day, he almost couldn't recognize her. The withdrawn caterpillar he had known had morphed into a dazzling butterfly.

The Tunggiya clan had lived among the Hans for many generations in northeast China and generally viewed themselves as Hans. In her childhood, Hexian had been taught Chinese literature and history by her father and Manchu history by her mother, who was from the renowned Manchu Heseri clan. She was thus fully bilingual and well-versed in the Four Books and Five Classics, Chinese poetry and calligraphy.

When the formal birthday banquet was over, Kangxi invited his cousins to his Palace for a reunion chat. Having ordered his eunuch to bring jasmine tea and dishes of sweet meats, he couldn't wait to show his cousins scrolls of his best calligraphy, each of which featured a different Tang poem.

Longkodo admired the works, while admitting that he had never previously read any of the poems. Hexian quietly looked at the first scroll, and with confidence, announced the poem's title and the name of the poet who had written it. She did the same with all the remaining scrolls. Kangxi was heartily glad to find that she had such deep knowledge of Chinese poetry. He heaped praise on her, and her face bloomed like a budding pink lotus. Planting his unabashed gaze on her, he was spellbound by her almond eyes, which were dark pools that drew in all the light and reflected it in a starry glint. The inner chords of his heart vibrated with her every smile. He tried hard to appear unaffected and engaged Longkodo in a chat about gyrfalcon hunting. The young lad responded enthusiastically and the two made a pact to go hunting together once the Feudal Lord Wars were over.

While they talked, he couldn't help now and then sneaking a look at the girl from the corner of his eye. The two young men began teasing each other about their childhood pranks, and she joined in without the slightest sense of reserve. Polite though she was, she didn't spare them the embarrassment of being reminded how they used to bully her.

They talked until near midnight. As the guests were rising to say farewell, Kangxi faced Hexian and handed her one of the calligraphy scrolls as a souvenir. It was a lyrical poem titled *Eternal Pining* by Tang poet Bai Juyi.

A few months later, around the lunar New Year, Hexian became Imperial Concubine Tunggiya. Once she entered the Inner Palaces, she quickly gained the favor of the Grand Empress Dowager who found her modest, gracious and cultured. Kangxi felt extremely comfortable around her and the two soon became inseparable soul mates. Thus, it was no surprise that before long she was granted the title of Noble Consort.

In the early spring of the following year, Kangxi's second Empress became ill. After struggling with the sickness for a month, she gave up and passed over to the other world. She had only carried the Empress title for six months. On Kangxi's order, Noble Consort Tunggiya took up the leading role in the Inner Palaces with no title change.

During the winter, one of the untitled Concubines, who had previously been a maid-in-waiting, gave birth to Kangxi's fourth surviving son Yinzhen, who would one day become the Yongzheng Emperor. Complying with Inner Palaces rules and with the birth mother's consent, Noble Consort Tunggiya, who was then still childless, took the role of foster mother to the infant son, whom she would care for and educate for ten years. At her request, Kangxi granted the birth mother the title of Imperial Concubine De.

By nature a kind and generous soul, Hexian employed tact, wit, diligence and devotion in discharging her duties as the head of the Inner Palaces. She set an example of frugality which pleased Bumbutai very much, as it reminded her of Shunzhi's Consort Donggo. While taking care of Prince Yinzhen and two of the other Princes, she also looked after the aging Grand Empress Dowager, and oversaw peaceful co-existence among the numerous Concubines. Whenever there was any dispute between two Concubines, she would patiently speak to each and ask: "Why are you doing this? How would you feel if the same were done to you?" And the dispute would somehow fade away.

As much as Kangxi treated her like an Empress in many ways, there were times when Hexian succumbed to bouts of jealousy. As Emperor, Kangxi naturally had unfettered freedom to sow his seed however he pleased in the Inner Palaces. Having exceptional good looks and a kind disposition just made him that much more of a fetish of worship in his harem. There was nothing she could do about the fact that she shared him with a host of other beautiful women. Still, acceptance didn't mean immunity from hurt.

On one occasion a couple of years into her Palace life, Kangxi's chief eunuch came to fetch her to the Emperor's bed chambers. As they passed the main chamber's latticed doors, she heard a woman's laughter ringing from inside.

While preparing her for the bed by brushing her hair and clothing her in a white silk robe, the eunuch, noticing her displeasure, explained that his master had summoned both

Imperial Concubine Rong and herself for that night. He said the Emperor liked Imperial Concubine Rong because she was fertile, having already borne the Emperor five sons and one daughter, although four of the sons had died in infancy. The eunuch's words touched a nerve in her and tears swelled in her eyes.

When Imperial Concubine Rong left the bed chambers, the chief eunuch quickly changed the bedding and another eunuch helped the Emperor clean himself in his private bath area. Then he came back to fetch her and ushered her to the bed. As she sat on the edge of the bed waiting for him, she could not stop her tears.

"What's the matter, Hexian?" he asked gently. "Why are you crying?"

"Your Imperial Highness, please forgive me," she sobbed. "I couldn't control myself. I was just thinking how nice it would be if you and I were commoners living an ordinary life."

Her words touched Kangxi profoundly.

"I know. Sometimes I think about that too. We could spend our days in a little house of our own. I would tend to the farm and you would take care of household chores. We could read poetry in our free time, or go riding in the forest… But you know I cannot change my destiny."

"Your Highness, a dream is only a dream and it's no good indulging in it. You were destined to do great things. It is your calling to take care of your subjects."

"No one understands me better than you do, Hexian. Tell me, what is bothering you? Your eyes tell me you're troubled."

"It's just that sometimes… I feel…..jealous…." She lowered her eyes.

"Oh, you mean Concubine Rong?"

"Yes. No… I mean sometimes… You have so many women, I'm not sure if you really care about me."

"Hexian, of course I care about you! You are so important to me. I could not go on without you. It's the truth." He wiped the tears from her face and tenderly caressed her cheeks.

"But the other Concubines must be important to you too?"

"Never as important as you. You and I understand each other well, we can talk all night and you have my complete trust. With the others, the relationship is purely carnal. I cannot talk to them. But I need them to bear me sons, for the sake of the Empire." He gently swept a few tendrils of her hair away from her face and kissed her on her lips.

"If I cannot produce a son, would you still care for me?"

"My feelings for you are from my heart, unconditional. If you cannot bear me a son, you are free to adopt one from the other Concubines. You and I will have many sons and daughters and many, many grandchildren," he said, and smiled cheerfully.

"Do you still miss your first Empress?"

He paused and a cloud passed over his face. "Yes, sometimes. But since you came, a lot less. Hexian, I would have made you Empress if not for a curse. I am a jinx… on my Empresses." He revealed his worst fear with reluctance."To protect you, I must not confer the title on you."

"Your Highness, isn't that a bit superstitious?"

"I knew you would say that. But my two Empresses both died young. I would not be able to stand it if my third Empress ended up the same way. I hope you don't mind…."

"You know I don't care about titles," she said. "All I care is that you will love me always. But I am so grateful for your concern for me."

For the first time, she saw a vulnerable streak in his eyes and she felt she would be willing to die for him. She certainly couldn't resist him now. As she snuggled up to him, he put one arm around her waist and used the other hand to pull down the bed curtains.

Wu Sangui had always cherished the dream of becoming an emperor. And in his quest, he had never felt the need for friends. He was a man of energy and even of violence, born to make war, and set little store in friendship. Thus his soldiers fought for him not because they honored him as a man of integrity, but because of his promise of material reward. He understood this well, and thus, in his steady slide towards disaster, clung to the illusion that promises of wealth could somehow work magic. After declaring himself the Great Zhou Emperor, he granted ministerial posts and honorable titles to his generals and high-ranked officials to lure them to stay with him. But the Qing forces prepared to lay siege to the loosely-guarded town of Hengzhou.

A few months later, Wu fell sick from exhaustion and was bedridden. His followers dissipated, but he did not forget that there was still one person who would be faithful to him regardless of what befell him. He had not seen her since their meeting in Anfu Garden several years before. Recalling the promise that he had made her, he struggled out of bed and wrote a letter to his grandson, Wu Shifan, asking him to come to Hengzhou to take up the throne and asked to be buried on Mount Shang in due time, leaving a space in his burial ground for Chen Yuanyuan. In a trembling hand, he also wrote a final letter to his beloved woman, begging her not to take her own life and entrusting to her care his only grandson.

Just days after the two letters were dispatched, Wu Sangui passed away, and his grandson arrived only to attend the funeral in a cursory ceremony taking up the throne of Great Zhou. But the town was on the verge of being recaptured by the Qing Army and Wu Shifan had to flee with the corpse of his grandfather in a coffin back to his redoubt in mountainous Yunnan. He selected a tranquil area on Mount Shang to erect a tombstone, and buried the coffin underground, leaving space on the side for another coffin.

It was deep autumn and the foothills of Mount Shang echoed in a lyric poem of crimson, amber and gold. Anfu Garden perched tranquilly on those foliage-clad hills as if it belonged to another time, another space. The din of wars and wails of human sufferings were mercifully held at bay, leaving this cloister in a kind of peace that was at once mystic and ordinary.

In her bed chamber, Yuanyuan was alarmed to see an envelope with a burned corner placed on her side table. She shuddered, being certain it was from Wu. Earlier she had heard news that Wu was losing his battles and had been anticipating this day. She shuddered and leaned on her bed post for support.

Picking up an ink slab, she mechanically ground it in the ink plate with a little water, as her head swam with disjointed thoughts. She felt compelled to write her afflicted life out before saying a final farewell. Through the whole night, her brush flew furiously over the sheets of paper in front of her, as she discarded draft after draft. By the time the final version of her poem was finished, shards of dawn were breaking in through the window. She blew out the candle. In the grey light, she read the poem aloud, unlocking cascades of emotions within her:

Hers was a life of sad songs that bring tears to the gods.
Her mother died as she was born; her father left her too.
Her scrawny aunt, poor as she was, took her in only to give her up.
To a brothel she went, where men feasted on her beauty not her soul.
Her flowering youth brought her no brighter hope.
Tossed between rich and royal lords, she was just an object sold.
Wu then came along, and a new page began.
But happiness was nothing but a short tease;
Soon molesting hands fell on her again, and into ignominy she sank.

When Wu disowned her that night in the battle camp,
Her heart died a death of a thousand slashes.
But for Yu Lin's merciful heart, she could not hope to see the light again.
Solitary mirth having now been tasted,
Her worthless shell must return to the netherland.

In the mid-morning, she took a bath and changed into fresh garments. Sitting on her bed, she chanted Taoist prayers for a long time. When that was done, she quietly closed the doors and from her wooden chest took out a long rope. Standing on a stool, she tried several times to loop it through the ceiling beam, but without success. She sat down on the stool to rest. Then a few more times she tried and when finally the rope looped over, she made a noose.

Barely had she put her head inside the noose when someone rammed open the doors and bolted in. It was the monk Yu Lin.

It happened that one of the two novice nuns had noticed the envelope and the devastated expression on her face. She had sensed something was wrong. When Yuanyuan did not appear for breakfast as usual, she had gone to take a peek inside her bed chamber through a chink in the door. She had witnessed the older nun's first fumblings with the rope, and had run all the way to the Temple of the Three Sages to fetch Yu Lin.

The monk grabbed her legs and eased her down while the novice nun who had brought Yu Lin went to fetch a cup of tea for her. Glancing at the unopened letter, Yu Lin picked it up and handed it to her, saying in a soft voice:

"Don't you want to read this?"

He tore open the envelope for her and as she began reading Wu's final letter, tears swelled in her eyes. Yu Lin had been her Taoist teacher for many years. All the tragic events that had scarred her life were well known to him.

"Yuanyuan, if you want to talk, I am right here to listen," he said.

"Master Yu, I made Lord Wu a promise and I just wanted to make good that promise," she said ruefully as she finished reading.

Yu took a quick look through Wu's letter and shook his head.

"Lord Wu is right," he said. "Taking your own life serves no purpose. Now that he has entrusted you with his grandson, you owe him a duty as an old friend. This is a chance too to practice compassion as a Taoist."

"I have to thank you, Master Yu, for saving my worthless life. I also owe you a big debt of gratitude for your teachings over the years. I tried hard to make Lord Wu understand those lessons too. It is a pity he was always too wrapped up in his worldly affairs."

"It is my calling to be your spiritual guide. I am just glad that I came in time to prevent a tragic mistake. Each one of us follows his or her predestined path. You must not blame yourself for his choices."

"Maybe you're right. I must take good care of Shifan. I owe my life to you, Master Yu."

"Each of us has his or her own worth. Even a small ant values its life. You must remember your own worth and value your life, Yuanyuan."

Yu Lin felt profound compassion for his world-weary student.

"Yes, as long as Shifan walks the earth, I have a duty to take care of him. I owe that duty to Lord Wu."

In the autumn three years later, the Green Standard Army, overran the remaining rebel-occupied parts of Hunan, Guangxi and Sichuan provinces and then forged its way into the mountainous province of Yunnan in a three-pronged attack. Han generals were the Commanders of all three forces.

On the rebel side, Wu Shifan was having a hard time leading his late grandfather's soldiers, who viewed him with distrust and disdain. Had the rebels been more united, the provincial capital of Kunming would have stood a good chance of resisting the Qing onslaught. But within a couple of months of the launch of attacks, the Green Standard Army breached the rebel lines at Mount Wuhua, the main defensive position, and laid siege to Kunming. Wu Shifan, young and inexperienced, had no one to turn to for advice as his army crumbled into total disarray. He was convinced his end was close but was anxious to first warn his foster grandmother, Madam Chen Yuanyuan, to take flight. She was his only close relative left and she had always been kind to him, regularly bringing him fresh fruit and vegetables that she grew in her garden.

He changed into peasant clothes, smeared dirt on his face and headed on foot towards Anfu Garden, two days' walk away. When he saw the aging nun's stooped silhouette by the side of the lotus pond, he felt a sting in his heart. Yuanyuan's face sagged as she saw him. He stepped forward and went down on his knees.

"Grandmother, the Qing Army has laid siege to the town," he wailed. "It is only a matter of days before they attack. I have come to tell you to leave while you still can…"

"No matter, no matter, Shifan," she interrupted him, and helped him back onto his feet. "No need to worry about me. What are you going to do now?"

"I will fight to the end with my soldiers," he replied as convincingly as possible.

Her legs felt weak and she had to sit down on the stone ledge of the pond. She tried to think but her thoughts were all tangled up. There was nothing she could do to save Wu's grandson. Her face went ashen white.

"It is the will of the heavens," she said feebly. "You are still so young. It's not fair for you...."

She took the young man into her arms and patted him on the back.

"I won't go anywhere, Shifan. This is my home, my only home."

When they had both exhausted all comforting words and tears, Wu Shifan bade farewell and left. He made his way to the small hill where he had buried his grandfather, knelt down before it and bowed three times. Then he took a vial from his sleeve, removed the lid and drank all its liquid content in one gulp.

With Wu Shifan gone, Yuanyuan stared absent-mindedly into the lotus pond, which was now dismally barren of flowers. After what seemed like a long time, she slipped quietly into her bed chamber, making sure not to be noticed. She took out the same rope from the wooden chest in which she kept her beddings. She was aware that both the novice nuns were in the garden outside her window tending vegetables, but she knew that this time her feat would not be bungled.

The next day, Wu Shifan's lifeless body was discovered by a soldier who had come to pay respects to Wu Sangui's tomb. He immediately reported the death to his superior and on the following day the rebel army waved flags of surrender on the look-out terrace of the fortress. The soldiers then opened the gates to the Green Standard Army and the eight-year long insurrection of the Warlords finally ended. In the aftermath, Wu Shifan's severed head was placed on a pike for public display in the main execution ground of Beijing. Wu Sangui's tomb was broken open and his corpse chopped into little pieces and placed on public display in all the southwestern provinces where the revolt had taken place. The Qing soldiers tried in vain to locate Chen Yuanyuan or her corpse.

Twenty-nine

With peace finally restored, Kangxi was considering promoting Noble Consort Tunggiya to the position of Imperial Noble Consort as a gesture of gratitude for her hard work in managing the Inner Palaces. When he went to his Nana to ask for permission, he had no idea that he was about to engage in his first-ever fight with her.

He found his Nana in her Palace garden tending to the lilies. After making obeisance, he told her that he wanted to grant his cousin the title of Imperial Noble Consort. She responded with a vexed expression.

"Why, Xuanye? In what way has she displeased you? I would have thought she deserved no less than the Empress title." She scanned her grandson's face for clues as to the reason for his inexplicable unfairness towards his beloved companion.

He winced at the retort and was lost for words, as he obviously was not prepared for such a question. He was reluctant to give the true reason, for fear that his Nana might think him silly.

"Well? What is the problem with making Hexian your Empress? The Inner Palaces have never been this orderly and peaceful as far as I can remember, and it is all due to her hard work and her wise diplomacy. She deserves the title. If you have someone else in mind, I would definitely forbid it." Her face hardened as she spoke.

"Nana, no, I don't have anyone else in mind. It's just that...."

the others are being promoted by one rank only. If I make Hexian Empress, it would a promotion of two ranks up for her. The others might see that as favoritism." It was a reasonable excuse.

"Xuanye, it is not that I wish to meddle with your Inner Palaces. I'm getting too old to care about these trivial things. But my judgment of people has not been impaired. All I want to say is that Hexian is an intelligent and generous woman and you need her right by your side for as long as you live. She deserves to be treated right."

"I know she does. No one values her more than I do. Trust me, Nana."

"The Empress post has been empty for three years now, and that is inappropriate. I have nothing further to say." She waved him away in exasperation.

It broke his heart to see her so upset. In his memory, she had never before shown disappointment in him.

"Nana, please believe me, there is no woman I love and respect more than Hexian. I know what I'm doing." He was desolate.

"I hope so, Xuanye. A great woman is not easy to find. By the way, have they found Chen Yuanyuan yet? Doesn't anybody know her whereabouts or what happened to her?"

"No, Nana. There is no news of her. But the search continues." He was glad that she had changed the subject.

"If she's still alive, I would very much like to meet her. I have heard that she is a brave woman with a mind of her own."

"My guess is that she probably killed herself out of loyalty to Wu Sangui."

"Oh, that reminds me. Xuanye, please summon the monk Yu Lin to come to the South Park Retreat to meet with me. I heard that he was a teacher to Chen. He should know what happened to her. I would like to talk to him."

"I will do so at once, Nana. If Chen is still alive, you would want to spare her life?"

"Yes, Xuanye, I would want that. She has had an unspeakably tragic life."

"You are right, Nana. We should spare her. Oh, before I forget, there is one more thing that I came to talk to you about. The Court and I have decided that you should be honored with two prefixes to your title for your invaluable advice during the rebellions." He was hoping this would improve his Nana's mood somewhat.

She looked tenderly into his eyes, her heart aching with love.

"Xuanye, over these eight years, you have sweated and toiled," she said. "With your wit and your careful strategies, you succeeded in ending the rebellions. If anyone should be honored, it is you. You must not forget to properly reward your generals and soldiers, especially those who lost their lives for you and the Empire. Please thank the Court on my behalf. My role has always been simply supportive and my place is in the Inner Palaces."

Kangxi was speechless at the consistency of her humility in spirit, words and actions. He could not but prostrate himself before her.

It was a long time since Bumbutai had last visited the South Park Retreat and she was elated to be back. It was a clear cold day in winter. Her meeting with Yu Lin was fixed for the following day and she had come a day early to savor the serene ambience of the vast expanses of snow-covered forest against a speckless cerulean sky. In a couple of months, she would be turning sixty-nine, but many of the events of her life seemed to have happened only a short while ago. It was hard for her to believe that she had aged so much.

She remembered most vividly that day she had come here with Little Jade. She had still been nimble and full of life then. This time, Sumalagu was with her, and they travelled together in a carriage instead of on horseback.

Upon arrival at the Park Retreat, they had a short rest and then headed out for a stroll together. They strolled slowly toward the spot where the elaphures were kept, on the riverbank. The snow made the walking a lot harder than it was in more clement weather, and when they reached the fences holding in the animals, Bumbutai was quite out of breath. Sumalagu, who had a stronger constitution, would have no problem with the walking if it was not for the formal attire she now wore. Several years earlier, Bumbutai had made her a princess and ever since she had been complaining about having to wear the stiff Manchu robes and how they impeded her movements. In her heart, though, she could not be more grateful, as it was the highest honor a maid could ever dream of receiving. Still she saw an opportunity to jest with her mistress.

"Your Highness, now you know why I prefer wearing maids' clothes! Don't you faint on me, now. I am not going to be able to carry you back to the Retreat in this stupid robe."

"Don't you worry, Suma. I'm quite alright. I only need… to catch… my breath. But you must dress… according to your…. status." She spouted her words intermittently, making a face at her beloved companion.

"Maybe we could borrow two horses from the forest wardens," Sumalagu suggested. "Riding should be easier than walking. What do you think?"

"That's a good idea. Go ahead and ask them. I'll wait here."

The old maid was soon back with two saddled horses, and having mounted them, mistress and maid trotted slowly side-by-side upstream along the riverbank, which sloped gently upwards into the densely forested hills. There was a vast aviary tucked away deep near a waterfall where gyrfalcons were kept and trained. Sufficiently trained falcons would be let free in the

Park Retreat and as their horses plodded on leisurely, some of these majestic birds hovered in a playful frolic over their heads.

"I'm so glad that Dorgon had built this beautiful hunting park," Bumbutai said. She was feeling talkative than she had for a long while. "It is here that I feel closest to Eternal Blue Sky. This place always welcomes me with open arms."

"You still miss him, don't you?" Sumalagu said in a half probing way, shooting an oblique glance at her mistress.

"I would be lying if I said I no longer do. A part of me will always miss him."

"He loved you to his last breath, although he was always too proud to show it."

"I guess he was torn between his love for me and his hatred of me. I never blamed him, because I understood better than anyone else why he was always so bitter. Sadly, I was part of the cause for that bitterness."

"Yes. Eternal Blue Sky sometimes plays jokes on lovers. If you two had been born in commoners' families, things would have turned out so differently." Sumalagu was the only one who knew Bumbutai's life inside out, or almost.

"Sometimes I still wonder what would have happened if you hadn't let Hong Taiji take away Dorgon's letter and brought it to me. Would I have eloped with him?"

"I dare say that you would have, at your age then. But Eternal Blue Sky had other plans for you. Everything was meant to be." The old maid was secretly proud that she had had a hand in deciding her mistress's fate, but allowed Eternal Blue Sky to take the credit, or the blame.

"After all is said and done, I'm grateful to Eternal Blue Sky for letting me keep a part of Dorgon....."

"I'm not sure I know what you're referring to?"

"My second daughter... Princess Shuhui... was... by him."

"Is that….. really true… Bumbutai? Oh my Buddha!" Sumalagu's sturdy body almost keeled over on hearing her mistress's shocking revelation.

"Swear on your life, Suma, that your lips are sealed on this," Bumbutai warned sternly.

"Yes, yes, I swear, I swear. But may I say that I'm happy for you?"

Sumalagu understood how much this daughter must mean to Bumbutai, especially when her eldest daughter had passed away three years earlier, and her youngest one had died in childhood. More importantly for her, Shuhui was Dorgon's flesh and blood.

"Suma, I'm just glad to have unloaded this burden of a secret at long last. I gave him a daughter, but I let him pass on without ever knowing it. That is why I feel I owe him so much." A cloud of deep contrition swept across her face.

"Bumbutai, you did a lot for him too. You protected him… And you did become his wife after all, didn't you?"

"He did make some big mistakes. But I also let my own interests guide me…"

"It was the timing and circumstances that tormented you two so. Neither one should take the blame. It was the will of Eternal Blue Sky."

"Sometimes I do feel that there are invisible forces that have pushed me along a pre-laid path. But I would be a hypocrite if I said I didn't make active choices in some situations."

"If you don't want to go insane, you've got to believe in something, be it Eternal Blue Sky, or Buddha, or the Tao."

"My only wish is for Shuhui to live happily in Mongolia with her husband. I will never burden her with my generation's miseries. I will pray to Eternal Blue Sky to keep her in its care."

"Sometimes it is best for a secret to forever remain a secret. Bumbutai, you had heavy obligations on your shoulders and you did all in your power to fulfill them. Mongolia and the Qing Empire cannot ask any more of you. They should take pride in you and honor you for what you've done."

"Speaking of pride, Xuanye is truly the pride of my life. I have to thank you, Suma, for playing a part in raising him."

Her face lit up the moment she talked about her grandson.

"He owes that to his hard work and talent," said the humble maid proudly. "I take no credit. He will be the greatest Emperor in history."

When they reached a clearing, they dismounted and sat resting on a flat boulder. As they chatted, the sun was preparing to take a rest. Both felt refreshed from the mountain air and the aura of the natural habitat. But a stinging evening chill began to graze their faces and they mounted their horses and cantered back to the Retreat.

The next day, Bumbutai met Yu Lin in the main reception hall of the Retreat. She had met him once before when he had appeared to report on his successful prohibition of Shunzhi being ordained as a monk. But she was surprised to see his radiant features despite his graying hair. He had about him an air that was tinged with poetic melancholy. When the etiquette of greetings was over, she asked him the direct question.

"Master Yu, the reason I asked to see you is that I would like to know the whereabouts of Chen Yuanyuan. I heard that you were a teacher to her for a while and thought you might have news of her."

"Venerable Highness, I am afraid I cannot be of much help, as I have been out of touch with her for a few years now," he said circumspectly, not daring to speak the truth lest the rulers had malevolent intent to desecrate Yuanyuan's remains.

Bumbutai's sharp skills of observation told her at once that he was lying. So she tried another approach.

"I have recently read the popular narrative poem *Song of Yuanyuan* by the poet Wu Weiye and am very much impressed. I think she is a remarkably strong woman who stood up to the worst of afflictions. I also heard that she is a gifted poet. So I was thinking that perhaps we might make her a study companion for the Emperor's Consorts."

The Empress Dowager's sincere tone had a disarming effect on Yu Lin and made him feel a lot more at ease.

"Venerable Highness, I beg your forgiveness," he replied in a choked voice. "I refrained from telling the truth because I wanted to protect Yuanyuan's remains." He couldn't hold back his tears as he prostrated himself. Bumbutai gently bade him rise and speak, saying there was no need for formality.

Then he told her all that had happened, starting from the day Wu Sangui first visited Yuanyuan in Anfu Garden up to the day she hanged herself for the second time. He did not forget to mention that she had tried her best to dissuade Wu from inciting the revolt. Yu Lin said he had buried her inside Anfu Garden, beneath the largest cherry blossom tree.

When he came to the end of the story, he took out a scroll on which Yuanyuan had penned her own elegy and showed it to the Empress Dowager. She read it eagerly, savoring every word. Her eyes became red-rimmed and she gave out a deep sigh.

"Life was cruel to Chen Yuanyuan. She was very much a victim of a bigoted society. But there was little she could have done to change things. She did nothing that was ignoble. In the end, she had the courage to live up to her principles. In my opinion, she was a much more respectable person than Wu Sangui."

She was in a pensive mood, recalling how Kangxi had tried to liberate Han women from the torturous and deforming practice of foot-binding. But his good intentions were no match for deeply entrenched ignorance that had calcified with time.

Then she turned to Yu Lin.

"Master Yu, you can rest assured that I will not reveal her burial place to anyone. I will order a halt to the search for her. She deserves to have a peaceful resting place."

"Venerable Highness, I bow to you on behalf of Yuanyuan for your great kindness."

"Master Yu, there was another thing that I wanted to speak to you about. I am interested in Laozi's *Daodejing*. Would you care to give me and the Emperor's Consorts Taoism lessons here, say four times a month? I would love so much to escape the Palaces and come out here for the fresh air."

"Venerable Highness, I would be too honored to be of such service." He greatly admired the Empress Dowager for her thirst for knowledge even at such an advanced age. He had been similarly amazed at Shunzhi's sharp intelligence, and knew now where it had come from. Never in his life had he encountered a more open-minded and more cultured woman. No wonder the Emperor loved and respected his grandmother so much. The Aisin Gioro clan, he thought, was fortunate to have such an enlightened educator and mentor for the reigning Emperor.

Thirty

When China was restored to relative peace, Kangxi set his eyes on the island of Taiwan, to which Zheng Jing had fled when the Green Standard Army had defeated his army along with the Fujian rebels. Zheng Jing had meanwhile died of illness and had been succeeded by his son, Zheng Keshuang. Kangxi felt that the coastal ports of Fuzhou and Amoy would never have peace until Zheng's Kingdom of Tungning in Taiwan was placed under Qing's control.

After consulting his trusted Han ministers in the Ministry of Defense, he appointed Admiral Shi Lang as the Naval Commander to lead a naval fleet of three hundred battleships to conquer Taiwan. Shi Lang had once served in Zheng Chenggong's naval force for a short time, and after he defected to the Qing thirty-seven years earlier, Zheng killed Shi Lang's father, brother and son. Kangxi knew there was no one more eager than Shi Lang, a skilled naval officer, to lead the Qing navy and see the Zheng family vanquished.

As a matter of courtesy, Kangxi consulted his Nana about his choice of Naval Commander, and she endorsed it without hesitation, being fully confident now of his shrewdness in decision-making.

After meticulous preparations, Shi Lang led his fleet and an army of twenty thousand soldiers out into the Taiwan Strait in the direction of the Penghu islands. Within days, his fleet had crushed the enemy's ships. Their incursion over the much larger island of Taiwan also met with little resistance and it fell under Qing rule.

While Kangxi had no mercy for two-timing traitors like the three Warlords, he was always ready to be lenient towards die-hard Ming loyalists who were prepared to pledge allegiance to the Qing. Granting him an honorary title of "Duke", Kangxi attached Zheng and his soldiers to the Green Standard Army.

Before the news of victory in the Battle of Penghu reached Kangxi, he had been dealt another blow in his private life.

Imperial Noble Consort Tunggiya gave birth to a beautiful daughter on an early summer day. She had been looking forward to the day so eagerly, it put a luminous glow on her smiling face. How she and Xuanye would love this precious child! She had waited for this moment for six years, and finally her most cherished wish was to be granted.

All through her pregnancy she had kept busy sewing and embroidering clothes for the coming infant. She knew Xuanye was just as excited as she was, although he had left a couple of days earlier with his Nana on a trip to the Kharahotun Mountain Retreat in Jehol. She was in labor for half a day when finally her bundle of joy made her grand entry. The little thing had large, dark almond eyes, just like hers, and silky soft, black, curly hair. Tears of gratitude filled her eyes as she looked down at her newborn.

On the tenth day, the baby bloomed into a little pink beauty whose nimble hands and feet wouldn't stop waggling to draw attention. The mother imagined her daughter would grow up to be a good rider just like her father. She was visualizing the expression on Xuanye's face when he got to see his infant daughter. In another twelve days he would be back.

Bumbutai had wanted to take this trip for a long time and she had been waiting impatiently for the revolt of the warlords to be put down so that Xuanye would be free to accompany her. She had just passed her seventieth birthday and her health was not as robust as it once was. While she could still move about with relative ease, she was anxious to visit once again the place where Dorgon's life had tragically ended.

Her life had always been lived for other people and never for herself. For her grandfather, for the Khorchin Mongols, for Hong Taiji, for Shunzhi, for Kangxi and for the Qing Empire. Yet for her most beloved Dorgon, she had given so very little of herself. She wanted so much to tell his spirit everything that had weighed on her mind for so long. She was convinced that his spirit lingered still in that place of death because there had never been a proper entombment of his remains, and she chose to believe what she wanted to believe.

Kangxi decided to bring only Sumalagu and a small team of bodyguards on the journey. He knew his Nana's wishes and selected an old guardsman who had been on Dorgon's last hunting expedition to join the party, so that he could lead them to the exact spot where his grand-uncle had lain, dying.

The two women rode together in a horse-drawn carriage while Kangxi and two guards rode in front on horseback and another two trailed behind in a wagon filled with food provisions and camping and hunting gear. They moved at a leisurely pace and made overnight stops in the evenings. Kangxi took care not to tire his Nana.

A few years after assuming full imperial power, Kangxi had built the Mountain Retreat of which Dorgon had first conceived. Possessed of a fervent passion for hunting just like his grand-uncle, he visited this haunt as often as he could.

Though he seldom spoke his mind about his grand-uncle, he maintained a secret admiration for his chivalrous, though forbidden, love for his Nana during his younger years. He often felt sorry for them both. Ever since his Nana had told him that he had eyes like his grand-uncle's, he had developed a fondness for him. But throughout his youth, people around him were strangely reticent about Dorgon and his deeds. Nana was the only one who sometimes let a few words about him escape her. What upset him most, though, was the brutal way his corpse had been treated. He could never understand the acrimony that existed between his father and his grand-uncle, and even less that between his grandfather and grand-uncle.

After six days' travelling, they reached the Mountain Retreat in Kharahotun. The cool mountain breeze was refreshing and a welcome change after the sweltering summer heat in Beijing. The travelers, who all had nomad blood running through their veins, took their time drinking in the serene and wild beauty, which made them feel right at home.

The Retreat was a modest complex of four annexed buildings, all sparsely furnished with bamboo furniture. The main building housed the lounge and dining area, and opened onto a large courtyard, while the east and west wings had three bed chambers each, with the remaining building in the backyard serving as the kitchen area and servants' quarters. The Retreat was nestled in a pine-forested ravine, right beside a crystal-clear turquoise lake fed by a nearby glacier.

Upon their arrival at the Retreat, a message was waiting for Kangxi, sent from the Board of Rites, announcing the birth of Imperial Noble Consort Tunggiya's first daughter. His face flushed with excitement as he read the missive. Relaying the happy news to his Nana, he bade Sumalagu prepare a big meal for the whole party that evening to celebrate.

The next day, Kangxi and two bodyguards left on a six-day hunting trip into the mountains, while Bumbutai and Sumalagu rested in the Retreat. They took daily strolls in the surrounding forest or spent time fishing in the glacial lake.

On the day following Kangxi's return from the hunting excursion, he accompanied his Nana, Sumalagu and the old guardsman to locate the camp site where Dorgon had died. The old guardsman had a good memory and within half an hour's riding, they reached the windswept plateau to the east of the ravine where the Retreat was situated, where Dorgon's expedition had camped on that fateful night. Although the sun tried to wrap its warmth around the forlorn plain, it was too engrossed in its own frigidity to respond.

Here, Kangxi, Sumalagu and the guardsman discreetly rode off to a nearby clearing to let Bumbutai have a moment alone.

It was thirty-two-and-a-half years since it had happened. The image of Dorgon lying unconscious in a pool of dark blood after his deadly fall flashed into her mind. She saw him clutching the pink bundle in his bloodied hand, and saw herself hugging his lifeless form in the mortuary. Burning the letter and the lock of hair over the candle. These images had never left her. They had been locked in the bottommost layer of her memory. Now she unlocked them and let them free.

At this moment a large golden eagle swooped into sight and circled above her head. She was excited to see it.

"Dorgon my love, can you hear me?" she murmured to herself. "I have come to talk to you."

She paced back and forth on the spot where Ajige's tent had stood. The eagle had landed atop the highest of the pine trees fringing the plateau. It squatted perfectly still on the crest.

"I am here to tell you how much I have missed you all these years," she continued. "I can assure you that it won't be long before I come and join you."

She glanced up at the eagle.

"There is something I wanted to tell you long ago but never did. I'm so ashamed that I kept it from you.... Please forgive me. Dorgon, I bore you a daughter, a beautiful daughter. Her name is Shuhui and she is now fifty-one years old."

She tried to find a rock surface to take the weight off her legs. Noticing a large flat boulder jutting out at knee level from hill slope within ten walking paces, she shuffled over and sat down. When she looked up, she saw the eagle still on the same perch, directly opposite her.

Without realizing it, she found she was fiddling with the butterfly buttons on the collar of her jade green robe. Sumalagu had made this robe with the same jade green silk as the Chinese-style waistcoat and skirt ensemble that she had worn the night when she performed a butterfly dance for Dorgon in Yongfu Palace.

"Do you remember that night when you came into my bed chamber soaked in alcohol? Hong Taiji was away fighting in a battle at Dalinghe. You would not leave..." She paused, deep in the memory.

"Shuhui is happily married and lives with her husband in the Khorchin Mongol State. For her sake as well as yours and mine, I kept the truth from everyone. It is only recently that I told Suma about it. Please forgive me, Dorgon."

The stately eagle flapped its expansive wings a few times.

"Through all these long lonely years, it is our lovely daughter who has kept me going. Ahhh, there was so much heartache and anguish that I was destined to go through, the tragic deaths, the maniacal hatred, the never-ending battles, the treachery .... But now I have completed all my duties. Your grand-nephew is a grown man and he is firmly set at the helm now. If you could see him, and I am sure you can, you would find that he has an air that takes after you."

During her pause, the eagle darted to the next tall tree and sat there, as if waiting for more. She drew out a pink kerchief with an embroidered blue swallow and put it on her lap before continuing.

"Dorgon, it was horrible what they did to your corpse. You didn't deserve that. I cried my eyes out for several days. I always took with me the drawing you gave me. It was the only thing that could give me a little comfort. Please forgive Fulin. He was under Oboi's bad influence. I am going to ask Xuanye to rehabilitate both your title and your tomb."

As she said this, a rivulet of tears escaped her eyes. In a husky voice, she carried on:

"You will be pleased to know that after so many years of turmoil, the Qing Empire is now finally consolidated under Xuanye's rule. If it hadn't been for your efforts and Hong Taiji's, this day would not have come. Dorgon, I hope you know that I meant every word in my first letter to you, and I still do. My heart has always only belonged to you alone. It is just that I had my own obligations and at times I was forced to make hard choices."

She raised her eyes again and was awed to find that the eagle had swooped down from its perch to the ground and was strutting on the spot of the tent site. Then it stopped in front of her and stood there quietly.

"My love, I knew that your claim to the throne was justified. You had opportunity to seize it after Hong Taiji's death but you didn't. You gave it up for my sake. This is a debt that I will never be able to repay you. Eternal Blue Sky willing, when my time here is up, I will come and serve you with my heart and my soul for eternity."

She stood up slowly and left her pink kerchief on the boulder. The eagle soared out of sight. Then she headed towards the party who were waiting for her. When she turned her head to look, the kerchief was gone.

After spending twelve days in the Kharahotun Mountains, the party was ready to leave. If Kangxi was anxious to get back to his Palace, he didn't let his impatience show. The party took the same six days for the return journey.

By the time they arrived at the Meridian Gate, it was early evening and Kangxi left the riding party to head straight to the East Palace where Hexian lived. It was the twenty-fourth day since the infant's birth. As he approached her bed chambers, he heard the sound of women wailing inside, and he felt his legs go weak.

His lovely infant daughter had passed away that morning from an unknown illness. Hexian had fainted several times during the day from heartbreak. Seeing his distraught wife, he stepped up to hold her in his embrace and did his best to comfort her, while hiding his own grief.

Hexian would remain childless right up to her death in the twenty-eighth year of Kangxi's reign. Kangxi would make her Empress on the day before her death, hoping that the auspicious event might pull her back from the Emperor of Ghosts. He would leave the post of Empress unfilled through the remainder of his life.

Four peaceful years quietly slipped by after the Kharahotun trip. Bumbutai's health was on a downward track during those years but she still kept up her studies. In the winter months of the twenty-sixth year of the Kangxi reign, she fell very sick and was bedridden.

Kangxi was crushed with grief over his Nana's illness. For thirty-five days in a row, he personally spoon-fed her herbal medicine and congee meals and slept on the floor beside her sick bed, keeping vigil overnight. He bade his Grand Secretariat not to submit Court memorials to him while he was at Cining Palace, unless they were of an extreme urgent nature.

One morning when she felt a little stronger, she asked Xuanye to sit on the edge of the bed and prop her up. She told him her last wishes:

"Xuanye, please listen carefully. I have two wishes that I want you to fulfill when I'm gone." She paused for a moment and then continued in a weak voice: "The first is that I would not want your grandfather's tomb in Mukden disturbed, and so I would rather be buried close to Shunzhi's tomb here near Beijing." She coughed heavily. Kangxi gave her some warm water to soothe her throat

"Yes, Nana, I'll see to it."

"The second is that I want you to promise to take care of Princess Shuhui for life after I'm gone." She was struggling to continue.

"You don't need to worry, Nana. I'll have her and her family brought here to live in the Palaces, if they are willing."

"Also, make my funeral as simple as possible."

"Yes, Nana, I know what to do. Now you must lie down and rest." He tried hard to blink back his tears so that she wouldn't see them.

When all the finest physicians had been consulted and her sickness still showed no signs of improvement, Kangxi sat down at his writing table and penned a long petition to the Shamanist deity.

In a praying ritual held at the Shamanist Shrine located to the southeast of the Forbidden City, a Shaman led the Aisin Gioro clansmen and Court Ministers in a group prayer pleading for the Grand Empress Dowager's speedy recovery. When the chanting was finished, Kangxi read out aloud the petition that he had earlier written, in which he specifically offered to have his years of life cut short in exchange for his Nana's recovery. As he came to the end of the petition, his face was drenched in tears. There wasn't a dry eye in the hall.

But as Bumbutai would often say, in the matter of life and death, there was no arguing with Eternal Blue Sky.

On her sickbed, she wandered into a dream and returned finally to her beloved homeland for the first time since leaving it at the tender age of twelve.

Chronology

1613 (March 28)	Birth of Bumbutai in the Khorchin State of Mongolia.
1625 (Spring)	Bumbutai becomes concubine to Hong Taiji.
1626 (February)	Battle of Ningyuan.
1626 (September 30)	Nurhaci, founder of the Later Jin Dynasty, dies.
1627	Hong Taiji commences reign as Khan, assisted by three other Beiles.
1629	Birth of Bumbutai's first daughter.
1630 (September 22)	Yuan Chonghuan executed by slicing.
1631 (September)	Battle of Dalinghe.
1632	Birth of Bumbutai's second daughter.
1633	Birth of Bumbutai's third daughter.
1634 (November)	Harjol becames Hong Taiji's Consort.
1635	Hong Taiji changed tribal name from "Jurchen" to "Manchu".
1636	Hong Taiji changes dynasty name from "Later Jin" to "Qing".
1636 (May)	Hong Taiji assumes title of Emperor.
1636	Bumbutai granted title of "Consort Zhuang".
1636	Harjol granted title of "Consort Chen".

1636 (December)	Surrender of Korea to the Manchu Empire.
1638 (March 15)	Birth of Bumbutai's son Fulin (Shunzhi).
1641 (October)	Harjol dies.
1641 – 1642	Battles of Songshan and Jinzhou (or Battle of Songjin).
1643 (September 21)	Hong Taiji dies.
1643 (October 8)	Fulin (Shunzhi) accedes to the Manchu throne, with Jirgalang and Dorgon as Co-Regents.
1644 (April 25)	Ming Emperor Chongzhen commits suicide on Prospect Hill.
1644 (May 27)	Battle of Shanhai Pass (at the eastern end of the Great Wall).
1644 (June 5)	Official surrender of the Ming Dynasty to the Qing Empire.
1644 (October 19)	Dorgon receives Shunzhi Emperor into Beijing.
1644 (November 8)	Formal enthronement of Shunzhi Emperor in the Forbidden City.
1645 (May)	Ten-day massacre of Yangzhou residents.
1645 (July 21)	Dorgon imposes "shaved head" order on all Hans on pain of execution for treason.
1645 (Summer)	Three massacres of residents in Jiading area.
1650 (November 24)	Massacre of Guangzhou residents.
1650 (December 31)	Dorgon dies in a hunting trip accident.

1651 (February 1)	Shunzhi assumes full imperial authority.
1651 (Summer)	Shunzhi weds his first Empress, Bumbutai's niece.
1654 (May 4)	Birth of Xuanye (Kangxi).
1659 (June - September)	Battle of Nanjing (river battle in which Koxinga's fleet defeated).
1660 (September 23)	Imperial Noble Consort Donggo dies.
1661 (February 5)	Shunzhi dies from smallpox.
1661 (February 7)	Xuanye (Kangxi) enthroned, with Sonin, Suksaha, Oboi and Ebilun as Regents.
1665 (October)	Kangxi weds his first Empress, Sonin's granddaughter.
1667 (August 25)	Kangxi assumes full imperial authority.
1669	Qing Court arrests and imprisons Regent Oboi.
1673-1681	Revolt of the Three Feudatories.
1678 (October 2)	Wu Sangui dies on sickbed.
1683 (Summer)	Battle of Penghu.
1683 (September)	Taiwan Kingdom of Tungning Surrenders to the Qing Empire.
1688 (January 27)	Bumbutai (Grand Empress Dowager Xiaozhuang) dies.

List of Characters

Qing Court:

Abahai, Lady, Nurhaci's favorite consort; mother of Ajige, Dorgon and Dodo.

Ajige, eldest son of Nurhaci and Lady Abahai.

Bumbutai, or Empress Xiaozhuang, a Borjigit princess of the Khorchin Mongol state; daughter of Jaisang; granddaughter of Manggusi; consort of Hong Taiji; mother of Shunzhi Emperor, Princess Shuhui and two other princesses; grandmother of Kangxi Emperor and Fuquan.

Daisan, second son of Nurhaci; First Great Beile of Later Jin.

Dodo, youngest son of Nurhaci and Lady Abahai.

Donggo, Consort, Imperial Noble Consort of Shunzhi Emperor (his favorite).

Dorgon, second son of Nurhaci and Lady Abahai; Prince Regent to Shunzhi Emperor.

Ebilun, of the Niohuru clan; one of the Four Regents to Kangxi Emperor; father of Kangxi's second Empress.

Fan, Scholar, a key Han adviser and teacher of Hong Taiji.

Ferdinand Verbiest, Flemish Jesuit priest; successor to Johann Adam Schall von Bell.

Gabula, Chief of the Imperial Guards; eldest son of Sonin; father of Kangxi's first Empress.

Harjol, a Borjigit princess of the Khorchin Mongol state; consort of Hong Taiji; daughter of Jaisang; sister of Bumbutai and Wukesan; granddaughter of Manggusi.

Hong Taiji, a son of Nurhaci; Fourth Great Beile of Later Jin; founder of Qing Dynasty; husband of Jere, Bumbutai and Harjol; father of Shunzhi Emperor; grandfather of Kangxi Emperor and Fuquan.

Hooge, eldest son of Hong Taiji; grandson of Nurhaci.

Hui, Consort, Imperial Concubine of Kangxi; niece of Mingju.

Hung Chili, a Han scholar of the Hanlin Academy; Minister of Rites.

Jaisang, a Borjigit prince of the Khorchin Mongol state; son of Manggusi; father of Wukeshan, Harjol and Bumbutai.

Jere, Empress, a Borjigit princess of the Khorchin Mongol state; daughter of Manggusi; sister of Wukesan; wife of Hong Taiji; aunt of Bumbutai.

Jirgalang, a nephew of Nurhaci; Second Great Beile of Later Jin; Co-Regent to Shunzhi Emperor for a short time.

Johann Adam Schall von Bell, German Jesuit priest; Director of the Imperial Observatory and the Tribunal of Mathematics; key adviser to Shunzhi and Bumbutai.

Kangxi, or Xuanye, son of Shunzhi and Consort Tunggiya; grandson of Hong Taiji and Bumbutai.

Lin, Scholar, a Han scholar; student of Scholar Fan; Minister of Documents.

Little Jade, a Borjigit princess of the Khorchin Mongol state; wife of Dorgon; half-sister of Bumbutai.

Manggultai, a son of Nurhaci; Third Great Beile of Later Jin.

Manggusi, leader of the Khorchin Mongol state; father of Jaisang; grandfather of Wukeshan, Harjol and Bumbutai.

Mingju, of the Nalan clan, a Senior Imperial Guard; Minister of Punishments; father of Xingde (a poet); uncle of Consort Hui.

Monggo, Consort, a deceased consort of Nurhaci; mother of Hong Taiji.

Nurhaci, leader of the Jurchen tribe; patriarch of the Aisin Gioro clan; founder of Later Jin Dynasty; father of Daisan, Manggultai, Hong Taiji, Ajige, Dorgon and Dodo; uncle of Jirgalang.

Oboi, one of the Four Regents to Kangxi Emperor.

Shi Lang, a naval admiral; Commander-in-Chief of the Qing naval fleet that conquered the Kingdom of Tungning.

Shunzhi, or Fulin, son of Hong Taiji and Bumbutai; grandson of Nurhaci; father of Xuanye and Fuquan.

Songgoto, a Senior Imperial Guard; third son of Sonin; coach of the *buku* young guards; Grand Secretary.

Sonin, of the Heseri clan; Head of the Four Regents to Kangxi Emperor; grandfather of Kangxi's first Empress.

Suksaha, one of the Four Regents to Kangxi Emperor.

Sumalagu, maid and confidante of Bumbutai.

Tuhai, a Senior Imperial Guard; Minister of Revenue.

Tunggiya, Consort, or Hexian, Imperial Noble Consort of Kangxi Emperor (his favorite and first cousin).

Wang, Chief of Staff of the Imperial Household Department in Shunzhi's reign.

Wang Xi, a Han scholar of the Hanlin Academy (who drafted Shunzhi's will).

Wu Liangfu, chief eunuch to Shunzhi Emperor.

Wukeshan, eldest Borjigit prince of the Khorchin Mongol state; son of Jaisang; brother of Bumbutai and Harjol; father of Shunzhi's first Empress.

Ming Court:

Chongzhen, the last Emperor of the Ming Dynasty.

Geng Jingzhong, Feudatory Lord of Fujian.

Hong Chengchou, a military general who defected to Qing after the Battles of Songshan and Jinzhou.

Shang Kexi, Feudatory Lord of Guangdong; father of Shang Zhixin.

Wu Sangui, a military general who defected to Qing at the Battle of Shanhai Pass; Feudatory Lord of Yunnan and Guizhou; husband of Chen Yuanyuan; grandfather of Wu Shifan.
Yuan Chonghuan, a military general; Governor of Ningyuan.

Others:
Chen Yuanyuan, a courtesan; favorite concubine of Wu Sangui.
Mao, a Zen Buddhist monk.
Mu, a Zen Buddhist monk.
Siu Mui, maid-in-waiting to Bumbutai.
Siu Fa, maid-in-waiting to Bumbutai.
Wang Fushen, a subordinate of Wu Sangui.
Xia, a Ming soldier who betrayed Hong Chengchou's army in the Battle of Songshan.
Yu Lin, a Zen Buddhist/Taoist monk.
Zheng Chenggong, or Koxinga, a Ming loyalist and naval commander in the Battle of Nanjing.
Zheng Jing, son and heir of Zheng Chenggong and father of Zheng Keshuang; founder of the Kingdom of Tungning in Taiwan.

Acknowledgments

My heartfelt gratitude goes first and foremost to my publisher Graham Earnshaw, whose faith in the novel has been priceless. Earnshaw Books' goal to bring to global audiences knowledge of Chinese history through fiction has been inspirational and encouraging. I happen to be a fervent supporter. My deep thanks also go to John Grant Ross, who read the manuscript at an early stage and offered me invaluable editorial input, and to Lydia Moed, who helped me improve the opening chapters. As well, I am indebted to my friends at Goodreads for their continual moral support throughout the writing process - you know who you are.

AUTHOR'S AFTERWORD

EMPRESS DOWAGER Xiaozhuang undoubtedly made an indelible mark on Chinese history, but her contributions as an influential leader and a champion for peace and humanity have been, I believe, greatly undervalued. I would even contend that without her charismatic guidance, the Qing Empire would not have survived its fledgling years. History also witnessed how the young Emperor Kangxi, under her mentorship, went on to become one of the most benevolent and liberal-minded Emperors in China's history. His oft-proclaimed deep affection and veneration for her, all well-documented, speaks volumes about this free-spirited and acuminous Mongolian woman.

While this novel is in the main an act of the imagination, it draws abundantly on the work of modern historians, both Chinese and Western.

Regarding the cast of characters, real historical figures predominate and real names are used as far as possible. There are a few characters, however, who are entirely fictional. These are: Bumbutai's Han maids Siu Mui and Siu Fa, Court Physician Sima, and Wang, the Chief of Staff at the Imperial Household Department. Naturally, episodes in which these fictional characters take part are my own creation.

In general, I have taken the liberty to flex my imagination where there are missing links, obvious gaps or only mere hints in the official historical texts. I have based my narrative on what I believe to be the psychological landscape of the key personalities as extrapolated from my research. In other cases, I have dramatized known facts a little.

As for historical facts, all battles and most Court intrigues included in the story are based on recorded events. I have tried not to deviate from the historical record. The one major exception is Dorgon's premeditated murder of Hong Taiji, which is my own conjecture. According to historical texts, Hong Taiji died on his sickbed in Empress Jere's Palace. In my defense, I would argue that the causes of death relating to Emperors and members of their households are often the most cryptic of secrets in the Imperial records throughout Chinese dynastic history, thus leaving room for speculation.

As the saying goes, sometimes fact is stranger than fiction. Incredible as it may sound, Johann Adam Schall von Bell's late-life melodrama is based on true events. The trial on trumped-up charges, the sentence of death by slicing, his near-death experience on the day of his execution, and the timely earthquake which saved him, are all well-recorded facts.

I should also mention that there is a centuries-old controversy over the question of whether or not Bumbutai, as Empress Dowager, married her brother-in-law, Regent Dorgon, after her son Shunzhi was enthroned. In this debate, there are two major camps. Conservative Chinese historians and academicians insist that there is no conclusive written evidence for such a marriage. One of the noted hardliners in this camp is Meng Sen, a well-known late Qing scholar and historian. The other camp, made up of mostly literary writers and common folk, earnestly believes that the marriage was a natural course of events, as a levirate union was a cultural tradition among Manchus and Mongols. Such a union, however, was generally abhorred in Han culture and hence, any documentary record might have been erased because it might denigrate the Qing Court.

This latter camp cites as evidence a particular poem written by the Qing era poet Zhang Cangshui, which describes the wedding in detail, and the fact that Dorgon used the title "Imperial Father Prince Regent" in Court documents. One key supporter of this camp was literary icon Hu Shih (1891-1962). He debated the topic with Meng Sen in an exchange of letters, saying that the title Dorgon used is itself an indisputable historical fact. Subsequently, Meng Sen admitted that the later Qing rulers had a habit of purposely destroying all written documents that they deemed as defamatory to Qing imperial figures.

For my research, apart from relying on newer editions of Chinese history publications (compiled from *The Twenty-Four Histories* and *Draft History of Qing*), I also consulted the following English non-fiction titles:-

Robert B. Oxnam, *Ruling from Horseback; Manchu Politics in the Oboi Regency 1661-1669*, 1975.

Frederic Wakeman, *The Great Enterprise: The Manchu Reconstruction of Imperial Order in Seventeenth-Century China,* 1985.

Pamela Kyle Crossley, *The Manchus,* 1997.

Evelyn S. Rawski, *The Last Emperors: A Social History of Qing Imperial Institutions,* 1998.

The Secret History of the Mongols: The History and the Life of Chinggis Khan, Translated & Edited by Urgunge Onon, 2001.

Jack Weatherford, *Genghis Khan and the Making of the Modern World,* 2004.

Cho-yun Hsu, *China: A New Cultural History,* 2006.

Jack Weatherford, *The Secret History of the Mongol Queens,* 2010.

1001 Battles That Changed the Course of World History, Edited by R. G. Grant, 2011.

Herbert Allen Giles, *China and the Manchus,* Revised 2013.

Alice Poon
2017

About The Author

Alice Poon is an avid reader of world historical fiction. Born and educated in Hong Kong, she grew up devouring Jin Yong's martial arts and chivalry novels, all set in China's distant past. That sparked her life-long interest in Chinese history. Writing historical novels set in Old China has been her long-cherished dream.

She is the author of the bestselling Chinese edition of Land and the Ruling Class in Hong Kong, which won the 2011 Hong Kong Book Prize. Canadian Book Review Annual selected the original English Edition as Editor's Choice (Scholarly) in 2007.

She currently lives in Richmond, British Columbia, Canada, and is working on her next Old China novel.

http://alicewaihanpoon.blogspot.ca
http://twitter.com/alicepoon1
https://www.goodreads.com/alice_poon